Beach Slapped

Beach Slapped

Barton Grover Howe

BGH Publishing
Lincoln City, Oregon
www.bartongroverhowe.com

Beach Slapped. Copyright © 2011 by Barton Grover Howe. All rights reserved. No part of this e-book may be used or reproduced in any manner whatsoever without written permission except in the case of brief quotations embodied in critical articles or reviews. For information, contact Barton Grover Howe Publishing, bartongroverhowe@gmail.com

Cover design by Sharalyn Hay
www.SweetPea4414@gmail.com

This is a work of fiction. Names, characters, places, and incidents either are a product of the author's imagination or are used fictitiously, and any resemblance to any actual persons living or dead, businesses, companies, events, or locales is entirely coincidental.

While the author has made every attempt to provide accurate contact information at the time of publication, neither the publisher nor the author assumes any responsibility for errors, or for changes that occur after publication. Further, the publisher does not have any control over and does not assume any responsibility for author or third-party websites or their content.

Acknowledgements

To Jimmy Buffett:
I hope you like the book

To the faculty at Anchor College:
Thanks for making my fiction real

And most of all to Allyson:
My editor, my friend, my wife, my life,
Who continues to make all my dreams come true.

Table of Contents

Thursday	9
Friday	91
Saturday	231
Sunday	387
Epilogue	527

Chapter 1
Callista Walker

THURSDAY

Callista Walker was being goosed by a sea lion. On any other day she might have found it funny. But since she was likely going to die in the next hour or so floating off the coast of Oregon, she was not exactly thrilled at the idea.

Pushing his snout right between her legs, the sea lion had been aggressive almost from the start. Bobbing in the 45-degree water, she was quite literally screwed, although the expression could apply on any number of levels.

As a young scientist with a master's degree in marine biology, she really wasn't surprised by the sea lion's behavior. Classified as a pinniped, California sea lions had a history of interaction with humans, some of it benign, some not.

Near Berkeley at Pier 39 in San Francisco, they took over the boat docks almost from the moment the pier opened to visitors. At first the pier owners were upset; they couldn't run them off because messing with a sea-going mammal is a federal crime. They changed their minds when they realized the sea lions were the biggest attraction they had going.

A boat owner further south in Newport wasn't as delighted when a group of them piled on his boat at dock and sank it. A 13-year-old girl in Australia even reported being attacked by one, although Callista suspected the sea lion was just trying to play. Not that Callista blamed the girl; it's not easy being the object of an eye that's attached to up to a ton of muscle and blubber.

Or a snout.

He'd made three passes now, and were it not for the wetsuit she was wearing, he'd have definitely gone where no sea mammal had gone before. (Or any mammal, for that matter, since Jerry Dixon, but that was another story.) If she lived through the day, perhaps she could start cross-marketing wetsuits as full-body, sea lion-proof condoms.

That seemed increasingly unlikely, however, and she wasn't thinking about neoprene condoms.

Callista wasn't in the water by choice. Just 30 minutes ago she'd been up the coast, catching some of the last waves of the morning on her surfboard. She was due to start her new job as an aquarist at the Surfland Aquarium of the Pacific in less than 48 hours. She wanted to get in some last moments of recreation before the demands of a new job took away her free time.

Having ridden her last wave nearly to shore, Callista was feeling spry and relaxed as she walked up the sand and to the top of the beach access ramp on NW Jetty Avenue. She'd left her camper van there alone while she surfed, though now there was a beat-up truck next to it. Sporting a white personalized tag, it clearly wasn't from Oregon, though the state and the meaning of the tag eluded her at the moment.

Maybe it belonged to the two men coming out of a house across and down the street. Giving them a jaunty wave as she continued on to her van, she resolved to satisfy her curiosity and go ask them just what the tag meant. Just as soon as she got her board put away.

That's when she noticed neither waved back, which did strike her as a little odd; everyone here on the coast had been very friendly. So, it didn't take much when she saw them arguing with one another for her to hurry up locking the board in the back of the van. And when one began walking determinedly her way, she knew it was time to get out of there.

Hurriedly, she got behind the steering wheel and locked the door. A split second later, a man with dirty blonde hair, one missing tooth and enough acne scars to attract a Mars Lander, started pounding on her window. He demanded she get out of the vehicle. She hit the gas instead.

Having only been in Surfland a few days she had no idea where she was going other than south. Looking back, she should have headed for U.S. Highway 101 through the center of town and stayed there, instead of trying to lose them on the meandering back streets that ran closest to the ocean. If she had, maybe she would have run into a cop, a fireman, heck, anyone, instead of a dead end street at the other end of town.

For a brief moment she thought she'd lost them, but just as she exhaled she saw the truck speeding down the hill behind her. Jumping out of the van, she headed for the beach again, knowing their truck would never make it through the deep sand. But that, too, proved faint hope as the man and the guy he was arguing with before began to run down the beach after her.

Normally, Callista could have outrun them without breaking a sweat. But still wearing her wetsuit her mobility was limited, she was sweating and panting profusely, and her booties, so perfect for sticking to a surfboard, were proving far less effective at running from two angry pursuers. She'd about given up hope when she saw the jetty sticking out into the ocean. Designed to protect the boat channel into Lenobar Bay, she hoped that its slick rocks and the pounding surf surrounding it would prove the deterrent she needed to wait the men out until she could think of something else. And it was — until a giant wave slammed into it and knocked her right off the jetty and into the ocean.

It was a miracle the tumble off the jetty didn't kill her and even more so that the waves didn't smash her back into the rocks. Indeed, they seemed to pull her away from the jetty and, for the moment, to safety. Coupled with the wetsuit she was wearing and the heat she'd built up during the chase, she didn't even have to worry about hypothermia, at least for a little while. Indeed, as hot as she was, her sudden dip in the ocean felt pretty good.

But the two men still watching her on the beach were another matter. Watching her through what looked to be binoculars, they had made themselves comfortable sitting on the driftwood, waiting to finish the job if the sea didn't.

Or the sea lion.

Now on his fourth pass, he was becoming even more aggressive, despite her best attempts to ward him off. Again, she knew this behavior wasn't totally unexpected. Women at sea had been reporting for years that sea-going mammals like sea lions, seals and even dolphins had seemed unnaturally interested in the most feminine parts of the human anatomy. In her studies, Callista had theorized it might have something to do with odors, as sea lions are known to have a keen sense of smell when they're not submerged. Still intellectually engaged despite the circumstances, she knew someone at the aquarium would find her suddenly empirical knowledge of the subject interesting.

Perhaps they could discuss it with her corpse.

Chapter 2
Bobby White

Bobby White brushed his dirty blonde hair out of his eyes for what seemed like the hundredth time. Kansas was windy, but nothing like this. And, as if to punctuate his misery, the fog began to roll in off the ocean. With any luck it would all be over soon, he thought, as he watched the young woman bobbing in the waves off shore. Although at this point he wasn't willing to assume anything.

After all, when he saw her tumble into the ocean off the jetty, he figured that was the end of her — until she surfaced.

Then, when he saw her fighting the waves next to jetty, he thought that had to be it; she'd be smashed to a pulp. But he was wrong then, too.

Finally, when he saw the shark circling her, he just knew that would be her death. He'd seen "Jaws" maybe 100 times on cable. Everyone died in that movie; at least he thought they did. Those were the only scenes he liked to watch.

But that joy was soon denied him, too — as always — by

his brother, Joey.

"That's not a shark," Joey said. "That's a sea lion. I saw one of them on the Syfy Channel in this movie where the Navy trained 'em to talk to space aliens and …"

"Shut up, God dammit!" Bobby barked at his brother. He was tired of being wrong today. Tired of the girl that wouldn't die. Tired of his damn brother always talking about some outer space nonsense. And — at the moment — tired especially of the wind that seemed to never stop. As he raised the binoculars for another look, he was especially tired of that.

God, he hated Oregon.

"Where the hell is Oregon?" Bobby asked into the phone. His uncle Shelton had offered to take care of all of his expenses if he would drive up and stay for a few weeks. But he had to admit, having never passed geography — or any high school class save for wood shop — he had no idea where that was.

Wherever it was, it sounded a long way from Hays, Kansas, and quite frankly, he wasn't sure he wanted to go. After seven years of working at Hays Supply he'd finally made assistant supervisor in charge of night stock. All the perks of (lower) management were his, including the ability to buy his Hays Supply belt buckle and bolo tie. With the raise that came with the promotion, he was now making close to $6.25 an hour. One more and he'd be able to afford hubcaps for all four wheels of his truck.

He had to admit, though, what his uncle proposed sounded kind of fun. A family legend, Uncle Shelton had been sent out of Kansas to live with some distant relatives in the west after he blew up a Topeka Toyota dealership when he was a kid. Something about getting revenge, and honor, although he wasn't really sure. In fact Bobby wasn't even sure about the Topeka Toyota thing, but he figured if all the guys in county lockup — a place he'd been more than once — still talked about it, it had to be true.

And now the legend wanted Bobby. Uncle Shelton had a big plan, he said. He just needed a few things taken care of, the kind of things that only a man like Bobby could really help with. They weren't the kind of things Uncle Shelton wanted talked about over the phone, but suffice it to say the money was good and the Milwaukee's Best would be plentiful throughout the job.

He almost took the job at the mention of the Milwaukee's Best. It was his favorite beer; let other men drink Bud and Miller. Bobby White was going to have only the best — it said so on the can — and Uncle Shelton was going to have unlimited amounts of it. But still, there were issues.

For one thing, it was already well into the middle of October, and Uncle Shelton wanted Bobby up there by the 18th. To make it, he'd have to have his younger brother, Joey, come with him, just so someone else could drive. His brother drove him nuts.

For one thing, Joey had finished high school, and nothing was worse to Bobby than an educated man trying to tell him facts and information all the time. If he wanted that he'd have stayed in school past ninth grade.

Even worse, however, Joey worked in a "Si Fi" bookstore. And while Bobby wasn't entirely sure just what those words had to do with books, he knew it made his brother even more annoying. "Outer space" this, and "warp speed" that. Everything that came out of his mouth seemed to come from a book, movie or TV show Bobby had never heard of. Why couldn't he just listen to Lee Greenwood like everybody else and shut the hell up?

Not that taking Joey didn't have some advantages: for one thing he was a good driver. Unlike Bobby himself, Joey had never put a scratch on Bobby's 1993 Dodge truck. In fact, it was Joey who showed Bobby how to buff out the scratches when he'd backed into the rolls of barbed wire fence outside Hays Supply last year. The fact that Bobby had just bought the almost-new truck with just 298,000 miles on it made the repairs all the more appreciated.

He and Joey had even been arrested together a few times. Nothing serious for Joey, of course, as his heart just never seemed to be into taking advantage of the opportunities life presented him. (The fact that those opportunities had put two felonies on Bobby's record, well that was just bad luck.)

But now Uncle Shelton was presenting Bobby with what seemed like a foolproof opportunity to make some money, have some fun, and drink beer just about all the time. What could possibly go wrong?

Of course, that logic was how he had gotten the first felony. Seizing a chance to date the girl of his dreams and shoot her new rifle, he'd taken both of them out to the woods to have some fun. Unfortunately, he'd neglected to tell her his plans, and next thing he knew he was arrested, charged and convicted of kidnapping. The judge said he understood and tried to give him the lightest sentence possible, but it was still a felony. So, Bobby had used his prison time to consider the danger of making decisions that involved guns, women and any combination of the two. (The other felony was pure bullshit; the guy said Bobby could have the tractor for free.)

He wished he could talk to his dad, but visiting hours weren't for another six hours, the jail didn't allow incoming phone calls, and Uncle Shelton wanted a decision. Now.

"You're sure I can get all the way to Oregon without having to eat at no damned Kentucky Fried Chicken?" Bobby hated any place that didn't use real chickens. He'd heard someone talk about it in jail once. "I ain't eatin' no mutant bird … Well, OK. That sounds good."

And with that the deal was almost done, save for telling Joey they were going to Oregon and picking up a list of supplies Uncle Shelton said they'd need once they got there. Both would be done within the hour, as Joey was home from the bookstore and Bobby's encyclopedic knowledge of the Hays Supply layout let him make quick work of the list.

They were off to Oregon by nightfall.

The girl continued to bob in the surf. How could anyone tread water that long? Bobby wondered. The one time he'd tried it in the Hays Community Pool he'd sunk right to the bottom, and if it hadn't been for the cloud of dust floating to the top of the water to signal the lifeguard, he might have died there.

But not this girl: she just kept floating in the waves, moving even farther north from the jetty, meaning she'd never even get smashed on the rocks. Damn, wouldn't this chick ever die?

Not that that had been his plan in the first place; he'd just wanted to scare her and maybe find out what she'd seen. But now that she was bobbing in the ocean, he did have to admit it would solve a lot of problems. Namely explaining all of this to his Uncle Shelton, or whatever the hell he said his name was now.

That was the first thing Bobby and Joey had learned when they got to their uncle's lake house in Surfland: he didn't go by Shelton anymore. Now he was going by the name "Shabazz T. Morton," and God help the person who left out even one syllable of that name. Even before telling the White brothers of his name change, he got so angry hearing the name "Shelton" that he stopped breathing for a moment and his face and chest turned bright red. He was so hot under the collar Bobby thought his uncle's gold chains might melt.

But after seeing his uncle breathe again, Bobby relaxed and went looking for the fridge. Whatever, he thought, I'll call you Willie Nelson if you want, just tell me where the Milwaukee's Best is.

But Joey couldn't leave well enough alone: he had to ask what the "T" stood for. And with a puffed up — and much paler — chest Morton told him: "Tiberius, you corn-puss, for the second Emperor of the Roman Empire, conqueror of worlds!"

"Did you know that's also the middle name of Captain Kirk?" Joey asked. "He saved the entire Earth on stardate ..."

Which was as far as he got before Bobby punched him.

Bobby had noticed his uncle's chest was turning red again, and since Bobby still hadn't found the beer, he was worried a heart attack would keep him from getting directions. Not that that was the only reason Bobby had hit his brother.

He was also tired of listening to Joey ramble on and on about every stupid thing for two interminable days of nonstop driving through multiple western states: Kansas: "Did you know there's really no such thing as a 10,000 pound groundhog?" Colorado: "Did you know all that stuff about Kentucky Fried Chicken is just an urban myth?" Utah: "Do you know why the Mormons came to Utah?" Idaho: "Did you know Lewis & Clark slept right here?" Oregon: "Do you know it rains anywhere from six to eight feet a year in Surfland?"

Bobby did not know who Lewis & Clark were nor did he know what a Mormon was, and he had never even heard of an "urban myth." And as to giant groundhogs, he knew it must be true because it was on a billboard on I-70, and he'd already verified the Kentucky Fried Chicken story with his dad, which meant that it must be true. Hell, they'd been in the same jail.

In the end, however, it all meant the same thing: Joey was full of crap. (All except the rain in Surfland part. Fall had arrived on the coast of Oregon with its alternating days — sometimes moments — of torrential rains and cloudless skies.

It was one more thing for Bobby to loathe.)

Which is why it wasn't too long until he stopped listening to Joey all together when they went out and did their work for their uncle. Hell, the only reason he took Joey at all was because he was afraid if he left them alone together again, Joey would start talking some space nonsense and his uncle would probably kill him.

That work consisted mainly of harassing one old widow named Alice Kauffman, who lived right down the street from his uncle's beach house. Every day it was pretty much the same thing: Wait in the beach house until the little old lady came home from her morning errands, and then go knock on her door asking if she was ready to sell to his uncle. They had done this several times a day, every day, for the two weeks the Whites had been in Surfland.

Every day she said no in that polite way little old ladies do — until yesterday.

"Boys, could you do me a favor?" she'd asked sweetly when they'd stopped by for what had to been close to the 80th time since they'd arrived. "When you go home tonight to see your uncle, if you would please tell him to drop dead, preferably in his shit-plugged toilet, I'd appreciate it. Thanks."

Bobby had Joey deliver the message; his uncle hated Joey anyway. And Shabazz responded exactly as Bobby knew he would: with a puffed up red chest, inflamed nostrils and a volume that ensured even Joey shut the hell up. It also promoted a change in methods, which was why when they went back to her house the next day, Bobby didn't bother to knock during their early afternoon visit.

Instead, he kicked in the front door and began verbally assaulting Mrs. Kauffman, an assault that might have turned physical had she not keeled over and died in Bobby's arms. Or at least it seemed like she had, Bobby wasn't sure.

He did know one thing, however: If she was dead, his uncle's life had just gotten a whole lot easier, because this job was all but over. Bobby could start filling up his truck bed with Milwaukee's Best now and be ready to get the hell out of this Godforsaken rainy state Sunday afternoon. Better still, he'd be away from his nut-job uncle. ("Legend, my ass," had occurred to him more than once.)

But Joey was about to deny him even that.

Just after Mrs. Kauffman had fallen to the ground, Bobby had run out the front door to make sure no one had been outside close enough to hear the altercation; a murder rap was definitely not what he needed. But before he could even begin to look, his brother came outside to tell him she wasn't dead, just unconscious.

Staring at his brother in stunned silence, Bobby saw Kansas getting further away every second. Which was when he saw a young woman carrying a surfboard near his truck waving at them.

Why the hell was she waving? How much had she heard? Was she on her way to the cops right now? If Bobby had learned anything from his encounter with his neighbor, it was that you couldn't trust any woman, and he wasn't about to trust this one.

"I'm going to get her," Bobby said decidedly.

"What?" Joey asked. "She's just waving 'Hi.'"

"You don't know that. She could put us away. Are you ready to go to prison? Are you ready for actual prison, Joey? 'Cause you're goin' down, too, if she busts us."

But Bobby never gave Joey a chance to respond, because by the time he'd opened his mouth, Bobby was already down the street and pounding on the window of the woman's van.

Two minutes later they were speeding after her down the backstreets of Surfland. Ten minutes later they were running down the beach. And five minutes after that they saw her get knocked off the jetty and into the sea by a wave.

That was 15 minutes ago, and save for Bobby breaking into the woman's van and stealing a pair of binoculars, not much had happened since, save for Joey's babbling about outer space sea lions, which was when Bobby aggressively told his brother to shut up.

As usual, it worked for a few minutes. But when Joey opened his mouth this time it wasn't about space aliens, warpies or any of that other crap that he was always babbling about.

"We're going to let her die?" he asked quietly. "We could still call the cops or the coast guard or somebody. We could do it without telling 'em who we are."

Bobby had thought about all of that himself. But the bottom line was he didn't know what she knew. He knew only one thing: Save her, and there would be all kinds of explaining to do to his uncle. He'd never get the hell out of this state. His decision was made.

"You got a better idea?" Bobby said. "You didn't sound to ready to go to prison back at the house."

Once again, Bobby gave him no chance to answer, as suddenly they both saw the girl in the water began to get pulled out to sea. Further and further she floated from shore until she disappeared into the fog.

And like that, Bobby was done on the beach with no regrets. Having made the decision to let her die, it was easy to watch her do so. "Let's get off this damned beach," he said.

"I'm going to put her binoculars back in her van," Joey said quietly.

"Good idea. We don't want anyone to think anything's missing when they find her abandoned van," Bobby said. "But hurry the hell up. I need a beer."

Chapter 3
Callista

"OOMPH!"

The sea lion had very nearly knocked the wind out of her as his powerful hind flippers struck her chest on his last pass. "I FINALLY get someone to make a pass at me…" she yelled out to no one in particular.

Talking to herself to help stay conscious, Callista was finding even her attempts at gallows humor were beginning to fade. "I always wanted more guys to hit on me, but this isn't exactly what I had in mind…" Indeed, whatever might have been funny was quickly slipping away with the cold reality of her situation, as even the jetty begin to slip off into the distance and fog.

She knew who would find it funny: her older sister, Arianna. Not the dying part; that might even make her sibling cry a bit. But that Callista's last encounter with a male was to be a fat mammal? That, Arianna would find just delightful.

The bitch.

*****

Callista Walker did not hate her sister; she just wasn't worth it. As their grandmother had often reminded them, hate was an emotion that required energy. If you truly despised someone, why waste all that energy on them?

So, as both were raised in the hills above Berkeley, California, what would have passed in any other family for hate became the simple rhythm of everyday life between Callista and Arianna. No matter what one did, the other usually did the opposite.

Callista became a bit of a tomboy, her long brown hair usually found under a baseball cap. Arianna became the blonde princess, never walking anywhere, but preening from place to place. (Unless she was getting a dye job; there, she slunk into the salon in a hoodie sweatshirt lest anyone see her going to bleach her strawberry blonde locks.) Callista spent her time on the bay and ocean, learning to surf, water ski, wakeboard and basically excel in any sport that touched the water. Arianna headed east to Lake Tahoe to snow ski, although Callista had heard she was usually more interested in sitting in the lodge and talking next to the fire for hours on end.

Separated by just a year in age, they were never far from each other physically or emotionally. Both entered puberty and developed from girls into young women about the same time, something that delighted Callista. ("Boy, Arianna, it's a good thing I came along, otherwise I don't know that the Breast Fairy would have ever found you.") And when Callista and Arianna's interests started to turn from Legos and Barbies, respectively, their roles at Berkeley High School changed as well.

Wearing jeans and sweatshirts, Callista joined the track team, Arianna the debate team in her mini skirts and tank tops (though — God forbid — never at the same time). Callista hung out with the "weird kids," the ones who didn't quite fit in with any other clique. Arianna kept company with the "best kids," the ones earning scholarships in everything from lacrosse to literature. Unless one knew their last name was Walker and they both lived in the same house, no one would have ever guessed they were acquaintances, much less sisters.

So complete was their separation that when both found themselves seated next to each other in biology class the teacher found the coincidence worth commenting on: "Look at that! Two Walkers right next to each other! Maybe you two were meant to be sisters! What are the odds?!" Pretty good, you twit, thought Callista, since it's an alphabetic seating chart. And if Callista had left it as a thought, that probably would have been the end of it.

But she didn't — in fact, she hadn't; she'd actually said it out loud. And within minutes Callista was on her way to the office. At first she was pissed; the last thing she saw before heading to see the principal was her sister smiling (sneering, really) from ear to ear. In the end, however, she was glad she did it, since it got her moved across the room.

Unfortunately, that was as far as they would get from each other when it came to their science classes. Even though Arianna was a year ahead of her sister in school, they constantly found themselves in the same class, as each jockeyed to get into the advanced classes taught by the best teachers. Because even though they were as different as could be, they both shared a love of the sciences.

Both excelled at all of them: biology, chemistry, physics, you name it. Both were brilliant, and each continued to stay out of each other's orbit, so most of their teachers never suspecting they were sisters. Having the 28th most popular surname in America had its advantages.

But where détente might have held at school, it was gloves off at home. And when the topic of pornographic sea lions came up — God bless CNN — Arianna already had all the answers, no matter what Anderson Cooper thought. Refusing to even consider that it might all be about smells, Arianna argued that it was a sign of higher intelligence — just as she did any time an animal did something interesting.

"You know," she lectured Callista during one of their breakfast-table debates, "the anatomy of a sea lion is a lot like a human's. There's no reason to think they don't have sexual desires just like us, too. If you ever actually had sex with a mammal, you'd know that."

Within minutes Callista did what she always did: She blocked her sister out, trying to distract herself with whatever was available: the newspaper, the TV, her silverware. Even the back of the Golden Corn Flakes box, with Leon the Lion pitching how healthy his cereal was. (Maybe he was right; Leon had nice biceps.)

It usually worked, and she could ignore her sister entirely.

Well, nearly. Because even if Arianna was completely annoying, transparent as a showroom window and morally vapid, Callista never thought her sister was stupid. Which is why when Callista heard the words "sea lion" and "porn" in the same sentence, she made a mental note to look it up.

And there it was: a story on the Internet about sea lions actually getting stimulated watching other sea lions have sex. A little more digging revealed a story from BBC News about a fur seal — a fellow pinniped — trying to have sex with a penguin. Watching the 45-minute act on tape — apparently sea lion scientists aren't opposed to a little voyeurism themselves — one scientist commented, "At first glimpse, we thought the seal was killing the penguin."

Callista smiled at the idea that she'd have another story for that scientist soon, a smile that disappeared as soon as she remembered her predicament. The sight of the beach now just a memory, she presumed even her attackers had given her up for dead. The cold water no longer kept at bay by her wetsuit, the first signs of hypothermia were finally starting to creep into to her 5-foot, 6-inch, 150-pound body.

And the sea lion was still out there, somewhere.

Strangely, she wasn't upset at the prospect of dying; perhaps it was the cold. Even the idea that her last moments might be spent reconsidering her sister's view — the only thing Callista smelled like by now was seaweed — wasn't that terrible. Even twits had to be right sometime.

At least it wasn't her father who might have been right;

conceding anything to the wisdom of the world's biggest asshole would have been something else entirely. And as she pondered her hatred for her father — sorry, Grandma — she found the burning thought warming her just a bit. Ironic: her father might actually be saving her life.

"God, just kill me now."

Chapter 4
Callista

Her realization momentarily holding off the chill, Callista took further solace in the fact that the sea lion had finally left her alone. Maybe her sister wasn't right after all, although that didn't really change two things. One: She was still going to die — albeit happier — and two: She was still thinking about her father.

Damn him! She meant what she said: If her last extra minutes on Earth were to be spent thinking of him, she'd rather just have died earlier, thank you very much.

It was her father who had driven her here to Surfland, Oregon. Not literally, mind you; she'd done that herself in her van. But the ongoing deterioration of his skills as a father and human being had spurred her to finally put as much distance between them as possible.

Not physical, mind you; there were a lot of places and aquariums further away from Berkeley than Surfland, Oregon. But with just fewer than 10,000 people nestled into one of the last rugged places in the lower 48 states, Surfland was as far karma-wise from her father as she could get. Indeed, if it had all gone according to plan, she might have been able to go months without ever having to think of him. Even longer if the cable TV went out around here as often as people said.

    He called himself Dr. Emerson Quincy Walker, Ph.D. — and he never skipped even one syllable of that — professor of political science at the University of California – Berkeley. He was a world-renowned lecturer, frequent guest on media talk and news shows and — if Callista could write his résumé — complete bastard.

    He'd come to Berkeley during the '60s as Emery Walker, an idealistic student, and had stayed on through more than 25 years to become one of the most powerful liberal voices in the country.

    His rise began just as he was finishing his doctoral thesis, a "thorough" examination of how pesticide corporations were solely out to kill not just the bugs of the third world, but all the people in it. On any other campus it would have been a liberal screed. At Berkeley it got him a teaching position. So, when Union Carbide accidentally released a toxic gas killing 3,800 people in just a matter of minutes in India, the young, telegenic professor became an overnight media sensation.

    And he knew it. Called the "Liberal Leopard" because of his tendency to lunge at the camera while on television, he became the unofficial voice of all things on the extreme left. As his fame grew so did his ego, until not even his fellow professors could stand to be around him. Which made perfect sense, since virtually no one at home could stand him either.

Married in the late 1970's to another idealist, Emery and his wife had two daughters by the early '80s. But the arrival of the autocratic, never-wrong Dr. Emerson Quincy Walker, Ph.D. on the national stage also brought about the arrival of a similar personality in the home.

On the same day Callista started kindergarten, her mother filed for divorce. Knowing she could never win a fight against the Leopard in the California courts, she gave her husband full custody. In exchange, he wrote his soon-to-be ex-wife a big check, which she used to move to Texas and go to work for an oil company or DuPont. Callista could never remember which.

With her mother out of the house, the Liberal Leopard was free to raise his daughters as he saw fit, which meant a lot of haranguing lectures around the table, sometimes up to three meals a day. (Making tens of thousands of dollars in speaking fees, Dr. Emerson Quincy Walker, Ph.D. rarely even taught anymore, something that thrilled his colleagues.)

Forced to sit at the table until he was done, Callista and Arianna were bombarded up to six hours a day with their father's opinion on everything: the greedy oil companies, the Godforsaken banks, the murdering government, just to name a few.

Arianna soaked it up, every word of it. If it came from her father's mouth, it must be the truth. Indeed, as she got older, her father's rants became less of a diatribe and more a chance to engage in a sick and twisted form of Socratic dialogue that would make Socrates himself glad he'd downed the hemlock.

Callista: "I went out to lunch with Carrie and Paul."

Dr. Emerson Quincy Walker, Ph.D.: "Where did you go?"

Callista: "Oh, just some fast food place. Burger King, I think."

Dr. Emerson Quincy Walker, Ph.D.: "Burger King is evil."

Arianna: "Why, Daddy? Must all fast food be evil?"

Dr. Emerson Quincy Walker, Ph.D.: "Fast food places are all owned by capitalist beings. All capitalists are evil. Burger King is evil."

Arianna: "Yes, daddy, I see. Don't you see, Callista?"

She saw, all right: saw that her father and sister were completely out of their minds, and as middle school turned into high school which turned into college, they got even worse. That's why when it came time to go to college, Callista went as far away as she could without leaving the coast, going to USC on full scholarship. That it was a great school made her very proud. That it was one of the most conservative schools in California and made her father and sister nuts, well, that was just a bonus.

Unfortunately, Callista couldn't spend every waking moment in southern California, although she did try. But there were only so many excuses one could give for having to work every major holiday, and eventually she'd have to go home to her father and sister, neither of whom had any clue just how much she despised them. Namely because she'd never told them.

She'd thought about it, of course. Looking at her friends

and how they had parents and siblings that actually functioned as human beings, she often dreamed of telling Arianna and Dr. Emerson Quincy Walker, Ph.D. to go screw themselves in the hopes that it might knock some sense into them. But then she'd go home for some occasion she couldn't get out of and realize it was hopeless.

Dr. Emerson Quincy Walker, Ph.D.: "Callista, did you see me on CNN today? I hope so. I explained how Wal-Mart is getting old people addicted to drugs with $4 prescriptions. I was quite brilliant."

Arianna: "Yes, Daddy, I see. Don't you see, Callista?"

So, Callista said nothing, year after year, as undergrad led into graduate school and one unavoidable visit after another kept her pretty much silent in her own home. Even when she left for her first job she said nothing, although she did notice that in the years since the sea lion discussion Leon the Lion's biceps seemed to have gotten even bigger. Probably steroids, she thought, which was the only smile she cracked that entire visit.

She was managing one now, too, although anyone who saw her would have thought she was a damned idiot: a riptide was now pulling her faster than ever from the jetty. The shore an even more distant memory, all signs of man and land had rapidly disappeared into the murk — and by all appearances, her chances at survival.

But having grown up along the coast, Callista knew something she was sure her visiting followers did not, even if they were still waiting: How to get out of a riptide. Which was why she waited, until the rip stopped pulling her out. That's when she could escape its grip by swimming sideways, parallel to the shore. And that's exactly what she did, heading north for several hundred yards until she felt it was safe to swim back to shore.

She would have made it, too, but the current had pulled her much farther from shore than she realized. And the cold that she'd held at bay with her wet suit, her fear and her anger for well more than an hour was finally taking its toll. She wasn't even sure she was swimming towards the shore anymore, the fog was that thick, her mind that addled from the cold.

It was not in her nature to give up, but it didn't seem to be in nature's nature to let her keep going. Even with the buoyancy of the wetsuit, each choppy swell now broke more above her head than below it, and every kick and paddle seemed to be less and less effective.

And she began to drown.

Cold and tired, Callista didn't figure it would take much to finish her off, and as she began to hallucinate, she knew the end was near. Strangely, she dreamed of her father's house and those horrible breakfasts around the table. Not of her father or sister — perhaps God was sparing her in death what she could never avoid in life — but of boxes of Golden Corn Flakes. And there he was: Leon the Lion and his enormous biceps holding her in his arms before she passed into the darkness.

Chapter 5
Fuzznut

Leon the Lion was in many ways your typical large cat: he had a huge mane of brownish red hair, a tan-colored body and a tail that twitched when he walked — and there the similarities ended.

Because behind that tail was a waistband that kept the tail attached, beneath the body was foam padding to give the appearance of a massive chest and muscles, and underneath the mane and head was the face of Fuzznut.

"Fuzznut." Just one word, one name. He was on his way home from Bo's Crab and Anvil, a seafood restaurant where he had been hired for a private lunch party. One of the most popular marketing gimmicks and kids' entertainers in Surfland, he was especially valued for his ability to make animal balloons while in costume. (That he could dress like a parrot and simultaneously make one boosted his hourly rate by $10.) Whatever costume Fuzznut was in, he was highly unusual — and not just as a performer.

A retired theme park mascot, Fuzznut had lived in Surfland more than a decade and no one had ever actually seen him. Because Fuzznut had a rule: never appear in public when not in costume.

He arrived at every job already in whatever mascot costume had been hired and took his breaks in private offices, closed rooms, the shadows of dumpsters — or, when necessary, bathroom stalls. (The larger handicapped ones were his favorite.) Often working up to a dozen jobs a week in the tourist-laden summer, Fuzznut's furry alter-egos were among the most famous faces in Surfland, but Fuzznut himself no one would ever recall seeing.

He booked engagements via e-mail and the phone (since mascots don't talk he never worried about someone recognizing his voice) and accepted payment through the mail or Pay Pal.

For jobs across town, he drove his '92 Chrysler minivan with tinted windows and changed in the back, always parking far enough away that no one ever put the van and his jobs together. When distance allowed, he preferred to stay in costume and ride his bike or — even better — walk. The only exception he made to this routine was rain, which admittedly in Surfland could be a lot.

Rain: it was what the Pacific Northwest, and the Oregon coast in particular, was famous for.

Seattle has built a whole image as a place where it never stops, (save for episodes of Grey's Anatomy, where it never starts unless it's directly tied to the plot). But the truth is, Seattle only gets about 32 inches a year, less than cities like Boston and Washington, D.C. — or at least that's what they tell people when they tour Seattle.

But the key thing about Pacific Northwest rain is not the amount the area gets, but how it gets it. In the east, and most parts of the country, when it rains it rains: add the moisture onto the annual tally and hope the crops grow.

In places like Seattle and Portland and Surfland, however, the rain can fall all day and never add up to anything. Indeed, when transplanted Californians run back to their sunny beaches after just one winter on the coast of Oregon, this is why.

Because not so much a rain, what happens on the beach is a mist that coats the skies and sands all day long, but never adds up to more than .05 inches of actual moisture. Not quite rain, not quite fog, but some weird thing in between, it is Seasonal Affective Disorder just waiting to happen, and a lot of people never adjust.

But what is anathema to some is paradise for others, especially those in hot sweaty costumes that run 40 degrees hotter than the surrounding air.

Fuzznut loved the mists that settled on the beach. A more regular occurrence now that fall was well on its way, he enjoyed this season immensely. Indeed, with Halloween — his favorite holiday — now two days in the past, he knew it was just a matter of time until the mists were all too often replaced with days of torrential rains.

Because while most days on the beach might be his

beloved mist, there were still times when the rain fell in sheets. (He hated those days; indeed he'd already lost a paying job to one such day last month when the Surfland Big Whig and Drag Queen Festival had to be postponed.) And there was nothing worse to a mascot than serious rain.

Heavy rain destroys mascot costumes. For one thing, the rain often dissolves the adhesives that hold the parts together in the head. Some children are frightened enough of a six-foot tall furry animal without a nose falling on them as they're shaking hands. (That was a very bad day for Fuzznut — a.k.a. "Surf's-Up Pup" — and the child, who he'd heard was still refusing to visit Disneyland even at 14 years old.)

The other problem is the weight. Because while rain does not destroy stitches and the like, a large furry costume can absorb up to 20 pounds of water in just five minutes of solid rain. Never designed to support that much weight, costumes stress and start to pull apart, causing split seams and holes everywhere.

That's why as much as Fuzznut loved to walk and ride his bike, if it was raining hard, or he thought it might, he would always drive his van. Parking near his final destination, he would make the last walk in costume with a giant golf umbrella. It was a pain in the ass sometimes. During the annual Benjamin Henry Harrison Pneumonia Days Festival in January he'd often have to park up to two miles away because there was no place to put his van near the lake.

But that wasn't today. It was the perfect weather for

mascots: a cool 53 degrees with a 15 mile per hour breeze bringing the fog in off the ocean. It was the closest his costumes came to being air-conditioned. And while he would have made the walk in costume even if it had been 80 degrees — he never made an exception to his rules save for rain — he had to admit this was a lot nicer.

Being slightly neurotic wasn't always easy.

Bouncing along with the breeze and very pleased with himself, Fuzznut was in a hurry to get home. He had a package due in the mail today, and he was anxious to open it up. Maybe that's why he almost missed the body floating in the surf about 50 feet from shore. Clearly a woman, her brown hair fanned out behind her, her wetsuit barely keeping her afloat even as the waves crashed over her face. Living on the ocean for more than a decade, he unfortunately had seen more than one body float in from the waves. Although he'd never had one come ashore just yards from his house, he had to admit he wasn't completely shocked at the sight.

And then she kicked.

If he hadn't been staring right at her he would have missed it, so feeble was the gesture. It was definitely there, however, and when she flailed again with her hand he knew this wasn't a dead body at all. But he also saw with horror that she soon would be: for as she weakly moved and the waves broke about her, she had gotten rolled over, and her face was now below water. Too weak to fight it, her head never moved in an attempt to breathe, and soon her arms and legs stopped moving, as well.

Fuzznut should have peeled off his mascot suit and run into the surf to get her, but getting the costume off took time, and he didn't think she had much more of that. So instead, Leon the Lion simply bounded into the surf, finally immersing himself up to his waist in the water. Scooping her up in his arms, he carried the woman out of the waves.

It almost killed him. Although mascoting kept him in pretty good shape, the fact was he was in his low 50s and carrying a 150-pound woman and 20 pounds of waterlogged lion fur through the sand. By the time he reached his house, walked up the driveway and punched in the access code that led into his courtyard, he thought he might pass out.

But then she drew a breath, and despite the adrenalin high that was rapidly fading, he managed a small smile. She was even managing to speak a little before passing out again, although he had no idea what the hell she was talking about: "Oh, Leon ... I am so sorry about the steroids thing ..."

Chapter 6
Callista

It was at least two hours before any of Callista's senses returned. It spoke to her exhaustion that even when she began to process her surroundings she could do nothing to react to the fear welling up inside her: She was not alone. For even though the curtains were drawn, she could still see enough to recognize a man at the other end of the room. An image of the toothless man with the acne scars flashed into her mind.

But just as quickly it went away, and oddly, she wasn't scared any more. Maybe it was the hazy sight of the man standing over a stove, busily working over something in a sauté pan. Perhaps it was his calm voice speaking into a cell phone, saying, "She's going to be OK." Or maybe it was the smells.

Some of it was clearly the scent of crab wafting through the house from the sauté pan. But it was something else, too; something that, while clearly synthetic and unnatural, was nonetheless comforting. Struggling to place it, she finally figured it out, and with that knowledge, she began to relax. "Wet teddy bear fur," she thought to herself and fell back asleep.

Chapter 7
Jackson Poe

About the time Callista was fading back to black, freelance writer Jackson Poe was on his way home from interviewing a sales rep about the exciting world of bathroom plumbing. One more soulless job to pay the bills, he was just south of the Surfland city limits when his phone rang. Normally, he didn't answer the phone when he was driving, but having just spent an hour talking about the finer points of toilets, he needed something clear his head. Besides, talking to Fuzznut was never boring.

"You found a *what* in the surf? OK, I'll be right there."

Never boring, indeed. Slipping his car into third gear and turning up the volume on his CD player, Poe pondered two things: How had Fuzznut found a girl floating in the waves? And more importantly, what was she doing in his house?

Fuzznut hadn't let anyone other than Poe in his house in all the years either of them had been in Surfland. Pondering that, Poe shifted into fourth gear and hit the accelerator, easily violating the 45 mile per hour speed limit. Fuzznut was not someone who dealt with meeting new people well.

Poe had met Fuzznut shortly after Poe and his girlfriend had moved to Surfland to become reporters for the local paper about 10 years ago. Although Poe had lost the exact details to time, he had almost killed Fuzznut on his first story assignment when something had gone very wrong with a golf cart at the Deals & Squeals Outlet Mall and Fun Center grand opening. Crushed up against the outside of the underwear outlet store, Poe was sure whoever was in that giant pig suit was going to sue him and his newspaper into non-existence.

Not a good first day.

But instead of getting mad, "Rooter" ("He's rootin' for good deals and fun!") just pushed the golf cart back and kept on shaking hands and making animal balloons for another three hours until the celebration was over. Amazed, Poe watched the pig the rest of the day. He even began to follow him when whoever it was in the costume began to walk out of the mall — and began to limp.

Now worried, Poe continued to follow the pig until he climbed into a white minivan with darkened windows and drove off. And that was the end of it.

Except to Poe it wasn't. Back at the newspaper, Poe asked his editor if she knew who the pig was, to which he got a funny look and a directive to get back to work. One day into his new job — and not really wanting to explain the full story of the limping pig — Poe didn't push it any further.

That night after work, however, he began to drive the

streets of Surfland looking for the minivan, and when the sun rose the next morning, he began looking again. His girlfriend thought he was nuts, telling him if he didn't stop he'd get them both fired. That's why when he was 30 minutes late for a planning meeting that afternoon, he told them both he got lost trying to get to know the bizarre streets of his new home.

The truth was, however, he'd found the van early that morning in the first part of the city he'd checked. Parked in a driveway on a dead-end street near the beach, it was almost invisible under a canopy of trees that seemed to cover the front yard as well. He had to look twice before he found the gate that gave him access to the front yard and the chance to knock on the door.

No one answered the first time, or the second or the third. Deciding no one was home, he was preparing to leave when he heard a moan from inside the house. Looking in a gap between the front window's drawn curtains, he saw a man in his early 40s lying on the ground struggling to crawl across the floor on one leg and two arms.

Opening the unlocked door, Poe entered and told the man who he was. Clearly in pain, he did his best to understand.

"So you're the sonofabitch asshole who ran me over," he said, and a friendship was born. Fuzznut — the man offered no other name — asked Poe to take him to the hospital about an hour outside of town to see a doctor. On the way home with a sprained knee that would take a couple of weeks to heal, Fuzznut asked Poe to please not tell anyone who he was or where he lived.

It was a promise Poe kept when he was 30 minutes late to his meeting, and for all of the ten years that had followed.

Rolling into Fuzznut's driveway, Poe parked behind the same van and opened the same gate he had a decade ago. Recalling his accidental introduction to Fuzznut, he hoped his new guest wasn't as freaked out by Fuzznut's "curious" attire as he'd been.

Not for the first time, Poe wondered if all that time in costume might not have wreaked a little brain damage on his friend.

But as he threw the gate closed behind him, Poe saw he had no reason to worry; the young woman was asleep in a chaise lounge on the front deck. How much longer she'd stay that way was anyone's guess; just inches from her nose was a steaming plate of crab cakes. Careful not to wake her, Poe tiptoed past her, unlocked Fuzznut's door quietly, and slipped inside.

And found himself face-to-face with a naked man holding a still-steaming pan and a pot of coffee. Again. (That Fuzznut had been crawling across the floor naked ten years ago was an image Poe had desperately tried to forget.)

"Fuzznut, I thought you told me you were going to at least wear an apron when you cooked," Poe said.

"Sorry, you caught me changing," Fuzznut said with no embarrassment whatsoever. "I spilled butter on the other one."

"Better the apron, I guess ..." Poe said, returning his attention to the girl out front. "Tell me she didn't see you like that."

"She didn't see me at all. She was unconscious when I fished her out of the ocean. She stayed that way while I brushed my lion costume — salt water's a bitch to get out of fur by the way — and threw it in the washer. And after mumbling a bit while I was cooking, she passed out again long enough for me to put her on the porch."

To Fuzznut it all made perfect sense, and once he explained the whole tale of how he found the girl, it did to Poe as well. More importantly, the girl apparently had no memories of Surfland's — and maybe the world's — only nudist mascot.

Some things were left better unexplained.

Poe's curiosity now moved to the girl. "Any idea who she is or how she got in the water?"

"Nope, that's why I called you, Mr. Reporter guy," Fuzznut said with more than a hint of sarcasm.

"But if it's all the same to you, I'd rather you do that somewhere else. I've got a new toy to play with," Fuzznut said as he pulled a large tube-like object from a box. "It's a T-shirt gun!"

At first Poe was stunned. Poe had never met a gun he liked, and neither had Fuzznut, one of the many things they had in common. But seeing the glee on his friend's face, Poe decided "T-shirt" was the key word here. "Where the hell did you get that?"

"Where everything good comes from: the Internet," Fuzznut said. "Just $299.95! Here, let me show ..." but he never got a chance to finish. On the porch, Callista had started to stir.

Chapter 8
Callista

Psychologists say of all the senses, smell is the most powerful when it comes to the ability to recall past events. Maybe that's why, despite the steaming crab cakes just inches from her nose, Callista was still thinking of wet fur when she began to wake up.

She didn't have many memories of her mother, but one thing she'd always remembered was her mom washing her teddy bear with unholy amounts of fabric softener. Still damp even after a cycle in the drier, Callista had come to associate the smell of her bear with better times. Even after her mom left, the smell stayed on the bear for years.

Perhaps it would still be there today if her father hadn't thrown out the bear when she was eight. ("Teddy Bears are named after a bear murderer," she was told.)

Gradually, however, the sweet smell of the past gave way to the scents of the present: the long-steaming crab cakes. There was something new, as well: coffee, held in the hand of a man standing at the foot of the chaise lounge.

"Good evening, miss. Coffee?"

Shaking out the cobwebs in her brain, Callista checked out the bringer of caffeine. A few inches under six feet with a small amount of gray at his brown-haired temples (and a bit of a roll around the middle, she noticed) he and his brightly flowered shirt seemed to tower over her as she lay on the lounge. Still, she managed to return the questioning tone in his voice: "A little late for the java, isn't it?"

"I'm not the one who's been asleep for nearly five hours."

And the morning came racing back to Callista: surfing, the race through town, the men chasing her onto the jetty, falling into the ocean and almost drowning.

The exceptional horny sea lion.

But everything after that was a blur. How she got onto this porch was a mystery, and although she vaguely remembered something about wet animals and a strangely dressed man — was he really dressed all in pink? — those memories were so much a weird blur she decided to not even mention them. The only thing that seemed real in the past several hours was waking up on this porch with a plate of crab cakes next to her, which she began to devour.

"Who are you? Did you make these? Who got me out of the ocean? Where am I? Can I thank them?"

Her questions came forth in a jumble and only stopped because she realized she was spitting crab onto the man's shoes. Not that he seemed to mind.

"I'll take the last one first: Unfortunately, no, he had a, uh, meeting he had to get to. That's why he called me to help you out," he said with a kind smile. "The rest, well, that's sort of complicated."

Chapter 9
Poe

Jackson Poe's life was complicated even before he met Fuzznut, as Poe had a knack for making decisions that made things more complicated. No one thought this more ironic than Poe himself, as in his mind every deliberative decision he had made was about the desire to keep his life simple.

He had grown up in Colorado in a small town about 30 miles north of Denver. Far enough away not to be a sprawling suburb, but still close enough to museums, concerts all the other things that parents drag their kids to when they'd rather be doing something else.

That gripe was minor, however, and in a world brimming with angst-ridden youth and adults who had never gotten over it, Poe was fairly content. Other than the fact that his parents both drove cars that were an utter embarrassment when they picked him up at high school and their tendency to hold hands and kiss in public places, it was a pretty good life.

When he packed off for college, he didn't go far, attending the University of Colorado – Boulder just a few miles up the road. Aside from being one of the most beautiful campuses in the country, it also had a great journalism school (and his mom could keep doing his laundry). Graduating in four years near the top of his class, he went to work in corporate communications when he discovered he could actually make a living that way.

He did that for nearly 10 years, eventually rising to the position of senior writer, a title that allowed him to travel, party all the time, and eventually get bored out of his mind. There were only so many stories you could write about an oil company.

So, he went back to journalism school, this time at the University of Missouri – Columbia. Here, two trends in his personality revealed themselves that continued to complicate his life to this day.

One: he liked the company of women. This wasn't news to him. Aside from intellectual curiosity once in Bangkok, he'd never wanted to have a relationship with anyone but a woman.

But after nearly a decade of traveling alone he found that having a woman in his life made things easier. There was always someone to talk to, always someone to hang out with on a Saturday night, always someone to keep him warm — and a few other things — in bed.

Unfortunately, the other over-riding trait in his life tended to make any kind of long-term relationship impossible: he was an uncompromising pain-in-the-ass.

Not that he hadn't always been; in high school he had a knack for ending up in the principal's office because he wouldn't just shut up in class or stop writing editorials in the student newspaper. It was even there his sophomore year in college, when he called one of his bosses a liar at a staff dinner.

But the closer he got to graduation in Boulder, the more he calmed down. Realizing that if he ever wanted to actually make a living at anything, he decided he'd better stop calling his bosses "sell-out spineless lap-dogs." (It just sort of came out in a meeting.) Indeed, by the time he graduated he had reformed himself enough that when the PR job came open at a Fortune 500 company (and the top 1 percent of the 500 at that), he easily got it.

Maybe that's why when he went to graduate school he reverted so easily to his defiant ways: after playing corporate suck-up for a decade, he was plain out of bullshit. Or maybe it was just more fun that way.

Whatever the case, Poe spent his two years in Missouri delighting some of his professors and editors with his writing style, while others made a point of throwing him out of their offices. Even on his last story, an investigation of the terrible way local cops and hospitals dealt with rape in Columbia, he made one editor so mad that the story had to be run while she was on vacation.

Indeed, the only reason it ran was because the other editor responsible for the story happened to be his girlfriend, Aly Oliviera. She was everything he wanted in a relationship, and after working together at the newspaper in graduate school, when their studies were done they headed off to build careers together.

Their first stop — and it turned out their last one — was Surfland. It was their last because neither had ever left and because there was no longer a "they."

Within weeks Poe's tendency to always say what he thought was getting him in regular trouble with his editor at the Surfland Siren. Never open defiance, it was more a constant questioning of the newspaper's priorities. And when Poe decided he'd rather spend a day following around a code enforcement officer who did everything but code enforcement instead of covering the latest bank to buy the honor of "Business of the Week" from the Chamber of Commerce, it was the end of his job.

It also ended his relationship with Aly. Willing to play by the rules, she was rapidly becoming the most trusted person in the newsroom. That Poe would put his personal crusades ahead of the paper, and in her mind, her, was more than she could accept. Just three hours after losing his job he moved out of their rented townhouse.

"You know, Poe," she'd told him on that night almost a decade ago, "I think I'll always love part of you. It's just the immature stupid part that I can't love at all, and since that's the bigger part of you, that's a problem."

"I'm not immature, just determined," he said. "You work there! You know how bad it is!"

"Don't give me that, Jackson. You were like this when we were in graduate school, you pissed off people as we left, and you started out this job ignoring the editor," she said, unknowingly clubbing him with a friendship he had never explained. "Your second day on the job you were late!"

"I told you, I got lost and ..."

"My ass, you were driving around town looking for that damned guy in the pig suit, even after your boss told you not to!" she said, exasperated. "I knew it, she knew it, everyone knew it! You couldn't go one day without doing your own thing — and here we are."

And that was the end of that.

He and Aly were still friends, and in a town of 10,000 it was a given they would run into each other a lot. Eventually, she became editor the Siren, giving her a front-row seat to one relationship after another of his, where eventually his need to be himself destroyed his ability to stay with anyone. His last relationship was the longest: three years, but that had ended a year ago when, once again, Jackson refused to compromise.

Since leaving the paper he paid the bills by freelancing articles for newspapers and magazines large and small. There was a surprising amount of money to made in writing about toilets and other grotesquely expensive things for the home.

Every once in a while he even got the chance to write about something he gave a damn about. The checks usually weren't as good as the stories about people being willing to pay $8,000 for a counter top that had a fern fossil in it, but at least he could put his real name on it: Jackson Day Poe. (Every other story got a pseudonym: Jack Ickes Ponell, his way of telling the world they'd been, "JIP-ped.")

He even made a few bucks here and there writing for small businesses. Though his days of being a corporate hack were over, he found nothing offensive about helping smaller businesses in town get their message out in the form of small press releases and websites. Indeed, when Aly had booted him out of the house, he spent the next year living in a small beach house where he got free rent in exchange for keeping the owner's website current. (Her annual April Fool's Day Gray Whale Feeding Festival was always good for at least two press releases and a slew of rentals in the other beach houses she managed.)

Fuzznut even dropped him a few bucks here and there; he always let Poe keep the change when Poe had to get something from the store for the recluse. When that was a $100 bill for a stick of underarm deodorant — mascots go through it quick — that meant a lot of money. Where Fuzznut got that kind of money, he never said, and Poe never asked, like most of the details of their friendship.

But it did mean that when Fuzznut called, Poe always tried to answer. Not because of the money, but because the two took care of each other in their own weird way. Fuzznut needed things from time to time — you can't order everything over the Internet — and Poe needed someone to talk to. (Fuzznut's aprons and occasional towel had helped a lot with that.)

Which is how Poe came to be standing on a porch on a cool Thursday evening staring at a woman who'd been rescued by a nudist in a lion suit.

Complicated, indeed.

Chapter 10
Callista

"I'm Jackson Poe," he told her as he shook her hand, and he explained to her as best he could what he knew. Although she suspected he was leaving some parts out — particularly when it came to his "friend" — she let it lie.

Whoever they were, they had saved her life.

When Poe got to the part where he had found her abandoned van at the end of the jetty road near the house, Callista began to tense up again. After eating the crab cakes she'd noticed a set of her own clothes and her rain jacket folded neatly at the end of the chaise lounge and wondered how they'd gotten there.

"How did you know the van was mine?" she asked, a bit more suspicion in her voice than she would have liked.

"The only people that come down this road are people who live here; the most popular public jetty access is further down the beach," he said, having asked Fuzznut the same question once. "When I saw all the women's clothing and the surfboard in back, I just kinda figured.

"What I can't figure is just how you ended up nearly dead in the surf. You weren't surfing, your board was in the van …"

Callista thought for a few moments before answering. After what she'd been through today, she had no reason to trust anyone.

And yet, she did trust this man.

There had been so many moments when she was at the mercy of Jackson and "his friend," tonight, and yet at each turn they had done nothing but what was right for her. Besides, there was still the mystery of why she had been chased down the beach and the possibility that they might come back.

"Speaking of complicated …" she began, and proceeded to tell Poe the entire story, from her first night in Surfland sleeping in her camper van to the hazy moments preceding their meeting on the porch. To his credit, Poe said nothing the entire time, and when she was finished, he simply said: "I need to make a phone call." And with that, he left the front yard, promising to guard the gate while she changed from her wetsuit into her clothes. When she was done, she let him know, and he came back into the yard.

"The first thing we need to do is stash your van. Whoever chased you may decide to come back, and we don't want them to find it or you in it. I think I've got that taken care of, although it does mean you'll have to spend one night on the couch at my place.

Callista nodded in agreement. Normally, she wasn't the kind to let a man she'd just met take charge of her life, but right now it felt comforting.

What he asked of her next, however, seemed far less so: after dropping off her van before the sun disappeared for the night, he wanted to drive back up to the north end of town. Whatever had spooked her pursuers, it had started there. From her description of the area, Poe said he was pretty sure he knew where to go. In fact, he thought he might even know which house it was, a thought that seemed to trouble him greatly as he opened the gate out of Fuzznut's yard.

She put that thought on hold, however, as she stepped into the driveway next to the house: "Oh my God, what the hell is *that?*"

Chapter 11
Poe

"That" as she put it — as everyone put it — was a 2011 Jaguar XKR convertible.

British Racing Green with a black top, it had every option possible, and even a few after-market add-ons just because Poe thought they'd be fun to have. Even standing still the car looked like it could achieve every one of its factory-limited 155 miles per hour (something else Poe had changed). Even people who knew nothing about cars and thought them a wasteful extravagance usually loved the look of this one.

"Poe," Callista said again. "What the hell is that?"

Like just about everyone before her, she just couldn't reconcile that the man dressed in an old aloha shirt, beat-up blue jeans and a cheap Casio digital watch could own a $92,000 car. And she was right.

"That," Poe said with a smile that belied his tone, "is death on my doorstep, my last relationship and any chance I'll ever have of driving a regular car again."

*****

Poe had never planned to own an exotic car. Hoped, yes. But planned, no.

Eking out a living the past decade as a student and a freelance writer, driving anything but his 15-year-old Toyota Celica convertible was pretty much a pipe dream. Even when he'd worked in corporate America, the money he made was never anything like what it took to afford a six-digit ride.

Truthfully, he was happy with his Celica. It had taken him through graduate school, made the trip to Oregon. Through one rainy winter after another, the top had always gone down quickly so he could enjoy those bursts of sunshine when they came. With a little 4-cylinder engine, it might not have been the quickest car in town, but it passed the RVs on the highway, and that was good enough for him.

Even some of the local kids thought it was a neat car; gearheads, they talked about turning it into a "tuner," one of those little Japanese pocket rockets in the "Fast and Furious" movies. Amused that teenagers would like his car, he always enjoyed taking it to the local high school, where he occasionally spoke to the advanced journalism class about what he did for a living.

About two years ago he'd completed such a visit when Ryan Nordin, one of the editors at the school paper, pulled him aside as he walked out of the building. He wanted to say thanks for all the visits Poe had made over the last couple of years. As a token of their appreciation, the staff had decided to get him a digital tape recorder.

That was the plan, anyway.

"Paxton was supposed to pick it up at the Sony store when he was in the Valley, but he forgot," Ryan explained. "So, he had his mom pull over at s gas station, and he spent the money on lottery tickets to give you instead," he said, clearly frustrated. "Paxton Dell may be a great writer, but he's a freakin' space cadet."

Poe just laughed, and told Ryan it wasn't a problem. "It's the thought that counts," he said as he took the tickets and put them in his back pocket.

But walking out of the building, it was a problem. Not the kids; they were just trying to say thanks, albeit in a screwed up way.

Rather, it was a problem for him. Poe hated the lottery, and he made sure everyone knew it. When they first started dating, Aly had given him ten tickets as a birthday present, having no idea how he felt about state-run lotteries. What resulted was a perfect dinner ruined as Jackson went off about the lottery.

"Lotteries are for states and voters who don't have the balls to raise taxes to pay for things," he said poking his fork alternately at the cous cous and Aly. "So instead, they start a lottery, and get every idiot to play.

"Sure, they say it's for parks or education or some wonderful thing like that, but as soon as the lottery money starts rolling in, they cut the money those programs used to get from the general budget. No one really gets anything extra except the jerk politicians who dreamed up the thing."

Aly, seeing her evening going straight down the toilet, tried to rescue it. "Well, maybe they're just trying to give people a choice."

She might as well have thrown gasoline on a fire.

"Choice! They know the only people who play these things are people that don't have any money in the first place!" he said, his arms now flailing with every word. "They are intentionally milking people's human weaknesses."

"You ever wonder why everyone who wins the lottery seems to be a hard-luck story that needs the money?" he asked. "If they're that poor, why are they plunking down $20, $30 a week playing a damn lottery!"

If Poe had stopped there, the evening might have recovered.

"And who the hell buys lottery tickets for a gift anyway?" he said to a woman who was starting to love him. "Boy, nothing says thoughtfulness quite like, 'Hey! I bought your present at a gas station!'"

And that was the end of the evening, as even Poe realized he'd gone too far — even before she sent a wine glass flying across the room. To his credit, Poe did manage to apologize in the days that followed. And when he backed his sincerity up with a massage at a spa near campus, she managed to forgive him.

She never did give him a lottery ticket again, however, and as Poe informed most everyone he knew about his hatred of state-run lotteries, no one else did either. "Most," however, did not include high school students; when he went to the school his job was to teach, not espouse his political beliefs.

That's why as he left the building, he planned to throw the

tickets out just as soon as Ryan was out of sight, and he would have, too. Instead, his phone rang and he forgot about them until the following Sunday morning when he pulled them out of his pocket and set them on the folding table before doing his and his girlfriend's laundry. (Surfland, Oregon, was a little far to still have his mother do it, though he never could figure out how she got his socks so white.)

The tickets were still there hours later when the news came on television. Getting increasingly frustrated with his girlfriend Vivian's delicates (he never had figured out just how to fold her lingerie), he looked up just as the winning lottery numbers went scrolling across the bottom of the screen. Still distracted by lace and frills, he absent-mindedly glanced at the pile of tickets, and had the top ticket been any other of the 30 in the pile, he never would have glanced again.

But he did glance again, because his six numbers seemed to match the numbers on the screen. Grabbing the remote, he rewound the TiVo and paused it: the numbers still matched. And just like that, Jackson Poe, publicly avowed Powerball hater and hugely vocal critic of all state-run lotteries, had won just over $4 million via the Oregon State Lottery. (He split the ticket with a family of seven living in a trailer in Iowa who were thrilled to win after 17 years of spending $25 a week on tickets.)

All the news stations wondered about the owner of the ticket, purchased at a Portland Chevron station, and waited for the owner to come forward. They waited in vain, however, because for months Poe wrestled with whether or not to even turn in the ticket. He didn't even tell Vivian, whom he had been dating for nearly three years. He had every reason to be conflicted: this money represented everything he hated about government and taxpayers who wanted everyone but themselves to actually pay for things. More than once he decided to just throw the tickets out.

But he never did, and as the reality of having $4 million sitting in his sock drawer began to sink in, his mind began to wander. It did not have to wander far; every time Poe drove into Portland he passed a Jaguar dealership. And one day he stopped and asked how much the convertible in the window was: $92,000? Another $20,000 or so for add-ons and taxes? Well that wasn't much compared to $4 million was it? (Well, $2 million after taxes. Whatever.)

And with the smell of leather in his nose and a six-speed stick in his hands, he made the decision to turn in the ticket. Was he a hypocrite? Yes. Was he going to hell? Yes. But by God he was going to drive there in style, and on a quiet Friday he walked into the lottery office in Salem.

He chose the day because it was the end of the week, and with any luck it wouldn't make the papers, not that it would matter if it did. Poe had rented a cheap apartment in Portland — for one month — and changed the address on his driver's license so when the e-mail went out to his "local" paper, it would go to the big-city Oregonian instead of the Surfland Siren, edited by one Aly Oliviera.

Which is how Jackson Poe, freelance writer and local fashion nightmare, came to drive what was arguably the nicest car in Surfland. "A rich uncle died," he told people, an answer most people accepted. Naturally, Aly wasn't one of them, but when Poe made up a good story with some of his relatives' names she knew, she let the matter drop.

His conscience was another matter. It bothered him to know that despite his high-flying morals — and the very vocal rhetoric — he could be bought. When he told people the car was death on his doorstep, he just let them assume he meant a relative, and not his soul.

It helped somewhat that he put the car in every local parade that existed and drove the homecoming queen every fall with the top down rain or shine. He had even returned some of the money from whence it came, setting up an annuity that would anonymously donate $20,000 a year to the high school journalism program.

And that was how he lived with himself, but it proved far too much for Vivian to continue living with him. When she found out what he had done with the ticket she was furious. Not that he had violated his moral code; she'd always suspected his arrogance had a financial tipping point.

But that he had spent it on a car. "A car? Jackson, have you lost your damn mind? We live in a tiny condo, have no damn room, can barely make ends meet, and you go drop a hundred thousand dollars on a car?"

She'd calmed down for a few minutes when she realized that even with his purchases and donations he still had more than half the money left. A million-plus dollars could still buy quite a bit, even in the expensive real estate market of Surfland.

But the moment was lost just as soon as Poe opened his mouth again.

"Actually, it's more than that," he said to her ever-widening eyes. "But I put the rest in some low-yield investments so I can always pay for maintenance and buy a new one every five years or so."

She moved out within the week, heading back to New Orleans to continue her massage therapist career. Just thankful she'd never told anyone about the lottery ticket, he didn't want to push his luck by offering her the chance to ride in the car.

He liked to think that would have changed her mind, but knew honestly that it wouldn't have. But that was OK, if a woman couldn't understand just why this car mattered to him — or at least acknowledge that it had a right to matter — then he didn't want to be with her anyway. Rationalizing a bit — he did miss her massages and discussions over dinner — he decided he was glad her misunderstanding ass had never been allowed to touch his leather seats.

Maybe that's why he was so careful about who he let in the car; anyone who was going to ride shotgun in the Jag didn't have to love it like he did, but they sure as hell better not bitch at him that it was a waste of money. He'd stopped a conversation with more than one person — attractive women included — who decided he was an idiot or, his personal favorite, "compensating for something."

Callista, he was thrilled to see, didn't fall into that category. After her exclamation and his explanation about the "uncle" and his qualms about spending his inheritance on a car

— he did tell the truth about Vivian — she said just one thing: "I better get a ride in that thing after we drop off my van."

Smiling, he promised her they'd do just that.

Chapter 12
Callista

Heading north on U.S. Highway 101 through Surfland in the Jag, Callista decided this was definitely better than her van.

If nothing else, she hadn't been living in this car for two weeks. (Volkswagen mystique or no, living in campgrounds and RV parks got old after a while.) Even not having showered since her two trips to the ocean, the 60 mile per hour wind going through her hair somehow made her feel clean. Coupled with whatever it was Poe was playing on the CD player — it sounded like a cross between reggae and the theme to Miami Vice — it was quite the contrast to thinking she was dead just a few hours ago.

It had been quite the half hour since she had met Jackson Poe.

After hearing Poe's car story — "Going off on a Jag" he called it — Callista groaned at the pun. But as she headed back to her van with Poe, she didn't let it tamp her enthusiasm for the ride to come one bit.

But she was quickly slapped back to reality when she

realized someone had gone through her van. At first she didn't notice; Poe had already told her he'd gotten the clothes out of the back.

But when she saw the binoculars lying on the seat instead of where she left them on the dashboard, she realized someone else had been through her things. It must have been the men on the beach.

Aside from the binoculars, someone had clearly tossed around her things. Her purse lay overturned on the floor, although it didn't look like they had taken anything. They'd even ejected the CD from the stereo, leaving it lying on floor mat. One of her favorites, she wrapped it in a piece of paper and stuck it in her jacket pocket.

Thankfully, she kept her identification and credit cards in the locked glove box, although that too had been tampered with: scratches marred the area around the lock. But had they actually gotten in?

Giving her wetsuit to Poe, she reached under the driver's seat as far as she could and pulled a magnetic lockbox off the seat springs. Taking a key from the lockbox, she was relieved to open the glove box and find everything still there. What had they been looking for? Poe was as clueless as she was, but suggested it might be best to get out of there, and she followed Poe in her van as he headed up the coast in his Jag.

After about a mile Poe turned off the street to park next to a large building with a huge courtyard out front. He said it was a bed and breakfast, although the parking area was hidden from the street by an adjoining stable and barn. Were it not already booked with a large group reservation, she'd be staying here tonight instead of his couch.

But it did make a good place to hide the van, and after grabbing a change of clothes and her toiletries, they headed north with the rapidly sinking sun to their left. When the song ended, Poe told her what was on his mind.

"The area where those guys saw you is full of beach houses that used to be managed by a friend of mine. She's just about the only full-time resident left, as most of the original even part-time residents have sold out and moved on."

"I miss their quilt-making parties," he said.

"You don't seem like the quilting type," she said, surprised.

"I'm not," he said, "but those women made some killer rum raisins."

Chapter 13
Poe

Left unspoken as he and Callista drove north was the fact that when Aly had booted Poe from their place, it was the lead quilter that had taken him in and let him work off his rent, since she was the owner of Surfland Haven Beach Rentals. Eventually, he had become the son she never had, taking time out of each day to check on her and make sure she was all right.

Her name was Alice Kauffman.

Poe's worst fears were confirmed as they approached Alice's neighborhood.

There, he saw her beach house, halfway down and across the street from the beach access ramp, surrounded by yellow tape, although it appeared the officers on duty were beginning to wrap up the scene.

"Oh my God," whispered Callista. "That's where those men were standing."

Poe said nothing as he parked the car near the house and

looked to see if anyone was on site who could tell him what happened. Two faces fit the bill: Pete Polanski, an officer with Surfland Fire & Rescue, and Julio Cruz, owner of a small contracting company that took care of Alice's properties. Pete clearly was busy, but upon seeing Poe, Julio walked up to the car.

"Julio, what's going on?" Poe asked him.

"Señorita Kauffman had to be rushed to the hospital," he said, clearly shaken. "I found her in her the living room when I came to talk to her about putting a new roof on her house early this afternoon."

Despite having been in Surfland for longer than Poe and having worked for Alice for nearly that long, he still talked about her with the Spanish honorific he thought she deserved. Speaking softly with the accent he still carried from his youth in Oaxaca, Mexico, it gave Julio's serious discussion about the older woman a sense of endearment that went just beyond boss and employee.

Indeed, after Poe had rounded up enough money to buy a place of his own, Julio had become Alice's next adopted son. She was his first customer when he began Oaxaca Workers, Inc., and watched with pride as his business expanded to three trucks and his young family grew into teenagers. When Julio needed someone to talk to because he was worried about his daughters, Alice was the first person he came to, as she had raised three of her own.

Lately, however, most of Julio's worries were about Alice herself.

In the last year she'd seen all of her neighbors accept outrageous prices for their homes and leave, the part-time residents' homes dropping out of her management program. It wasn't about money; Julio knew she had plenty even without their commissions.

But even as part-time residents, they had been her friends, and they were gone now. He'd discussed this with her, but she told him not to worry, that change was the way of things. Even in the past few weeks, when she'd seemed particularly distracted, she told him not to worry about it.

And now he felt terrible. Telling Poe about his concerns, he wondered out loud if she might have collapsed from those unknown worries.

"And those two men couldn't have helped, either, always bugging her about this and that," he said, suddenly looking like he'd eaten a rotten lemon. "Just because she used to manage those houses doesn't mean she knows everything about them."

At the mention of two men, both Callista and Poe audibly caught their breath. "Julio, what two men?" Poe asked.

Failing to notice their startled reactions, Julio told them how they'd been asking Alice all kinds of things about the houses of her former friends. She told him not worry or do anything that would jeopardize the flow of work his company had been doing for the men.

Not that he was proud to call them his clients.

"Actually, they just work for the guy who pays me," Julio said. "He used to pay me himself in cash by mail, but the past two weeks those two guys have been doing it. The one missing his front teeth is the bad one. Every time he pays me he keeps threatening to have me deported.

"He's the one that should leave the country, maybe then he could find himself a dentist." At that remark, Poe wanted to ask him more about the men, but he lost his train of thought when Pete came over to the car.

"Well gentlemen," Pete said, addressing both Julio and Poe, "you'll be happy to know Alice is going to be all right. It looks like it was just a minor heart attack, although they are going to keep her overnight at the hospital, just to be sure." With the news, Julio, Poe and Callista all exhaled deeply, a sound that finally alerted Pete to a new face in his midst.

"So, Poe, who's your friend? You wouldn't even let me ride shotgun for the first three weeks you owned the car."

"That's because you drop ketchup on the seats every time a fire truck drives by," he said with a laugh, before becoming a bit more serious again. "This is my friend, Callista Walker, and has she got a story for you."

Chapter 14
Poe

In truth, Callista's story was probably better made for the police that were also on scene at Alice's house. But he'd decided to have Callista talk to the police later; at the moment they appeared to have their hands full taking Julio's statement, anyway. For now, he wanted to fill Pete in on what was happening.

In Poe's brief time at the paper, he'd come to know Pete first as a source and then a friend. Yes, there was Pete's obsession with collecting anything and everything related to fire departments, fire engines and firefighting tools. But that really only counted as one obsession, and in a place like Surfland, that meant you were actually pretty normal.

Asking Callista and Poe to come with him to his Jeep, Pete listened as Callista told her story. She had gotten better at telling it since the first time, and save for the momentary distraction of watching Pete brush the stuffed Dalmatian he kept chained into the passenger seat, it took only a few minutes. After adding on what Julio had told him, Poe wanted to find out just what Polanksi knew that might help him make sense of a mess that was rapidly beginning to involve more than just one of his friends.

"How do you know she was attacked?" Poe asked, even though he didn't really believe it. "Even a minor heart attack might have put her on the floor."

Pete's reply was straight to the point: "Heart attacks don't kick in doors," he said, before taking Callista and Poe over to the house.

The police investigating the scene had no problem letting Poe in; it was well known he and Alice went way back. But it didn't take a trained crime scene investigator to see Polanski was right about the door; the frame was clearly shattered from the door jam outward. Looking at Callista, Pete asked her if maybe she'd seen it happen.

"No," she said, looking back towards the ramp that she'd walked up what seemed like a lifetime ago. "I just waved at the two guys standing on the porch. I had no idea being friendly could be such a problem."

Poe finished her unspoken thought. "Not unless the people you're waving at have just committed a crime. They must have thought you saw something, although I can't imagine getting caught robbing an old woman would make them want to kill you."

Pete ended that train of thought just as soon as it started, however. "The police don't think robbery's the motive. Nothing's missing from the house, and there's a lot of valuable stuff here."

Looking around, Poe saw he was right. Not only was nothing missing, nothing had even been moved, something Poe found curious after the ransacking of Callista's van.

The vases from China, the German tapestries, even the gold statues from Peru were untouched. Even an idiot who knew nothing about art would have to know the gold was worth a fortune. Hell, bronze had become so valuable to meth heads, that the addicts were ripping statues out of parks with trucks so they could melt them down.

No, thought Poe looking around the room, robbery was definitely not the motive.

But what was it?

In the background, he could hear Callista finally getting a chance to talk to the police, and as she ran through the story for the third time in 90 minutes, he could detect weariness in her voice. Whether it was from being tired of constantly retelling the story or just because she was tired, Poe detected a fatigue in her voice that wasn't there when she told Polanksi the story.

Not needing to hear it again himself, he stared at the splintered door's frame and made a note to have Julio come over and fix it before she got home. It would never be the beautiful hardwood of the original, but with the right stain Julio should be able to make it match.

Built with a hardwood that Poe was sure had long since passed onto an endangered species list, Poe gazed around the room one more time and noticed that, indeed, every square inch of Alice's home was the real thing. No cheap woods around the doors and windows, no simulated parquet on the floors, no

Home Depot lamps on the ceiling: everything in this house was exactly the way Alice's late husband, Walter, had built it in the early 1950s.

Even angrier now at the damage to Alice's home, Poe resolved to keep it the way Walter had built it.

Next time Poe saw Fuzznut he'd ask him to find an authentic piece of wood that matched, maybe on eBay. If the man could find a T-shirt gun, he could certainly find a piece of wood, Poe thought, as he took a six-inch piece of the splintered wood and slipped it into his pocket.

That's when he found Callista standing behind him. He'd been so wrapped up in his thoughts he hadn't noticed she'd finished with the police.

Five minutes later, after saying goodbye to Pete, he and Callista were on their way to Poe's house, and less than ten minutes after that Callista found herself in Poe's half-bath brushing her teeth.

Returning to the living room, she saw Poe had already folded out the hide-a-bed — sheets, pillows and all. Mindful of how tired she must be, Poe excused himself until morning. Which was why he was surprised when she said she was still too wired to sleep. "I did sleep five hours this afternoon," she said defiantly. "You've got a DVD player. Let's watch a movie."

"Oh, Callista, you just said the magic words," and with that, a devilish grin lit Poe's face from side-to-side.

Walking slowly across the room to the light switch, he suddenly seemed to be hypnotized, yet with a purpose. Turning down the lights, the room was now lit only by the glow of the blank TV screen. Crossing back across the room in the near darkness, he opened a cabinet and gently removed a small box. Slowly, he left the cabinet and moved to take a seat in a chair next to Callista's hide-a-bed.

As he opened the box slowly in front of Callista, he couldn't believe this was happening. After Vivian's enraged departure he despaired of ever doing this again with a woman. Lifting the item from the box, he sat it in Callista's lap and getting down on bended knee asked her a question he'd been longing to ask for one year, one month and four days (he'd kept track).

"How do you feel about Steve McQueen movies?"

Chapter 15
Joey White

FRIDAY

Captain James Tiberius Kirk had been through a lot of crap.

He'd been dematerialized into an alternate universe, had a monster try to remove all of the salt from his body with giant sucker hands, been altered by transporter accidents, and even had his consciousness switched into a woman's body.

At the moment, any of those seemed like an improvement to Joey White. For one thing, no matter what Captain Kirk went through, it seemed like he got to kiss some space chick at the end of every episode.

More importantly, though, Captain Kirk never had to spend time with Joey's Uncle Shelton — Augh! Shabazz T. Morton — which seemed to make all of the good captain's travails seem to pale in comparison. (Save making out with the green space chick; that was a little much for Joey.)

Because from the moment they'd gotten back to his

uncle's house on the lake, there had been nothing but yelling and screaming, mainly between his uncle and brother. Sitting slumped in the kitchen as his brother as explained their seemingly murderous morning, each new piece of information from Bobby seemed to make his uncle madder and madder:

"Mule-sputum! You kicked in the door?"

"Sheep-grease! You killed her?!"

"Shit-squelch! You killed the girl, too?!!"

At the last two questions, Joey did raise his head from the table. Not to say anything, but to look out the window and think.

First, he was horrified that he had actually gotten used to his uncle. The man got almost giddy as he started nearly every conversation with his efforts to make an original insult. The fact that he did it three questions in a row this morning, well that was just crappy icing on the cake.

But secondly, and more importantly, was real horror: Hearing his uncle say "killed" twice. It was really the first time Joey got the chance to think about what he had done, and it hit him hard.

Certainly, Joey had gotten in trouble before.

A little shoplifting from Wal-Mart when he was a kid, and then there was the time he'd urinated off the Ferris Wheel during the county fair a couple of years back. He'd gotten a slap on the wrist for the first one, but the second one landed him with 50 hours of community service cleaning up I-70. Although there's never a good time to pee on people from 40 feet in the air, there are particularly bad ones, like when the district attorney's daughter is sitting in the car under you.

But his time picking up trash along the interstate gave him the chance to think. First and foremost was that his brother was a bad influence; both times his brother had prodded him to do it.

Second was that people let some really strange things go flying out of the car. That purple box of round white sponges didn't look like anything he'd ever cleaned a toilet with.

Clearly, his brother was a bad influence on him. Even knowing that, however, didn't change the fact that Bobby was his older brother. Sure, Bobby had a mean, stupid side, but didn't everyone? Even Captain Kirk did mean things. Heck in that one episode where the transporter accident split him into a good half and an evil half, Captain Kirk discovered he couldn't live without the evil half. (Maybe that was the one that made out with the green chick.)

And if it was good enough for Captain Kirk, it was good enough for Joey.

He knew that from working at Space Case Books in Hays. It had opened Joey up to a whole other world of thinking, and clearly Bobby's criminal ways and stupid decisions were just his bad — but necessary — side acting out. But Captain Kirk had learned to control his bad side and so would Bobby, he assumed.

Hoping to nurture that side, he'd said "yes" when Bobby asked him to go on a trip.

In truth, it had been more of a demand — "We're leavin' for Oregon in an hour. Get a map and pack your shit." — but he did want to go. His dad even had a special assignment for him; during a special phone call from jail, he asked Joey to deliver a box to his uncle but tell no one, not even Bobby.

These were the kind of adventures Captain Kirk went on. And even if Oregon wasn't Rigel VII, it promised to be a great adventure.

That certainly was not what had happened.

Bobby had seemed to get meaner with every passing day and can of Milwaukee's Best. When Joey had noticed a mailing tube sticking out of the mailbox at the beach house, he took the time to go get it. Bobby responded to the gesture by berating Joey for taking other people's stuff, though it didn't seem to stop him from opening it.

When Joey started talking to the foreman of the carpentry crew that was working for his uncle, Bobby told him to shut up, then let loose a stream of racial names that would have made a Klansman blush. It was becoming obvious that Captain Kirk was far better at controlling his evil side than Bobby White.

That's why when he took the girl's binoculars back to the van he let his brother believe it was so they wouldn't get caught. (How Bobby thought someone would just dismiss the spilled purse and scratched up glove box, Joey had no idea.) Clearly, if Bobby had no remorse about scaring a woman to death or letting a woman drown, putting the dead's binoculars back would mean even less.

And now that he began to think about it again, he had to accept what he'd done: he'd been responsible for the deaths of two people. No, he hadn't killed them, but he could have saved them.

The guilt was incredible, but for the moment disrupted, as his uncle was going ballistic again. Now, however, his rage seemed to cover anything and everything since he and Bobby had arrived two weeks ago.

The girl, again: "Do you even know who she was, wheat-snot?!"

Bobby's drinking: "Another six Goddamn cases of Milwaukee's Best, pigeon-shit?"

Bobby's spending: "Genital-scrape! What the hell is this $85 charge on my credit card from EBay?!"

Bobby tried to explain each, some more successfully than others: He'd searched her van for her ID but couldn't find it. Yes, it was six more cases, but before Bobby agreed to come out that was the deal. (The local Quik Mart had started to buy it in bulk.) And yes, that was his charge; he'd found a Hays Supply sweatshirt/underwear/socks and sandal combo for sale and had to have it.

The last answer seemed to make their uncle the maddest; Bobby had put nearly $400 on their uncle's credit card in the past two weeks, buying nothing but Hays Supply memorabilia. Bobby said he was just showing how proud he was of where he was now in lower management. His uncle said he was just showing that he was another hick whack-job from Kansas.

That was just about the only thing his uncle had said that made sense. His uncle's next question, however, put him right back in the nutcase category in Joey's opinion: "You broke the door trim?! You worm-cunt!!"

Did worms even have those? Joey wondered, before he returned to just how nuts his uncle had gotten.

More than two murders, more than hundreds of dollars down the toilet for his brother's stupid vices, the damage to the door seemed to make him the maddest. And Bobby, as always, did nothing to help.

"Screw that, all that stuff will be gone by this weekend anyway," Bobby said, cracking open his second beer of the morning. "And it's not like some dead geezer gonna need it until then."

And that's when Joey saw his uncle began to get really mad.

His face redder than ever and that big vein over his eyebrow beginning to pulse, Joey lowered his head again and tried to block out the verbal eruption. Focusing instead on his brother's continuing slide towards his darker side, even Joey had to admit that the salvation of his brother — or himself — wasn't going to be found in the fantasy world of Star Trek.

Maybe Star Wars …

Chapter 16
Poe

As usual Jackson Poe was up early to make breakfast, although it was the first time in more than a year he'd actually made it for two. Since Vivian left there'd been no one in his life, not that he figured Callista would be next.

For one thing, he was (almost) old enough to be her father. And his growing need to help her get to the bottom of this mess was more like a brother protecting a sister.

But even if she'd been older and less vulnerable, he doubted anything romantic would have developed. His relationship with Vivian had ended with the realization that she didn't understand him at all, and he'd become more than a little cynical about relationships.

The fact that Vivian was barking at him on the phone this very second didn't help, either.

"You still haven't sent me that jewelry box I accidentally left behind, and it's been six months since I asked," she said with exasperation. "What, your car too nice to park at the post office?" That was pure sarcasm.

Her crack notwithstanding, Poe went to the post office all the time. He just couldn't seem to remember to take the jewelry box when he went. A Freudian thing, probably. "I know, I know, I just …"

"Let me guess, you're too swamped with your 'busy writing career,' to take the …" and Vivian went off on one of her tears about how he needed to get a real job. It was yet another reminder that the car had been the final straw, not the first one, and Poe began trying to figure out a way to gracefully end the conversation. He wasn't having any luck when the solution presented itself, sort of.

"What a great night!" Callista said, rising out of the hide-a-bed. "I really needed that after our adventure yesterday." Only then did she notice Poe was on the phone and discover what Poe often remembered at inconvenient times: his phone had one hell of a sensitive microphone in it.

"Who the hell is THAT?" Even without the phone, Poe was pretty sure he could have heard her from New Orleans. Why Vivian would be angry a woman would be in his condo more than a year after they broke up he had no idea, but she clearly was. At least he assumed so; she'd hung up.

"I am soooo, sorry," Callista said, "I had no idea you were on the phone."

"No problem, she gets like that sometimes," he said, acknowledging that she'd probably stop calling if he'd just send the jewelry box. Maybe that's why he didn't send it; he liked talking to her. No, that was too much Freud — and horror

— to contemplate. He quickly changed the subject.

"So, now how do you feel about Steve McQueen movies?"

Last night's movie was called "Bullitt," and despite the question, he was asking about far more than the iconic actor. Poe didn't own another Steve McQueen movie; he wasn't even sure he'd seen another one. But the film contained what he considered the best 9 minutes and 42 seconds ever put on celluloid: a car chase through the simple past of one the greatest cities on Earth.

Behind the wheel of a new dark green 1968 V8 Ford Mustang, McQueen chases two suspects in their black 1968 V8 Dodge Charger through the streets and hills of San Francisco. Hitting speeds of up to 110 miles per hour with icons like the Golden Gate Bridge flashing in the background, it is widely considered the best car chase ever put on film. In one scene, the Charger is so out of control it actually crashes into the camera that's filming it.

Poe first saw the movie when he was 13, at his neighbor's house. The richest family on the block they were the first to have a VCR, and when they popped "Bullitt" in one afternoon he had no idea he was about to see automotive history. Only half watching until the car chase scene, he had them rewind it so he could see it again.

When Poe turned 17 he used his birthday money to buy his own VCR and a copy of "Bullitt." He watched and rewound the chase scene so many times he broke the tape and had to buy another copy of the movie. (The later invention of the DVD player had probably saved Poe at least $50 in "Bullitt" tapes he didn't have to replace and countless hours he didn't have to spend rewinding.)

Part of it was the cars. The black Charger was cool, but the Mustang was exquisite. For a kid whose parents drove a bright blue Pinto station wagon and bug-gut — his dad's description — green Mazda pickup, the idea that such vehicles existed was a pleasure all in itself.

But more than that, it was the essence of the chase itself. Set in a San Francisco that never ages from 1968, the city seems uncluttered, almost empty, compared to the megabuck landscape that sits on the peninsula today.

Couple that with two cars simply flying off of the paved hilltops and cornering on the curves. No hidden ramps to get more air, no random cars thrown in just so they can get smashed to pieces, no exploding cable cars (although Poe loved the chase scene in "The Rock," as well).

None of that crap: just two cars gunning their engines as fast as they can until one of them explodes. (Thank God it was the Charger.)

Simple: just the way Poe tried to keep his life, and after everything that had happened with Callista, it was the perfect antidote to a chaotic day. It was something not too many people understood. Aly did, Vivian didn't, and now he hoped Callista would as he asked her what she thought of the movie.

"Well, it made me kind of depressed," she said. "It made me realize I was born about 15 years after I would have really loved the city of San Francisco." But seeing his face starting to fall, she quickly added: "But I loved the car chase scene; there've been days when I've wanted to drive that way myself."

Poe immediately felt the beginnings of a frown turn into a smile, even when she began to dissect the movie: "Is it just me, or did they pass the same Volkswagen Bug like three times?"

Far from being annoyed, however, he was thrilled she'd been paying such close attention, and it gave him an excuse to tell her more about the movie.

Actually, they'd passed the same bug four times and a blue sedan with a black top three times. Also, the Charger lost six hubcaps, and as the chase proceeds body damage mysteriously appears and disappears from the black car. With every hill jump and hard turn shot from different angles and then cut and spliced in a different order to make the chase seem longer, he told Callista "'Bullitt' may have been a automotive tour de force, but by no means was an editing one."

"My God," she said. "You really have watched this a thousand times. How long did it take you to figure all that out?"

"Not as long as you'd think. I got it all off of Wikipedia about three years ago," he said. "I was always too busy drooling over the Mustang to really pay attention to all that crap."

Letting out a huge laugh, Callista had just one other question: "Why all the ceremony with the DVD in a wooden box? When you got down on one knee, you had me wondering if you were going to propose marriage, although I'll admit in that size box it would have been one helluva ring."

Now it was his turn to laugh. "That's just because I'm not normal. It's kind of a requirement for living here, if you haven't noticed."

Chapter 17
Oregon

Perhaps it's the human desire to be different from the other six billion people that occupy the planet that makes everyone want to believe they are "not normal." Even in places as demographically average as Ohio, residents are more likely to tell you why they are different — and hence better — than everyone else.

Take Hamilton, Ohio. In a desire to set themselves apart, town leaders once renamed the city Hamilton!, and asked the post office and mapping agencies to include the exclamation point so other people would know how exciting they were.

Alas, the government told them no, and they had to go back to being just another city in the Midwest, one known mainly for being a massive speed trap that funds its government on speeding ticket revenue. (Town leaders were not as anxious to put this on maps.)

Oregon does not need an exclamation point.

Even from the outside, the residents of the other 49 states hear enough about Oregon to know it's a bit different. (OK, 48;

the residents of neighboring Washington seem to hate Oregon, even as their RVs fill the state's beaches.)

Television personality Stephen Colbert called it "California's Canada," in response to its liberal leadership in environmental law and other more quirky things, like being one of only two states where it's illegal to pump your own gas and the first state to allow physician-assisted suicide.

(If Poe would allow a bumper sticker on his car, he would give the one that reads, "Oregon: Where it's legal to gas yourself but not your car," the best spot. If someone would bother to make it, anyway.)

No, Oregon is definitely not normal.

But not so simple, either. Because despite one news clip after another of tree-hugging liberals running amok in the forests, there are just as many people in Oregon who would be happy to take a chainsaw to the huggers instead of the trees. Just as many people who hate smokers polluting their air but hate even more the state telling all those people to not do it anymore. (Oregon was the last state on the Pacific coast to pass a smoking ban, and even then didn't make it take effect for 16 months, probably to let people calm down.)

Some call it the fierce spirit of independence, others stupidity. Whatever you call it, however, Oregon's past has been "not normal" since humans first walked its soil.

The first trace of humans in Oregon is from a feces pile. States like Virginia get the mighty Algonquian people to mark humanity's arrival in their history and New Mexico gets the stone-carved Clovis point from more than 130 centuries ago.

Even Ohio has the Mound Builders who built, well, mounds for ceremonial and practical reasons as far back as 3,000 years ago. Oregon gets a human crap pile in the back of a cave.

True, Native Americans eventually filled the state, including the coast around what is today Surfland, and lived largely peaceably for thousands of years. But although they made an effort to get along with the white arrivals, they, too, must have thought these newcomers were not normal, seeing as all of them seemed to be looking for something other than what was actually here.

Captain James Cook arrived on the coast in 1778, looking for the Northwest Passage. Not finding it, he went home. Lewis & Clark were looking for the same thing, but after spending the rainiest winter in centuries on the Oregon coast they, too, went home. (If it would make any of these men feel any better, there is finally a Northwest Passage from the Pacific Ocean to the Atlantic now that global warming melts the polar ice cap every summer.)

When the Oregon Trail began in the mid-1800s, thousands of settlers set out from the Midwest — though one presumes not from Hamilton! — to get free land. In that sense they probably were normal, not that it lasted long. In their mind, the natives were not normal in that they were not Christians, so they set about converting them.

For their part the natives — thinking themselves perfectly normal — killed a bunch of the self-proclaimed missionaries. By the time of statehood in 1859, some 52,000 people (to whom it seemed perfectly normal to force the natives onto reservations) had followed the trail to Oregon. Although this seems like a lot of people, especially in a state that was largely empty, the reality is five times that many travelers opted for other places like California.

Looking at it statistically, Oregonians are not normal.

What that left, however, were a unique bunch of people. Kit Carson commented on the type of people that survived the arduous journey to Oregon: "The cowards never started, and the weak died on the way."

Indeed, it's thought up to 10 percent of the people who started the Oregon Trail died before they could finish it, leaving a very fit — and probably slightly crazed — 90 percent to settle the state.

Just one more explanation for why Oregonians are, as Jackson Poe put it to one of Oregon's newest immigrants, "not normal."

Some are over the top about their lack of normalcy, like people who dance around in public in animal costumes for a living. (The nudism and other quirks, well those are just a bonus.)

Others do it in small ways, like keeping their favorite movie in a walnut box or having a stuffed dog ride around in their Jeep so they can get one step closer to believing it's a fire truck.

And others do it in ways that seem to broadcast their refusal to conform even as they go about the basic tasks of everyday life. People like Rip Rockford, P.I.

Chapter 18
Rip Rockford

A private investigator named Rip Rockford: to even the most clueless about '70s television, the name just sounds like someone who should be out investigating something. The name was no coincidence.

Born Rip Van Winkle Snodgrass to a Scottish father and a mother who loved the writings of Washington Irving, Rip had hated his name since he first learned what it was. The first day of school was always an unmitigated hell as each teacher felt compelled to read out his entire name while calling attendance, ensuring relentless teasing from his peers through at least Christmas break.

He'd always viewed his name as a double curse: Rip Van Winkle was bad enough. But why couldn't he have at least gotten one of the cool Scottish names, like McCloud or McTavish? Playing sports in high school was a particular hell; the other team never got tired of screaming, "Snodgrass ..."

and then adding on whatever asinine thing they could think of (and there were plenty).

Maybe that's why as he progressed through school in Salem, Oregon, he gradually retreated into his house, spending his time watching television and messing around on the computer.

The TV affected him earliest: watching endless hours of cop and detective shows, he got addicted to them, foregoing most activities so he could watch his shows even as he went through college. "The Rockford Files," "Mannix," "Starsky & Hutch," "Kojak," "Hawaii 5-O": he as much consumed them as he watched them. Even when he graduated with a computer science degree and moved to Seattle, he spent as much time with the likes of "Magnum" and "Miami Vice" as he did with his job.

That's why at the age of 40 he decided to cash in his stock options, bail on Microsoft and move to Surfland, where his family had vacationed when he was young. Drawing cues from the heroes of his past he started wearing Aloha shirts like Magnum, bought a red 1976 Ford Torino like Starsky, and got himself a P.I. license — and name — from his all-time favorite, Jim Rockford.

Unfortunately for Rip, crime in Surfland, Oregon, doesn't quite measure up to the fictional worlds of Honolulu, Bay City and Los Angeles. Indeed, Rockford had to admit, it didn't even measure up to the reality of Salem, and cases were few and far between. Not that Rip needed the money; his stock options had seen to that, but he was bored.

So, he engaged his second love, computers, and as the booming world of the Internet brought all the information of the world literally to his fingertips, Rip built a nice side business doing background checks and digging up information for anyone who was willing to pay — in a variety of ways.

Because with money not the object, Rip didn't have to do anything he didn't want to for anyone he didn't want to. And for those he wanted to help but who didn't have much money themselves, Rip often did it for free or in the form of trade. He'd had his car's transmission (supposedly) fixed three times after helping his mechanic through a nasty divorce.

Having been through the process three times himself, he was particularly sympathetic. And staunchly against ever getting married again, which his current significant other was perfectly OK with.

A couple for more than eight years, her name was Katrina — with name issues of her own after the hurricane — and both were perfectly content to share a life together without a marriage certificate. Keeping an apartment together at the top of Katrina's Seabiscuit B&B on the beach, he ran the occasional background check on deadbeat customers for her, and Rip was happy, his Torino's transmission notwithstanding.

"Damnit!" he cursed from under the car, once again up on blocks out in back of the B&B. "How many times does my mechanic need to get divorced before this thing runs right?" Legs sticking out from under the car, Rip didn't really know whom he was talking to, he just knew there were three sets of legs, although he assumed one of them was Katrina.

Sliding out from under the car he discovered it was Katrina, his friend Jackson Poe and the young woman who had dropped off her van yesterday evening. He remembered now: she was going to be staying here for a couple of days until a few things got straightened out.

Just as when Poe was working on an investigative piece, Rip knew his friend saw him as one of the few people he trusted to help. For that reason and many others, Rip knew he would do all he could to help figure out just what Callista had gotten herself into. As Katrina helped Callista move her things from the van to her room, Poe told Rip everything that had happened.

Both agreed it would make sense to do a background and records check on the folks in Alice's neighborhood. Maybe it would tell them something, although Poe did feel a little weird about having his own friend checked, especially as she was lying in the hospital. Unfortunately, that was as far as they got, and it didn't get them any closer to knowing just who might be after Alice and Callista in the first place.

By now, Katrina and Callista had returned from her room. Laughing as they approached Rip and Poe, Katrina took note of their clashing Hawaiian shirts. "Again: You two shouldn't be allowed to stand together," she said, pretending to shield her eyes. "You look like Walt Disney threw up."

Poe was the first to respond: "Hey, not my fault. I was wearing Hawaiian shirts long before this guy ever became a Magnum wannabe."

Rip was quick to respond, of course. All four talked and

laughed for the next ten minutes about how both men had enough Aloha shirts to wear them every day for three weeks and never put on the same one twice.

Truth was, Rip was glad for the diversion for a few minutes. He and Poe had decided that if they were going to get any further with figuring things out, the key lay with Callista and what else she might be able to remember, something Poe had mentioned he was reluctant to do; he knew how weary she was getting of telling the story.

But hoping that maybe a night's sleep had jogged something else loose, Rip used a lull in the laughter to broach the subject and asked her if there was anything else. To his surprise, there was.

"The truck had one of those license plates," she said pointing to a car with Washington tags in the parking lot. "Well, maybe not exactly that, but it definitely had blue in it."

His hopes lifted and then just as quickly dashed, Rip tried not to be too dismissive. "Half the tourists in Surfland have Washington tags," he said. "Not to mention all the other states that have blue on their license plates."

Again, Callista surprised him. "True, but how many have 'H-Y-S-P-L-Y' on them?"

Chapter 19
Bobby

The blue (and light brown) license plate that jogged Callista's memory was at that very moment sitting on the other side of town, attached to Bobby White's 1993 Dodge Ram and a very visible testament to his pride in his role at Hays Supply in Hays, Kansas. Bobby had worked there since he was 15, which was a bit of a miracle since he was in most every way the most incompetent employee Hays Supply had ever hired in their 72 years of operation.

When he started on the loading dock, opening boxes off the shipping truck, he regularly sliced into whatever was in the box. Even when they discovered he was using a switchblade instead of a box cutter, he continued to decimate their supply of Carhart overalls; any box Bobby opened usually had to have at least one pair put on clearance because it had slices in it.

They tried him next in the rental yard, checking that the equipment was ready to go after someone brought it back. But when it was discovered that Bobby was using Skoal spit to lubricate the weed-eaters, they yanked him out of there, too. (The settlement with Mrs. Gormson after she was blinded in one eye by flying chew had cost the company thousands, even after the insurance company got involved.)

Finally, they tried him in customer service. Placing him at the entrance, they hoped he could handle the sheer act of saying, "Hello." That, too, was a bust.

Just three days into the job he told a customer to, "Take his dark ass back to Mexico," when an extremely tan man came in eating Taco Bell. The fact that it was Mr. Gormson only made it worse, and by the time the store was done writing checks, he and Mrs. Gormson were off on another Caribbean vacation, where he got an even better tan.

Clearly, Bobby White was costing Hays Supply a fortune, and had he not been the favored relative of a member of the Kansas State School Board, he would have been gone a long time ago. But Hays was not a terribly large place, and the managers of Hays Supply knew letting Bobby go might mean all kinds of problems for the school, particularly when it came to funding the basketball team.

Which is where things stood, when the general manager of Hays Supply called Bobby into his office. Not quite sure just what to say to the biggest financial disaster to hit the business since a tornado had filled the store with pig shit from a neighboring feedlot back in '72, he tried a simple question.

"Bobby, why couldn't you just tell him where the Weed-B-Gone was?"

"I don't like them damned Mexicans coming into this

country and takin' all our jobs," Bobby said, slumped in his chair. "I'd be rich now workin' for Burger King if it weren't for them."

"Bobby, Mr. Gormson's lived in this town for nearly 62 years. He's even a Baptist. Did you just not know where the weed killer was?"

"Hell no! I knew exactly where it was, aisle 18, shelf 9, section 3! I just got confused on account of his eatin' foreign food. You won't find Lee Greenwood eatin' no damned Taco Bell."

And that's where Bobby White saved his job and ensured that within the decade — about as long as the managers could put it off — he would be promoted to assistant supervisor in charge of night stock. That was because despite having no social skills and the brain of a gecko, Bobby had an encyclopedic memory of anything and everything in Hays Supply. In just his three days in customer service he had memorized the location of everything in the store, down to the smallest washer nut.

Working solo at night — and with just a car key to open up taped boxes — Bobby would unload the trucks and then stock every last item. On nights when there was no truck to unload he would walk the aisles looking for stray items and then returning them to their rightful place. Even the people at Hays Supply who hated Bobby — well, everyone — had to admit that the store was much more efficient with Bobby working.

Bobby had even helped reorganize the store, first suggesting that they move the masks and nose plugs next to the manure and peat moss selection. At first they were stunned that Bobby would notice such things; rarely showering, he often smelled of manure himself.

But he was right, and when sales of nose plugs and masks nearly doubled, they let him reorganize other things, like putting a test track in the middle of the store for lawn mowers. Sure, it meant removing aisle 11, but coupled with placing Budweiser and Tide stickers all over the tractors, NASCAR fans started buying John Deere's in record numbers.

This last creation led to one of the greatest moments of Bobby's life: a Hays Supply embroidered denim shirt with his name on it. And as much as Bobby was taken with his name, he was even more impressed with the Hays Supply name written on the shirt. Management even gave him an extra three, on account of his good work, they said.

All his life, Bobby had wanted to belong to something.

In middle and high school he could never make the athletic teams because of his grades and the ridiculous rule that didn't allow drinking after games. As an adult, he tried to buy clothes with fancy names on them, like Kmart and Tastee Freeze, but every time he went shopping they'd ask him to leave on account of not wearing shoes, or a shirt, or some other damned fool thing.

Hell, if had a clean shirt he wouldn't need to go buy one, now would he?

But with his Hays Supply denim shirts he now belonged, and deciding that he wanted to show the world just how important he had become — just let Goodwill turn him away now! — he decided anything and everything that had Hays Supply on it had to be his.

In just a matter of weeks, he bought everything the story had to offer: promotional T-shirts, canvas bags, baseball caps, even a pair of women's shorts left over from the "Daisy Duke" promotion, where a bunch of girls washed cars to pay for Edna Jean Raynud's electrolysis.

Hanging out at the little league ballpark, he even offered the biggest kid on the team sponsored by Hays Supply $20 for his jersey. Buying it from an 8 year old with a hormonal problem was a risk, Bobby knew, but the shirt just fit.

But having bought everything there was to buy in and around the city of Hays, Bobby still wasn't satisfied. So he tried EBay, where his brother had helped him buy a truck once. At first, there wasn't anything with Hays Supply on it. But after a couple of weeks of trying, things did start to appear: a belt and a bolo tie, sweatshirts, underwear and socks, and even sandals. (What the hell Bobby needed with sandals he had no idea, but it said "Hays Supply," and that was enough.)

So, when Uncle Shelton had called Bobby and asked him to come west, Bobby left with mixed feelings; his career at Hays Supply was clearly going somewhere. But he went because his uncle was a supposed legend and at the very least he could keep buying his Hays Supply merchandise from just about anywhere that had a phone line and a computer, and his uncle had agreed to pay all his expenses.

Not that his uncle saw it that way.

Going through last week's mail, his uncle had already

discovered the $85 he'd spent on the sweatshirt/underwear/socks and sandals combo. With the mail delivered to the house on the beach, his uncle often just picked it up, threw it in his car, and went through it in bulk once or so a week.

On the upside, it gave Bobby extra time before his uncle noticed what he'd done with his credit card. On the downside, it often meant his uncle opened the bills for his different credit cards all at the same time.

Today was definitely a downside.

"God damnit! Squirrel-nugget!" his uncle screamed, his face turning crimson for what must have been at least the third time today. "What the hell is this $108 charge on my MasterCard from EBay? It better not be more of that Hays Supply shit!"

Had Bobby been smarter, or not drunk on his second six-pack of Milwaukee's Best, he might have just let the question be hypothetical, rhetorical, unanswered, or something. Bobby, however, was both stupid and drunk, and none of those possibilities entered his head, even if he had known what they meant.

"Damn right it is! I got the world's last case of Hays Supply condoms! I even made sure they was checked for authenticity!"

At this his uncle's face got even redder, and as he looked at the piles of Hays Supply memorabilia already scattered around the living room, Bobby thought that the vein in his forehead might finally explode. Instead — and to Bobby's delight — he turned his wrath on Joey. "And you, Space-sputum! Where the

Beach Slapped

hell is Thursday's mail? Did you get the goddamn mail again? How many times have I told you not to get the mail?!"

At first Bobby thought his brother would try to turn the subject back to Bobby. "Well, at least I didn't open it like Bobby," he thought Joey might say. But Joey didn't; maybe he figured that would only make things worse for both of them.

Not that it stopped their uncle.

"I have been waiting weeks for some drawings! How the hell am I supposed to get them if you keep getting the mail?" he asked, looking directly at Joey. The gaze didn't last long, however, as whatever momentary break Joey had gotten his brother was forgotten in Bobby's alcohol-impaired brain.

"Oh yeah, those came. I was lookin' at 'em before we rousted the old lady," he said, as he cracked the top on another beer. "That thing looks real nice." At this, Shabazz exploded in rage again.

Drunk and smiling as he cracked open yet another beer, Bobby was actually somewhat proud that no matter how stupid the act, he could usually figure out some way to do it.

Chapter 20
Fuzznut

Fuzznut was not mentally ill, paranoid, or any of the other descriptors that people like to use when they think someone is crazy.

True, he only appeared in public in mascot costumes. And equally true was his tendency to walk about the house naked. (Yes, he had taken to usually wearing an apron, but only because he spent most of his time cooking one crab dish or another.)

But in most other respects he was relatively normal. He watched primetime television shows on broadcast and cable. He liked to surf the Internet, whether to check up on the world or to buy things. He had friends, although save for Poe they mainly came in the form of e-mail pen pals.

He kept his door locked most of the time.

The latter of these came from his days growing up in Southern California; even a half-century ago it wasn't the kind of place you didn't keep the deadbolt turned. In 21st century Surfland it kept out random squatters who often checked homes on the beach for a place they could crash while the owners were away, often for months at a time.

Not that many bothered to check his home, he knew. With large shrubs and fences surrounding both the front and back yards, it wasn't exactly a place that beckoned people in. The only chance people would even have to look in his house was if they pulled down the driveway and tried to glance in the south window. Even that would have been fruitless, however, as Fuzznut kept it covered with a gauzy curtain that let him see just enough to know there was a car pulling up next to his house.

In the summer, it was usually someone using his driveway as a turnaround once they discovered his street was a dead end. In the off-season, once a week or so, it was a very determined salesperson who went away once they got no answer at the front door. And twice it had been Pete Polanski, racing to the beach to rescue someone stuck in the surf when they illegally drove their car into the ocean.

But more often than not when a car appeared in the driveway, usually about every other day, it was Jackson Poe in his British Racing Green Jag. Since Poe was considerate enough to turn down his stereo before pulling up, Fuzznut knew the distinctive purr of the V-8 engine as well as any sound in his world. Sometimes he'd glance to see the blur of green outside the window, sometimes not. The window curtains didn't allow much more than that anyway.

So, when Poe came by for the second day in a row, it was more often than usual, but not extraordinarily so, and Fuzznut took no more than a second's notice of the spot of green in the driveway. He was equally undisturbed when Poe unlocked the front door and let himself in the house. Poe had the only other key to the house, and they'd been friends long enough to know what to expect. (Today, he was wearing only a Louisiana-themed apron in honor of the Cajun Crab he was making.)

Like most of his visits, Poe was bringing Fuzznut something. But today it wasn't ketchup or eggs or any number of other things Fuzznut occasionally ran out of. It wasn't even edible; it was a piece of wood.

"A little big for a toothpick, don't you think, Poe?" Fuzznut was also not without humor.

Setting the wood on the table, Poe ran his finger along the edges of Fuzznut's cooking pan and came right back at him. "A little spicy for a man with exposed privates, don't you think?"

"Why do you think I wear an apron? After that episode with Dave's Insanity Sauce and the ham you don't have to tell me twice," Fuzznut laughed.

"Actually, I did."

"Whatever. So, what's the wood for?"

Poe told Fuzznut about the break-in at Alice's house, the resulting damage to her home and the hopes that Fuzznut might be able to find a piece of wood to replace it. A friend of Alice's, too — he'd performed at more than one Fourth of July carnival at Surfland Haven — Fuzznut was happy to help. "It looks like redwood, but not."

"Yeah, I was thinking the same thing," Poe said. "I was hoping maybe you could figure that out."

"Sure, but you've got to do me a favor first ..." Fuzznut said, his voice trailing off before crossing the room to pull a two-foot long silver tube out of the closet.

"Oh God, not that damned T-shirt gun again." But that's exactly what it was, and Fuzznut wanted to do a little testing.

Powered by expelled carbon dioxide, T-shirt guns might be the greatest thing ever invented for mascots involved in the distribution of T-shirts. Ranging from $200 to $2,000, they enable mascots to stop expelling energy throwing and spend more of it dancing, frolicking and doing all the other things mascots do to entertain crowds.

Because depending on the size of the gun and the CO_2 charge, a T-shirt gun can propel a T-shirt anywhere from 100 to 500 feet through the air. Packing an enormous amount of power, they are capable of propelling even an XXXL into the second deck of a baseball stadium all the way from the outfield.

"Hey, Poe, you make fun of this all you want," Fuzznut told him as they walked to the backyard. "You weren't the mascot trying to throw those damn things into the second deck of Dodger Stadium. I almost fell off the wall and killed myself."

What Fuzznut needed to know today, however, was how far the gun would shoot horizontally. So, sending Poe out the back gate onto the beach, Fuzznut pulled the trigger and shot a T-shirt just over his back hedges while telling Poe to see how far it went. Returning a couple of minutes later, even Poe was impressed. "That thing must have gone 200 feet," he said, checking out the T-shirt gun with a bit more respect.

"Perfect! That's more than enough to launch from the dock onto Bo's back porch. I've got a job there Sunday dressed as a bear, and I was hoping to try this thing out. You and that girl should come by. Where is she anyway?"

And for a moment, Poe was taken aback. This was the first time he'd ever heard Fuzznut talk about wanting anyone coming to see him other than Poe and reporters with cameras. Within moments, however, Fuzznut was back to his normal self: "You're not going to bring her back here are you? And don't you dare tell her my name. You didn't tell her my name, did you? I mean any of them."

"No, I simply told her you were, 'a friend,'" Poe said calmly. "And since you asked, she's back at The Seabiscuit. Katrina hooked her up with a room for the next few days. I figured she could use the rest while I talked to you and go see Alice."

"Well, OK." Fuzznut was calm again, and began picking some flowers from his garden in the backyard. "Give these to Alice for me, will you? Tell her they're from you, though."

Chapter 21
Poe

Heading north, Poe had the top down on the car and the stereo up, this time playing the soundtrack to "Robin Hood." Kevin Costner's English accent may have been horrifying to listen to in the movie, but the score was wonderful, Poe thought. With winter coming, the number of days he could keep the top down was getting limited. In fact, it was supposed to rain tonight.

But ignoring for now the dark clouds building to the west, Poe was enjoying life. Granted, he still had no idea what was going on with Callista, the two men in the truck and the attack on Alice, but he often found the sheer act of driving the Jag could help him make sense of things.

That, and a good cup of coffee.

Located a mile or so north of his house, Bendovren Coffee was among his favorite java stops in a town full of them. Cheryl had owned the shop for a couple of years now and along with always remembering his favorite — 20 ounce triple-shot with sugar-free white mocha and caramel and skim milk — her son Ryan was the journalism student who had given him the lottery tickets.

"Hey, Cheryl," he said pulling up to the drive-through window. "My usual, with an extra shot. I have a feeling it's going to be a 'day.'"

"You know, when you order something every day with an extra shot, it really stops being the usual," Cheryl gently chided him.

"No grief, too early."

Changing the subject as she squirted the syrups into the cup, she mentioned her son. "Ryan told me you were by the school the other day again. He thinks you're about the greatest guy who ever lived. Why is that?"

"No idea," Poe said, though he had some sneaking suspicions. "I must teach good journalism," he continued, and he dropped a $20 bill in the tip jar while Cheryl wasn't looking. Two minutes later he and his four shots and were headed to the hospital on the west side of the lake.

Upon arrival, Poe was stunned to discover that Alice had been moved from the general population into the critical care ward. As soon as he arrived at Alice's room, however, Pete was there to put him at ease. She'd been moved after a minivan full of elderly Swedes had hit a herd of elk. They'd taken up both beds in every room in the west side of the hospital, forcing Alice into the critical services wing on the east side, not that her condition really warranted it.

"They're in group counseling together," Pete explained. "Apparently, a lot of them are having some type of antler-related PTSD. Thank God they don't live in a country where Rudolph visits the mall at Christmas."

Walking into Alice's room, Poe had opened the door quietly, not wanting to risk bothering her. He shouldn't have worried.

"Look, I don't care if no one there remembers," Alice said barking into her cell phone. "When I bought that mug at McDonalds they told me it guaranteed free coffee refills for life. Is it my fault none of your employees have been alive long enough to remember the promotion? Yes, you call me back," she said, turning off the phone.

"I swear, Poe, whatever happened to the meaning of 'for life'?"

"Alice, I didn't think you were allowed to have a cell phone in here."

"That's what they keep telling me, so don't you start."

Happy that Alice was clearly fine, he didn't. Then, he told her about everything that had happened to Callista, including his visit to the house. Wrapping up the story, he mentioned offhand Juan's problems with the men who'd been visiting her.

"Well, I think we can move it up from 'visiting,' although that is what I told Julio," she said with a tinge of regret in her voice. "They were the two that attacked me."

"I wondered," Poe said. "Who are they?"

"It's really more just one of them; the smaller one never seems to say anything," she said. "But in truth I have no idea.

They showed up on my door a couple of weeks ago saying they represented the anonymous man who wanted to buy my house.

"I told him no, and I told them no, dozens of times. I haven't said 'No' to anyone that many times since Johnny Gadnecki asked me to date him in ninth grade," she said, chuckling lightly. "Boy, he was a well-muscled thing."

Happy to see Alice's spirits still up, he felt safe pushing the conversation a little further. "Why didn't you tell Julio that? He's like a son to you."

"I didn't want to burden him. His oldest daughter is driving him crazy, he's constantly worried about immigration trying to expel even his legal workers, and even though those rednecks were jerks, they were paying him to do a job. Never turn down a check, you know."

"Yes, I know, you told me that every time I got angry at someone who edited my stories," Poe said, smiling. Her patient prodding had been the only thing that had kept him from telling the editor of most every home and style magazine on the coast to go screw themselves. "What was Julio doing for them?"

"You know, I have no idea. Every day Julio's men would go into one of my neighbor's old houses, make a tremendous racket, and then come out hours later," she said.

"There was one curious thing, though," she said, very much the voice of a woman who thought it her job to keep watch over the neighborhood.

"Every couple of days a big panel truck, you know, like a U-Haul or something, would back up to a different garage door on my street in the middle of the night," she recalled. "A couple of guys would hop out and take a whole bunch of stuff in, and then take a whole bunch of stuff out, filling the truck back up.

"They never turned on any lights, so I have no idea who they were or what they were doing."

Once again: another piece of information that made no sense. If he'd wanted to be this discombobulated, he would have drunk decaf this morning. Nevertheless, he went on. "Were they the same men that attacked you, or maybe Julio's?"

"Either, neither, both; although, as mean as that one boy was to Julio's men, I doubt that," she told Poe, clearly frustrated. "It was just so dark."

Poe excused himself from Alice's room as her phone rang. As he left he could hear her arguing again. "That's right, FREE COFFEE FOR LIFE … Look, is there anyone there over the age of 25? …"

Outside of her room, Pete was waiting for him with the news Poe expected: the police had figured out about as much as he had. Even having fingerprinted the entire place, there was nothing to go on. With Alice due to be released from the hospital in just a matter of hours, it worried Poe that her attackers were still out there.

"Pete, how much trouble would it be to keep Alice here for a few more days? Maybe tell the world she's not doing so well. If someone out there still wants to get her, I'd rather they think they all but finished the job already."

"Well, I'll need to see if the doctor will go along with it," Pete said, the gears already turning in his head. "But you need to make sure Alice is OK with it. She's about ready to kill the next nurse who tries to take away her cell phone."

And with that, Pete was down the hallway, looking for the doctor. Poe returned to Alice's room, calculating that he'd figured out the magic words to get Alice to stay put for a few more days. "Alice," he said sweetly, "I think I've figured out how to get you your free coffee."

Chapter 22
Callista

"... I promised the doctor I'd drive his daughter in the Starfish Days parade," Poe told Callista over the phone. "She's the queen, and she doesn't want to ride in a dory on a trailer like she did last year when she was princess."

"Sounds like a pretty easy deal for keeping Alice's secret for a few more days," Callista said.

"Yeah, not too bad, only now I have to explain to the drag queens why I can't drive them. Maybe they'll be at opposite ends of the parade and I can drive both. The route's short enough, I think ..."

And with that, Poe and Callista's conversation dropped off into the distinctly non-normal realm that she was quickly discovering passed for normal in Surfland. Having already discussed what Poe had learned from Polanksi and Alice, they decided that Poe would leave her at The Seabiscuit for the rest of the day. Strangely, despite the craziness of the past day, there really wasn't anything more she could do for now.

If only she could say the same for the rest of her life.

She was supposed to start at the aquarium tomorrow, and she just didn't see how that was going to be possible. Aside from the mental strain, her body was still physically beaten up from her time in the ocean. Clearly, she was going to have to ask them to delay her first day, something she wasn't excited about at all.

This was supposed to the job she where she got to start over.

That's why she'd come Surfland in the first place.

Chapter 23
Oregon & Surfland

If Oregon was the state where most people were not exactly normal, the coast might be considered their sort of protected national park. A place where everyone is free to live as they please, largely in defiance of whatever might be happening — or had happened — in the world at large.

Certainly, the coast of Oregon is not alone in this respect. Just a dozen or so hours south along U.S. Highway 101 is San Francisco, a city famous as a final chance to get it right, a final stop when people fail. That there are suicide hotline phones at both ends of the Golden Gate Bridge doesn't stop more than two dozen people a year from throwing themselves off the bridge into the bay.

But the coast of Oregon is no San Francisco; for one thing there is no bridge anywhere towering 250 feet above the ocean. More than that, though, is that people don't come to the Oregon Coast to die, they simply come to start over.

Because coming to coastal Oregon is a lot like throwing

out the standard map of America itself, or at the very least falling off the edge of it. Community populations hardly ever top 10,000, and most are much smaller than that. The nearest city of any size is Portland, which is 90 minutes to six hours from the various towns of the coast.

In the winter, landslides, windblown trees and floods often close the highways in and out of town leaving the area isolated (although not as often as the Portland news stations — the bane of tourism promoters — would have people believe.)

So, whether it's someone running from their past or just making a leisurely stroll toward a different future, the Oregon Coast attracts all kinds of people. Seeking a chance to wipe the slate clean, they come to this psychological refuge on the wettest edge of the United States, hoping this is where they might finally fit.

And nowhere more than Surfland.

For one thing, it's one of the youngest towns on the Oregon coast: parts of it were founded by people who are still alive. Very few people in Surfland have a history going back more than a generation or two, so even newcomers fit in relatively quickly. There is no sense that one must have lived for 50 years in Surfland with 28 relatives in the town cemetery before they can be considered a local.

Another thing is that Surfland is, well, kind of unattractive. In contrast to the historical ambiance of Astoria, the fun of downtown Seaside, the funky weirdness that is Yachats, or the vintage charm of the riverfront in Old Town in Florence, Surfland seems more like an urban sprawl of motels interrupted by occasional bursts of quaint urban redevelopment and ugly rock and gravel yards. Anyone looking for the idealized romance of a Pacific Northwest beach will certainly go somewhere else.

And in the mind of Surflanders, they are more than welcome to.

Because the people who choose to call Surfland home don't live there because of aesthetics, bragging rights in magazines or any of those other things people like to yap about. Not that the city doesn't have things to brag about; some of the best restaurants in the state are in Surfland, along with all the exciting things that come with having a casino at one end and a bustling bay at the other.

But people have to make an effort to find those things (the casino's endless marketing notwithstanding). And while it can be an effort to appreciate what Surfland has to offer, the people who live there find that effort is almost always rewarded. Because with very little sense of history other than the one they are creating at the moment, everyone in Surfland feels pride in it and feels invited to take part in it.

Even those people — perhaps especially those people — who are trying to start over.

Their pasts two decades or two months behind them, people who move to Surfland can get involved in everything. Whatever they might have done before, it is understood that their history began again when they got to Surfland.

When Aly became editor of the Surfland Siren, she briefly proposed doing background checks on all city council candidates, because that's something she'd learned to do in grad school. But after talking with Rip, she realized that was a terrible idea. Not that anyone had anything terrible in their past, but some had a litany of curious financial choices, relationships gone very bad (and public) and other oddities.

What she also noticed, however, was that all of them had clean records once they arrived in Surfland. And she decided to do what most residents of Surfland do — let people's pasts stay in the past.

Curiously, when the candidates got wind of what Aly was thinking, very few of them objected. For some, it was that they just didn't care anymore. For others there was nothing there they figured their friends didn't already know.

Because as much as people in Surfland might be trying to get away from their pasts, they know it is very much a part of them. And although when they arrive in town they might be tight-lipped about who they were and what they had done outside the refuge of Surfland, eventually they tell someone. Everyone seems to know everything, while at the same time not letting it change things.

It's a curious balance, maintained because with very few exceptions everyone in Surfland has a similar story to tell.

Callista Walker was no different.

Chapter 24
Callista

Showering in her room at The Seabiscuit, Callista pondered the choices she'd made that had led her to Surfland and her job at the aquarium.

Upon graduation from USC, she'd wanted to stay in California, so she'd taken a job at Sea World working with the pinnipeds, where not one of them ever tried to molest her. Even so, she tired of the job quickly; the corporate nature of the place never really suited her personality.

Not that it was all bad. She liked talking to tourists about maritime environmentalism, especially the kids. But as in any place that has stockholders and Wall Street to impress, the mission to entertain as well as educate was always there. Eventually, it just got to her, and on a busy day one August, she finally snapped.

Despite being asked not to bring food near the seal tanks, one particularly obnoxious guest insisted on bringing his ice cream in close. Coupled with a droning conversation via cell phone with his stockbroker, he not only dropped his Rocky Road into the tank, he didn't even notice.

Not so when Callista smacked two well-aimed dead fish across his face from about 10 feet away.

"I figured since he needed to share his snacks with my seals, the least I could do was share theirs with him," she told her boss about 30 minutes later. (It would have been quicker had her boss not been busy trying to convince the man that the flying fish were because of a violent arm spasm.)

And that was the end of her job at Sea World, although her boss did agree to write her a stellar letter of recommendation. He did suggest, however, that she go to work somewhere that was not owned by a beer company or fronted by Mickey Mouse.

That led her to the Georgia Aquarium in Atlanta. Although the largest aquarium on Earth, it was created with a quarter of a billion dollar donation from the creator of Home Depot. Existing as a separate non-profit, it was something Callista thought would appeal to her.

So, packing up her van, she headed to Atlanta — and lasted three months. She liked the aquarium and the people on both sides of the tanks, and the job was everything she thought she wanted. But it was too far from the west coast she loved and too big for her tastes. With an 8.1 million gallon tank as the main attraction, the place was huge, leaving Callista with a perpetual feeling of being overwhelmed.

She headed back to Southern California, and crashed on a flight attendant-friend's couch for what she figured would be a few weeks as she sorted out her options. Clearly, the corporate thing wasn't her, nor was the big thing, or the east coast thing. It left a short list of places she might want to work.

Two she considered were the Steinhart Aquarium in San Francisco and the Monterey Bay Aquarium. She'd crossed them off her list early because both were far too near to her father and sister in Berkeley, but realizing her options were growing limited, she applied there anyway.

What she discovered, however, was that they had crossed her off their lists. In the three months since the incident at Sea World, she had become infamous in aquarium circles. Her fish-flinging incident had been recorded on someone's cell phone and put on YouTube. Although it hadn't gone viral in the world at large, everyone in the aquarium community had seen it. Although they might have silently approved of what she'd done, publicly no one would even talk to her about a job.

So, with a growing sense that her career might be over less than a year after she started — wouldn't her family love that — she sent out one last application to the Surfland Aquarium of the Pacific. A small aquarium that attracted fewer that a half-million visitors a year, it was a non-profit that was so committed to education above entertainment that they didn't even name the behemoths swimming in the shark tank. (Not that the guests didn't give them their own names, but that was another story.)

Six months went by and Callista heard nothing. She was growing weary of working part time at Starbuck's and her friend had been laid off by the airline, so even her free rent was probably over soon. Thinking perhaps she might be able to make a go of it as a high school science teacher — they were always looking for women — she began flipping through course catalogs and planning a return to school.

It was her last afternoon in her friend's place, and as she moved her things to her van the phone rang. The Surfland aquarium was calling, and they had an opening. Not willing to trust her fortune, Callista came right out and asked about the YouTube video.

"You've seen it, right?" She didn't want to get there and find out they'd made a mistake.

"Of course I have," said the man who would be her boss. "I've got a still of the fish hitting the guy in the mouth on my wall."

"And you're OK with that?"

"Would you do it again?"

"If someone drops ice cream on my seals again, I might."

"Good, that's what I was hoping you'd say. You start in two weeks."

And instead of heading for UC Riverside — no way could she afford USC without scholarships — she headed north up I-5 to Oregon.

She stopped off in Berkeley just be courteous and was reminded again of why living anywhere near her family was a terrible idea. With her father's connections, Arianna had started and acted as the spokesperson for "Free Animals and Sea Creatures in Storage Tanks, Now!" a new anti-aquarium group hell-bent on getting every fish and mammal in every tank returned to the ocean.

Within minutes, her family's one dinner together turned into the tag-team lecture Callista had become so familiar with.

"You know, Callista, all aquariums are really just fish prisons," her father said.

"You know, Callista, they beat their whales at Sea World," her sister said.

"You know, Callista, they just raise those fish in tanks so they can feed them to tourists," her father said.

"You know, Callista, 'Free Animals and Sea Creatures in Storage Tanks, Now!' is going to make sure people like you never hurt another animal again," her sister said.

For about thirty minutes of this, Callista simply took it like she always did. But in the last few years she'd learned a lot about aquariums. She knew the truth. Although she might not have loved her past employers, she knew they were not bad people and that they treated the creatures in their care with respect.

And she'd learned a lot about herself. She was not willing to be browbeaten into submission anymore by her domineering father and sister, not willing to listen to their lies that other people were too coward to question. Brandishing their degrees like a sledgehammer, her father had made a career of scaring people out of questioning him, and her sister was doing very much the same.

No more.

Rising from the table, she quietly took her plate and silverware to the sink. She did not counter their arguments with facts or try to change their minds; either effort would have been useless. Reason, she found, never changed the mind of a zealot.

Instead she simply walked to the door to leave, for what she planned to be the last time ever. And as she opened the door, she turned over her shoulder and looked at Arianna to speak. "You know, you really might want to get a different name for your group," she said with a wry grin. "Acronyms can be a real bitch."

It had been about 10 days since she'd left her father and sister with that dumb look on their faces. It was rare, and it had felt so good at the time. But that was all gone now, she thought as she toweled off from her shower. Knowing that the longer she put it off, the crazier it would make her, she wrapped the towel around her middle and called her new boss.

Answering on the first ring, he seemed thrilled to hear from her, which at least gave her a good place to start her story. And she did, telling him everything that happened from the second she walked out of the water with her surfboard to being dropped off at the B&B. It took about 15 minutes, and through it all he said nothing. Praying that her cell phone hadn't dropped the call somewhere along the way, she waited several seconds for him to respond.

"I think," he said quietly, "that when you see those guys next you should throw a fish at them."

Callista burst out laughing, relieved that at least part of the past couple of days wasn't going to end disastrously. Telling her to take all the time she needed, he asked her to call back on

Monday and let him know when she could start.

"November's not exactly our busiest time," he said. "Besides, when you get here you're going to have a helluva story to tell, if you want to. You'll fit in just perfect; everyone here's kind of a lunatic, anyway."

Thrilled that maybe she had finally found a place she might fit in, Callista laughed again, feeling unburdened of a major weight. Although the fact that two men might still be trying to kill her kept her from fully enjoying the moment, she did feel good enough to ask one last question.

"I was wondering if I might able to stay away from the sea lions for a while?"

Chapter 25
Shabazz T. Morton

Shabazz T. Morton had been in the background long enough.

Not wanting to be too close to what would literally be the scene of the crime, he'd brought in his brother's sons to do the last little bit of dirty work. He'd assumed that they'd acquired Denny's criminal mind and would be able to do what was needed.

Shabazz had been half right: Bobby was a criminal, and Joey had brains.

Unfortunately, Bobby's mind seemed motivated by drinking huge amounts of Milwaukee's Best and spending as much of Shabazz's money as possible on Hays Supply shit. And while Joey did seem fairly bright, all he ever did was babble about "Space Trek" or some nonsense like that.

If there'd been any justice in the world, he thought in one of the more perverse concepts of the word, the two of them together would have been able to do something right. Instead, Joey had managed to ensure the one piece of mail he had to get had been left on the other side of town in the beach house. And Bobby had cost hundreds of dollars to both his credit cards and even more in damages to the old woman's house.

Thinking back to the moment they arrived, other than actually making it here from Kansas, he could think of only three things they hadn't screwed up. Bobby had gotten the supplies just like he'd asked from Hays Supply, Joey had brought in a lock box Denny had sent out with him, and their efforts — no matter how screwed up — ensured Alice Kauffman was still in critical condition and not expected to live.

In a small town it was easy to find out how people were doing, and it was nice to hear she wouldn't be doing much of anything much longer. He hoped in their grief her relatives would want to sell quickly, although with just two days to go, it was probably hopeless.

And again, he was reminded of the non-solution the White brothers had been. Maybe he should have had Joey do the talking, at just a bit over 5-and-a-half feet tall, he was a good three inches shorter than his brother and Alice probably would have liked him better. That he also had a full set of teeth and washed his hair more than once a week was also a plus.

And they were ultimately the reason he'd not even thought about having Joey come out in the first place. Shabazz had tried being reasonable with Alice, making her dozens of over-priced offers for her house. She'd turned every one of them down.

That didn't change the fact that he wanted her house; each one he could acquire was pure profit. So he'd called up Denny in the hopes that his brother could come down and "persuade" her to sell by becoming her virtual shadow, a constant reminder that life would just be a whole lot easier if she'd simply sell.

But Denny was where he often spent his time these days: in jail. It wasn't much, just a misdemeanor for horse theft, but given Denny's long criminal record — and the unfortunate ways he was found to be using said horse — the judge gave him the maximum sentence. Never one to let a good criminal opportunity pass the family by, however, Denny recommended his son, Bobby.

"Now he's no criminal genius like me, " Denny told his brother during his weekly phone call from jail, "but he is in management now at Hays Supply, so he's got somethin' goin' on up there. He's even good with computers. Spends all his time with e-Babe, or somethin' like that. I think he's lookin' for a wife.

"Anyway, it'd do him good to learn from 'The Legend,' himself. Lemme get his number. I got it written on my arm here some place …"

"The Legend," as Shelton Todd Morton came to be known, got his start when he was 16 years old and bought a cheap Japanese car from a dealer in Topeka only to later set it afire right across the street from the dealership.

Soon, word spread that Topeka Toyota had done Shelton wrong, and that in a raging revenge he had taken the car back and then blown it up in protest. In a circle of friends and extended family where the only question that mattered was, "Ford or Chevy?" he quickly became a hero. (The fact that he had bought a Toyota in the first place mattered little.)

Shelton's parents were somewhat less thrilled. Their hands were already full with their older son, Denny. Having turned 18 just six months earlier, he was already compiling a lengthy adult rap sheet, not to mention a reputation for unsavory activities with hoofed mammals.

They feared Shelton would head down the same path, so they sent him to live with his mother's cousin in Portland. The distance they hoped would keep him away from the criminal element he seemed to favor. Oregon worked because everyone knew it rained all the time, which would be a perfect since a young arsonist would have serious problems lighting things on fire.

It half worked: Shelton never burned anything again. As to separating him from the criminal element, Shelton simply switched time zones, although not before his base nature — a loud-mouthed ass — asserted itself in ways that would affect him for years to come.

Arriving at his new high school in downtown Portland in the mid-'80s, Shelton encountered more African-American people on that first day than he had in his entire life. He handled the situation as anyone would whose understanding of black culture extended to what he'd seen on "Sanford & Son."

"Damn!" he said to no one in particular during first period math, "I had no idea you people were so short. How the hell are ya'll ever going to play basketball?"

Second through sixth period were handled with equal sensitivity, and by the time he got to seventh period gym class everyone in the school knew about the new kid from Kansas. So when Shelton observed in the locker room that, "Everyone of ya'll coulda been in 'Roots' if you just had some whip marks on your backs," it was all the jocks around him could do not to dog pile him.

Indeed, they probably would have had not the young man right next to Shelton smashed him across the back of the head with a Calculus book. "I got three classes with this idiot," he said. "I can put up with a lot, but don't insult LeVar Burton."

When Shelton came to in the nurse's office, it was informally decided that anyone who irritated a National Merit Finalist scholarship winner to the point of violence probably had it coming, and formally nothing was done. Although it was suggested politely to Shelton's guardians that he might want to shut up for a while; the vice principal had been in Language Arts when Shelton had said: "I know why the caged bird sings: 'Cause he's too stupid to have agreed to do community service."

At this point Shelton did learn something: how to shut up in the name of self-preservation. For a brief time, he even tried to fit in, hanging out at football games and trying to flirt with the cheerleaders.

But what had worked in Hays didn't fly in Portland at all. No one was impressed that he could turn a handful of wires and Kleenex boxes into a set of speakers for his portable cassette player. (On foggy nights in the wheat fields of Kansas there was nothing better than Waylon Jennings, a six-pack of Schlitz and a girl who he had convinced he was 21, simply by dabbling the place where he should have had facial hair with a fine-tip Sharpie.)

By the third game of the season he basically did nothing but hang around the concession stand and beg for leftover hot dogs at the end of the night.

Eventually, he found himself keeping company with the kinds of people his parents had wanted him to get away from. What the school administration liked to call "disaffected youth," they had quite an effect on Shelton.

Impressed by the legend of what he'd done in Topeka — he had news clippings — they liked hanging out with him. He taught them everything he knew about electronics and wiring and how to use those skills for fun and profit.

In turn they taught him where to find largely unprotected areas all over the Portland metropolitan area where he could jimmy locks and hotwire vehicles. Starting with Chevys and Fords in the high school parking lot — Shelton was out of Kansas, what the hell did he care? — he even started poking around the docks, seeing what fun he could have with the occasional boat.

By the time he graduated, Shelton was a one-man crime wave and his method was a simple one: steal a vehicle and find someone to buy it for next to nothing. Whether it went to a chop shop, got new counterfeit paperwork or any number of other illegal things, Shelton didn't care. Selling the vehicles at

25 percent of their actual value, there were always takers.

And Shelton did a lot of taking. Spreading his activities across the entire Portland metropolitan area, his enterprise went largely undetected by the authorities, and he could usually snag and sell five to six vehicles a week. (And whatever he couldn't he was more than happy to ditch in one of Oregon's many rivers and lakes.)

By the age of 22, Shelton was richer than he ever thought he would be growing up in Kansas. (Never paying taxes helped a lot.) And so he began to indulge himself. But instead of just going out and buying any old thing that struck his fancy, Shelton decided to recreate who he was. Curiously, his blueprints were the very people that had so intimidated him when arrived in Portland: African-Americans.

True, Shelton had never learned any sensitivity about African-Americans. Indeed, Shelton himself never called them African-Americans; "Blacks" was as far as he had gotten, which, all things considered, was a radical improvement over what he'd said to his science teacher in third period on that fateful first day of school.

He had been banned from every KFC and Popeye's in the Portland area, because every time he entered one he insisted on speaking to "the people who have all the rhythm — and watermelon." This, despite the fact that at least half the time there were no African-Americans in sight. "What? They have to be here," he'd scream. "Where else do they eat?"

But despite his inability to communicate with African-Americans, he was fascinated by their culture — or at least what he thought was their culture. Accepting broad stereotypes based on the likes of Mr. T and whatever rap star happened to be appearing on TV, he saw them as the epitome of life as he thought it should be.

He bought a 1986 four-door Cadillac Seville with a landau roof and chrome wheels. He wore gold chains, even going so far as to carry around a picture of the cast of "The A-Team" so he could tell jewelers what he wanted.

He even got a new name: Shabazz T. Morton. It was a combination of "Shakur," a rapper he knew of who'd recently been killed, the letter "b," just because it sounded cool, and "jazz," a music he knew African-Americans listened to. He didn't know what the middle initial stood for yet; but as long as he left it "T" he wouldn't have to change the monogram on his custom landau roof. (He'd paid extra for that.)

And so it was that Shabazz T. Morton continued the criminal career that Shelton Todd Morton had begun. But with the new name came fatter targets, and like a junkie who needs to keep taking in more and more to get the same high, Shabazz got more daring. Expensive cars valeted at steak and seafood restaurants, yachts on the Willamette, even an airplane once at Pearson Field across the river in Vancouver were fair game.

But it was this last stunt that finally got Shelton — Shabazz was never a legal name — dragged before a judge. In all his planning to steal the Honda six-passenger jet, he neglected to cover one thing in his discussions with the partner who'd come up with the idea: "What do you mean you can't fly this thing?" Shabazz asked incredulously after they'd managed to pick the locks and get into the plane. "That's why you're here!"

Whether the partner thought Shabazz had a license or he truly thought they could just drive it to their customer at the Vancouver Mall — as he told the judge — it really didn't matter. Within two minutes of Shabazz's ill-timed discovery in the cockpit, the cops were all over them.

The sentence was stiff. Although most of the crimes he had committed were never connected to Shabazz, his most recent thefts — an Aston-Martin Vantage, a BMW M6 convertible and an 1100 horsepower cigarette boat — were. Their value put him in felony territory and in the crosshairs of the IRS. (Never paying taxes hurt a lot.) He got twenty years.

During his time in prison, Shabazz did what Shelton had learned to do in high school: shut up and survive. Coupled with his electronics skills — he could fix anything — he largely avoided the types of trauma that prisons are famous for. (Although he did get worried once that a CD player he was fixing for a "big date" might be for him; he'd heard that the owner thought Carrie Underwood was from Kansas.)

Aside from having to always sit at the far end of the table because he was left handed — electronics whiz or no, one only needed to elbow-jab a serial killer a certain number of times before things got ugly — Shabazz's time behind bars went fairly smoothly. He spent most of his time watching television, drawn particularly to home improvement shows (what he didn't know how to wire, he did now) and the History Channel, which is where he finally figured out what the "T" should stand for.

"Tiberius." It had a nice ring to it, he thought. The Roman name of Tiberius Caesar Augustus, he was the second emperor at the time of the birth of Christ. "Shabazz Tiberius Morton": now that's a real man's name. It spoke of conquering and commanding, a name to be feared.

And sure as hell not the name of some dumb space nut, Captain Jerk, or whatever his nephew said the guy's name was.

Just the mere thought made him angry again; at least he'd punched Joey when he'd said it. That made him feel a little better, and so did finally deciding that he needed to start taking control of things again. He'd still use Bobby and Joey, but the days of just sending them out on their own were over.

Yes, Shabazz T. Morton had been in the background long enough.

Chapter 26
Surfland

Technically, the town where Shabazz had chosen to work his latest criminal enterprise wasn't much older than Shabazz himself. The youngest city on the Oregon coast, it was incorporated in just 1965. And while its true roots did go farther back than that, they didn't by much.

The oldest part of the city was begun as its own town in the early days of the 20th century, while the youngest was developed as another town in the late 1930s. In the intervening quarter-century three other small towns popped up nearby, taking advantage of their sites along the Roosevelt Military Highway.

By the 1960s, the five communities occupied a largely unbroken six-mile strip of stores, shops and homes along what was now called U.S. Highway 101, The Pacific Coast Highway. Every year more tourists came, more people moved there, and eventually the communities found themselves in deep shit, literally.

For although each community had been founded on its own — and had the rivalries to prove it — they all shared one very important commonality: totally overwhelmed sewer systems. Their community's plumbing systems a patchwork of septics, hastily laden pipe and aging water treatment facilities, each community found itself desperately in need of a better way to flush the toilets.

Banding together as one city was the way to do it, because with enough people the federal government would pay for it. It required three votes among the residents of the five communities to make it happen, so contentious was the idea to some people. Maybe that's why residents started so quickly sporting bumper-stickers with their city's new — and completely unofficial — motto: "Bonded in Crap Since 1968."

Nevertheless, it did pass, leaving one question unresolved: What to call the new city?

To just name the new city after one of the old towns was never a consideration. That would have made residents of the four communities that weren't selected so angry the measure to join the towns never would have passed. So, a contest was held, and the name that got the most votes would became the name of the new city.

The town's school children immediately did what many of their parents could not: they all quickly agreed on something. And with every child filling out a ballot, the name "Surfland," was the overwhelming choice. But calling this choice "too honky-tonk," the mayor and the new city council threw it out and substituted the far less popular "Colton City," named after the city's location in north Colton County.

It was a decision they quickly regretted. Parents were furious as their elementary students cried, and their junior high school students said it violated the democratic process. The high school students said it was just one more example of "The Man" trying to put down America's youth, never mind that "The Man" in this case was a mayor who made his living installing toilets. (He won in a landslide, his campaign slogan, "I Know Crap," perfect for a town investing heavily in sewers.)

The council quickly reversed their decision at the next council meeting, a decision that pleased most people. The high school students notwithstanding — who had hoped to drag things out a little longer so they could re-enact the nude scene in "Hair" as a protest — the name was changed back to Surfland, a name it has been happy with ever since.

Mostly.

As late as the 1980s one resident still protested the decision by refusing to use the sewer system, going so far as to only go to the bathroom in a portable toilet. He made sure when he emptied it to always take the contents to the other end of town where he dumped it in an empty lot. Only upon his death — and the later discovery of the most well composted lot in Surfland — did anyone ever become aware of what he'd been doing for 20 years.

Even today, among the older garages in town, visitors can still occasionally see a bumper sticker reading, "Bonded in Crap Since 1968." There are a few dozen scattered around, although most are in what's now called the Harrison District.

This is not surprising, since it was the town of Harrison that began what is now Surfland in 1909. Indeed, it was the only one of the five towns whose majority never voted to merge. Forced to accept the will of the majority, however, they became part of Surfland with grudging acceptance.

This was for two reasons, and the first was obvious: Even the most ardent non-merger supporter had grown weary of the sewer backing up into Lenobar Bay, the heart of Harrison. It's very hard to attract tourists when they run the risk of human feces ending up in their crab traps.

But the other had more to do with community pride: they demanded that the name of the school stayed the same. The first school in north Colter County, Harrison High School had been the destination of thousands of school children for more than 50 years, and the people of Harrison wanted it to stay that way.

To this day, even though the separate histories of the five districts that make up Surfland are largely forgotten, Harrison High School remains a daily reminder of one man's perseverance — and another's abject stupidity.

Like so many people who would grow to call Surfland home, Luther Alfred Lattulans arrived in Colton County, Oregon, in 1907, hoping for a new start. His previous ones having all gone nowhere.

The second cousin, once removed on his mother's side, of former President of the United States William Henry Harrison, Luther had become obsessed with founding a town that he could name in honor of his relative, dead now these 66 years. As his failed efforts over the past two decades in Missouri, Utah and Idaho had proven, it was quite the challenge. He'd even failed in California, which was sprouting new towns faster than it could seem to name them. (He was particularly frustrated when despite his best efforts, town residents chose "Soapweed" as the name of their town west of Lake Tahoe.)

His travails were readily understandable, although obviously not to him. This is because William Henry Harrison is perhaps the most undistinguished, unmemorable, uneventful president in American history. This is not to say bad, corrupt or anything like that; there's probably a reason no one has ever named a town after Richard Nixon.

Rather, William Henry Harrison earns his distinction by having the shortest presidency in American history: one month, from March 4, 1841, to April 4, 1841. Giving the longest inaugural address in history on a cold and wet day without the benefit of an overcoat probably had something to do with it.

For while in today's lexicon a politician speaking 8,444 words for nearly two hours might be called a lot of hot air, this is still only a figurative expression. Because just a couple of weeks after his speech, President Harrison fell ill and eventually died of complications of pneumonia.

Not exactly the most distinguished moment in the history of the American presidency.

Still, the man was a President of the United States, and Luther thought that should mean something, and for this reason he was committed to founding a town in his relative's name. Everyone else thought he should just be committed, and this was just as true among the people he met on the coast of Oregon.

But Luther worked hard, opening a town store and barbershop, and people saw that while Luther might be a little crazy, he was in fact a good man. When another local businessman asked for a loan from Luther to build a small hotel a couple of miles north, Luther instead just gave him the money.

Knowing that growth of the area would ensure his own town's success, he asked only one thing: that the town be named in honor of President Harrison's political party. This is how the Whig City District of Surfland eventually came to be.

But it was the town of Harrison that was Luther's true love, and it was he who lobbied the U.S. government endlessly for a post office, the only thing that really mattered when trying to literally put a town on the map. In 1909 his dream came true, and the tiny town of Harrison was born.

Tragically, Luther only lived to see his town on that map for two years. He died of heat stroke in 1911, a record late summer heat wave killing the man who — for fairly obvious reasons — always wore a top coat, and sometimes two. His last joy was cutting the ribbon at the grand opening of the community high school.

Proud again that his relative's name would be remembered despite an early death, Luther slipped into the great unknown the next morning. Ironically, however, as much as his relative's name defined the town, it was Luther's name that would come to stand for something 31 years later, and nowhere more than the high school that didn't bear his name.

It would not have made him happy.

Chapter 27
Poe

Getting Alice's coffee problem solved was a simple matter of a five-minute phone call to the owner of the McDonald's franchise in Surfland as Poe sat in his living room. Indeed, the longest thing about the process was scrolling down through the phone's contact list to the "Y" listings, where Dick Yelpers' phone number had gone unused for more than six years.

He'd profiled Yelpers for "Dine and Dash Daily," a nationally known publication in fast food circles that was recognizing Yelpers' purchase of his 10th McDonald's franchise, despite his disability. (Yelpers had burned off all his taste buds and half of his palette in a tragic reheated pizza accident as a child.)

The story had made Yelpers a minor celebrity amongst processed chicken fans — he'd almost invented the dinosaur-shaped chicken nugget — and he'd been grateful to Poe ever since. "If there's anything I can ever do for you," he wrote

Poe on the back of a tray liner, since speaking wasn't Yelper's strong point, "you let me know."

And now Poe had, by getting Yelpers to fax a letter to all his coastal McDonald's outlets letting them know that any senior with the special sunrise mug should get a free cup of coffee. (Yelpers even promised to throw in free dino-hash browns, once he got those through corporate.)

"Ann-tim, Poo!" Yelpers said, before Poe hung up the phone — making Poe wish he'd hung up just one moment sooner. For while well intended, Yelper's remarks had the side effect of not making Poe feel well at all.

Poe didn't like calling on old sources for personal favors. Having written hundreds of stories over the years about people big and small all over the Pacific Northwest, his phone list was huge, and he never hesitated to use it when he needed help on another story. That was business.

But every time he made a phone call for something personal, he felt like he was using his connections as a journalist for personal gain. Not that it was a lot of gain, or even personal.

He'd never used his sources to get anything for himself, just friends, and he'd never gotten anything monetary even for them. The most "valuable" thing he'd ever done was get a dentist to replace Ryan Norcross's molar for free.

That's why Yelper's send-off bothered him so much: it wasn't just that he'd done it, but that he knew he'd probably do it again.

Of course Poe wasn't the only one who was bothered. It

had made Vivian nuts, although not for the same reasons.

With Poe's wealth of contacts — there was more than one Fortune 500 exec in his directory — it made Vivian furious that he couldn't take better advantage of things, especially considering Poe's money situation. Namely, that he didn't have any.

Not to say Poe was poor. He paid his bills and always had just enough to take care of the things he had to, like fixing the roof, feeding the pets and keeping a ready supply of microbrews in the refrigerator. But he never had more than that, and every time he had a brush with wealth it made Vivian nuts that he couldn't take advantage of it.

No wonder she left when he bought the car.

But the lottery money paid for the car only, and save for the money he gave to the high school each year, nothing else. Sure, he tipped big once in a while and donated more than he should to pet causes, but the lottery money was never to be used for anything else. He was very strict about that.

Which was why even at 6 a.m. on a Friday morning, Jackson Poe, owner of a six-digit British supercar, was finishing up a story for "Beach Fashion and Faves" magazine, one of dozens of magazines up and down the coast that he wrote for under his pen name.

Titled "Tee Up Your Toilet," it was a 600-word piece about how for just two or three thousand dollars people could turn their bathroom into a faux-putting green. (Floating balls were highly recommended.)

Soulless writing, it took him only half-an-hour to write,

but it was a $250 paycheck, with another $50 thrown in for the sidebar about who made the best floating golf ball for the commode. ("Title-pissed.") And as he e-mailed the story off to an editor he'd never met in a city he'd never been to, he gazed out the window at the Jag just to assure himself that having some standards was worth it.

Reviewing his morning, it had already been a long day, even before noon.

He'd started with the story, Vivian had made her regular call to suck the joy out of life, Callista had awoken to put some back in, and he'd visited Alice at the hospital just to remind himself of how confused that life had become.

And as he finished his conversation with Yelpers and headed for the car, he mused just how quickly things could get weird in less than 24 hours.

Hopefully, that was about to change; he was on his way to the B&B to talk to Pete, who had learned a few details behind the license plate Callista remembered seeing. Maxing out the volume on the Jag's CD player with the theme to *Jurassic Park*, he was in The Seabiscuit's driveway in less than five minutes. What he learned, however, dashed his hopes as quick as he'd taken the corner out of his driveway.

"Kansas? They take a wrong turn on I-70 looking for wheat?"

Gathered around a table outside of the kitchen with Rip, Katrina and Callista, Poe sent his coffee mug flying across the room as his arms failed to contain his frustration.

"Tell me there's more than that," he said, his foot now wiping up the floor with a paper towel.

There was, Rip said, but what their uncle, a convicted felon named Shelton, a.k.a. "Shabazz," Morton, might have to do with it, he wasn't entirely sure. Handing Poe another cup of coffee, he ran through Morton's criminal record.

"'Shabazz?' Like the late civil rights leader?" Poe asked when Rip was done. "Is this guy African-American?"

"No, he's definitely white," Rip said, giving Poe a full-page copy of Morton's mug shot. "He popped up in my search because he inherited a beach house about a half-block down from Alice. I wonder if she knows him."

"I don't think so. She didn't mention him, and he doesn't look like either of the guys Alice or Callista described," Poe said, as Callista also signaled she'd never seen Shelton, Shabazz, or whatever his name was.

"But I'll bet he's the one who's been trying to buy her house, and the one who sent our friends with the Kansas license plate," Poe speculated. "Although why he'd want a house half a block away and not even on the ocean when he already has a beach house, I have no idea.

"You sure there's no other local connections for any of these guys?"

"I have not yet begun to search," Rip replied, and with that Poe knew he'd be getting more answers. Even Callista smiled a little, although at this point, Poe figured going back to bed would be the only thing that would truly put some spring back in her step.

For his part, Poe still had a life to lead, errands to run and stories to write. Someone had apparently figured out how to incorporate the remains of flora into a marble countertop, and the readers of "Fashion and Faves" needed to know.

Grabbing Morton's picture as he headed back to the car, he told a grateful Callista he'd see her in the morning and walked into the parking lot where a light rain was starting to fall. But backing out his parking space, Poe stopped short when he saw Katrina standing behind him. As he rolled down the window, she simply walked up to the car and handed him his coffee.

"I'd recommend finishing this before you get to the high school," she said with a small smile. "You burn one of those kids in the crotch and they may sue this car right out from under you."

Even Poe's best friends always seemed surprised that he never worried about taking the Jag to the high school. Whether it was wanton vandalism, an accidental fender bender, or just some kid leaning up against his car in their studded jeans, people could envision no end of traumas that could befall an exotic car in a high school parking lot.

But Poe knew something about high school kids that his friends did not. They were basically the same as every day people when it came to his car: they were scared to death of it. It was something Poe relied on, even while at the same time lamenting that most people would believe just about anything.

Because as a result of watching hundreds of hours of television, most people believed his car was armed with an alarm so sensitive that merely getting near the car would set it off. Horns would blare, cops would be called, and everyone within a 50 mile radius would know who had done what. Poe's favorites were people who had watched too many James Bond movies: "Don't touch the door handle; it'll explode."

In reality, he had a basic alarm like a lot of people, which registered collisions, broken windows and attempts to break into the car. And as for the errant rivet from a pair of jeans or a passing backpack, those things were easily buffed out.

And so as Poe pulled up in front of Harrison High School, he didn't worry for one moment about leaving it right in front of the school as he grabbed his coffee and headed inside. Even as he got out of the car, he heard a new rumor — "If you get near the mirrors, it'll zap you right in the balls." — and he did nothing to discourage it.

Poe had come to Harrison High right after leaving Callista at The Seabiscuit. Knowing that her job was no longer in peril had taken a huge weight off her shoulders. But she clearly was still tired and distracted — people trying to kill you tends to do that — and Poe was pleased to see she thought staying at the B&B was a good idea, too.

Not that Poe minded being with Callista; he was enjoying the friendship they seemed to be building. Funny, smart and attractive, she never even asked him about the weird music he liked to play when they were in the car. But he had a lot to get done today, and she'd probably be bored stiff through most of it; both would be happier with her at the B&B.

As it was every Friday, his first stop in the afternoon was

the high school, to return the journalism stories he'd edited after meeting with the kids on Tuesday. The students knew the routine, and as always, Ryan Norcross was there to meet him at the main office and collect the papers.

"Hey, Poe. You want to go to Seattle for the journalism conference with us?" asked Ryan, causing Poe not for the first time to momentarily stop breathing.

It was not because Ryan called him "Poe" — most everyone did — but because Ryan always made Poe think Ryan knew where the money that funded his class's field trips came from. How he would know, Poe had no idea, but ever since the anonymous donations had started coming, Ryan almost never missed an opportunity to invite him on the big annual trip to the student journalism convention. Yet another byproduct of a guilty conscience, Poe surmised.

But just as he always did, Ryan quickly changed the subject: "Hey, thanks again for getting that doctor to replace my tooth," he said, baring the left side of his jaw to show Poe.

"No big deal; just a phone call to an old friend," his conscience nagging him for the second time in 10 seconds. "Just don't try to chew a fan belt in half again. Someone who knows cars like you do, you'd figure you'd know that," he said, laughing.

"Don't worry, I'll never take a bet from those guys again," Ryan said, smiling, knowing full well he'd let some jerks on the football team get the best of him. "And thanks again for helping edit our stories."

"No problem, " Poe said, as he handed over the papers,

and dropped them all over the floor.

"Maybe you shouldn't try to drink coffee and talk at the same time," Ryan laughed.

"Yeah, I keep hearing that," Poe replied.

With that, Ryan leaned down to pick up what turned out to be more than just journalism papers. Poe had mistakenly grabbed the photo of Morton as well from the seat of his car.

"Hey, I know this guy," Ryan said. "He comes to all the football games."

"He does?" Poe asked not believing his luck. "Who is he?"

"I've got no idea, but he sucks," Ryan said with his nose crinkled up into an uncharacteristic sneer. "He always does the all-you-can-eat for $10 thing at the hot dog stand and then spends all night stuffing his pie hole along with the two guys he always brings with him. We lose, like, $20 every time he shows up, and I'm sure we will again tonight.

"He's the worst thing to ever hit the boosters, and that says a lot, knowing our football team," Ryan said, once again back to laughing at his own humor. "You're not doing a story on this guy, are you?"

"No, nothing like that," Poe said, his mind now a million miles away. "Just a photo I accidentally grabbed from a friend's place," he said, the gears in his mind slowly beginning to form a plan.

"That kid I was working with the other day — Paxton — he's really good," Poe said, speaking the truth.

But now there was more than one reason he wanted to talk to Paxton. "Do you have his number?"

"Unfortunately. The guy's a great writer, but about as reliable as a 12-year-old Fiat," Ryan said, while punching the buttons on his cell phone. "Here's his number, but good luck getting anywhere with him. I never know where that guy's head is."

Chapter 28
Paxton Dell

Paxton Dell was 150 miles southwest of Surfland, 30,000 feet in the air and racing home at close to 700 miles per hour. There were more than 300 lives in his hands — including the entire cheerleading squad — and only he could save them now.

Looking to his left, he saw Portia McDonald was already looking at him. On any other day she would have been the prettiest girl on the squad, but now she was his co-pilot, and she was scared.

"I wish I could have saved the pilots, too," he told her, giving her hand a little squeeze. "But there were just too many terrorists. Don't you worry, though, I'll get us down."

Checking the air speed once again, Paxton knew he was pushing the giant 747-400 to the limit, but after playing flight simulator for hundreds of hours, he knew what he was doing. Sure, any faster and he'd break the sound barrier and tear the plane apart, but people were dying.

"Ryan!" he barked into the pilot's headset to the only other still-conscious person still on the plane. "What's going on back there?!" The first-ever joint cheerleader-journalism class trip from Harrison High School was quickly unfolding as an epic nightmare. "Ryan! Answer me, damnit!"

The news wasn't good. Although Paxton had single-handedly disarmed all six terrorists from his hidden base in the first-class bathroom, he hadn't stopped them until they were well into dispersing the gas throughout the cabin.

Thank God he, Ryan and Portia had all been in different bathrooms. But now Ryan had been reduced to a quivering mass of jelly, and all Portia could seem to do was look to him to save her and the other 300 people on Oceanic Flight 999 to Tokyo.

But it was a look Paxton had been expecting, one turning from fear and terror, to love and passion, as she realized that this man she'd failed to see for so long would now bring her back to the surly bonds of earth. Reaching out her arms towards him, Paxton longed to hold her, to bathe her in the surety of his heart, soul and loins.

But not now. Now he had to deal with two F-16 Hornets streaming in on his port and starboard sides. They were to escort him to Portland International Airport, where he would burn off his fuel and land on autopilot. At least that's what they thought, anyway.

Paxton Dell had other ideas.

"No dice, Portland," Paxton said as Portia gazed into his eyes. "The doctor says the passengers are getting sicker. I'm bringing her in now." Ignoring the screaming in his headset from the President, he began his descent.

What Paxton planned would to any other man be suicide: he was going to bring 1.1 million pounds of plane and people in for a belly landing on Lenobar Bay. If he timed it just right, he could touch down at the south end of the bay, and bring the plane to a stop just before the condos and restaurants on the north side of the bay. An expert in linear physics, he'd done the math, and he believed in himself.

And so did Portia, who held him tighter as he began speaking into his headset again. "Fine! Shoot us down, Portland, I dare you! We're all dead anyway!" Now, completely out of the co-pilot's chair, Portia was almost in his lap, and Paxton knew if they were to die, at least it would be together.

Then, surely sensing his determination and command of the crisis, both fighters began to peel off to the east. In the lead plane, the pilot saluted Paxton and wished him luck through the headset.

"God speed to you, too, Maverick," Paxton whispered back before returning to the task at hand.

Massaging the controls like a pilot who'd made a thousand landings, Paxton brought the belly of the giant plane down perfectly at the south end of the bay. It was torture trying to control the reverse thrust of the four massive engines manually, but that was the only way to do it.

"AUGHHH!" Paxton yelled as his muscles screamed against the pain spreading through them. "Dear, God," he thought for a brief moment, "we're not going to make it." But just as quickly it passed, Portia gazing into his eyes, giving him the last bit of strength he needed.

And the jet began to slow: 500 miles per hour, 400, 300, 200, 100 ... and by the time the jet reached the north end of the bay, it had come to a stop with the emergency door touching the pier. A professional pilot could not have done what Paxton Dell just had.

All around the plane boats were circling, helicopters hovering and emergency sirens blaring. Even the sea lions swimming near the evacuating passengers seemed to bark their approval.

But Paxton Dell saw only one thing: the light in Portia's eyes and a passion that burned only for him. Neither of them spoke for the longest time, neither having to. Their love forged by tragedy and triumph would burn forever.

Rising from the floor, she locked the cockpit door, and began to unbutton her shirt. Eyeing him with a raw sensuality that comes only from knowing a room's sole access point is secured against terrorists, she continued slipping out of her clothes until only a pair of Victoria's Secret panties and a Nike sports bra remained. Slowly, she eased down on the floor and leaned back to put her head in his lap.

"It's time for six," she said, her pouty lips whispering to him.

"Oh, baby" he said, moaning loudly. "Are you sure?"

"Yes, I'm sure! Number six! Mr. Dell! What is the answer to number six?"

And just like that, the plane was gone.

As were the terrorists, the helicopters and every other sign that he was a hero. Only three things appeared to him now: Ryan Norcross, who was shaking his head in a mournful way; Portia McDonald, who was laughing hysterically, (definitely with all her clothes on); and Mr. Payne, who quickly moved on to someone else, though not before pronouncing sentence on his daydreaming student.

"Mr. Dell, just where is your head?"

A random poll of the students coming out of Mr. Payne's trigonometry class that Friday afternoon would have revealed three possible locations of Paxton Dell's head.

The most popular — and a unanimous choice of the football team — would have been "Up his ass." And next in popularity would have been "In space," a place Ryan knew from personal experience that Paxton spent a lot of his class time.

The last choice would have been the selection of just one person, cheerleader Valeria Cruz. The oldest daughter of Julio, she alone was a good enough friend of his to know that when he spaced out he was simply dreaming of a world where he was the person he wanted to be.

After one particularly bad day of self-loathing, Paxton had actually asked her why she even bothered to be seen with him. She must have better things to do than hang out with the school's biggest weirdo.

"Paxton, you're sweet and funny, and even if you are a bit naïve, you're a survivor," she said. "Because no matter how much everyone around you calls you a 'space cadet,' 'loser,' 'ass,' or every other thing, you never stop dreaming of better things."

She'd even called him a "relentless optimist." It almost made up for all the people who now hated him even more after his latest daydream in class.

Almost.

"Watch where you're going, dip-shit," Portia McDonald sneered at Paxton as she elbowed her way into the hallway past her would-be suitor. (She was definitely a member of the "up his ass" voting bloc.) "Valeria, why do you hang out with this toad? You could do so much better," she said, not even bothering to listen for an answer before she pushed her way down the hallway.

Drowning again in self-loathing and admittedly looking for a rescue, Paxton looked to Valeria. Another cheerleader and certainly cute in her own right, he repeated the question to her, although taking care to leave out the toad part.

"You make me laugh," she told him, and while he'd found he made a lot of girls laugh, when Valeria said it she didn't mean it as a put down.

"Paxton, why do you like her so much?" Valeria asked as they walked down the hallway to the media center. "She's a bitch. Trust me, I see her at practice every day."

"I know, I know ..." Paxton said, and he did.

Portia McDonald had made it abundantly clear she'd rather die in a plane crash than ever be saved from one by the likes of him. Once, she had been kind to him, but he found out later it was just a ruse to see if she could make him have an erection in the middle of gym class. (She could.)

But in that five minutes of gym class, Paxton had become enraptured, and no matter how horrible she was, how dismissive and cruel, he couldn't get Portia out of his mind. Valeria constantly tried to get him to move on, and more than once he'd resolved to wash Portia from his consciousness.

But then he'd hear some song that reminded him of her, see some movie that made him think it was still possible. Indeed, "The Princess Bride" was his favorite movie, and having seen it at least 100 times he knew anything was possible.

Just like he and Portia, Buttercup had loathed Wesley, but Wesley never gave up. Sure, he had to get mostly dead and fight off killer Rodents Of Unusual Size before they could live happily ever after, but Wesley never gave up, never stopped believing.

And neither would Paxton.

True, there were very few opportunities to have to fight off giant rats while saving a damsel in distress in the 21st century. But he convinced himself — outside of his fantasies anyway — that reality was enough. That if he just had another five minutes he could make her see the real him, the heroic him, the one that would do anything she wished.

Which was about four minutes and 58 seconds longer than he'd gotten in the last year.

He'd even become the high school mascot just to be near her at football games. At the first game, the plan had gone pretty well; he'd actually gotten her to hug him.

But at the second game he held onto the hug a little too long, and when it was done one of the football players noticed what had been all too apparent in gym class. ("Hey, why's the mascot got a tail in front and back?") By the time they got done pummeling him, everyone knew Paxton was the mascot.

Now at the games it was understood that if he got anywhere near Portia, the football team, most of the cheerleading squad and even one-third of the pep band would beat him senseless.

Fortunately, Valeria stood at the opposite end of the squad from Portia, so he could still be near her when he was in costume. It was the only thing that made it bearable, something he was counting on since there was another game tonight.

"Valeria, you want to grab a burger tonight after the game like usual?"

"I can't," she said with a sigh. "My dad says I have to come home right after the game."

"Tonight? It's a Friday!"

"He thinks we spend too much time together," she said rolling her eyes. "He said it's not proper for a girl my age to have a boyfriend." At that last word, Paxton burst out laughing, and within seconds Valeria was as well. "Yeah, I know, but just try telling my dad that. To listen to him, boys didn't even talk to girls in Mexico."

"Maybe if I just introduced myself to …"

"NO!" Valeria pleaded, "He'd lock me in my room forever. He'd think you were asking for permission to …" But now it was her turn to get cut off as Paxton's cell phone rang. Looking with puzzlement at the caller ID, Paxton waved goodbye as Valeria left, leaving him to respond to his caller: "No, I don't think I can put my head in the washer …"

Chapter 29
Poe

Contrary to what some might expect, the weather on Friday afternoon was one of the reasons Poe loved owning his Jag in rainy coastal Surfland.

Having been several days since there'd been any moisture, the light mist that had begun to fall as he drove to the high school was welcome. It gave everything in town a nice sheen, seeming to wash the dust off of everything. The pink-colored ice cream shop on Lenobar Bay seemed to shine a little brighter, the ferns in the yards seemed a rise a little higher, and the grime of the road seemed to fall from the Jag a little faster.

It made Poe smile, and even though he always preferred to have the top down, it was his opinion that British Racing Green never looked better than when it had beads of rain racing off the side of it.

Happy: it was a good disposition to be in since he was about to ask Fuzznut for a favor. Because just asking would probably put a serious damper on his afternoon, no matter how loud he might play the theme to "Waterworld," before getting to his friend's house.

It was necessary, however, now that he knew Shabazz Morton — and hopefully the two men who had attacked Callista — would likely be at the football game tonight. If Morton was like most people, he'd start talking about things while lulled by the perverse anonymity of a public venue, one made even better by the fact that not a lot of people actually went to HHS football games.

It was an unforeseen opportunity that Poe couldn't miss, but he was going to need Fuzznut's help if he had any chance to find out more about what was going on. Because no matter how relaxed Morton might get, he seriously doubted that he would be able to just take a seat next to them in the stadium and eavesdrop.

But a skunk sure could.

Chapter 30
Surfland

Periodically in the 30-odd years after Luther Alfred Lattulans' death in 1911, the students of William Henry Harrison High School would rumble and grumble about the rather banal name of their town and school, unimpressed by their namesake's 32-day presidency. But their parents and eventually grandparents remembered the role Luther had played in putting their tiny town on the map, and the controversy would go away.

That all changed in 1942. Not because Harrison's status was being debated, but rather Luther's.

It began innocently enough, when a new student from Eugene was sent to the office for suggesting in history class that Karl Marx might not be such a bad guy after all. The principal's first thought was to have him expelled then possibly beaten in the ravine south of the school, and not necessarily in that order.

But it was pointed out by the superintendent that the

student's father was a major backer of the student band. Unless the principal wanted the students marching naked during football games, beating the crap out of his son would probably be a bad idea. Besides, seeing as the student's father was a retired poli-sci professor from the University of Oregon, the kid had probably been raised mentally deficient anyway.

Instead, the young rebel was forced to dust and clean all the trophy cases in the school, a daunting task, given that in the early decades of HHS most of the athletic teams weren't truly God-awful. And that's why, behind the football trophy for winning the 1924 Crab Cup tourney and the plaque denoting the school's 1938 participation in the Salmon Slapping Festival, he found the oldest photo in the school, one taken the day they cut the ribbon on the new Harrison High School.

Protected from exposure by all the other crap piled atop it, the picture was almost as clear as the day it was taken. Luther, the two topcoats, and even some massive beads of sweat that were a sign of Luther's imminent demise: all were clearly visible. But of more interest to the student was the dog standing with Luther, who looked to be panting almost as much as his owner.

It was a German Shepard, and while in 1911 it had been his innocuous constant companion — no woman had ever been able to appreciate the ninth president to Luther's satisfaction — to a rabble-rousing student it was a gold mine. Because even though the German Shepard had been the school's mascot since 1911, if there was anything hated in the U.S. in 1942, it was Germans, the SS and by extension their animal enforcers: the

German Shepard.

Within days the student and his father had whipped the town into a furor: Harrison was clearly a Nazi! He and his dog were the very symbol of oppression! Never mind that the picture was taken in 1911, well before the Nazis were even a thought. Never mind that the dog itself — "Luv'ums" — was mostly known for peeing on campfires and sleeping in the street. In the fervor of World War II, people began clamoring to dump the mascot, change the name of the school and possibly the town itself.

As the year wore on the situation did improve somewhat; the realization that the Japanese might actually bomb Harrison and other coastal towns from offshore submarines gave people other things to worry about. And having checked the trophy cases for any pictures of alumni with Japanese fighting dogs, the principal began to relax some.

He didn't for long, as another part of Harrison's history came creeping into the future.

It started when the call came for scrap iron and other recyclable materials to help the war effort, and the people of Harrison aggressively went about salvaging what they could. Unfortunately, this included a few things people were still using, like sewer pipes.

In all fairness, the pipes had been empty, dry and unused for years when people began dragging them off. But when exceptionally heavy spring rains began overflowing into the places the pipes used to be, it became very clear that the water in Lenobar Bay had gotten very unclear.

Certainly, from even the earliest days, the people of Harrison had fought the problems of bad septics and heavy rains. Indeed, even when all the plumbing was working there were some pretty ripe days that only the eventual merging of the towns would fix. (And even then not always, to the horror of the Chamber of Commerce.)

But with the wholesale removal of most of the major plumbing infrastructure that dealt with flooding, the smell was unholy, and the scent of human filth often filled the town. It was said Edna Rylans died from it when the pig lot next door gave her a heart attack. Which was still better than Billy Doolans, who passed out and fell face-first into a stream of sewage while trying to walk to work. Although he survived, most people agreed that the irreparable damage to his nostrils forever changed him as a man.

At the high school on the side of the hill, the school was spared the nightmare in the bay below. But when the wind came from the south, it pushed the smell through the hallways like a bulldozer through butter. The students now had something else to complain about, and ample time to get creative as their teachers tried to teach classes up in the woods on the worst of days.

Maybe that's why it's not known who first figured out the alliterative similarities between the name "Lattulans" and the word "flatulence," but by April 1942, every student knew the "new" name of HHS: "Flatulence High School." To no avail, the administration tried everything to return Luther Alfred Lattulans to his rightful place of respect — especially after students added the first two names of "Lethal All-farts."

The principal even made good on his earlier threat, having his young Marxist — and his lefty father — beaten in the ravine south of school. With the added bonus that the ravine was now full of sewage, even a decade later all involved agreed it was worth having the marching band in nothing but undershirts and castaway fishing pants for the next six years.

But even the sudden decision to bolt town by the now-stinky leaders of the protests — and the subsequent law that required that everyone put their excess sewage in tanker-trucks — couldn't make all the controversy go away.

So, a compromise was reached. The students agreed that Harrison High School really was a good name for a high school. Yes, Harrison was an idiot, but at least he wasn't Herbert Hoover. In return, the students were allowed to dump the German Shepard as the school's mascot, and vote for a new one.

But with "Flatulence High" still fresh in their minds, if now banned from their mouths, they unanimously chose a fitting new mascot. The Harrison High School Fighting Skunks were born.

At first town and school leaders were shocked, but in the end it was decided that since there were hundreds of the things running around the hills anyway, it might not be so bad. Indeed, over the years the community came to embrace the normally unappreciated malodorous rodent.

"Skunk Pride" signs appeared in windows all over town. Plush skunks wearing HHS shirts became big sellers among even the tourists, who admitted that they had nothing like it at home. And at the games, the students' favorite cheer became, "We stink! And so do you!"

Unfortunately, what seemed ironic in the '60s and '70s when HHS teams were among the best in the state, had become truly pathetic by the 21st century when the school's teams had long established a record for futility and incompetence. When ESPN published a survey saying being a team mascot was the 10th worst job in sports, nowhere did people agree more than in Surfland, Oregon.

At away games the mascot was the subject of constant derision. Instead of doing the wave, someone would lift the skunk's tail while everyone in the stands made fart noises. At home games things were better, but not much. In 2004, two science students synthesized a gallon of skunk spray and poured it on the mascot. It was thought the football team bet them to do it.

That was the last straw for the girl in the suit, who quit the job and eventually transferred to a school in the Valley, since everyone in Surfland said she smelled, even after 14 showers. As a result, for nearly six years the Fighting Skunk costume hung in the closet, because even after the smell was gone, no one was stupid enough to wear it.

Until a lovelorn teenager came along, anyway.

Chapter 31
Poe

It was Poe's hope that he could convince Paxton to let him borrow the skunk costume for tonight's game. He'd tell Paxton he wanted to wear it for a story he was working on, but of course neither was true. (There went his conscience; now he was lying to high school kids. Again.)

Because Poe wasn't going to spy on Morton, Fuzznut was — if he could talk him into it.

"No way in hell," Fuzznut said, before going back to playing with his T-shirt gun. "I've got better things to do, Poe."

"Like shoot your balls off with that damn thing?" Poe said. "At least point the open end away from your crotch."

"OK, good idea," he said turning the gun around in his lap. "But I'm still not wearing that damn mascot costume to the game. I don't wear other people's costumes."

"Oh, please ..." But before Poe could get any further, Fuzznut pointed at the tip of Poe's nose and said just two words: "Remember that?"

Poe knew immediately what he meant: One night, when he and Fuzznut had been knocking back one too many beers and crab cocktails, Poe told him about the worst moment of his high school life. That he had gotten a giant pimple on the end of his nose, one so big it actually gave his nose a ramp at the end. It stayed there for almost 10 days before it had finally gone away. What it had to do with a skunk costume, however, he had no idea, and he said so.

Fuzznut was ready: "You know what happens when you wear a costume someone else has sweated in? When you wear it, all the dried sweat oozes back out of the suit and gets on your skin," he said, admittedly making Poe feel fairly clammy.

"OK, I'll admit that's gross," Poe said. "But what's that …"

"I'm not done! Did you know everyone's sweat has a different pH factor?"

"No, I didn't," Poe said, now getting more than a little exasperated, which was saying a lot given his normal relationship with Fuzznut. "Are you going to get to why this means you can't help Callista, or not?"

At this Fuzznut paused for a brief moment, but then continued right on, almost as if he didn't hear Poe. Rising from his chair, Fuzznut was now trying to move about his living room. And on another afternoon, it might have been funny: an over-50-year-old man trying to walk while still holding a T-shirt gun between his legs while totally naked but for a red apron.

Actually, it was funny, Poe decided. And he began to

smile.

"Don't you laugh, nose-zit boy!" Fuzznut said. "When you get someone else's sweat on your skin, if the pH factors are too dissimilar it makes you break out. If that boy's the sweaty kid I think he is, I'll have enough acne to be my own Clearasil commercial. No thank you!"

At this Fuzznut sat down, and Poe realized he'd have to take a different tack, but he had an idea. Because in the midst of Fuzznut's rant, Poe had noticed that one pause, when he mentioned Callista's name. It was the second time Fuzznut had seemed concerned about Callista, and he was hoping that would be enough.

"Fuzznut, I promise I'll have the kid thoroughly wash and dry the thing before tonight," he said before getting to his point. "I'm sure Callista would really appreciate it …"

At which point Poe thought he'd overplayed his hand; Fuzznut had never particularly demonstrated any concern for anyone, save for Poe. Indeed, in all of their conversations, Fuzznut had never even mentioned another human being, not counting the people who'd harassed him in costume over the years.

"Don't think I don't know what you're doing, Poe," Fuzznut said. "You think just because I saved that girl's life you can guilt me into doing something for her.

"Well, you're right," Fuzznut said, now running down a list of conditions.

Poe knew not to press it further, thoroughly glad that the only thing he had to do now was convince Paxton Dell to meet

Fuzznut's set of demands.

Although Poe normally didn't call the students he worked with during class, Ryan had told him Paxton had a free period during sixth period, so he felt OK trying to contact him. With Fuzznut sitting next to him, to make sure the conditions were met, it took only two rings for Paxton to pick up.

The first part of the conversation went fairly well: Paxton was thrilled to not have to be the mascot tonight. And Poe could almost hear him choke when Poe told him he'd pay Paxton $200 if the kid could make sure some other things happened as well.

"Can you put the head in the washer?" Poe asked. "No, well, OK. Can you just Febreze the crap out of it?" he said, as a nodding Fuzznut gave his approval.

"Next, the thing has to be washed and dried, using only Nuzzle fabric softener, you know, the one with the cute bear on the label."

"Why? Uh, why …" Once again looking to Fuzznut for an answer, Fuzznut waved his hand under his nose and produced a big smile. "Because it, uh, smells good, you know, like a bear, I guess."

To this response, Fuzznut simply rolled his eyes. But it must have done the trick, because after another minute Poe was off the phone and smiling.

"Well, he'll do it. He thinks I'm wearing the costume and I'm supposed to meet him just down the hill from the stadium at 6 p.m."

"And he has no idea I exist, right?" Fuzznut asked with caution.

"No, but I think he may want to hire you," Poe said.

"For what?"

"Honestly, I have no idea," Poe said with more than a little bewilderment. "He just wanted to know if he gave me back the money if I'd be willing to put on a giant rat costume and attack the cheerleaders."

Chapter 32
Julio Cruz

Paxton Dell was not a normal person.

That was plainly obvious to Julio Cruz. Normal people did not drive around in circles with a giant black-and-white pelt flapping out the back window of their car for 28 minutes. (Julio had been counting.) And this was the boy his daughter wanted to date?

Not that Julio was feeling terribly normal, himself, at the moment.

It wasn't like he'd made a habit of following his daughter's suitors around town, but this boy was different. He was the only one that Valeria had ever asked him about twice after he'd told her, "No."

"But please, Daddy?" she'd asked him two hours earlier, after school in his company truck. "I swear, there is nothing going on. We just want to get a burger."

"Valeria, I came to school because you forgot your

cheerleading rain jacket this morning, not to argue with you," he said, getting more frustrated by the minute. After another day of asinine projects for that ignorant redneck — the check finally came in the mail — arguing with Valeria was just more than he could take.

Teenagers! Girls! Why couldn't her mother talk some sense into her?!

But even as he asked himself the question, he knew the answer: her mother was working. A blackjack dealer at the casino, Soledad Cruz worked Wednesdays through Sunday from 4 p.m. to midnight. Julio had been opposed to this, of course; a lifetime of tradition told him his wife should be home with the kids.

But more than a decade of life in Surfland said something completely different: it was expensive as hell to live here. In the end that spoke louder than tradition, although he still wished she wasn't working at the casino. "Can't you get a job somewhere else with better hours?" he'd asked her. "I hate to think of you out late; it's dangerous."

"Dangerous? It's Surfland," she said with a dismissive laugh. "The biggest problem here is getting killed by a senior citizen in an RV, and they're all asleep by the time I get off."

"The kids need their mother," he said, trying his best to use his macho Latin male voice.

"They do. But right now, they need health insurance more. Especially since you insist on teaching Anna how to bullfight by riding your bicycle at her," she said with loving disapproval.

"A child is never too young to learn the traditions of her

family," Julio said defiantly.

"Well, you've done a wonderful job there; at eight years old she already knows how to call 911," she said before turning serious again. "Julio, you and I both know the benefits and money from this job mean you can finally start your own business.

"Now, be a man, and go get the children so we can tell them how you're going to be their mother," and she laughed again as she heard him grumbling on the way out of the room.

Six years later, he was still grumbling. Yes, all the benefits of the job had borne themselves out.

But every time he and Soledad had talked about her taking different hours at the casino, they realized she made the best money right where she was. (The woman made more in tips than anyone else on the casino floor.) College funds and braces for the kids, new trucks and tools for the business: they all had to be funded.

And so she worked nights, and he got to play Mr. Mom to three daughters, the oldest of which was making him completely nuts as she started her sophomore year at Harrison High School. He knew this would happen when she became a cheerleader; boys were always trying to have sex with cheerleaders. (They didn't have cheerleaders where Julio grew up, but he knew as a young man if they had, he would have been trying.)

Of course, even her becoming a cheerleader was proof that Julio had increasingly lost the ability to control his daughter. Because six months ago, when she had come home saying she wanted to try out for the squad, he had initially said no. Actually, it was something closer to, "Hell, no."

"I did not bring you all the way to this country so you could jump around like that Brittany Sears person."

"Spears, Daddy, it's Spears," she'd said, chidingly.

"I don't care, she's still a *prostituta*," and as far as Julio was concerned, that was the end of it.

But Valeria didn't give up. And after a tearful discussion with her mother produced a late-night conversation with her father, both were surprised to find Julio had changed his mind.

In reality he had not.

But he knew she'd probably never make the squad, and even if she did, there was no way she could come up with the $745 it took to pay for uniforms, camp and all that other crap cheerleaders had to wear. (What idiot had invented mini-pom poms for shoes?) He and her mother sure as hell weren't going to pay it; that much they agreed on.

But when she made the squad and then did dozens of hours of odd jobs around town, Julio realized he'd gambled and lost. Secretly, he was proud of her. When she'd been willing to clean out all the grease traps at Bo's Crab & Anvil just so she could sell the oil as bio-fuel, he was proud of both her work ethic and ingenuity.

But he was always worried, and boys like this Paxton Dell were why. He'd seen him talk with Valeria often when he picked her up after school, and he didn't like it.

At best, boys like Paxton were a distraction from the education Valeria was supposed to be going to school for. At worst, he wanted to steal his daughter's virginity. Either was unacceptable, and when Valeria persisted in her desire to see this boy who was allegedly "only a friend," Julio realized he had a serious problem on his hands.

He would not underestimate his daughter again.

"This is why I didn't want you becoming a cheerleader," he said. "I didn't bring you to this country so you could prance around for a bunch of dumb boys who don't even know how to play real football! They use their hands! Who uses their hands in football?"

"American boys do, Daddy …"

"Exactly, and pretty soon Paxton will be wanting to put his hands on you!"

"Daddy, he's not a football player, he's not even a jock. He's the mascot."

"The mascot?! They're the worst of all! Have you seen that episode of CSI?!"

At that, even Julio realized he was rambling. He knew CSI was about as close to real life as Jose Cuervo was to real tequila (although the people in that furries episode were truly bizarre). And, honestly, he loved American football; he'd even taken the family to see a Ducks game in Eugene when a client had given him five tickets they couldn't use.

These boys, though … *Mecachis!* They made him crazy! But when Valeria had run from the car crying he finally decided to find her in the cheerleading room to try and work things out.

Well, he almost did. Because just about two minutes after Valeria went in the entrance to the school, he saw Paxton Dell coming right out of it. The boy was running, stuffing papers into a large black bag slung over his shoulder — and singing. It wasn't a song really, just words and a melody:

"She's gonna say, yes!
"She's gonna kiss me!
"My life's not a mess!
"She's gonna love me!"

And Julio knew exactly whom he was talking about, and all thoughts of apologizing to his daughter evaporated. Briefly, he considered that Paxton didn't know there would be no burgers, no kissing and no loving tonight. But they must have seen each other in the school; they used the same door, and the school wasn't that big.

There was only one other explanation: Valeria hadn't told Paxton, "No." After he'd told her that she couldn't see the boy, she had ignored him. Five minutes ago, he would not have thought such a thing possible, but why else would this boy be so happy?

The kid was obviously a deviant; maybe that CSI episode wasn't so far off, after all. Damned costumed perverts. He'd been trying to get into his daughter's pants for weeks, and now it was so close he was singing about it!

Which is when reason went out the window and Julio starting following the boy home.

Even as he followed Paxton's car out of the school driveway, Julio knew he was overreacting. Especially when Paxton's first stop after the school was the grocery store, where after just five minutes he came out with nothing but a gigantic yellow bottle of something. With a giant teddy bear on the side, Julio had to admit it didn't look terribly perverted.

Parking in front of Paxton's house was even less interesting.

For the first hour he'd sat in his truck while nothing had changed save for the light rain that seemed to be letting up a little. No one had come, no one had gone, and aside from a once-every-ten-minute rain check during the second hour, the most Paxton could be accused of was an interest in laundry and precipitation.

And for the second time that afternoon, it occurred to Julio that he was a bit off the deep end.

He had to admit he'd been distressed the last few hours. Just this morning his 11-year-old daughter, Selena, had nearly given him a heart attack at the breakfast table.

The morning had started off like every morning when his wife was still asleep after working overtime: he was in charge of breakfast, which meant bowls of Golden Corn Flakes for everyone. He was eating his own bowl and thinking to himself — not for the first time — "Man, that Leon the Lion's got some nice biceps," when Selena spoke up.

"Daddy, what's a penis for?"

Almost choking on his flakes, he managed to whisper, "What?" Which was the wrong thing to do because she said it again.

"A penis. They were talking about it in gym today," she said, totally unaware that her father currently had seven individual Golden Flakes lodged in his windpipe. "Someone said Billy Dawson's got really big when someone hit him with a croquet mallet."

Having regained his composure (and the ability to breathe), Julio told her to ask him again at dinner. Only in fifth grade, she accepted that, but Julio knew he had only postponed the inevitable. Indeed, as he stared at Paxton's house, he decided that his desire to follow Paxton wasn't so much about seeing what the young man was up to, he just didn't want to go pick his daughter up from the babysitter.

Which was about the time he realized he'd been paying overtime rates to the babysitter for the past half hour. (She charged $10 per hour, per child after 5:15 p.m.; "Not to be cruel, " she told Julio, "but at that point, I need a martini more than I need your kid.")

So, Julio decided to leave, knowing he was going to have to have a serious talk with Valeria tonight about this boy.

But just as he released the parking break, the rain stopped and Paxton came running out of the house. He was carrying what looked like a giant skunk pelt, and upon reaching the car he tucked the end of the sleeves in the rear left window before rolling it up. Then, he hopped behind the wheel and tore off down the street.

Julio decided to follow, admittedly more curious than concerned at this point. Calling the babysitter, he begged her not to charge him and promised her he'd bring her a bottle of Absolut. She accepted, and he started up the engine prepared to follow a very strangely adorned white 1992 Nissan Sentra about town.

Shifting the transmission into drive, he thought again: Paxton Dell is definitely not a normal person behind the wheel.

And Paxton wasn't when he got home, either, Julio thought.

Back in front of Paxton's house, Julio saw the boy grab the costume and run in the front door before the rain started to fall again, this time harder than it had all day. Less than two minutes later he was out the door again, this time wearing a rain jacket and carrying the same giant black bag he'd left the school with earlier.

Julio surmised the costume was in the bag, which even he had to admit seemed normal enough as he followed Paxton back to the high school, where the game was just 30 minutes from starting. What Paxton did next, however, made him think the boy might be into something far more serious.

Because instead of pulling into the school parking lot as Julio expected him to, Paxton passed the high school and drove down the hill. About a half-mile later he stopped in front of a white minivan with tinted windows. Once again carrying the bag, he got out of the car and knocked on the back door of the minivan. The door opened just enough to pull the bag inside. Julio had no idea what he was seeing, but he knew it couldn't be good.

What he saw next confirmed his worst fears.

It was a hand, reaching out of the backdoor of the van and putting dozens of bills into Paxton's hands. Immediately, Julio knew whatever he thought had been in the bag, it definitely wasn't a skunk costume.

His mind began running through the possibilities, but soon only one thought filled his head: "My God, my daughter's in love with a drug dealer!"

Almost as quickly as he had the thought, he tried to dismiss it. Julio was a protective father but not a crazy one.

He'd known some bad people in his life; that idiot from Kansas came immediately to mind. And no matter what his intentions towards his daughter, Paxton Dell definitely didn't seem like one of those people.

There had to be another answer! What kind of drug dealer drove around with a skunk costume hanging out of the window?

The kind who's trying to signal someone, he found himself thinking. Fully aware that he'd just seen drug dealers doing weird things on CSI: Miami a week ago, he tried to dismiss it like he did everything he saw on television. (He had to stop watching those stupid forensic shows.)

But there was no denying the shadowy exchange at the back of the van, or the wad of bills that had changed hands. The running joke was that most kids in Surfland couldn't afford drugs, but now he wasn't so sure.

What occurred to him next, however, frightened him even more: Was his daughter into drugs? Quickly, however, he dismissed that idea.

He'd been a good parent and read every anti-drug pamphlet the school had to all his kids. More importantly, she didn't show any of the classic signs of drug use. Hell, she was the one who shot him with a squirt gun every day for two years until he stopped smoking.

What then could she be doing with Paxton Dell? Clearly, she had no idea who this so-called "friend" really was.

He was tempted to get her right now and tell her what kind of boy she had hooked up with, but he realized that she was already performing for the pre-game crowd. It was going to be bad enough telling her. He wasn't about to pull her out the game to do it.

Besides, the safest thing he might be able to do for his daughter right now was to keep watching Paxton. Pulling out his cell phone, he called the babysitter back to let her know she was about to have the most financially rewarding night of her life, and he waited for the boy to make his next move.

For a moment, he thought about calling the police. But in reality he knew he had nothing. And hopefully, he'd get something concrete enough that he could call the police with more than just suspicions. (That, and he wasn't exactly eager to explain why he'd been following around a heretofore harmless teenager.)

Which is why Julio was still sitting there two hours later with what he had started with: nothing.

Paxton had done nothing after running back to his car. He had simply sat down and began singing, which he continued for the entire time Julio watched. Again, Julio was as confused as he was suspicious; he'd never seen Horatio Caine have to shoot a drug dealer who sang as he committed a felony.

This kid was a damn freak.

And it just got worse. Eventually, Paxton was singing — and drumming his hands on the steering wheel — so loud that Julio could actually hear it through the windows of both cars and the pounding rain. The melody was the same as before, although the words had changed a little.

"She's gonna love me!"
"And that's that!"
"She's gonna be mine"
"Even without a giant rat!"

Paxton Dell was definitely not a normal drug dealer.

Chapter 33
Shabazz

Three hours before the game and four miles northeast of the high school, Shabazz T. Morton had found that taking charge of things was more annoying than could ever be imagined. Because as Shabazz did more, the White brothers did less, which gave them far more time to make him regret ever calling his brother. (Why couldn't Denny have just tipped the cows like everyone else?)

Bobby was the worst, of course; even in the wildest dreams of incarcerated criminals, he could never have imagined someone could put down so much cheap beer. Worse yet, no matter how much Milwaukee's Best Bobby put down his gullet, he was exactly the same as he was when he was sober: a complete asshole.

It didn't even slow him down; instead of dozing off like a lot of people do on a cheap beer buzz, Bobby just kept on going. Even his fingers remained unimpaired, giving him ample time and ability to buy more Hays Supply shit on EBay.

("Hubcaps! There's even three of 'em!")

As for Joey, Morton wished he'd get drunk. Maybe then he wouldn't be such a boring geek. Although he seemed to have stopped talking about Captain Turk, or whoever, now he was going on and on about saving Bobby from the dark side.

"I know there's still good in you," Joey had told Bobby. At which point Bobby belched in Joey's face so loud it caught Shabazz's attention in the other room. From the spittle on Joey's forehead, it appeared the only thing in Bobby was Milwaukee's Best and bits of pork rinds.

And it was here that Joey demonstrated the one thing he and his brother had in common, besides a farm-animal loving father and a mother who had the good sense to get the hell back to Kansas City: neither one was deterred by anything. For now, having picked up on one of Shabazz's phone conversations, Joey began to blather again.

"You know, I heard you say 'Landau.' Is that Martin Landau?" Joey asked, now roaming the kitchen completely oblivious to the growing amount of umber in his uncle's face. "You know, he was in 'Space: 1999,' and in 'Ed Wood,' where he …"

"BOBBY!" bellowed Shabazz. "Get in here and punch your book-germ brother again!"

"Screw you," Bobby yelled back. "It's your turn."

Whether it was or not, however, was immaterial; Joey was gone now. And still boiling with anger, Shabazz made himself calm down before placing another phone call. His partner was not the kind of man Shabazz wanted to scream at.

By 6 p.m. Shabazz had calmed down a lot. He had a lot of reasons to be happy.

Despite massive bungling from the auto-body shop, his new car was sitting in the driveway. His partner had agreed to meet him at the football game to discuss progress. And the Fighting Skunk Boosters were once again offering all-you-can-eat hot dogs at the game.

Even the White Brothers were out of his hair at the moment, not that it hadn't been a pain in the ass making it happen. Even though he'd had them doing the same thing every night since they got here, the return of airborne moisture to Surfland had Bobby bitching.

"It's raining!" Bobby said, as if this was shocking news.

"No shit, scrote-choker; it's Oregon," Shabazz said. "Just wear this goddamn rain jacket and you'll be fine."

"This sissy thing? What kink of fruit wears this stupid plastic crap?" He sneered, before letting loose another belch.

While thankful that the Columbia jacket was there — it kept the pork rinds off his shirt — Shabazz was rapidly losing his patience. "Then don't wear it, I don't care, H-2-hoe!" he yelled. "You're spending all your time in the garage anyway. Just get the hell out of here so I can get to the damn game!"

Tossing the jacket to the ground, Bobby marched towards the door as he grabbed another Milwaukee's Best from the table. Turning to yell at Joey to hurry the hell up, he instead found his uncle's red face yelling at him again: "And don't forget to get the goddamn mail from the other house!"

Right then, Joey slunk by both of them, distracting Bobby long enough to kill the conversation with his uncle. Thank God that boy can drive drunk, thought Shabazz as the two left in Bobby's truck.

Picking up the jacket off the ground, Shabazz dusted it off before putting it on himself. (Bobby had never actually let the inside touch his skin, thank God.) Grabbing the keys to his new car, he hustled out to the garage and headed south to the stadium. He couldn't wait to show his partner his newest toy; his partner appreciated cars.

Shabazz knew this because he'd tried to steal one from him.

About six months before getting arrested, Shabazz had been trying to steal a four-door Jaguar sedan out of a valet lot in downtown Portland. The lot was several blocks from the restaurant, and on a busy Saturday night the attendants were doing all they could to keep up with cars coming and going. Slipping into the Jag in the dark, it would be an easy heist.

Or it would have been, if the owner hadn't been lying in the backseat having sex.

"Who the hell are you?!" The demand so startled Shabazz that he simply froze. Two seconds later a gun lodged at his temple ensured he stayed that way. And how the man managed to put his pants back on, shoo the woman from the backseat and get back to vertical without ever moving the gun a millimeter, Shabazz would never know.

But it wasn't the last surprise. Because instead of calling the police — or shooting him — the man in the backseat told him the last thing he expected to hear: "After I get out, I want you to steal this car," he said, the gun finally beginning to lower from his temple. "I hate this goddamn English thing. My wife made me buy it, and after eighteen years I hate her, too."

It made sense to Shabazz. He was only stealing the car because a chop shop wanted it; he thought it was damned ugly. What kind of moron put a cat on the hood?

And as to the man's wife, well, he obviously didn't know anything about her. But unless his armed now-benefactor had married her when she was still an embryo there was no way the leggy blonde he saw slip into the dark was this man's spouse.

More than a decade later, not much had changed. The man was still married to the same wife, he was still having sex with barely-legal teenagers, and he still did business with Shabazz T. Morton. And what had started with a few more car thefts before Shabazz was arrested — the man's wife had leased a lot of crap he couldn't stand — had become a full-fledged partnership as Shabazz put his grandest plan into action.

His partner hadn't wanted to come to the game. Hot dogs weren't his favorite, he couldn't stand Bobby White, and the pouring rain had made the two-hour drive from Portland take closer to three.

But with the plan less than 48 hours from its most important phase, Shabazz wanted to see him. And while he couldn't do anything about the rain, he had made sure the White brothers were busy tonight; there would be no one belching on his partner this time.

Pulling into the back of the now-crowded parking lot, he

pulled up the hood on his rain jacket and sprinted from the car. Running across the parking lot, he saw his partner running to the gate as well, barely missing someone in a skunk costume sprinting from a white van.

Chapter 34
Fuzznut

Even at 50-plus years old, Fuzznut could still haul ass when he needed to. That's why just three seconds after exiting the van, he was at the top of the steps and in the front gate of the football stadium; a soaked costume meant an end to the Harrison Fighting Skunk and Poe's plan.

But if the run had not left him extremely wet, it had left him winded, and he paused once he was inside the stadium. Standing for a minute to catch his breath, he was punched three different times by high school students, the last two of whom called him, "boner boy."

Momentarily forgetting he was supposed to be Paxton Dell, he almost retaliated. Fortunately for his assailants' testicles, Fuzznut was distracted by two men running into the stadium. One he did not know, but the other he recognized from the picture Poe had showed him: Shabazz T. Morton.

Following them across the top of the stands, Fuzznut stood close by as Shabazz first stopped at the hot dog grill and then took his seat in the nearly empty visitor's section. Over the next three hours, Shabazz would return to the grill more than 14 times.

Fuzznut expected this; Poe had told him that's where he was likely to find Shabazz and possibly the two men that had attacked Callista. But 14 times? Shabazz wasn't even feeding the guy with him, and he never put into the tip jar once. Fuzznut couldn't imagine how much Shabazz cost the boosters when he'd brought his nephews.

Fortunately, the grill and the visitor's section weren't terribly far apart, so it wasn't obvious that a giant skunk was staying close to just two people. And while in any other stadium it might have been strange that the mascot never went into the home section of the stands, Paxton's reputation ensured that the visitor's section was exactly where the Harrison Fighting Skunk was supposed to be.

"Hey, Paxton," a band member whispered to Fuzznut while they stood near the grill. "You just remember to stay away from Portia, or I'll personally shove this up your ass," he said patting his instrument. And as the band member walked away with his tuba, Fuzznut once again wondered about the young man who normally wore this costume.

For the first two hours of the game, that was the most interesting thing Fuzznut heard. Shabazz and his partner talked about cars, women they had known, and anatomically impossible things in the backseat of a Lexus convertible. Fuzznut would have been bored out of his mind if the man's voice hadn't been driving him crazy.

Not Shabazz's; He sounded like the Kansas-bred hick he was, while trying desperately to sound like a man from a place far hipper. "They call me, 'Shabazz,' 'cause I'm soul-full," Shabazz told his friend.

"Didn't Malcolm X pronounce it differently when he converted to Islam?" Shabazz's partner asked.

"Malcolm who?"

No, it was the partner whose voice was driving Fuzznut crazy. It was incredibly familiar. Although nasal and even a bit whiny, he'd heard it before in a place very different than this, but exactly where remained a mystery. Closing his eyes seemed to help, but it still escaped him, the idiocy of Shabazz often breaking Fuzznut's train of thought.

"You should see my car," Shabazz said for the eighth time tonight. "I even have my initials stitched on the side."

Pounding his forehead against the inside of the skunk's head, Fuzznut found it hard to believe this idiot could be involved in anything short of not wetting himself. Even Shabazz's partner seemed to be growing weary.

"Look, Shabazz, I didn't drive all this way just to have you tell me about your damn car," he said. "I realize actually buying one for you is a big deal, but just tell me that everything's still on track."

"Fine," Shabazz said like a petulant child who'd been called to task. "The appliances are in, the wiring is set and untraceable, and the only hold-out is nearly dead in the hospital. I'd wanted to get to her house, too, but only one out of 18 isn't too bad."

"You can still get the property, though?"

"I'm sure of it," Shabazz said, before jamming another hot dog in his mouth. "All her family lives at least 1,000 miles from here. When we drop a nice offer on them, they'll be happy to get rid of whatever's left of their mom's house.

"You just make sure to drop off the last of the million this Sunday," Shabazz said, while showering his partner with the last of his hot dog. " And, you'll be good for ten times that by this time next year."

The partner seemed content with that, not even seeming to notice as he wiped bun crumbs and ketchup from his jacket.

Both then gathered their things to leave the game; suffering a 49–7 drubbing, the Fighting Skunks weren't exactly worth staying for. Shabazz also wanted to head for the grill one more time before it closed.

Fuzznut followed him, and as he shook hands with yet another 6-year-old Fighting Skunk fan — elementary school kids still liked the mascot — Fuzznut pondered what he'd just heard. Clearly, something big was up with Alice and some other properties in Surfland. Just what and when he had no idea. Clearly, however, Callista had stumbled over something that was going to continue to make both she and Poe's lives more difficult.

Which frustrated Fuzznut more than he'd like to admit. While he would never call it a soft spot — he didn't get those for women any more — he did care what happened to Callista. It would have been a real shame to get his lion costume soaked with salt water just to watch her get herself killed some other way.

At least that was what he told himself over and over again.

His train of thought was broken once again as Shabazz left the hot dog grill with three more hot dogs. The parents and students working the stand looked ready to kill, but did nothing. Fuzznut, however, did.

Noticing Shabazz's wallet sticking out of his rear left pocket, Fuzznut intentionally bumped into Shabazz as he headed out of the stadium with his hot dogs. Careful not to disrupt the food — ketchup was bad for faux-fur — Fuzznut used his paw to knock Shabazz's wallet out of his pocket. Shabazz's reaction was immediate, and just what Fuzznut hoped for.

"Fungus-waste! Watch where you're going, you goddamn furball!" he yelled. "I paid good money for these hot dogs!" Pre-occupied with ensuring his food was there, he never noticed his wallet lying down on the ground, or that the skunk picked it up as he and his partner headed back into the rain.

Keeping the wallet wrapped in his furry hand, Fuzznut headed for the handicapped stall in the stadium bathroom. He'd give the wallet to Poe; maybe it had some information Poe could use. They money, however, he pulled out and wadded up in his left hand. When he exited the restroom, he made sure to only shake with his right hand until he got back to the hot dog grill.

Once there, he deposited the money. He was careful to make sure that the kids, parents, four band members and two cheerleaders next to the grill saw just what the Harrison

Fighting Skunk had done. Taking a bow before he headed out of the stadium as well, he was pleased to hear a very loud, very shocked voice.

"My God, boner boy just donated $718!"

Chapter 35
Poe

Although the game still had 10 minutes to go in the fourth quarter, the Harrison Fighting Skunk had left the stadium.

As Poe expected, Fuzznut was ready at the stadium gates to run down the steps. Down by 42, he figured that no one was going to be much in the mood to celebrate at this point in the game. Within seconds of Poe's arrival, Fuzznut was down the steps and into the van.

"I hoped you were listening to the game on the radio," Fuzznut said, pulling off a now very sweaty skunk head. "When you're that far behind, being the mascot's about as much fun as being the cheerleader at a funeral."

"I was, although you know how much I hate local radio," he said turning it off. "Although it's better than that crap they normally play on weekend nights. If I hear one more person dedicate 'Wind Beneath My Wings' to the love of their life, I may have to submit Bette Midler to a ritual killing."

Taking care to hang up the costume parts on various hooks

around the edge of the van, Fuzznut was wearing nothing but a skin-colored unitard as he took a light brush and managed to work out most of the rainwater that had stuck to the costume. When finished, he put it back in the bag. As he did so, he told Poe what he'd heard and done, including his stunt with Shabazz's wallet and the money inside it.

With this Poe smiled; Paxton could use a break. But soon he was back to being frustrated. Other than Shabazz's Oregon driver's license and a business card for a wholesale appliance dealer in Kansas City, Kansas, (yes, there was one) there was nothing to shed light on what Fuzznut had heard between Shabazz and his mysteriously familiar yet unfamiliar partner.

Hearing voices outside the van, Poe looked out the front windshield and saw the game was over. The other team had scored another three touchdowns, and as Fighting Skunk fans left the stadium, their team outscored 10-to-one in the pouring rain, it was a quiet crowd.

Except for one fan.

Knocking on the back door of the van exactly five minutes after the end of the game, Paxton Dell was very excited, and as Poe told him about the large donation in his name, he got even more so. Almost tearing the bag out of Poe's hand, Paxton ran back to the stadium, virtually bouncing as he went. He might even have been singing.

Closing the door again, Poe was getting ready to head back to Fuzznut's house where his car was waiting, before he noticed a pile of papers on the floor of the van. They were Paxton's; they must have fallen out of the bag. Noticing they were the same papers he'd returned to the school earlier in the day, he knew Paxton would need them. Stuffing them inside his jacket as he left the van, he ran through the gate into the stadium.

Finding Paxton was easy; the stadium was almost empty, save for a gathering of cheerleaders, a few football players and a dozen or so band members at the bottom of the home stands. All them were gathered around the school's much-maligned mascot performer.

But instead of being reviled he was regaled; clearly the skunk's donation had taken him from goat to hero: "Dude? Where'd you get that money? You rock, boner boy!"

Well, almost a hero, Poe thought.

Starting to work his way down the steps so he could return Paxton's papers, Poe stopped when he saw Paxton take one of the cheerleaders aside. Getting down on his knee before her, Poe noticed Paxton could barely look at her as he asked her something. It was unbelievably corny, and from the cheerleader's immediate reaction, he knew she was about to break his heart, despite what "he" had done that night.

But just before she said the inevitable, she instead walked back over to the gathered group. After a brief conversation she returned to Paxton, still down on one knee, and put her finger under his chin. Whatever she said next was obviously what Paxton wanted to hear, although if there had been any doubt, his scream of, "YES! FINALLY!" would have removed all doubt.

"I'LL PICK YOU UP AT SEVEN!" He yelled as he ran up

the stadium steps. "WEAR A DRESS!"

His speed was enough that he was taking four steps at a time. He ran right by Poe, Paxton never even seeing him as he reached the top of the stadium.

"I'll get these to you later, then ..." Poe said to no one in particular, as Paxton raced out into the parking lot. Poe was again humorously reminded energy was wasted on the young.

Still watching Paxton as the boy headed out into the parking lot, Poe saw him blaze by another cheerleader. Like Poe, she tried to get his attention but he never even broke stride. Perhaps it was just as well; her father seemed very angry, and more than once he yelled at her to get into his truck. Only as she climbed inside did Poe focus on windshield long enough to notice the girl's father was his friend Julio.

Clearly, he was irate. Poe knew he was having problems with his oldest daughter, but he'd never seen Julio this furious. Whatever she'd done, it must have been pretty bad. Maybe he'd ask Julio about it next time he saw him.

And then again maybe he wouldn't; even over the rain he could hear Julio's voice as he peeled out in the rain-slicked parking lot. Genuinely mystified, Poe prepared to run back to the van when another set of squealing tires got his attention, although this time they were racing towards him. Finally stopping with a loud application of anti-lock brakes — Poe knew the sound from his own car — what stopped in front of the stadium was without a doubt the greatest abomination of God he had ever laid eyes on.

He almost wept for Steve McQueen.

Chapter 36
Poe & landau le toit

At some point in the history of automobiles, *landau le toit* — the landau roof — served a purpose.

A retractable cloth covering, in the '20s and '30s they acted as a retractable top on the back of touring automobiles. In the 1950s they worked as a kind of mini-convertible on a small number of vehicles. A descendant of decades of coach building, even as far back as the horse-drawn carriage period, they were a functional need, even if not always the most aesthetically pleasing one.

But like most of the American auto industry, things went horribly wrong in the world of landau roofs by the 1970s. Not content with just killing off the American convertible, manufacturers used landau roofs to make it appear all kinds of cars had a convertible top.

Suddenly, vinyl began appearing both inside and outside of every car that someone wanted to make appear more "elegant."

Even some Japanese compacts started sporting them, proving that even Toyota could make mistakes.

They were hideous, all of them, and as Poe grew up in Boulder he noticed that just because people had money didn't mean they had taste. Even worse, as the dry climate dried out the plastic in the tops, they began to crack and the padding inside began to virtually ooze out of the roof.

Not that Detroit didn't make it worse.

Because not content with just making two-door faux-convertibles, they began putting landau roofs on every kind of car imaginable. Soon, all kinds of four-door cars were sporting landau tops. Never mind there was no actual four-door convertible; people just wanted the "sophistication" that a landau roof brought to their cars.

Poe's theory was that it was a way for the perpetually pathetic to own a pseudo-limousine. So, no matter how offensive it might be to an automobile purist, if people wanted it, Detroit would build it. Not until Chevrolet put a meaningless trunk bulge in the '90s-era Monte Carlo would Poe again be so offended by the stupidity of the auto-buying public.

And, like so many things that annoyed Poe, his feelings tended to get him in trouble.

He'd been walking with Aly and an editor from the St. Louis Post-Dispatch one night in the spring before their graduation, slowly making their way back to Poe's car. Noticing a Ford Taurus with a landau roof — and chrome accents, to boot — Poe offered up his unsolicited opinion: "Wow! There's really nothing like vomit on wheels, is there?"

Later, Aly told him she couldn't decide which made her madder: That he'd had to say it, or that he didn't notice the editor getting into the Taurus as he had. Either way, not one of their job applications that spring ever made it out of the Post-Dispatch's human resource department.

Moving to Oregon hadn't mellowed Poe on the subject. Because even on the more humid coast, old landau roofs looked awful; exposed to rain nine months a year, instead of cracking they simply faded. It was, Poe had to admit, a bit of an improvement; instead of reminding him of shaved dog with furry pinstripes, they looked like an old T-shirt that had been accidentally bleached in the washer.

Poe vowed that no matter how long he lived, not he nor anyone he cared about — not even a little — would own one. Two years ago he'd even given Aly $2,000 so she wouldn't have to buy an Accord with an after-market landau roof. ("Yes, I know it's good deal, Aly. But no one but you and a 72-year-old Alzheimer's patient with glaucoma would buy this thing.")

But standing now at the entrance to the football stadium, Poe knew Aly would be as horrified as he was. Even someone as sanguine about cars as she was would acknowledge that what lay before him was an offense against man and God. *Le toit?* More like *le toilet*.

It was — or had been — a 2011 "Bullitt" Mustang. Inspired by the car Steve McQueen had driven through the streets of San Francisco more than 40 years ago, it was a 315-horsepower V8 monster. Painted a Dark Highland Green with the classic chrome gauges and their narrow numbers, inside and out it was as close as a human could come to buying one of the most famous street-legal muscle cars in the world.

But where the green roof should have been was a mucus-colored landau roof. Running from just above the windshield to the base of the rear pillars, it even had initials monogrammed into the sides and roof. Lettered like towels in pretentious bathrooms, the middle initial was twice the size of the first and last letters. "SMT," it read, and while Poe knew those weren't really somebody's initials, he immediately decided it was appropriate. This was a smutty — and shitty, and anything else one could think of — thing to have done to a beautiful car.

The stitches were even in gold, for God's sake.

As Poe stared at the car, he got angrier and angrier. He would have punched the editor of "Vanity Fair" for driving this mutant. Perhaps that why he was so surprised to find that he wasn't really surprised to see who got out of the car and ran into the stadium: Shabazz T. Morton.

Poe was horrified. He was nauseated. He was in shock.

And he was glad he had a Swiss Army knife on his key chain.

Chapter 37
Poe

SATURDAY

Poe had nightmares all night about the Mustang.

Even though he'd managed to make a few dozen deep slashes in the top before he and Fuzznut took off in the van, he'd tossed and turned all night. Trying to sleep, he couldn't get the image out his head. Even when he finally began to doze, his REM sleep was punctuated by thoughts of Morton violating his car in the same way.

At 5:30 a.m. he gave up, and rising from the bed, he went to the door to the garage and opened it, just to be sure nothing had happened to his car. Returning to the kitchen to grind some coffee beans, he was once again glad he'd chosen not to get a tan-colored top on the Jag. This morning, it would have been just a little too close for comfort.

Ten minutes later, Poe was at work on his story about dead

things in counter tops, another testament to the fact that some people just had too much damn money.

For years, a staple of school science classes has been looking at the marks left by plants millions of years ago on various forms of stone. When Poe was a kid his neighbors had pieces of flagstone with black fern patterns on them cemented into their patio. They were interesting, but by the time he'd partied at the same house during the Fourth of July in 1992, they were common enough that he didn't think twice about peeing on them when the bathrooms were full.

He didn't think the owners of the fern stains he was writing about this morning would be so calm. Selling for hundreds of dollars a square foot, people up and down the coast were now installing all kinds of fossil-laden stonework in their homes. Spending up to $30,000 for a wall hanging, anyone could now have something no one else had; every fossil was different they were told — and sold.

Never mind that a fern was pretty much a fern, and in the end every piece of stone said the same thing about each subsequent owner: I can buy more than you. Incredulous even as he typed the story, Poe laughed as he imagined how much fun it would be see the look on someone's face as they found the centerpiece of their living room the same piece of stone that supported someone's toilet.

Maybe he wasn't the only one peeing on fossilized ferns, after all.

Sending the story off to his editor, he would concede that at least the reporting and writing had gotten his mind off just what to do next about Callista's problem. But other than that, it was a soulless paycheck and nothing else.

It had begun by meeting a "Fernstone Design Consultant" at a show house in north Surfland, so she could show Poe just how this marvelous product could be used. Mindlessly walking from room to room, he quickly typed the important things — not much — into his phone's keyboard. Having written dozens of these kinds of stories, he'd learned most of what these people said could easily be poached from their websites.

The only time he ever really noticed what they said anymore was when they said the word "only" followed by a huge sum of money. A house that was "only $675,000," a refrigerator that was "only $5,400," or in this case, a bathroom counter that was "only $8,000."

If "only" he could strangle them.

Growing up in Boulder, he supposed he should have been used to it by now. But then as now he had never understood how people could so blithely throw around massive sums of money like they were nothing. Especially when it was being spent on such meaningless crap as a bathroom counter or a piece of rock to hang on the wall.

Early on he'd been tempted to ask the people he interviewed if it their customers were struck by the fact that the more they spent on being different, the more likely they were to run into someone just as vapid as they were. But just as early, he'd figured out that the people he interviewed were only on his list because they'd already bought an ad in the magazine he was writing for.

So, he fantasized and said nothing, knowing that sooner or later one man's kitchen would be another man's toilet.

Fortunately, not all his stories were so empty and dull. His relationship with Rip had given him the resources to be a pretty good investigative reporter, too.

In the beginning it was simple things, like Aly hiring him to check out rumors about potentially shady real estate transactions. More than once he'd turned nothing into a great story, as when Rip had told him that the new owner of the $4.5 million beach house overlooking Lenobar Bay had just laid off 50 percent of his employees. His $50,000 kitty litter box was of particular interest to readers.

In time, Poe was known as the go-to guy in the Pacific Northwest if you wanted someone to do some freelance digging. Some even paid well, although Poe found himself just as often working for next to nothing because he believed in what the story was about. (He'd given his fee from the $4.5 million beach house story to the laid-off employee that tipped Aly off in the first place.)

It helped that Rip never charged Poe for the information he gathered. This was partly because Rip was a great guy and partly because much of what Rip dug up wasn't exactly public record. Neither of them wanted any kind of paper trail, so instead Poe bought Rip a lot of beer and agreed to play racquetball with him at least once a week, where Rip regularly cleaned up the court with Poe.

Oddly, he and Rip's regular willingness to step — and occasionally vault — over the legal line didn't bother Poe one whit. More than once Poe had tried to reconcile the guilt he felt whenever he lied to someone like Ryan about his car with his complete absence of remorse after doing something as illegal as sneaking into someone's house. (People don't just leave diamond-encrusted kitty litter boxes sitting on the porch.)

Sipping his coffee, Poe realized his mind had been wandering. But as so often happened when he stopped thinking about things, he found the answer he was looking for. Heading off to the shower, he hoped Shabazz T. Morton, known car mutilator and likely scumbag, was just as careless as a millionaire with a very spoiled cat.

Chapter 38
Poe

As Poe pulled into the driveway of The Seabiscuit, the rain continued to fall, though not as heavily as the night before. Pulling out his cell phone, Poe called Paxton to tell him he had his homework, but no one answered. Sent to voice mail, Poe told Paxton how to reach him, noticing only at the end of his message that Callista had been watching him the whole time from the front door, a cup of coffee in her hand.

A day and night of rest had accomplished what Poe had hoped. She looked rested, and for the first time since Thursday's adrenalin rush had worn off, she seemed alert. Holding the door open as he came inside, she was clearly glad to see him.

"Have you already had your first three cups of coffee today?" she asked him, holding out the mug. "Or would you like some?"

"Yes I have, and yes I would," he said taking the mug from her hands. "Never tease an addict."

"So," Callista said, pouring herself another cup of coffee. "What's on tap for today?"

"How are your pole skills?" he asked.

"Dancing?" she replied, with a smile, while bouncing her eyebrows like Groucho Marx.

"No," he said, amused. "I was thinking climbing, actually."

Fifteen minutes and the two main themes from Star Wars later, Poe and Callista were outside Shabazz's beach house. Trying to stay low profile, they'd parked behind Julio's truck in Alice's driveway. Whatever was the matter last night clearly hadn't kept him from work this morning, although Poe didn't actually see Julio anywhere.

Walking quickly down Jetty Avenue to the address Rip had told him was Shabazz's beach home, Poe and Callista took one more quick look around before heading to the backyard. Opening the gate and entering quickly, it took no more than five seconds for both to be out of sight.

Like many beach houses, the back door of the house was a sliding glass door. Built when seeing the world was more important than blocking it out, it remained even though all it looked out on now was a six-foot-high wooden fence. Grabbing the handle, Poe checked to see if it was locked and it was, just as he'd figured.

"Now what?" Callista asked. "You act like this was all part of your plan."

"Watch, and be amazed," he said as he pulled a pair of rubber-lined gloves from his back pocket.

Walking slowly among the wooden 4x4s that supported the

porch above, he finally stopping at the one nearest the house. Putting on the gloves, he reached up the pole, using it to steady himself as he stepped up onto the gas meter, where he waited another few seconds to steady himself. Reaching one hand now onto the railing of the deck above and another onto the deck itself, Poe pulled himself higher and higher until he was straddling the rail.

Seconds later, he was opening an unlocked sliding glass door.

Taking care to wipe his feet before he went back downstairs, he parted the curtains on the lower door, opened it, and had Callista come inside. Taking time to wipe her feet as well, she eyed him suspiciously. "You do that often enough that you carry gloves?"

"You only have to get a two-inch splinter wedged between your fingers once to never want to do it again," he said, now returning the gloves to his back pocket.

"And how many times have you done this?"

"Including this time? Never," he said, starting to look around. "Nobody ever thinks to lock the door off the deck, especially when there are no stairs."

It was a pretty basic beach house for this part of town. Like Alice's house and every other home on this block, it had been built by Alice's husband when they first came to what was then the small town of Ageya. For all Poe knew, Alice's late husband had sold it to Morton's mother, just as he had to all the other people who used to own homes on Jetty Avenue, long after Ageya had become the northern district of Surfland.

Like Alice's house, there was a living room set apart from the entryway, with a small bathroom and galley kitchen rounding out the first floor. Upstairs were three small bedrooms and a bathroom. Nearly 1,800 square feet, it was huge for the time in which it was built, though now it would be considered tiny compared to the monster homes that were popping up in Surfland these days.

Poe liked what Alice's husband had come up with better. He recalled the hours he'd spent in her house, the unique touches and quality construction, signs of a time long since gone. He could relax there, in a way he guessed he'd never be able to in the showboat houses he spent his time touring these days. He suspected if he could come back to this house as a guest instead of a violator he might feel the same way.

Well, maybe not; clearly cleaning was not Shabazz's strong point. Nothing shined the way it did in Alice's house. Even the light fixtures looked unkempt, almost cheap. As he had after breaking up with Aly, he mused that men just never seemed to be able to keep things truly clean.

Walking into the kitchen, things were dingy in here, as well. Only a new stove sparkled, and even it had more than its share of dust on it. Used microwave popcorn bags were scattered everywhere, the only sign that anyone had been here save for the small pile of mail on the table. Noticing an open mailing tube with Shabazz's name on top of the pile, Poe pulled what appeared to be a poster out of the tube.

Unrolling it, he scanned the full-color computer-rendered drawing of a massive condominium complex. But other than the words "Tiberian Shores" written across the top of the drawing, it meant nothing.

"Lord, that's ugly," Callista said, looking over his shoulder. "It's like two giant boxes with windows and shingles. Is that in Surfland?"

"Not in this universe," Poe said with equal disdain, starting to roll it up so he could return it to its tube. "But if it's important to Shabazz, it's important to me," he said, tucking it under his arm. "Come on, let's see if there's anything upstairs."

The top floor of the house seemed much the same as the lower floors: everything was where it should be, just dirtier and shabbier than anyone who cared would ever let it get. Wanting to confirm that no one actually lived in the house, Poe opened one of the antique dresser drawers: empty. Frustrated, Poe started talking with his hands again.

"Do you get this at all?" Poe said gesturing around the room. "A fully appointed house with no one in it. No signs of life but one piece of mail and dozens of popcorn bags." He was definitely wound up now.

"Original antiques and fixtures everywhere. But a brand new stove in the kitchen!" Slamming his hand down in the drawer, he waited for the sound to punctuate his anger. Instead, it went right through the bottom of the drawer leaving a hole the size of small plate.

Poe was stunned and suddenly silent. Callista was simply stunned: "I suppose this is more of the 'watch and be amazed' part?"

Chapter 39
Julio

"A drug dealer?!" Valeria Cruz cried across the breakfast table. "Daddy, I know you don't like him, but how can you say that?!" she cried, now fully in tears.

Julio never got a chance to answer, because within moments she was out of the kitchen, running up to her room, and slamming the door.

As Julio had suspected would happen, this conversation had not gone well. He had hoped waiting to talk to her this morning would help. After the game she was tired and soaked to the bone — so much for the raincoat — and he was still so upset (and admittedly perplexed) by what he'd seen last night that he didn't trust either of them to be able to talk rationally.

And it had all started out so well.

For the first time in days all five members of the Cruz family had been gathered around the table. And even though Julio was ready to burst, he held his tongue until his wife had taken the other two girls upstairs to clean their rooms. He started his conversation about Paxton the simple way he always did: "I don't want you seeing that boy anymore."

"Daddy, why are you even bringing this up again," she asked, as she cleaned the dishes in the sink. "I went to the game. You drove out of the parking lot like a maniac. I came home. End of story."

"Yes, I know, and I appreciate that," Julio said trying to be understanding while laying the groundwork for what was coming next. "But I don't even want you talking to him at school, or anywhere else for that matter."

This inevitably brought the question of, "Why?" And while Julio was absolutely sure of what he'd seen during the money exchange, he was not ready to explain where he'd spent his evening. It had been bad enough lying to his wife about what he'd been doing, thanks to his youngest daughter.

"Mommy, you should have seen Mrs. Jenkins last night," Selena said, as her mother made breakfast. "She was farting so loud it scared the cats."

"Selena, it's not nice to make fun of other people," she said, lightly chiding her daughter. "I'm sure she can't help it."

"I don't think so; she does it even when she's awake," Selena said, innocently. "I think those funny drinks she has with olives make it worse when she falls asleep."

"She was sleeping in the middle of the afternoon?"

"No, she was just farting then. This was last night ..."

Seeing a train wreck coming, Julio tried to head it off: "I forgot to tell you, honey, I had to work late last night, so I left them at the babysitter a little longer."

"You know I don't like it when you do that," Soledad told him. "Mrs. Jenkins is close to 80 years old. She doesn't do well after six o'clock."

"I know, I know ..." Julio pandered, looking for an excuse. "But that job over on Jetty Avenue kept me out late last night. It's almost done," he said hoping that Soledad would drop the subject; she knew his distaste for the client on that job. "I wanted to be able to wrap some things up without having to deal with that redneck."

His dodge worked, and his wife seemed content to let the matter drop. "I understand. Just try not to do it too often," she said. "Day care's impossible to find in this town, and I don't want to kill Mrs. Jenkins, literally or figuratively."

And that was that. Almost.

"But tell me you didn't buy her another bottle of vodka," she said. "I'd rather we not add to her need for 'funny drinks with olives.'"

"Not one," Julio said, which was the truth; by the time he'd picked up the kids she'd demanded two. Why couldn't she just drink the cheap crap, like everyone else?

Lying was expensive in so many ways. And it made him even less anxious to tell his daughter why he knew what he knew about Paxton.

Even more than lying to his wife, however, he really didn't want to tell Valeria the truth, but for different reasons. He didn't want his daughter to think he'd become one of those "creepy dads," who were as much stalker as parent. He'd tried very hard not to be one, last night notwithstanding. So, as much as it pained him to lie, he knew the truth would be even more damaging — again.

"Daddy, I asked you, 'Why?'" Valeria asked again, bringing him back to conversation.

"Let's just say I've heard some things," he said hoping that would do, but knowing it wouldn't.

"Is this about what happened when he was in the skunk costume at the first football game?" she asked incredulously. "Daddy, that happens to boys. Don't tell me it never happened to you."

Having no idea what she talking about, but willing to run with it in the hopes it would get him out of trouble, Julio tried to play along: "Valeria, that may be, but I was never a mascot. You saw what they did on that episode of C.S.I."

"What?! You watch a show about murders, rapists and drug dealers and you tell me to be scared of the mascots?! Well, I understand now! Would it make you feel better if I was friends with a drug dealer?"

"He is a drug dealer!" Julio yelled, finally releasing what he'd wanted to warn his daughter about all night and morning. But the way it came out ensured the conversation was over, and as she slammed her door, Julio knew he'd lost all chance to talk with his daughter for the morning.

Finishing the dishes, Julio decided he'd try to talk to her later. She was working this morning and afternoon at Bo's before she came home to take care of her sisters tonight. Maybe he'd try to stop by and see her on her lunch break. Time might give both of them the ability to talk more rationally. He wanted to get this conversation over with; he didn't like to leave things hanging with his daughter.

Besides, the day was going to be busy enough and crappy enough as it was. First, he had to get back to the project on NW Jetty Avenue and make sure his crews were ready to wrap up. Honestly, he hadn't really done much work there himself; it was a simple enough job that he'd let his men handle it. But dealing with that racist idiot from Kansas had been a drain all by itself, and he didn't want to leave any reason to have to talk to him again.

After that he'd need to spend at least a few hours at the house overlooking Nelta Lake, where he was building a rooftop deck. True, he had weeks to work on the project, as the owners of the house weren't due to stay there again until Christmas. But the rain was supposed to break this afternoon, and after the deluge of the past couple of days he felt like he was getting behind.

Finally, he had to decide what to do about Paxton Dell. Again, he was tempted to call the police, but held off for the same reason as last night: He really didn't know anything. Calling too early would not only make him the "creepy dad" but creepy neighbor, as well, and that would be bad for business.

He needed to know more.

Checking his watch, he realized if he hurried he'd be able to make a stop at the camera store before getting over to NW Jetty Avenue. He knew just the way to keep an eye on Paxton Dell.

Chapter 40
Joey

Joey was more than happy to ride in the backseat of his uncle's car. Anything to get him further away from the man, who was angry as he'd ever seen him, which said a lot.

Usually, he'd get angry, his face would turn an unnatural shade of red, and then he'd go back to normal, the massive vein in his forehead returning to normal size.

But from the time his uncle got home last night, all the way through this morning and even now in the car, that vein — he could see it in the rearview mirror — had never gotten smaller, never stopped pulsing red. It reminded him of the red alert light on the Starship Enterprise, although he'd discovered lately not to say things like that.

Indeed, if Joey had learned anything in the past few weeks, and the past few hours in particular, trying to say anything to his uncle was useless: at best he got ignored, at worst he got punched. With his uncle clearly still near apoplectic about the damage to his landau roof, Joey decided any conversation today might get him killed.

Joey still held out hope for his brother, however. True, Bobby had become far more of a nightmare here than he'd ever been in Kansas: breaking and entering, beating up little old ladies, watching women drown. Joey had never seen his brother this bad, and just about anyone else would have considered him beyond redemption.

But hadn't Darth Vader done far worse things? He'd destroyed entire worlds, choked his own wife, and even tried to kill his mentor — twice. Yet his son had never given up on him, even after Darth Vader chopped off Luke's hand and turned him over to the emperor. Luke Skywalker had believed that there was still good in his father, and Joey would do no less for his brother. Hoping the Force could be strong in him, Joey knew he just had to wait for the right time.

"Hey, Mexican!" Bobby yelled down the street. "Come 'ere!"

Well, so much for the Force right now, Joey thought. And still thinking about his problem, he shuffled away from the car with his brother as the light rain continued to fall.

Parked near the other end of the street from his uncle's beach house, it took Julio a couple of minutes to reach the sidewalk to talk to them. Julio had walked slowly, which didn't surprise Joey at all. Bobby had treated him horribly, and while Joey felt badly that he'd never done anything to stop Bobby, Joey felt he could at least look Julio in the face.

"Hello, Joey," Julio said to him, managing a small smile, before Bobby cut in.

"Hey, don't look at him, Mexican! I'm the one you gotta deal with! Now, you get the job done? I don't wanna have to call the gov'ment and have any of you deported."

"Yes, sir, all 17 houses are finished," he said, now looking mostly at the ground.

"Damn right! And I'm glad to see you payin' me the proper respect, seein' as if it weren't for me, you and your boys would be so poor you couldn't even buy Taco Bell," he said spitting something brown and pointy on the ground. "Hell, you'd probably all have to swim across the Oregon border back to Mexico!"

Joey was impressed, once again, that Julio never rose to his brother's level of ignorance. As Julio had mentioned numerous times, everyone with Oaxaca Workers, Inc. was in the country legally, but he clearly understood that to say anything to Bobby would just invite more, so he stayed quiet.

And had Joey been Julio, he'd have kept his head down, too. Easier to keep the stuff that came flying out of Bobby's mouth from hitting him in the eye that way. Managing a small smile, Joey noticed in fact the only place Bobby's breakfast had gone was on Bobby himself, where evidence of his fried chicken breakfast now covered his Hays Supply Athletic Club T-shirt.

Noticing Joey's small smile, Julio smiled back a little, before finally responding to Bobby's diatribe: "Yes, sir."

"Damn right! And I'm glad to see ... Oh, yeah, I already said that," Bobby said, taking another slurp from the Milwaukee's Best in his hand. "Well, whatcha waitin' for?! Get the hell out of here! Lazy damn Mexican."

Managing a small tip of his head to Julio before he turned to follow his brother, Joey went from one verbal assault to another: "Joey, why the hell don't you ever say nothin' to that guy? Why do I always have to be the one coverin' your lazy ass. Damn, you're worse than those Mex'cans."

Not for the first time Joey considered what a tough task he had ahead of him: Darth Vader may have been a murderer, but at least he killed everyone equally. Resolving once again to watch all six Star Wars films on his iPod, he hoped the Force would be able to tell him something about combating racist rednecks.

But somehow he doubted it.

When Joey and his brother returned to the driveway, Shabazz was still staring at his mangled rooftop. The man appeared to be almost catatonic, Joey thought, though from the looks of the vein in his head he suspected an eruption was imminent.

"Tell me they're done with the houses, rat-nads," he said, not waiting for an answer. "They sure as hell should be; they never had to touch that old bitch's house."

"They're done," Bobby said, taking another long swig of his beer. "He's just packin' up the last of his shit now down there."

"You better not have paid him for that last house. If you did, I'm taking it out of your share," he said, starting finally to head for the door of the beach house. "I'm tired of waiting for that old crone to die."

Joey had heard his uncle call the hospital at least a half-dozen times in the last 24 hours, hoping every time they'd tell him Mrs. Kauffman had finally died. Obviously, that never happened — much to Joey's relief — not that his uncle would have actually told him such things.

His uncle had told him very little, in fact, the entire time he and his brother had been here. Whatever his plan was, it stayed between he and Bobby and whatever mysterious partner he had in Portland. Joey simply did was he was told.

Every night he and his brother would make several trips with a large flatbed truck filled with stuff from the lake house to the beach house and each time back it up to the garage of one of the houses. Once there, they would take what was on the flatbed and put it in the garage and put what was in the garage on the flatbed. Then, they'd take that stuff back to the lake house.

Over a period of weeks, everything in the massive six-car garage at the lake house and the items continually being replenished in the smaller one-car garages had switched places. They'd done this at 17 houses, with each one rotating its own quantity of boxes, lumber, paneling and all manner of household goods.

At first, it took them two or three days before they'd move onto another house; his uncle's insistence that they only transport the goods at night seemed to make the process last forever. But soon, Julio's men had become so proficient at their jobs, they were often moving items too and from two to three houses a night.

Although the increased workload came close to exhausting Joey — Friday night had been particularly bad in the rain — he was impressed by how fast Julio's men could complete their work. Indeed, from what Joey could determine they'd finished early, although that might have just been because they apparently never got a chance to work on the old woman's house.

But what the work was, Joey really had no idea. Indeed, from what he could tell, Julio's men were doing busy work: every box, piece of furniture, paneling and fixture Joey moved out of the garage looked to be pretty much the same as the ones he'd moved in. The only things that had seemed at all different were the stoves: old ones came out of the houses while 17 brand new ones all went in.

It obviously made sense to his uncle, however. And just as he had every time he'd come to the beach house, he looked behind the stove and smiled. This time, however, he appeared to be making a more deliberate inspection of everything. Indeed, as he knocked on wall panels and peered at the dusty light fixtures, it seemed to Joey that the vein in his forehead was getting a little less red.

"Oh, yeah," he said to no one in particular. "This is just perfect."

"Yeah, those Mex'cans are real hard workers when they're not bein' goddamn lazy," Bobby said.

As he so often did these days, Joey thought that was about the stupidest thing he'd ever heard. Even his uncle seemed taken aback for a moment, finally looking at Bobby a full second before speaking again.

"Listen mouth-groin, just shut the hell up and get the mail," he said before wandering into the living room. "That's the whole reason I had to come here in the first place: because you two in-bred frog-crotches can't remember to bring me my mail."

Joey dreaded what was about to come next. Because looking now to the table where he'd sat the mailing tube and Bobby had left it after opening it, there was nothing but empty popcorn bags and two pieces of junk mail.

"It's not here," Joey whispered to his brother.

"What do you mean it's not here?" Bobby whispered back. "What did you do with it you it, you idiot?!"

"Nothing! You were the last one to have it on the table!"

"Me?! I am gonna take your space-case head and stuff it so far up ..."

Joey never got a chance to hear just how his scalp was going to boldly go where no one had gone before. His uncle was now bellowing from the living room: "Bobby! Get your ass in here!" How the hell had his uncle heard them? Maybe that vein was increasing the blood supply to his ears.

Following a few feet behind his brother, Joey was barely inside the room when Bobby started making excuses. "Joey's a goddamn retard! He must have put the mail in my truck!"

Joey started to protest; as angry as his uncle was right now, Joey wasn't about to take the fall for something he didn't do. But before he could even utter a syllable two things surprised him.

First, Bobby elbowed him in the stomach — that wasn't the surprising part — and then whispered out of the corner of his mouth, "Shut up! I'm just trying to get him off our backs!"

It was the first thing Bobby had said in weeks that made Joey feel like he had a brother. It gave him hope that his brother's good side might still be within reach.

The second surprise was his uncle's reaction: he was calm. Not calm like the Dali Lama, more like the calm in the eye of a hurricane. But given the explosion Joey was expecting, it was remarkable.

Scary actually.

"Bobby, Joey: Did either of you forget to lock the back door when you left here last night?"

More than just a little terrified of their uncle's freakishly calm demeanor, both answered quietly, "No." Taking their answer at face value, he saw his uncle turn back to the door and begin to open it.

Before he did, however, Joey saw what had caught his attention: closed between the door and the frame was the curtain. Had he done that? Joey wondered to himself. If anyone was guilty, it would be him; as much as it had been raining there was no way Bobby would have gone outside.

His uncle, however, had taken his, "no," as the truth, and there was no way Joey was going to change his answer now. Watching his uncle carefully, Joey saw him standing out on the back deck and turning his head slowly, like he was looking for something. After a couple of minutes of this he had still said nothing.

Only when he returned to the living room did he speak. "Fine, just make sure you get that mail tube out of your truck when we get back." And that was it. No cussing, no red face, no throbbing vein warning of a massive coronary. No, it wasn't small, but it didn't look like it might rupture like a garden hose under a truck tire, either.

For the first time in weeks, Joey thought things might finally be getting back to normal. Not his life in Kansas normal, but Oregon normal, where he was still miserable but not always scared to death. Even his brother had showed something resembling kindness. Smiling a little, he began to follow his uncle out the front door — which was when his brother punched him in the side of his head.

"Joey'll find that mail he lost!" Bobby said, racing past him to his uncle's side. "If he doesn't, I'll shove that iPod so far up his ass you'll be able to plug earphones into his dick!"

Careful to stay out of reach of any more random fists, Joey followed them both outside to the car. The rain was falling harder now, the forecast notwithstanding, and moments later he found his shoes ankle-deep in a puddle. Sighing, he reminded himself that even Luke Skywalker had to go regroup in a swamp once in a while.

Chapter 41
Callista

Standing behind Julio's truck, Callista and Poe were peering through the cab windows. From there, they had a clear if somewhat distorted view of the Whites and Shabazz leaving the beach house where the two of them had been snooping just minutes earlier. One of the brothers was climbing into the backseat of the Mustang while the other berated him, something about wet shoes being easier to shove … somewhere. With her jacket's hood up against the rain, it was hard to understand just what he was saying.

But hood and rain or not, Callista knew exactly whom she was listening to and seeing: they were the two men who had chased her and left her to die in the ocean. And while she couldn't be sure, she would be willing to bet the man who was yelling now was the same one who had been yelling in the beach house just minutes ago, and pounded on her van window two days ago.

She was more than happy to see them speed away in their uncle's mutilated car. Especially since just ten minutes ago it looked like she and Poe might wind up with another up-close opportunity to see the worst dental work since Mike Meyers in Austin Powers.

Thinking back to their discovery upstairs, she remembered it had taken Poe about five seconds to regain his composure after he plunged his hand through the bottom of the drawer. "Not exactly quality construction," he'd said, before he began to look around the room again, almost as if he'd never seen it before.

Finally, he'd walked over to one of the redwood walls and begun to knock. After a couple of seconds a weird look came over his face. If one could be said to look satisfied and constipated at the same time, Poe had that face now.

But before he could explain the unique look he had given her, they heard a car pull up in the driveway below. Careful to stay out of sight, Poe looked outside through the front window and smiled. "Well, well, he said, if it isn't our Mustang Molester, Shabazz T. Morton," he said quietly. "And, if I'm not mistaken, his two nephews, "Missing" and "Link."

Gesturing Callista to the window, he had her look out to confirm they were the two who'd chased her. As the two men walked into the street she could only see their backs. But all the larger one had to do was yell — "Hey, Mexican! Come 'ere!" — and she'd known these were the guys. Seeing the light of recognition on her face, Poe pulled her away from the window and led her downstairs.

Careful not to make any noise, they made their way to the back of the house and slipped out the lower sliding glass door. Raining harder now than when they'd entered, they opened the door as little as possible and slipped through quickly before slamming the door shut. Moments later, they were outside the fence and next to the house.

Callista's first reaction was to run. Whether away from the men or towards them so she could beat them senseless she wasn't sure. Poe had another idea, and he had them hide behind a corner of the house where they could hear what was being said in the street without being seen.

It turned out to be the perfect location; not only could they hear the conversation with Julio in the street, but when the three men came back to the house, they could hear those conversations clearly, too. Poe remarked several times how this shouldn't be — these old houses were solid as a rock with a lot of retro-insulation, as well — but he seemed to be making the comment to himself, so Callista said nothing.

It didn't hurt that whenever the men inside the home seemed to have a discussion they did it at maximum volume. In fact, it was when things suddenly got quiet that Poe decided they should put some distance between themselves and the house.

Choosing to run first along the beach the length of the street, two minutes later they were climbing up the dune. They rested there for a minute, and after checking to make sure the street was still clear, both ran across NW Jetty Avenue to Alice's house, where they now found themselves hiding behind

Julio's truck.

Even after the Mustang pulled out, Poe had Callista wait behind the truck. Aside from wanting to insure the brothers and uncle were long gone, he wanted to see if Julio was inside Alice's house before bringing her out into the open. While he was gone, Callista continued to stare mindlessly through the windows, noting that the cab was immaculate, with a new set of binoculars still in the box the only sign that anyone had actually been in the truck.

Callista was still lost in her thoughts when Poe returned and told her it was OK to come into the house. "Well, that certainly gives us something to think about, doesn't it?" Poe continued on. "I think I might even might be starting to understand something."

Following him in the house, Callista said simply, "I know exactly what you mean." But she wasn't speaking to him or Julio, or anyone else within 636 miles for that matter.

It was 637 miles from Berkeley, California, to Surfland, Oregon, and Callista Walker spent every one of them being pissed at Dr. Emerson Quincy Walker, PhD. and Arianna Walker, who had no fancy title, but was arrogant enough to make people assume she did. Together they were sanctimonious enough for 10 normal people, and while Callista remembered her grandmother's admonishment about hating people, she remembered her later addendum, given during their most recent phone call.

"I know you want me to stay in California, Gram," she'd

told her. "But this job in Surfland's just too good to pass up."

"That, and you want to get away from your father and sister," she'd said with the bluntness that usually only octogenarians can get away with.

"Now, you know that's complicated ..."

"It's not complicated: They're assholes."

"Gram! That's your son!" Callista said, stunned. She'd certainly heard her grandmother use foul language. She did it a lot. But Callista had never heard her say it about her own offspring.

"He may be my son, but he's also a self-serving asshole," she said. "I see him on TV, railing against fast companies and corporate America. But when we go out to dinner, you know what he does? He takes me to Carl's Jr. and spends all his time haranguing the manager."

"Well, that does sound like Dad," Callista said, wondering where any defense of her father came from.

"Honey, he buys me a kids meal, while both he and your sister get a Six-dollar burger."

"Oh."

"But you'll notice I still don't hate them. That takes too much energy."

"How do you deal with it, then?" Callista asked, hoping for some wisdom she could use.

"I just remember that in the end anyone that stupid and arrogant is bound to hang themselves," she said, laughing. "Oh yes, they'll get theirs, and I just hope I'm alive to see it."

And so Callista drove north to Surfland, desperately

hoping that someday they'd get theirs. Hoping that her grandmother was right, while still saddened that she would not, in fact, be there to see it. It was a bitter pill to swallow.

Now, walking into Alice's house, it tasted even worse.

From the moment the Whites had run her onto the jetty, something larger had been bothering her, and now that they'd forced her to run again, the feeling was all the more acute. The wrong people were "getting theirs."

Julio was getting berated in the street, Alice was getting cooped up in a hospital, and Poe was getting run all over town trying to clean up a mess that wasn't his. True, he seemed to be enjoying it — slicing up Shabazz's roof had seemed to really cheer him up — but her grandmother's addendum didn't seem to be paying off for anyone.

Whether it was her father and sister yelling at her as she went out the door (she knew her comment about acronyms had fallen on deaf ears), Shabazz yelling at his nephews, or Bobby berating Joey and Julio, the world just seemed to be full of mean people using their existence to make everyone else miserable.

Suddenly, she was tired again. Tired of abusive rednecks. Tired of arrogant sisters and know-it-all fathers. And most of all, she was tired of running from all of them.

"God!" She yelled out loud. "Why do people take this crap?"

"Well, I take it because I have to," Julio said, clearly surprised she'd asked.

"Huh?" Callista said, suddenly aware she was no longer

talking just to herself.

"I take it because I need to work," he said, clearly continuing a conversation he and Poe had already begun. "And even though all my workers are legal, many of their family members and friends are not. None of them need ICE crawling around here asking questions."

"Oh," she said, now feeling more than a little ashamed. Even Poe seemed to be giving her a worried glance, as her cheeks began to flush red. "I'm sorry if I was rude."

"Are you kidding? I ask myself that same question every day," Julio said, starting to laugh. "I just get past it by imagining a shark tearing that redneck's body into pieces, starting with his little *pene*," he said, clearly imagining Bobby getting his. "It would make a fine toothpick, I think."

Finally able to laugh herself, Callista chuckled as she rose from the couch. "I think I know a sea lion that might be able to help, as well." Out of the corner of her eye she noticed Poe was smiling back at her again.

"Now, if you don't think Alice would mind, I'm going to get a glass of water," she said, walking to the kitchen. "How it's possible to get dehydrated when it rains 87 inches a day, I'll never know."

Listening as she went to the kitchen, she heard Julio finish explaining to Poe just what work his men had been doing on this block of NW Jetty Avenue and how little he'd personally had to do with it. Indeed, he said, allowing for the repetitive ease of the work, it had been a very simple job.

"If it had been anyone else but that racist redneck paying

the bills, and late, too, I would have given them a partial refund," Julio told him. "We were supposed to keep working today. In fact, they told me to meet them here at Alice's house. But then they called me last night and told me the job was done."

"No idea why the change in plans?" Poe asked.

"No, I just know they'd been telling me since we started we had to be done tonight," he said. "I can't imagine what other house they'd want us to do. We got every house on this block save for this one, and as you know there's really no other houses in town like these."

Looking around again at Alice's home, he had to agree, though he was beginning to suspect the block as a whole wasn't quite as unique as it had been. "No idea what they've been up to? " Poe asked. "I didn't even know one person owned all these houses."

"I'm not sure someone does. The man who hired me for all of this said he was just a middleman for the new owners. He had the keys and the money, so I just told my guys what he told me."

Finishing her glass of water, Callista was about to ask Poe what was clearly running through his head, but before she could his phone rang. From the conversation, she could tell it was Rip calling with more information: "… So, every house on this block of NW Jetty Avenue is owned by Shabazz? He did it with holding companies? Maybe he's not so stupid after all," Poe speculated to his friend on the other end of the phone call. "Yeah, that kind of all makes sense in terms of what Julio's been telling me, although I still can't figure out what the hell the guy is really up to. It's almost like he's trying to lose money ...," he said, his voice trailing off.

"Look, could you do a little bit more digging? I need to know where these guys are actually staying, because it sure as hell isn't here. Julio tells me no one's lived in these places for months," Poe said, adding, "Thanks," and ending the call.

As he hung up Callista prepared once again to ask him what was on his mind — just in time for his phone to ring again. This time, she had no idea who he was talking to.

"Yes, I know you have to go be an otter ..."

"Yes, I've hurt the children of the world ..."

"Yes, you're a very busy person ... Hey! You called me! What, did you spill some Chinese pepper extract sauce on your crotch again? ..."

"Oh, it was curly redwood ..."

"No, I had no idea it was that expensive. Thanks for ordering some ..."

"Yes, I'll pick you up some pine nuts at Safeway."

Hanging up the phone, Poe turned back to Callista. "Well, that was interesting. Now, what were you going to say?"

"I have no idea," she said, truly drawing a blank after three minutes of phone conversations that mostly made no sense at all.

Pinching the bridge of her nose between her fingers, Callista was adding herself to her list of people of people who were getting theirs. Which right now meant one mother of a headache.

Chapter 42
Shabazz

For Shabazz T. Morton's part, the journey back to the lake house was a quiet one. He had a lot to think about, and save for Bobby's constant haranguing of his brother — there just had to be more than one orifice of Joey's that Bobby could threaten to exploit — he was able to figure out a few things on the long drive around the east side of the lake.

The first was simple: he'd have to go home via the northern route for the next few days, along Highway 101. With all the rain, a 100-foot stretch of East Nelta Lake Road was almost underwater. Even after it stopped raining, the runoff from the Coast Range mountains would have it two feet under the overflowing creek by late afternoon, where it would stay for hours, maybe days. Not exactly the best thing for a sports car with only a few inches of ground clearance.

The next thing he decided was that when he found the kid who'd vandalized his car he'd have Bobby beat them until they were unconscious or $3,854 fell out of the kid's pants. That's what the auto-body shop said it would cost to fix the roof — the roof they'd just finished putting on less than 24 hours earlier. God, cars were a pain in the ass; no wonder he usually just stole them.

For a minute or so he considered doing exactly that; stealing a car always gave him a rush and made him feel better. There was a nice Range Rover just down the road. Maybe he'd just hotwire it, drive it around for a few hours and then crash it into a wall. Hell, the owner would probably thank him; he'd seen that thing on a tow truck more than he had in the owner's driveway.

God, how he hated British cars.

But soon his thoughts returned to a more immediate problem: someone had been in the beach house, he was sure of it. Yes, Bobby lied all the time about what he'd been doing, and Joey could have just as easily left it open thinking it was a portal to another universe, the space shuttle or some stupid thing. But he didn't think so.

And if that was indeed the case, were the intruders just a bunch of dumb kids looking for an exciting place to have sex for the night? Lots of kids did it. Hell, he still did it, when he got someone drunk at the bar.

It occurred to him his paranoia was probably an overreaction. But that was thinking about it logically, and thinking, he'd found, was never a good thing in the world of Shabazz, or Shelton for that matter.

From his earliest days, Shabazz had known he wasn't exactly the smartest person in the world. Between the time he first became sentient at the age of 14, he could only remember one thing that thinking had made better. His brother had asked him to work the midnight shift with him at the dairy farm, and he'd decided that really wasn't a good idea given what his brother wanted to do with the udders. (Not until his brother came clean years later, did Shabazz learn that they didn't even have those kinds of jobs for elementary school kids.)

Later, 11th grade testing revealed that when it came to higher-level abstract thinking, he wasn't even the smartest kid in the resource room. Considering that included at least a dozen kids who were 20 years old and still in ninth grade, he realized he'd better just stick to rewiring things for fun and profit. (He still thought he should have gotten extra credit for showing the teacher how to rewire the phone so it wouldn't receive calls from the principal.)

Yes, he'd always known that his brains weren't going to get him very far in life, so he'd learned to trust his instincts.

And right now they told him someone was on to him, although who that might be he couldn't imagine. The only two people who had accidentally gotten close to him were either dead in the ocean or nearly so in the hospital. Still, someone had been in the house and the mailing tube was gone.

He needed to do something, but what? He felt almost dull, with even his instincts failing to give him the direction he was used to. The last 14 hours had been one hit after another: the car, the beach house, the mail, his wallet disappearing with $700 in it. (My God, that had been an expensive football game.)

He realized he'd managed to stay calm because he was in shock, but he'd better snap out of it soon, because he needed to make a plan.

"Soon," as it turned out, arrived less than 15 seconds later, delivered by the pile of worthless flesh riding shotgun that Shabazz hoped once again, by some miracle, he wasn't related to.

"Joey, you got 30 seconds once we get home to find that tube in the truck," Bobby was yelling at his brother in the back seat, "Or I'm gonna shove a socket wrench so far up your ass …"

Shabazz went off: "Wheat-stain! If you say that one more time, I'm gonna bury you up to your waist in the sand head first and wait for the tide to come in," he growled. "Shove it up his nose, his mouth, his goddamn ear for all I care," he said even louder, feeling the blood now filling his face. "But you say 'asshole' again, and I'm going to sew yours shut, starting with your tongue."

"And you," he shouted to Joey in the backseat, "if I hear one more word about 'the dark side,' 'The Force' or any other goddamn thing that comes out of a book with little green freaks, I will run your head over and let your brother shove any goddamn thing he wants in any hole you have!"

God that felt good, he thought as pulled into the driveway. "Now go look for my goddamn mail," he told them both. He knew they wouldn't find it, and then he'd tear into them again, which would make him even happier.

It wasn't quite stealing a car, but it was close.

*****

There was one place Shabazz's instincts did not serve him well in his youth: his mouth. Mainly, that he never controlled what came out of it.

If he hadn't been bragging, no one would have ever known why he'd blown up his first car. If he hadn't insulted every African-American he met, he wouldn't have been banned from two different major fried chicken chains. His prison sentence might even have been shorter if he'd just gotten off of the plane when he first arrived in Oregon, went straight to jail and shut up.

"Hey, whore," he'd said to the plain-clothed woman who was riding shotgun in the police car on the way to the couthouse. "How about we do it the backseat?"

"I'm a detective, you degenerate," she said.

"Great. We can both bring a gun in our pants."

The judge made note of this at Shabazz's sentencing, deciding to add on another two years just because the accused had been such a prick. A fair judge, however, he did want to give Shabazz a chance to explain himself — except that Shabazz never actually made it to his sentencing.

After calling the bailiff's wife a "government supported slut with a polyester fetish," it was decided Shabazz probably shouldn't be let back into the courthouse. (Although most were in agreement that at 350 pounds the bailiff's wife really should stop wearing bright pink track pants.)

All of this was why everyone familiar with Shabazz T. Morton was so surprised that once behind bars he became a model prisoner. Because instead of becoming one prison gang leader's girlfriend or another's bitch — even money was on both — Shabazz mostly kept to himself.

Even long-time prison guards were amazed. Eventually, they even let him work in the electronics shop, having decided that the often-tragic combination of metal TV antennas and 6-foot, 8-inch rapists didn't produce an undo threat to Shabazz's colon.

Indeed, every day Shabazz was observed doing pretty much the same thing: watch TV, repair electronics items for both the prisoners and the guards, and make the rounds of the courtyard during exercise time, usually talking quietly to some of the newest prisoners.

The observers were mostly correct.

But what prison officials saw as just a quiet stroll around the yard, Shabazz knew was actually stress release. Because in truth, prison had not taught Shabazz to control what came out of his mouth; he'd simply learned to control when it came out.

For example: He'd learned the cafeteria and shower, among giant men who could molest him for a week without stopping, was the wrong place to say anything. But the yard, among terrified new prisoners, was the right place, and Shabazz usually started with the smallest prisoner.

"Listen to me, you goddamn piece of white-collar shit ..."

"I robbed a gas station," said the bewildered prisoner.

"Then why are you wearing a shirt with a white collar, you idiot?"

"It's prison issue," said the new prisoner, now more

confused than scared.

"Just shut up, OK? You see that huge black guy over there? Well, I fix his CD player, and I'm going to tell him I couldn't finish because you wanted to have sex with me.

"And don't even think about telling anyone, 'cause I'll have someone bend you so far over in the shower you'll be licking your own ankles."

And with that the new prisoner usually quietly nodded, back now to just being scared.

And so it went: "Fresh meat" arrived in the prison, Shabazz verbally abused them out in the anonymity of the yard, and no one was any the wiser.

He slipped up occasionally.

Once, near the end of his sentence, he picked on a midget, which was when he'd discovered that the man really didn't like being called "clit-midget." Having failed to notice his latest target had developed enormous arm muscles as a vine-swinging primate-like creature in the latest George Lucas movie, the diminutive prisoner almost crushed Shabazz's testicles before Shabazz had a chance to step back. (Only by promising to turn the "little person's" clock-radio into a device capable of sending Morse code did Shabazz manage to escape with his act — and genitals — intact.)

Shabazz's status as a model prisoner with a gift for electronics repair had other benefits as well: as someone who could repair any TV in the prison, he got to watch them all the time. His favorite was the History Channel, which eventually produced his middle name of Tiberius.

What he also "learned," however, was that when you were a great man doing great things you could say and do anything you wanted to anyone you wanted. Watching "Saving Private Ryan," he was enthralled by the fact that everyone in the movie could be as much of a loud-mouthed racist as they wanted to be and still get to maim people. That he had completely missed the point of the movie was lost on him.

As it was with everything Shabazz saw on TV. Watching "All in the Family" reruns on TVLand, he thought Archie Bunker was the smartest man on television. From James Bond movies on Spike he decided it was always best to just get rid of people instead of talking to them. From "March of the Penguins," on Animal Planet, he concluded that the smart penguins were the ones that headed for the ocean and never ever came back; who wanted to spend their winter freezing in the dark with a stupid kid?

But it was in viewing the dozens of home improvement shows that peppered television in the early 21st century that Shabazz learned his greatest lesson: There was a lot of shit out there. It was a discovery that would form the basis of his plan for post-prison redemption, and it was a discovery he almost missed.

He'd been about seven years into his 20-year sentence and had just finished repairing the television from the main recreation area. One of the larger inmates had been trying to stab another one to death when he missed his target's head and hit the television. Trying to tear out his victim's heart with nothing but a plastic spork required a tremendous amount of force, and when he'd missed, his hand had gone right through the buttons for changing channels.

Replacing the keys and the circuit board behind it took Shabazz all of about 10 minutes, including running through all the channels with the keypad. Discovering there was a glitch while at channel 27, he stopped there for a minute to tighten a wire. And there he saw the thing that would change his life: Fake stalactites in a basement.

They were the ugliest damn things he had ever seen.

Watching until a commercial, he discovered he was seeing "Trading Spaces," where two different couples each agree to decorate a room in the other one's house. Obviously retarded, Shabazz thought, one of them had turned the other couple's basement in a make-believe cave, complete with Styrofoam rocks and stalactites. It was hideous beyond words, and both couples absolutely loved it.

And as he watched more shows, he realized that no matter how ugly, no mater how boring, no matter how ridiculous, if people thought they were getting something "special," they were thrilled.

After spending his adult life stealing some of the most expensive cars on Earth, it was shocking for Shabazz to discover that there were actually people out there who thought vinyl looked good enough to use as a wall hanging, that creation had actually allowed people to reproduce who would cover a wall in wet plaster and then throw hay up against it, thinking it gave off a barnyard vibe. (Never mind the fashion statement, Shabazz thought: Who the hell wants to live in a barn?)

Fascinated, he checked the listings for more home "improvement" shows and eventually came upon a "Flip this House" marathon. It was a daylong broadcast of a show where people would buy piece-of-shit properties, work their asses off fixing them up, and then sell them for a profit. The first episode bored the crap out of him.

Two girlfriends had bought one house and their husbands had bought another and were now competing to see who could finish the fastest and make the most profit on their sales. But instead of being about how to flip a house, the show became each pair figuring out how they could sabotage the other pair's efforts. By the middle of the show, the brothers were clearly frustrated by their wives' actions but had no idea what to do next.

Not Shabazz. Momentarily forgetting where he was, and screaming out loud at the TV, he told them what to do: "Shoot the bitches! Why don't you just shoot the bitches and sell both houses?! Goddamn! Get a cock, you two!" Fortunately, no guards were nearby, and the next episodes proved more informative.

From them, Shabazz learned that in a desperate desire to make a boring house look interesting, people would buy just about anything. If they had the money, they'd buy something from someone else's house and put it in their own. Whether it was picking over the dead at estate sales, or just paying through the nose on eBay, the older and rarer something was, the more someone had to have it to make themselves appear authentic as well.

Of course, not everyone had a ton of money, so those people would just fake it. Need a piece of stained glass? Paint a piece of regular glass with puff paint and watercolors. Need an old Persian Rug? Buy a new one, tatter the edges and maybe even spill some shit on it. Need an old baseboard? Buy the same crap everyone else did and just stain it a custom color.

That most of these shows were sponsored by massive big-box stores didn't surprise Shabazz at all. People could spend as much (or as little) as they wanted and with some work make their home into an original creation that only every other person in America who'd shopped at the same chain store could have.

Surely, there had to be a way to make some money off this, Shabazz's instincts told him. And then four things happened in his ninth year of incarceration that helped him put it all together:

First: His great aunt passed away, leaving him her beach house in Surfland, Oregon. When he'd first been sent to Oregon they'd spent a lot of time out there together, and she'd decided to leave it to him in her will. And even though many times in the ensuing years she'd made the decision to change that — since her Shelton had clearly become a hoodlum — encroaching dementia ensured she never did.

Second: Watching another hybrid home improvement/contest show — "Tell to Sell" — Shabazz had seen how the question of improper stove installation had kept an Oregon woman from selling their beach house before the other contestants. Not informing homeowners about potential problems was wrong and illegal, the host said. (Shabazz disagreed: If someone was stupid enough to buy a house and not inspect the stove, they should get blown up. Dip-shits.)

Third: Shabazz's friend with the overactive backseat libido and wife who couldn't stop leasing God-awful cars stopped by to see him in prison. His latest real estate development deal was in trouble because all the stolen cars had destroyed his credit rating. Hoping at least two of them could "turn up" so he could clear his record, he needed to know just what lake Shabazz had rolled them into.

And Shabazz told him — for the price of listening. Because just 48 hours before his soon-to-be partner had walked in the prison gates, Shabazz had learned the fourth thing: he was being let go early on account of good behavior. (Shabazz had no idea that was possible.)

And less than a week later he was: now very much a man with a plan — with his sights set clearly on Surfland, Oregon.

A little over a year later, everything Shabazz had learned in prison was about to make him rich. Even his ability to control the timing of his mouth came in handy whenever his partner started getting a little too pushy. (He'd come this close to telling him to go drown himself in one his own faux-marble toilets at the football game.) For Shabazz, prison had been exactly what society told him it should be: it had made him a new man.

Granted, turning him into an ever more aggressive and

violent felon probably wasn't what the state had in mind, but Shabazz didn't care. And now he was about to exercise the one other skill he'd acquired in prison, although ironically enough it was never one he'd used while there: excessive use of volume.

As Shabazz's reaction to his outburst at the TV behind bars had reminded him, even though he might be able to say anything he wanted in the anonymous world of a large prison, he could never say it as loud as he wanted. If he'd ever been caught yelling as he let his temper run amok, the carefully crafted life and lie he'd built for himself in prison would have been over. So he was quiet: all day, every day, for most every moment of 10 years.

But almost like a soda bottle that keeps getting shaken, the pent up decibels bubbling inside Shabazz kept building higher and higher. Upon his release, every time he could let his voice go, he did. And even if it didn't make him think better — admittedly, it wouldn't have taken much — it did make him feel better.

It had started literally the first minute he was standing outside the prison gate. For just moments after he stepped into freedom, an inmate had been plucked from the prison exercise yard with a helicopter. (Later investigation would reveal the prisoner had somehow used his clock-radio to signal the chopper.)

Shaking his hands at the sky, Shabazz began to scream: "Incar-stabators! You couldn't keep in a five-year-old in a wheelchair you penitentiary-probes!" And he kept screaming all the way down the street until he was out of sight of some very stunned guards, very proud as well that he'd actually started making up his own insult words.

It had felt sooooooo good then to just let it go, and it had ever since, especially when he unleashed it on two people as annoying as his nephews. Screaming at them had given him the clarity he needed to plan: they would go back to the house tonight and wait. If someone were coming to the house, he would know.

"Hey, sheep-creams!" he yelled out the door. "Get out of the goddamn rain and get in here. And where's my mail?! You haven't found it yet?!"

Oh, yeah, it felt good to have a plan.

Chapter 43
Poe

Jackson Poe had home improvement shows on his mind, as well.

The brand new stove among all the older appliances and dingy environment of Shabazz's beach house was bugging him; he knew he'd seen it somewhere before. But from the time he and Callista had snuck out the back door, and all the way through his conversation with Julio, he just couldn't remember where.

But as he and Callista had headed back to his house for lunch and a hot shower — the rain had them both chilled — the car and CD player acted as they always did: as an elixir for clear thought. And by the time the orchestral theme from "The Lion King" was finished, he had his answer.

Walking through the front door, he began rifling through file drawers full of old notes, where he finally found what he was looking for: an episode of "Tell to Sell" on DVD. Broadcast a couple of years ago, it was a televised weekly contest to see which homeowner of three different beach homes could sell their house first. Episode 23, featuring "Old, Classic Houses of the Oregon Coast," had one of the houses Alice's husband had built, just two doors down from where Alice still lived on NW Jetty Avenue.

The problem was, there were no other old, classic houses for sale anywhere in Surfland at the time, and after weeks of looking, the producers went to plan B: lie. Picking two houses that weren't even for sale — one wasn't even in Surfland — they went through all the motions of having each homeowner try to "sell" their house. Given a nice check for playing along, each figured it would be harmless fun.

Choreographed down to even the "candid" expressions, the host seemed to take particular glee in telling one of the "sellers" that they lost their sale because they had failed to disclose that their new stove had a history of problems. Chastising them on the air for being dishonest, the host was thrilled to tell viewers that the house on NW Jetty Avenue had sold first.

When it was broadcast, it showed Surfland as a perfect little town where the sun always shone and any moment it seemed Norman Rockwell might strip down to his skivvies and go running into the azure Pacific. (God bless editing, leaders of the Chamber of Commerce thought.) It had made everyone in Surfland very proud to be on the famous home improvement show.

Well, almost everyone. The seller who had been chastised on the show for trying to improperly sell something she wasn't even selling was furious. And after weeks of being kidded and insulted on the streets of Surfland, she called her neighbor, Alice Kauffman. And Alice was all too willing to listen; the producers had tried to get her to "sell" her house, too. She'd said no then because what they were doing was dishonest, and now even angrier that her friend had been caught up in the lie, she called the one person she knew would do something about it: Jackson Poe.

And he did. In a story he sold to the Oregonian, Poe exposed the entire show as a sham. With research, he'd found this wasn't the only town they'd done it in. Not since a self-proclaimed TV survivalist had been found to be spending his nights in five-star hotels had such a crap-storm rained down on a reality TV show.

Now that was a story Poe had loved to write.

He hated those damn home improvement shows, with their sense of mass-produced taste and judgmental hosts telling everyone what was supposedly attractive. These were the kind of people that had fossilized ferns in the bathroom and bought the magazines he prostituted himself to write for.

"God, I hate those friggin' bastards," he mumbled a little too loudly to himself as he clicked through the DVD menu.

"OK," said Callista, coming out the bathroom dressed but still with a towel wrapped around her head. "I guess now it's your turn to talk to the ether?"

"Sometimes my passions get the best of me; there's just not usually anyone here to hear me go off," he said, sheepishly.

Accepting that, Callista turned her attention to the TV:

"Why are you watching this God-awful show? Don't you know everything is rigged?"

"Yeah, I'd heard that. No, what I'm looking for is something else ... here," he said clicking on the last menu.

Popping up on the screen was the obnoxious host who'd chastised Alice's friend for not disclosing the stove — the exact same stove that Poe had seen in Shabazz's beach house. And now he remembered: the model as made was safe, but the original directions had been so poorly written that it was possible to hook the stove up in such a way as to make it basically a ticking time bomb.

The solution was simple: get new directions and do it right. But as the host had pointed out, not everyone had gotten those directions and a lot of homeowners might think they had a safe stove when really all it would take was one surge of gas pressure to blow the thing apart.

Indeed, even Alice's neighbor had conceded that had been one silver lining: her stove had been installed wrong. Whether a few weeks or months, her house probably would have gone up just like a townhouse development in Cleveland had not the connection been fixed.

Turning off the TV, Poe got off the couch and started pacing the room. "That can't be just a coincidence. But again, this makes no damn sense!" he said, starting to wave his arms again, noticing that Callista had moved herself between him and the espresso machine.

Stopping, Poe made a show of backing off from the coffee. Suddenly, however, he remembered something: the business

Beach Slapped

card he'd found in Shabazz's wallet.

Pulling it out of his own wallet, he now began to smile, and three minutes later a phone call to Kansas City, Kansas, confirmed what he'd suspected. Someone — he couldn't get the salesman to tell him who — had bought 18 of the stoves three months ago at an incredible discount.

It confirmed at least one thing Poe suspected: Shabazz was cheap.

But it didn't change one basic fact: even though Poe knew what Shabazz had done, he still had no idea why.

"He got a hell of a deal on those stoves; nobody wanted the things after all the bad press," he said to Callista, the act of finding at least one answer calming him down a bit.

"I mean, look at what he's done: He's taken the original fixtures, the original paneling, even the antique furniture where it was left — everything — and pulled it out of every house on that street. He'd have done it to Alice's house, too, but she wouldn't sell," Poe said.

Now it was Callista's turn to be confused. "Well, doesn't that make sense? All that stuff's worth a fortune, and he'd going to sell it," Callista said. "We're talking a lot of money here, right?"

"Oh yeah, according to a friend of mine, a two-inch thick, two-foot by six-foot piece of curly redwood goes for more than $700," Poe told her. "And Alice's door and window frames, cabinets and baseboards are all made of this stuff. God only knows what it's worth."

"Then why isn't that the answer?" Callista asked.

"Shabazz is a greedy S.O.B. that wanted Alice's house so he could gut it. When he didn't get it, he tried to beat it out of her with his two nephews."

"Because all of that stuff is worth a lot more in the house than outside of it," Poe said.

"How's that possible?" Callista asked. "Hell, my van would be worth as much as your car if I could sell every part in it for full-retail value."

"Don't ever say that again, that's blasphemy," Poe said, tossing her a look of mock sternness. "On a car that's true, but these houses are no mass-built car. Sure, he's got the raw material, but in tearing them out of the house, he's destroyed all the original workmanship, the value of having a truly unique and classic home. It would have made a lot more sense to just sell the houses intact, if money is all he's after."

"True," Callista finally agreed. "But we've already established this is the guy who put a Landau roof on a new Mustang," she said, trying to get him to smile again. "Bricks are smarter."

"That, I can't argue with," he said, remembering how happy it had made him to carve up the top of the Mustang; he thought Steve McQueen would approve. "But I still think there's something we're all missing here."

"Maybe, but that still doesn't mean we shouldn't just have them all arrested," she said. "Those two guys beat up Alice, and I'll bet they'd tell you their uncle put them up to it," she said smugly. "There we go: everyone goes to jail, and I go back to my life. Sound good?"

And she was right, Poe conceded. At this point he should be willing to let this go. Let Callista get on with things, let Alice come home, and let himself get back to writing stories for terrible little magazines read by people he'd like to drag under his car.

And yet he could not; he didn't think Alice or Callista were safe yet. Worse, he couldn't shake the feeling that Surfland itself was in trouble and that the very thing he had come here for was very much at risk of disappearing forever.

Chapter 44
Poe & Surfland

After leaving graduate school, Poe and Aly had briefly considered moving back to his native Colorado. (Missouri was definitely out; the Post-Dispatch editor with the butt-ugly car seemed to have e-mailed every editor between Kansas City and St. Louis to tell them what a bastard Poe was.) Taking a week to himself while Aly went back east to see her family, Poe headed home to his parents' house outside Boulder.

Having recently moved, their new house was hard to find, located at the end of a cul-de-sac amidst a whole bunch of houses where every third one looked exactly the same. Even the colors were the same, or damn close: all a variant of brown. Finally finding it after passing it twice, he pulled into the driveway after his dad had walked down to the street.

"Sorry I'm late," Poe told his dad as he gave him a hug. "I was looking for your flagpole. When are you putting that up?"

"I'm not."

"But why? That's the coolest thing ever, and you've got

flags from all over the world," Poe said, laughing. "You made my year when you hung up that Union Jack on the Fourth of July."

"I'm not allowed to have it," he said, obviously a bit depressed. "It violates the covenants."

"God damn ..." Poe said, and what followed after that was even less appropriate for a neighborhood full of families and pets with decent hearing.

And as Poe spent the rest of the week amongst the rapidly growing suburbs of Denver and Boulder, he saw the identical creeping sameness everywhere he went. Whether they were inexpensive condos or massive 4,000-square-foot homes, every house, every yard, every development looked alike.

From their insipidly bland earth tones on the outside to their faux-European architectural details on the inside, every home just bled conformity and a lack of originality that came only from planning a community by committee.

Driving out of Boulder to the southeast along the turnpike was a particularly horrible example: row after row of staggered boxes all painted exactly the same color, their patios and decks all in exactly the same place. And he knew: he would never live here again.

The small town of his youth was gone.

Packing up to head back to Missouri, Poe asked his dad if he had even bothered to ask about the flagpole. He had; the enforcer of the neighborhood rules lived just next door, ensuring he couldn't even get away with raising a small pole in the backyard.

Beach Slapped

So, late that night — Poe always made the drive overnight to avoid trucks and cops — Poe did two things: He boxed up all his dad's flags and put them in his trunk, promising to raise them somewhere else, some other day. And he painted the next-door neighbor's garage florescent orange, using a special paint designed to mark highways and protect the space shuttle upon reentry, or so he'd been told.

It was just a few months later that Poe and Aly found themselves in Surfland, heading into town from the south. Cruising through their new home, Aly was the first to speak: "Where the hell did you move me to?" And Poe could see exactly what she was talking about. Whereas suburbia was being overrun with covenant-controlled blandness, the people of Surfland seemed to have never even heard of one.

Because as a result of being five towns that merged into one city, Surfland's design could at best be called "eclectic," although Aly had her own description: "Poe, this is butt-ass-ugly ... My God, is that a day care center or a nail salon?"

"I think it's both," Poe said. "Isn't it great?"

Despite his enthusiasm, she did not agree, and like the thousands of tourists before her, Aly's first reaction was to go somewhere else, and if she hadn't already had a job she probably would have.

In the years to come, Poe would tell people that Surfland, "is a wonderful place to live, but you wouldn't want to visit there." That was an exaggeration of course; if Surfland had any more visitors it would probably topple into the ocean.

But the truth was that while most of Oregon's coastal

towns have a certain look, Surfland looks like a random mix of bad civic planning and boring back-lit plastic signs, pock-marked by hopeful islands of city-managed urban renewal.

And whether it was Aly in the '90s or the hoards of RV drivers in the 21st century, when people came through Surfland on Highway 101, what they mainly saw were ugly motels, strip malls, used car lots and even the occasional rock and gravel yard. More than one travel magazine pointed out that Surfland was largely a wonderful place to pee on the way to somewhere else along the beach. (Although in Poe's experience, one didn't need to be leaving Surfland to pee on the beach; he did it all the time.)

Not that visitors were the only ones who noticed Surfland's shortcomings. Even the head of the visitor's bureau was embarrassed that they had so many cheap hotel rooms dotting the city. The head of the Chamber of Commerce spent $6,200 on flowers and trees trying to hide the fact that their office was in a single-wide trailer.

The reason for all of this was simple: here — as was so often the case — Surfland's curious past was playing itself out in the present. Because merger or no, much of the area was still as fractured geographically and stylistically as it had been before the city had bonded in crap in 1968. No one could agree on anything, and so really nothing changed.

The gaps between districts remained: the city visitor's bureau had even taken to putting up signs in the most barren parts, reading: "Surfland: You're Still Here!" And where they did built, people put up pretty much anything they wanted.

Even Poe had to admit that having an RV without wheels right next to a school right next to a 3,500-square-foot house didn't make a whole lot of sense. Indeed, as the city had upgraded its zoning regulations in the past decade, Poe had been all for it.

But as Poe had known from the moment he met a hermit-nudist-mascot on the backstreets of Surfland, the heart of Surfland wasn't in what immediately met the eye or in what lay on Highway 101. It was in the quirky little neighborhoods that hid behind the highway. The aging drag queens that lived in Whig City, the kids who liked to run barefoot (sometimes all the way to their necks) along the bay when the tide was out, the little beach cottages that framed the rolling hills of Harrison and the beautiful old houses that framed both sides of Jetty Avenue in the Ageya District: these were the places that made Surfland special. Some were beautiful, some were ugly, but all of them were unique.

And no one gave a damn whether or not you raised a flag or what color you painted your house.

Somehow, that seemed to be at risk with Shabazz T. Morton in Surfland. Clearly, he liked that kind of boxy, style-free crap, as evidenced by the poster of Tiberian Shores that Poe had taken from his house. Thinking of all of the houses Alice's husband had built being gutted so Shabazz could refill with them with ferns in wall hangings, putting greens near the toilet and $8,000 countertops made Poe want to throw up.

"Sorry, but I'm not done yet," Poe said to Callista, finally answering her question. "I know that stylistically deranged asshole is up to something, and I'm going to get him."

"Do I still get to play?" Callista asked, teasingly.

"Only if you want to. You might be right; maybe I should just leave this to the police," Poe said, as he headed for the garage. "But he's attacked my friends and my town, and quite frankly I'm just not mature enough to let that go."

"Count me in, although I have no idea just what that means."

"Neither do I," Poe said, now walking back past her without looking. "But I do know what happens first." And opening the back door, he walked out into the rain and ran something up the flagpole. He was back inside within a minute.

"What's that?" Callista asked him, as he closed the door. "We declare war," he said, as he went to the bathroom for his own shower.

But now it was her turn to look past him — at the Union Jack flying in the wind.

Chapter 45
Paxton

Listening on the phone to Valeria Cruz, Paxton Dell's heart crashed into his stomach.

"Paxton, Portia only said, 'yes,' because of a plan she made with the football team," Valeria told him, as he sat on a bus returning from Portland. "You can't go through with this."

Paxton knew this had been too good to be true.

After getting the $200 from Poe last night, he'd finally been able to craft the perfect date: He'd go to Portland and rent a Corvette, drive Portia around town, and then take her to a picnic right at the base of the bluffs in Harrison. A romantic fire, some shrimp and scallops on skewers, and s'mores for dessert. Closing his eyes, he could imagine her licking the marshmallow off his fingers just before those same lips passionately kissed him.

Was it a long shot? Sure, but Paxton was on a hot streak, and as he headed to the bus station at 6 a.m. to catch the bus to pick up the 'Vette at the Portland airport, he figured anything could happen. The money from Poe, the donation to the boosters that everyone thought he'd made — although he liked to think he'd have done the same thing — the band members who had stop threatening to beat him up: how could he lose?

Yes, they were all still calling him "boner boy," but at least it was with affection, sort of. And if the whole school could change their minds, he was sure Portia would, too. He just knew that once she saw how wonderful he was, how she was the center of his universe, she'd literally fall into his arms. (He'd started lifting weights just so he could lift her when that happened.)

He even had their second date planned: another picnic, this time on a sunny afternoon overlooking the lake at Yacht Club Park. Not that there were any yachts there; it was just a fancy name, but it was still romantic as long there hadn't been a fish die-off recently.

And now all of that was getting shot to hell.

"A bet? Are you sure?" he asked Valeria.

"Yes, I'm sure," she said, feeling awful that she had to be the one to tell him. "One of the girls I work with at Bo's is dating some guys on the football team, and I heard her talking about it on her cell phone. You're going to kiss …"

"I'm going to kiss her!" Paxton said hopefully. "That can't be all bad."

"Paxton, you're going to go to kiss her, and then just before it happens, the football guys are going to slide down the cliff, tackle you, paint you black and put a white stripe down your back."

"Oh ..."

"Paxton, are you OK?"

"Yeah, I guess," he said quietly, before mercifully changing the subject. "How about you? You seemed pretty upset when you ran by me yesterday after school, and your dad seemed pretty mad last night. Everything OK?"

"Me? I'm OK, my dad's just worried about some stuff," she said, not sounding entirely truthful. "It'll be fine, Paxton ... Paxton? Paxton?!"

"Valeria, I'm losing you! Valeria?" Paxton yelled back into the cell phone.

"'Can you hear me now,' my ass," Paxton said, and realizing how loud he'd said it, decided to slump down even lower in his bus seat.

Perfect, just perfect: which was pretty much par for the course since he'd gotten to the airport. Because other than the weather forecast calling for a clear night on the beach after 24 hours of almost nonstop rain, everything else had been crap.

The date was a joke, the football team was out to paint him like a skunk, and Portia had no intention of kissing him. On top of the fact that he'd gone all the way to Portland to rent a Corvette, just to be told he had to be at least 21.

It was official: life sucked.

All that work! He was going to go through that whole date thinking she liked him and then he'd get totally screwed!

Or would he?

Valeria had said they were going to wait until he tried to kiss her to make their move. That gave him the whole date to change her mind! If he could impress her enough, maybe she'd call off the bet; she had to have some kind of signal to call it off. Of course she did! Was it crazy? Sure, but his original plan had needed a lot of luck, now he just needed some more.

And with that he sat back upright in his bus seat and went back to planning, this time how to super-size his date. Humming Frank Sinatra's "New York, New York," he paused occasionally to nod "yes" and mumble to himself. Oh, yes, this could work ...

Of course, failing to rent the Corvette was going to force him to scramble when he got home. His nearly two-decade-old Nissan Sentra wasn't exactly a dream machine, but he could fix that.

Now, if he could just remember where the sheepskin and duct tape were ...

Chapter 46
Julio

Five minutes earlier and 52 miles west in Surfland, the weather forecast had borne out: sun was starting to poke through. Enjoying a break from the crowded restaurant inside, an employee of Bo's Crab and Anvil stood on the deck overlooking the water, a tiny figure silhouetted against the waves on the bay and the clouds in the sky.

But to Julio Cruz the figure wasn't tiny at all: it was his daughter, and she was talking on her cell phone. Looking through his new binoculars from the scenic viewpoint beside the bay, he could see her as clearly as if she were standing next to him.

He'd never planned to spy on his daughter with the binoculars; they were for watching Paxton Dell, so he'd have proof the next time Paxton made one of his drug deals. But he'd wanted to see just how well they worked, and the scenic overlook offered the perfect spot. Better yet, it was easily on his way to Bo's, where he planned to talk rationally to his daughter about his concerns regarding Paxton Dell.

But she must have gotten her break early, and as Julio took a close-up look at each tourist on the deck outside Bo's — why did men insist on trying to wear a comb-over on a windy beach? — he saw his daughter wander into his field of vision and pull out her cell phone. Whoever she was talking with, she seemed to be sad: several times she pinched her nose and ran her palm across her forehead and up through her hair.

But it was what she did at the end that caught his attention. Because even though he couldn't hear her, the words on her lips were unmistakable: "Paxton ... Paxton ... Paxton."

Paxton! And as it had the last time he'd been caught surprised by the existence of Paxton Dell in his daughter's life, he dropped any plans to talk to her or be reasonable about this very wrong young man. (God only knows what he did in that skunk costume at home.)

Watching his daughter put the phone back in her pocket and go back inside, Julio went back to work himself, slowly making his way up Highway 101 towards the lake road and his job building the roof-top deck. But even as he did so his mind was on what he would do next.

Take care of Paxton Dell.

Chapter 47
Callista

At least in its initial phase, Jackson Poe's war on Shabazz T. Morton didn't appear to Callista to begin too radically different from everything else he did: they were in his Jag flying through the streets of Surfland with the CD player blaring some bombastic instrumental music that came from God-only-knew-where.

One thing was different: the break in the rain allowed them to put the top down. But with the temperature hovering in just the 50s, Callista was still wearing the same jacket she had been all week. The locals had told her she'd be able to take it off in July.

Following the signs to the hospital, they turned right onto West Nelta Lake Road, the compliment to the similar road that ran up the east side of the lake. But unlike the eastern road, which ran through the low ground next to the lake, this road began immediately climbing a hill. As the car slowed down, she noticed Poe was waving at just about everyone, before finally he stopped to talk to someone.

"Hey, I've got a mother of a crimp in my neck," he said to a woman raking her yard. "How about a massage next Monday night before the city council meeting?"

She responded to Poe as just about everyone seemed to: "You're sure that pain's not lower? Like in your ass? I can't fix that without a special tool," she said, laughing.

"Fine, just meet me in the mayor's office."

Even after three strange days with Jackson Poe, Callista couldn't help but be surprised: "Do you always get massages in the mayor's office?" she asked him.

"You do when the mayor's your massage therapist," he said, once again getting the car moving up the hill. "She's the best in town, although the lady she shares the office with is close."

"What's she? A city councilperson?"

"Nope, just a massage therapist, although she does moonlight as a clown and bartender."

"At the same time?" Callista said, just to be a smart-ass.

"Only once that I know of," Poe said, with a shit-eating grin now going ear to ear. "Hold on, I've got to talk to another weirdo ... Pete!"

Stopping the car at the top of the hill, Poe was waving at Pete Polanski. Waving back, Pete was putting the final touches on his bright red Jeep, which he had just washed off in the spreading sunshine.

"Hey, Poe," Pete called back. "See you got the top down and the same crappy music playing." Now turning to Callista, he continued the good-natured barrage at his friend: "Is he submitting you to his God-awful movie soundtrack collection?"

Not even giving her a chance to answer, Pete went right back to Poe: "What schlock is it this time?" Why can't you just listen to normal Lynard Skynard like every other 40-something with a convertible?"

"I'll stop playing my music when you stop trying to put brass fire-hose fittings around your gas cap," Poe said. "You are not a fire truck. And by the way, where's your dog? Did it crap a fur ball in your seat again?"

As both of them eased out of the car, Pete and Poe continued to badger the other about what were clearly mutually bizarre — yet appreciated — eccentricities, all the while Pete's real dog, Dexter, snoozed at their feet, ignoring them both. Eventually, however, their conversation turned to Alice and everything Poe had learned about the men who'd assaulted her.

Having heard the conversation more than once, Callista let her mind wander to more normal things, like the amazing view.

Polanski's house was one of two atop what had to be one of the highest and steepest hills in Surfland; she even noted a parabolic mirror at the top so people could see who was coming up the other side. And even in the mirror, you could see unbroken all the way from Pete's driveway to the beach, less than a quarter mile away.

More than anything it reminded her of home, or at least San Francisco across the bay. There, one street after another seemed to run straight down the hill and into the water. When she was a kid, she found herself wondering if she got up enough speed in a car whether she could actually jump all the way to Alcatraz.

Smiling, she recalled watching "Bullitt" and wondered if Steve McQueen had thought the same. Or if maybe Poe had. Her train of thought momentarily interrupted by Pete — "You sure you don't want to get the police in on this?" — she scratched Dexter on the head and walked back to the car where Poe was already behind the wheel.

"No," he said. "My instincts tell me this is like a good story: you'll only screw it up if you rush it." And with that, the car was once again racing east on West Nelta Lake Road, down the steep hill, slowly curving to the left above the lakeshore.

"Hey, Poe, is this your favorite road in town?"

"Huh? Why do you ask?"

"Because it looks just like those roads in "Bullitt": lots of curves, hills and places to go screeching around corners like a heathen with your hair on fire," she said, noticing for the first time she could see Nelta Lake to the east. "For a guy with a dark green car that hauls ass, that seems irresistible."

"You noticed, eh?" he said, pointedly shifting the car into fourth gear. "Let me just say that while I compliment you on your powers of observation, the behaviors you've described are highly illegal, and would be irresponsible." He shifted into fifth gear. "And any such similarities that might you think you might have noticed between Surfland and San Francisco are merely coincidences of topography and not a sign that God loves me."

"OK, paragon of virtue," she said now totally relaxed by the wind racing through her hair, "just how many times have you coincidentally taken your car hauling ass over that hill in front of Pete's house."

"Zero."

"Zero? Oh, come on! Don't tell me you haven't wanted to take this thing airborne just like Steve McQueen."

"Wanted? Yes, in my more deranged moments. Done? No," he said, slowing the car back down and downshifting as they approached a curve. "McQueen's Mustangs had modified brakes and suspensions so they'd survive the jumps. A regular car could never survive that."

"You said, 'Mustangs.'"

"Oh, yeah, they used two for the filming, and one had to be sent to the scrap heap, it was so badly screwed up," he said speeding up and returning the car to fifth gear. "You ever watch the 'Dukes of Hazzard'?"

"My dad told me it was 'stereotyping a lower class that had been held in intellectual serfdom,' and I was banned from watching it. So, yeah, I saw it all the time."

"They went through more than 250 Dodge Chargers on that show. Every time they made one of those high-flying 'Yee-Hah!' jumps they pretty much had to roll the car into the scrap heap," he said, sounding almost sad. "You can actually see the car bend on impact if you slow it down on the DVD."

"I take it you've done that."

"I own every episode; I decided to limit myself to jumping cars off of hills vicariously," he said. "This car may end up on the junk heap someday, but I'll be damned if it's going to be at my hands."

Chapter 48
Callista

After the massage therapist mayor, Callista figured she was done with Surfland's peculiarities, at least on this drive. But as Poe parked the car and put up the top, Callista found she was wrong again: "This is the hospital? It looks like an office park."

Sitting on the shore of Lake Nelta, St. Gangulphus Hospital was a one-story structure no bigger than a small suburban office building. For someone like Callista, whose familiarity with hospitals pretty much began and ended with "ER" she couldn't believe an entire hospital could fit into something this small.

"I take it people don't get really sick or injured," she asked Poe.

"Oh, they do; there's a lot of stupid people out on the highway," he said, as he leaned over and pulled something out of the glove box. "They just better hope the helicopter to Portland goes faster than they do."

"Does that happen a lot? How do you deal with that?"

"Yeah it does, and you just learn not to be an idiot when

the cloud ceiling's under 200 feet. That, and pray to only have a massive heart attack in the summer."

Within two minutes they were in the hospital and standing in Alice's door; Poe was one of the few people who could get to Alice without question. For the first minute after they arrived, however, Alice didn't even notice them. She was too busy watching a public relations spectacle unfold on CNN.

"So you deny that you're fascists?" Anderson Cooper asked the bearded man and young woman on television.

"Yes, Anderson, as we've explained, that was an unfortunate acronym created by a member of our organization, a member that has been soundly reprimanded."

Watching from the door, Callista saw a tiny sideways disapproving glance from the man to the woman. It was something only she would notice — as she watched her father and sister get taken apart on national television.

"Well, Dr. Walker, you say that, but as I read through some of the transcripts from you and your daughter at 'Free Animals and Sea Creatures in Storage Tanks, Now!' meetings, I see that you advocate imprisoning all marine theme park workers, even the teenagers selling stuffed animals," Anderson said, clearly enjoying hanging the "Liberal Leopard" and his preachy cub with their own words. *"That certainly sounds like fascism to me."*

"Anderson," Arianne said, clearly trying to dig the pair out of the hole her new organization had put them in, *"you need to take those comments in context ..."*

"Miss Walker: just what context should we take you

saying, 'Salmon should have just as many rights to be fed farmed fat people,' in?"

And with that, Callista could hold it in no longer, and burst out laughing, which finally brought them to Alice's attention.

"Oh! I'm being rude, let me hit the mute button," Alice said, bringing an early end to Callista's fun.

Still chuckling, Callista walked into the room with Poe, hoping that she could buy a copy of what she'd seen from CNN.

"Alice," Poe said, "this laughing young lady is the woman I've told you so much about: Callista Walker."

"How nice to meet you," Alice said, extending a handshake that demonstrated a woman who had very much recovered. "'Callista,' what a lovely name, although those fools on TV seem to be making a mockery of your last name. It must be terrible to have a common last name and have to share it with people like that."

"You have no idea," Callista said, managing to keep her reaction to a smile.

"Alice," Poe said, changing the subject, "I'd like you to stay here another day or so, if you don't mind. I think I've just about got this figured out, but I'd feel better if I knew you were safe here."

"No problem," she said. "Just keep the great food and coffee coming, and I'll stay for a week." Noticing Poe's surprised reaction, she chided him lightly: "Now, Jackson, don't tell me you didn't plan that," she said pointing to a massive bouquet on the desk.

"The owner of McDonalds sent me that yesterday and has three meals and a fresh carafe of coffee delivered to me every day. Really, it's too much."

"Uh huh, no problem," Poe said, wondering what this little piece of largesse would cost his mortal soul, or at the very least his journalistic one. He had the feeling Dick Yelpers was about to invent another shaped potato and "appreciate" any coverage he could get.

"Well, since you're clearly in a good mood, maybe you could tell me a little something about this," he said pulling a piece of curly redwood out of his back pocket. "Is all the trim and cabinetry made of this stuff?"

"Everything inside the house is."

"'Everything,' meaning what?"

"Meaning everything: the walls, the furniture, the cabinets. If it's made of wood in my house, it's curly redwood."

"My God, your husband trucked up redwood trees to build everything in your house?"

"Oh no, dear. It was just one tree," she said clearly remembering the day nearly 60 years ago when he'd done it. "He had about a 320-foot redwood with a 23-foot diameter quartered and sectioned so it would fit on trailers to go up Highway 101 from northern California."

"He built the entire interior of your house from one tree?" Poe asked, incredulous.

"No, he built every house on our block of NW Jetty Avenue with that tree, and a few more around town I think," she said, clearly lost in the past.

"There was over 60,000 board feet of lumber in that tree. I remember it well; Walter never would shut up about it," she said with a smile.

"My God, does anyone know that?" Poe asked. "What are those houses worth?"

"Well, the people that bought them from Walter knew. As I say, he never stopped talking about it," she said. "For a while in the '70s we actually stopped getting invited to block parties."

"But as to what they're worth, I have no idea, really," she said. "But they're sure not worth what they sold them for; that's why all my neighbors sold so fast, the prices they were getting offered were 20 percent more than anything they ever thought they'd get. At our age, you don't pass that up."

"But you did," Callista said, finally speaking up, as Poe still seemed too shocked to really say much of anything. "Why didn't you sell out?"

"Well," she said, giving Callista a sly eye, "just because I like getting invited to block parties doesn't mean I wasn't proud of the old fart. I plan to die in that house, although I'd prefer it if potential buyers wouldn't try to rush me along."

Smiling, Callista simply took her hand and squeezed it, an understanding passing between them. Poe, now back among the mentally living, rejoined the conversation, and Callista took it as an excuse to back away from the bed and take a seat in the chair.

Watching them, she heard Poe try to disguise the shock and concern Alice's answers had given him, and as the conversation meandered to other topics — Alice wanted to know how she might be able to get all her friends McDonald's coffee mugs — Callista knew Poe's efforts had succeeded in relaxing her again.

Turning back to the TV, the sound was still muted, but Callista didn't need to hear what Anderson Cooper and his guests were saying to know what was happening. The screen split into two portions, she could see Anderson was now largely sitting quiet, as her father and sister did all the talking. To her joy, her father was actually lunging at her sister, although both of them had their fingers pointed and mouths open in rage at the other.

That's when it occurred to her: My God, they did get was coming to them, and I got to see it. Everyone did.

And as she thought about everything she'd been through the past few weeks, she began to believe that if the people who had attacked her before Surfland could get divine justice in the end, maybe the people who attacked her in Surfland could, as well. Certainly, stranger things had happened in the world.

Which meant in Surfland they probably would, and a giant smile spread across her face.

Chapter 49
Bobby

It wasn't too often that a smile spread across the surly visage of Bobby White. In a perpetual state of being pissed off at the world, his general expression was one of drunken malaise occasionally punctuated by fits of rage that proved at the very least neither he nor his uncle were adopted.

But this afternoon was different; the UPS truck had arrived with Bobby's latest EBay purchases. Even having brought all his Hays Supply memorabilia with him to Oregon, he was all ready to buy more (especially since he'd gotten a hold of his uncle's credit card numbers). And as so often happened, his latest purchases had arrived on the same day, even though he made the purchases days apart. The first was the Hays Supply condoms his uncle had been so angry about.

As the listing said, one package of 12 had been opened so he could check for authenticity, something Bobby quickly did, even though it meant setting down his can of Milwaukee's Best. "Yep," he said to Joey, who was sitting across from him in the kitchen, "there it is. "Damn, you gotta like that quality. The words are a little blurry, but you gotta expect that on such delicate stuff, don'tcha, Joey? ... Joey!"

Damn his brother! Once again, he was off in some la-la-land with space aliens and other dumb shit Bobby had no use for. He'd flipped through his brother's comics once, hoping to find some outer space babe with three boobs or something, but all he ever saw was space ships and hairy dudes with three eyes.

"Joey! Wake the hell up! I'm showin' ya my condoms!"

"They're very nice, Bobby," he said, with no apparent enthusiasm. "I don't think I want to do this anymore."

"Do what? Babble about the dark side an' savin' people?" Bobby said, now carefully checking to make sure he'd gotten the more than 1,000 condoms he'd paid for. "Good, 'cause you been talkin' about that all day. Thank God I've been drinkin' or I would have actually had ta listen to ya."

"No, I don't mean that," Joey said, with an exasperated sigh. "I mean this work for Uncle Shelton, or Shabazz, or whatever his name is now."

"How you gonna quit what you never started?" Bobby said with a sneer as he cracked open another Milwaukee's Best. "You ain't done shit since we got here. I've been the one doin' everything."

"Then maybe you should just go back to the beach house with him alone tonight," Joey said hopefully, although knowing what the answer would be.

"Shit, no! Last time I left you alone to go get beer you

charged $15 in pay-per-view movies to watch some damn fantasy thing about gardening!"

"That was Harry Potter," he said. "I was hoping to learn how Dumbledore helped Snape ..."

"I don't care! Your damn movies cut into my beer money; did you know that?" he asked, now fully turning his attention to Joey. "So, all I want is for you to shut up and do as you're told for the next 24 hours! Then, we can get the hell out of here, and I can get my money just like we planned."

"I don't even know what the plan is," Joey said quietly.

"And you're not supposed to," Bobby said, now tearing into the other box. "Uncle Shabazz and I just decided you'd screw it up, just like you did the mail. So don't whine to me! If you hadn't lost it, we wouldn't even have to go back to the house tonight ... Damn, looky here at this ... this is the most beautiful thing ever."

"It's really nice," Joey said hopefully, trying to find anything to calm his brother down. "It looks just like that belt-buckle you wear every day, so I think it's good that you have two."

"Belt buckle?" Bobby said dismissively, before taking another huge slurp of his beer. "That shows you what you know, shit-head. I paid $117 for this, and it ain't no goddamn belt buckle."

Chapter 50
Hays Supply

Sixteen hundred miles southeast of Surfland, the employees of Hays Supply were toasting — again — that anyone could be stupid enough to pay $117 for a belt buckle with some Velcro on the back. Indeed, it was their third such toast tonight, and they'd stopped counting the total number long ago.

Bobby White was one stupid man.

The manager of Hays Supply had noticed Bobby's penchant for Hays Supply-marked goods shortly after they'd given him his denim shirt when he became assistant supervisor. He wore it everywhere he went, and while they appreciated the company pride, they were becoming increasingly concerned that his lack of hygiene coupled with wearing the same shirt seven days a week was sending the wrong message to potential customers who might encounter Bobby around the city.

They'd considered firing him, of course, but no one could

stock like Bobby. He knew where every last thing in the store was, down to the section and shelf. But by limiting him to working nights when no actual people were around, he could both replenish the store in half the time as any other employee and not gas out potential customers.

They solved the problem of Bobby smelling in public by giving Bobby two more shirts and having him clean one of the hot tubs at least three times a week with "special cleansers" while in his clothes. Although it wasn't the same as showering, and he always smelled like chlorine, it largely did the trick.

It also highlighted the degree to which Bobby would go to in order to slap the words "Hays Supply" all over his body. Because as Bobby crawled out of the tub one day, he found the mailing label from the crate holding his special hot tub cleanser and was carefully reading every word.

"Hey, boss man! What's the deal with this thing?"

"Uh, what do you mean, Bobby," he asked, fearful that their little plan to keep Bobby clean was about to literally get blown out of the water. "All the pool cleaners come from Suave and Ivory."

"No, not that," he said holding up the laminated label to the light. "It says 'Hays Supply' in real fancy lettering. I think it'd look real good on my wall."

Relieved that they weren't going have to come up with a plan to start dousing him with a fire hose, his boss flipped back an answer: "Yeah, those are a limited edition mini-poster, you know, like from the car magazines. I'll sell it to you for ten bucks."

And a scam was born.

Eight months and three more mailing labels, seventeen T-shirts, one belt buckle, a bolo tie, four pairs of socks, 17 feet of rope, four sweatshirts, 492 tongue depressors, one kitty litter box, countless pairs of hunter's long underwear and a "Hays Supply Athletic Club Members Only" package (including T-shirt, mini-barbells and workout bag) later, Bobby's spending on Hays Supply "memorabilia" had totaled well in excess of $2,000, even before he left for Oregon.

Of course, continuing to come up with memorabilia for Bobby was a job in and of itself. Not even Nike had all that merchandise for real. So, it had become common practice during slow periods at the store to see what else the staff of Hays Supply could come up with next to sell to Bobby.

Some things were easy; whenever someone would return a pair of long underwear that were illegal to return to the shelves, they'd just staple a return address label inside the waistband and sell it to Bobby. They'd done the same thing with the tongue depressors, which they'd gotten in trade when a destitute medical supply truck driver needed a new alternator.

It made for one hell of a beer fund, something that management realized they were about to lose when Bobby announced he was "driving somewhere west to one of those ocean states." Here again, however, Bobby's innate stupidity rescued them.

Just four months earlier, Bobby was looking to buy a truck on eBay, after his brother showed him how to use the auction website. As Bobby followed the bidding on one particular truck for nearly two weeks, all he could do was rave about how his "new" 1993 Dodge Ram was going to have less than 300,000 miles on it and would be just like one of the Peterbilt trucks with the big flared fenders.

"You should see this thing, man, it's a beaut'," Bobby bragged one night as he came on to his shift. "It's only got primer on, like, five of the body panels."

"Bobby," his boss asked, "Are you sure the '93's the new body style? I don't think they started doing that more modern look until later."

"Hell yes, I'm sure. I called the guy, and he just told me it looks like that 'cause it was an early prototype or somethin'. He said all I gotta do is call Dodge and they'll send me the right fenders for free since I got the test model," Bobby said, now leaning over to pull up his Hays Supply socks.

"How stupid do you think I am? Hmmm, I think the writing on my socks is coming off," he said now starting look around. "You'd think they'd have used a better crayon at the factory."

And with that, the staff of Hays Supply had realized Bobby would continue to buy anything, especially on eBay. So, about once a week they would post "new" merchandise, and then spent the next two weeks bidding it up during their lunch breaks. (No one else was bidding, that was for sure.)

Their latest creations were among their most successful, although the 1,263 condoms, which Bobby had purchased for $108, were problematic for some; they were horrified at the idea of Bobby even trying to procreate. They went ahead, however, when they'd all agreed that should that terrible event come to pass, it would be ideal for everyone if he did wear a condom. And it was pure profit, too. The condoms, leftovers from a misguided local clown who found it was virtually impossible to teach safe sex and make animal balloons at the same time, required just five minutes and a tiny fine-tipped Sharpie pen to become "Hays Supply Classics."

Even more amazing was the $117 they'd gotten for the belt buckle, their first attempt at trying to sell Bobby something he already owned. They simply removed the belt and then attached a giant two-sided Velcro patch to the back. Calling it, "An authentic Hays Supply Horn Cover," the online description explained how it had been specially handcrafted with raised metal lettering just for 1990s Dodge vehicles. (Bobby still would not admit he'd bought the wrong truck.)

And as they'd boxed up the condoms and "horn cover" for shipping, they'd begun to imagine all the other things they could sell to Bobby. Of particular excitement was the potential for "Hays Supply Wooden Erector Sets," seeing as the store still had more than 10,000 tongue depressors in back.

If they could sell all of those, it would be more than enough to keep the beer fund going and cover the cost of the hot tub after the tax deduction.

Given its "prior history," the health department suggested they donate it to the local college. They planned to use it in their physical therapy program for pigs, for which the college was eternally grateful.

In fact, they were so thrilled, they agreed to have two

interns assigned to Hays Supply on a permanent basis to help with night stock and inventory. Interns that proved so good at keeping inventory and restocking — and showering — that it was quickly discovered that what they may have lacked in the ability to memorize was quickly redeemed by their ability to read and not piss people off. (Mrs. Gormson's lawyer was now suing for post-traumatic stress disorder, claiming his client now lost bladder control anytime she saw a billboard with chewing tobacco on it.)

So, they toasted Bobby again, thrilled that the money would keep coming, at least until Bobby discovered he'd been fired, while thoroughly in hysterics at the thought of what Bobby might do with the condoms — and still praying it had nothing to do with sex.

They'd have been laughing even harder had they known how confusing their customer was finding the concept of Velcro patches.

Chapter 51
Joey

Despite Joey's best efforts, he couldn't keep a small smile from his face as his brother tried in vain to attach the "horn cover" to his steering wheel. Every time Bobby would stick the Velcro to the steering wheel and then the cover to the Velcro, both would just fall off.

At first it had taken almost 30 seconds for the adhesive on the back of the Velcro to come loose from the plastic horn. (Joey suspected it was covered with syrup and sausage grease; Bobby thought Pigs-In-A-Blanket were finger food.)

But with each subsequent attempt to reattach it, both the cover and Velcro fell off quicker and quicker until finally the adhesive had been so thoroughly destroyed that it failed to hold at all. Nevertheless, Bobby tried another 17 times, figuring that pounding and screaming would accomplish what following directions had not. (He'd even put down his beer the last three times.)

Not that Joey hadn't seen this coming.

For one thing, he was still convinced it was a belt buckle, and that it would have been of far better use keeping Bobby's butt-crack out of public view. (Clearly, wearing one belt wasn't doing the job.) Also, he'd kind of figured this was going to happen when he'd noticed the "directions" were handwritten on the back of a Toro weed whacker warranty card.

Instantly, however, Joey felt badly that he was finding joy in his brother's misery; he really wanted to be a better person than that. But after the nightmare that had been the past few weeks, he found himself enjoying his brother's rage being displaced on something other than him.

The peace didn't last long.

"Goddamn it, nubbin-cunt!" his uncle screamed as he came out the front door. "How many times are you going to honk that horn?!"

"Until this goddamn thing works, that's how long!" Bobby snapped back. "You'd think somethin' made in Cambodia would work right!"

"Do you even know where Cambodia is, you scrote-choker?" his uncle asked.

"Yeah, it's in Missouri or somewhere, asshole!"

And on they went, with his uncle conceding that Cambodia was in fact in Missouri, and Bobby all the while screaming at the belt buckle, pounding on the steering wheel, and cussing some more when it fell to the floor. Thank God Bobby's truck didn't have an airbag, Joey thought, or it would have gone off in his face by now.

Finally, after 19 more fruitless attempts with the Velcro,

Bobby announced his intentions to go get some epoxy from the garage. Screaming after him, his uncle told him it was time to get over to the beach house, since he wanted them there by dark. The only response that greeted him and Joey was a slamming door.

Two minutes later, Bobby returned with a tube of epoxy in one hand and his black denim jacket in the other. With "Hays Supply" written boldly across the back in gold spray paint, this was the first time Joey had seen it since they'd gotten to Oregon.

"What the hell is that?" Joey's uncle asked.

"This is my real jacket, not that sissy plastic shit people wear out here," Bobby said. "I wore it every day in Kansas, and I'm gonna wear it here, 'cause I'm sick of all this Oregon bullshit."

"Fine with me, maybe at least the jacket doesn't smell like the rest of your clothes," his uncle said, now walking by Bobby on the way to his car. "Jesus, don't you ever shower?"

With that, Bobby lifted his arms for a moment and stuck his fingers in each armpit before drawing his digits back to his nose. Inhaling deeply, Joey saw him shrug his shoulders before climbing back into his truck and returning to work on the steering wheel.

"Cow-puke!" his uncle screamed at Bobby. "Let's go! I want you there by sundown! What good's it do to watch the house after dark if you aren't there by dark?"

"I'm gonna attach my horn cover first! Besides, what the hell are you doin'?"

"I've got to go check something out first — I told you that!"

"Like hell, you did!" Bobby yelled back, and for a second, Joey thought Bobby might say more. But like a puppy suddenly remembering a thrown stick, he immediately went back to fiddling with his horn and the epoxy.

"Now you listen to me, goose-spooge. If you want to see even one penny of that $50,000," Shabazz growled loudly, "you got five minutes, then you will drive over there, park at the far end of the street and then wait for me in the car. You got that, pig-shit for brains?"

Bobby mumbled something that Joey took for acceptance, although it was probably the number that made Bobby actually shut up.

For his part, Joey decided the best thing to do was just get out of the way, so he climbed into the truck to wait. As he fastened his seatbelt, he figured anything he could do to make his uncle think he was listening was a good thing.

As usual, he was wrong.

"You damn meat-smelt! What are you fastening that for?!" his uncle yelled at him.

Joey knew there was absolutely no right answer to the question — especially in his uncle's universe — so he decided instead to just sit and wait for the onslaught. It didn't take but a few seconds.

"Only pussies wear seatbelts! What if your car explodes? What if you need to jump clear of someone while you're driving?" his uncle screamed. "You ever notice that more people die now in cars than in 1920? Now, why do you think that is, corn-whore? Goddamn seatbelts!"

Joey knew the answers to these things, of course. And living next to I-70 in Kansas, Joey had seen enough accidents to know his uncle had clearly lost his mind, but he once again just sat and said nothing.

"And don't get me started on airbags! Those things will blow your goddamn head off! See my car over there? I disconnected 'em," he said proudly. "Not gonna find my brains all over a bag! You're not gonna find my brains anywhere!"

And with that, he marched to his car. Not for the first time, Joey noticed that as Shabazz stormed off from his latest berating he seemed to almost have a bounce in his step. As his uncle peeled out of the driveway onto East Nelta Lake Road, Joey wondered what kind of man got his jollies from verbally attacking other people — and if it might not go beyond just verbal.

"Hey, asshole! Come 'ere!" Bobby yelled at Joey. "Get me another beer — and some paint thinner. I just glued my hand to the steering wheel."

Sighing, Joey walked back into the garage, wondering just how many of his uncle's behaviors might be genetic. Maybe Luke Skywalker was adopted ...

Chapter 52
Fuzznut

It wasn't too terribly often one could actually see the sun set over the Pacific Ocean, off Surfland. If it wasn't raining or overcast, there was still usually a layer of clouds and fog hanging over the water so that the sun disappeared from view long before it fell behind the watery horizon. This was true even when the entire day had been all but cloudless.

Nevertheless, every clear evening people would watch the setting sun, hoping that direct sunlight would continue to shine right up until the very end. Tonight was no different, although on most nights there would not have been an otter on a bicycle watching it as well.

He was on his way home after appearing as "U Otter B," a mascot for the Surfland Visitor's Bureau. Dressed head to toe in brown fur, Fuzznut had spent his afternoon at the south end of town near the aquarium handing out brochures to tourists reading, "U Otter B fishing in Surfland" and "U Otter

B antiquing in Surfland" and any number of other shameless plays on his name to promote the city. (Fuzznut's own creation, he was very proud of it, especially since they paid him $25 an hour to do it.)

As mascot jobs went, it was pretty simple: stand in front of a building and shake hands, although at four hours, it was long enough to get boring when it got slow near the end. Fortunately, Poe stopped by to let him know how Alice was doing and that he and Callista were off to Shabazz's beach house one more time to confirm a theory Poe was working on.

If anyone thought it was strange that a grown man was talking to an otter that just nodded a lot, no one said so, as even Callista seemed to be lost in her own thoughts as she waited for Poe about 20 feet away.

Indeed, Poe left right as Fuzznut's time was up. Waving goodbye to his friend, Fuzznut laughed to himself as he heard Callista asking Poe for a favor: "You don't suppose we could listen to my CD? It's right here in my jacket ... No? OK, no problem ..."

Fuzznut had known the answer to that as soon as she'd asked. Poe wasn't predictable in most ways, but when it came to his car's CD player, some things were set in stone.

Now walking behind a large tree on the side of the aquarium, Fuzznut unlocked his bike — it had taken him forever to find a combination lock he could work with furry hands — and headed for home.

He'd originally planned to drive to the job, but when the sun peeked out just before he left, he decided to ride his bike instead. Wearing webbed feet, it was a challenge, but it had been raining hard the past few days and he'd missed the sun, even though he never actually let it touch his skin.

But now that sun was largely gone; the cloud deck was high off the ocean today. And to make matters worse, before he could ride out a busload of Japanese tourists wanted him to autograph every brochure and pose for pictures. He admitted to himself he was nervous about being on the road after dark, since he hadn't brought his bike light with him. Sometimes being a neurotic mascot was a real pain.

He was tempted to ride mostly up Highway 101; it would have been a lot quicker. But from experience he knew that when people saw a mascot on a bike they became complete idiots and were just as likely to run him over as wave hello. (Actually, most people on 101 were idiots anyway; the costume just made it worse.) So, he rode where he could on the backstreets, most of which, while poorly lit, had the virtue of being largely empty of traffic, especially here in early November.

Not that visibility was the only problem with Surfland's backstreets. Riding there also doubled, even tripled, the distance he covered to get home. Yet another artifact of one city that used to be five towns, not one street in the city, save for Highway 101, ran the entire length of Surfland.

To visitors it was maddening: streets seemed to begin and end without reason, while some of the avenues that covered the length of the city were in fact just a few hundred feet long in sections before petering out again. Whether it was the streets running east to west or the avenues running north to south, more than one Surfland tourist had found themselves ready to pull their hair out when the address they were looking for — say 1700 Oar Avenue — couldn't be reached by the street with the same name just one block away, like 1600 Oar Avenue.

Residents, too, found it to be a pain in the ass; when Highway 101 jammed up with traffic, there was no way to get around it by using the side roads. Even traveling from one neighborhood to another could be complicated, since you might have to drive 20 blocks just to go somewhere that was really just five blocks away. (Going to neighborhood potlucks, people learned to never cook anything you had to take in a car.)

Tourists, residents, even the cops found it aggravating to get anywhere — trainee officers had to memorize a street map before they could get off probation. But in the end, most people came to accept it as just another part of life in wonderfully weird Surfland, Oregon, even it meant still getting lost after being in town a decade.

Which was happening to Fuzznut now. Growing darker by the minute, he wasn't completely sure what street he was on. Getting more and more confused, he considered doing the unthinkable: taking off his head so he could get a better look. (He also had a tiny fuzz ball in his right eye, and it was killing him.)

Right then, however, a car came over the hill behind Fuzznut and lit up the street like Christmas. Momentarily blinded by the high beams, Fuzznut turned away and began riding again, letting the car light the way. Normally, he would have been angry that someone was using their high beams in a neighborhood — it was always tourists looking for an address — but he appreciated the gesture.

Or at least he thought he did.

"Hey, you, fuzz-fart!" Fuzznut heard the driver yell. "Get out of the way!"

Now pissed, Fuzznut did exactly the opposite, slowing down to almost a crawl and meandering about the street. Logically, Fuzznut knew this was not a good idea, but this was his town and he'd be damned if any tourist was going to tell him what to do.

"Masc-slut! I am going to run your ass over! I will put fur all over my tires and use your fuzzy head to clean my windshield! Are you listening, fur-hole?!"

Fuzznut was in his zone now. Perfectly spacing himself between the parked cars on the narrow street, he slowed even more, while still managing to miss the puddles that remained from the rain. (Damsels in distress were worth getting wet for, not tourist assholes.)

He could have done it all night, but he knew where he was now, and the turnoff to his street was coming. Besides, as angry as this guy was getting, Fuzznut wasn't completely sure he wouldn't get run over.

Turning left, Fuzznut thought about flipping the driver his middle finger as he drove by, but then remembered he didn't have one amongst his webbed hands. So instead, he just waved as the driver screamed, "You piece of rodent gleek!" and raced on by in a green Mustang.

*****

Thankfully, the rest of the drive home was uneventful, and with it now completely dark, Fuzznut rolled his bicycle past his white van and into his backyard. As he locked his bike up, he peered through the slats in his fence at a bonfire about 100 yards down the beach.

As he watched a young man unpack a huge picnic basket next to the fire, he smiled. Even though he'd sworn off romance in his life, he knew a date when he saw one.

Sitting at the base of the Harrison Bluffs, they were in a popular spot and largely isolated from view, since the houses were about 25 feet above the beach in that area. Had he been a voyeur, Fuzznut surmised he'd have seen more than one young man get his first kiss there – or first something else.

Which of those this young man might have in mind, Fuzznut had no idea. But with the amount of gear the kid had brought – he was unpacking a huge backpack now – he clearly had a major evening planned. Two chairs, a blanket, a small cooler, even a small boom box: within five minutes he had a nicer set-up on the beach than Fuzznut did in his living room. (Although just why the young Casanova had brought along an inflatable building, he could only imagine, though still preferred not to.)

But just as Fuzznut liked his privacy, he tried to respect other people's, as well, and he turned his thoughts to what he'd do for dinner. (He had to admit, some Manhattan clam chowder would be pretty good.) But just as he began to go inside, he heard something that jarred him so thoroughly he pulled his head off just to make sure he'd heard it right.

"*Good evening, I'm Ron Blaine, and I'm happy to sponsor 'Love Lines,' Oregon's favorite song dedication show. And remember, when you're ready to buy a home, now you've got a friendship you can build on.*"

It had come from the boom box on the beach, but that's not what startled Fuzznut. It was the voice: it was the unknown yet still familiar voice from the football game. Smacking his forehead, which he decided would have hurt less had he still been wearing his padded head, he wondered how could he have missed that omnipresent voice?

It was Ron Blaine, home developer and consummate abuser of Portland's airwaves. For more than 30 years Ron Blaine had been advertising on the radio with the same annoying voice and the same annoying tag line: "Now you've got a friendship you can build on."

There must have been something to it; the man had been in business for more than three decades. But as to whether or not friendship had anything to do with it, Fuzznut seriously doubted it. In a recent Internet poll, Ron Blaine's advertisements had not only been voted onto Portland's Top 10 Most Annoying Commercials, they took five of the top six spots. (A mattress saleswoman with a creepy dog took third place.)

Part of what made the ads so horrible was the voice itself: it was nasal, annoying and whiny, made all the more so by its placement up to six times an hour during morning and afternoon drive time. That anyone with such a grating voice could be all over the radio just blew the mind — and produced all kinds of speculation.

Why was he only on the radio? Why didn't he ever go on TV? Why weren't there any pictures of him?

A few people came up with fanciful ideas. Some believed he was a scumbag on the run from the law. While at the other end of the scale he was a mob witness in the government's relocation program. ("Portland's where I'd go," said one radio wonk. "Everybody in New York thinks the country ends at the Hudson River.")

To most people, however, the answer was obvious: he must be hideous, probably from an accident or something or maybe a birth defect. Fuzznut had figured it was probably something really embarrassing, like his lips were shaped like a vagina or something.

Well, so much for that theory, thought Fuzznut, now leaning up against his bicycle in the backyard. He'd seen Ron Blaine at the game, and he didn't look like a mutant at all, although if he was doing business with Shabazz T. Morton he probably was a scumbag — and Poe would want to know.

But as Fuzznut took one more glance down the beach at what seemed to be an increasingly weird date — the inflatable building was gone, but now the young man appeared to have lit his nose on fire — he realized he was tired. His revelation about Ron Blaine could wait until tomorrow, he decided, and with that he went inside, stripped off his clothes and tried to figure out how to mix crabmeat into a Manhattan clam chowder.

Chapter 53
Shabazz

It had taken Shabazz T. Morton forever to get from the lake house to the beach house. Because the south end of East Nelta Lake Road was still flooded, he'd had to go all the way to the north end of the lake and then come back through town. Then, on his way south, there'd been an accident as a minivan pulled out onto the highway and speared a Suburban, which then bounced into a BMW Mini.

Forced to a dead stop in the middle of the accident scene, he heard everyone yammering at the police and he didn't know which of the victims he hated more. There was the idiot in the minivan who decided to text her Crate and Barrel list to her nanny while she drove. Or there was the couple in the Suburban who could have avoided the accident if she hadn't been "looking in his lap," for something while they were doing 45 miles per hour. And finally there were the four hippies from Eugene, who despite having virtually no damage to their vehicle, thought the couple should be arrested because "only having two people in a Suburban was a crime against mother Earth."

Pounding on his steering wheel in frustration, Shabazz's face was as red as it ever got when the traffic finally began to flow again — as did his mouth: "Crate-and-Bare-Whore! Get bent over mini-bar! You two Suburb-verts, get bent somewhere else! And you, duck-mucus! Go back to Eugene and shut your goddamn liberal holes!"

And with that he floored it, trusting that the cops' and rescuers' duties at the accident would keep them from chasing him down. He was right, of course; Surfland only had two cops on duty on most fall nights, and within five minutes he was in the back parking lot of Harrison High School.

As he suspected, it was empty. Even with a community event in the gym tonight, there was no one parked out here, and he knew that would be true tomorrow morning as well. It would make a perfect location for his last money drop with Ron Blaine, something he'd been concerned about since he'd discovered their former meeting spot at the beach house had been compromised.

Smiling at his brilliance and coming wealth, he pulled back onto Highway 101. But within minutes he realized he was about to hit the same traffic jam he'd just come through, now going the other way. Wanting to avoid to traffic (and everyone he'd just pissed off) he turned west onto a side street — and within minutes was lost.

God, how he hated the streets of this stupid town!

Beach Slapped

Thinking to himself that if he couldn't design a city any better than this he'd cut off his own balls (or at the very least the urban planner's), he turned on his high beams and sped down the street. Within a few minutes he had actually managed to find himself back in a spot he recognized.

Looking at his watch, however, he realized that his idiot nephews had likely been at the beach house for at least 10 minutes, and God only knows what stupid thing they might do next. (If Shabazz had to see one more condom, he was going to pull it over Bobby's head and suffocate him; he'd seen it done.)

But just as he was about to floor it, he realized there was a cyclist wearing some kind of furry suit riding in front of him. He dealt with it in his typical manner: "Hey, you fuzz-fart! Get out of the way!" Infuriatingly, it just made the guy go slower.

Now quickly ramping up to maximum hate, Shabazz alternated between thinking things in his head: "I'll bet he does it with his bicycle seat in that costume!" and screaming things out the window: "Masc-slut! I am going to run your ass over!"

But unlike the fresh meat prisoners in the exercise yard and his cowering nephew Joey, not only did his screaming not have any effect, it seemed to make the guy go slower. Now as mad as he had ever been, Shabazz began to seriously debate running the guy over when the cyclist suddenly pulled off to the left.

"You piece of rodent-spooge!" he screamed as he went by, now driving so out of control that only the traction control on the Mustang kept him from plowing right through someone's front-yard collection of plastic flamingos and mermaids.

Fortunately for the citizens of Surfland and their yard ornaments, Shabazz encountered no further difficulties on the backstreets of Surfland or accidents on Highway 101 when he returned to it. And when he finally pulled onto NW Jetty Avenue, he was even relieved to find his nephews had parked at the north end of the street, just like he told them.

But after parking his car behind their truck, he discovered they weren't actually in the cab. For a moment, he thought they might have already gone into the house, but soon he heard whispering in the darkness up ahead.

"Joey, I dare you to touch it."

"I'm not going to touch it."

"That's 'cause you know if you do it'll shoot your balls off."

"It will not, but I'm still not touching it, Bobby."

Not even daring to wonder what they were talking about, Shabazz crept forward another 100 feet or so before he saw what they were talking about: a green Jaguar XKR. He'd stolen at least two of them, and while he knew the alarm wouldn't electrocute anyone — he couldn't be that lucky — he also knew that it didn't belong on this street.

"Goddamn," he said to himself, the vein in his head now starting to throb again. "I hate British cars."

Chapter 54
Julio

Fuzznut wasn't the only one watching Paxton Dell's date unfold. Sitting on the bluffs directly above Dell's fire, Julio Cruz was watching what he had decided was the strangest date he had ever seen — and he'd seen it from the beginning.

It had begun three hours ago, with Julio finding himself parked in the same place he'd been about 24 hours earlier: in front of Paxton Dell's house. Honestly feeling guilty, Julio couldn't believe he was making a habit of this. But he was convinced Paxton Dell was about to complete another drug deal, and he wanted to be there so he would have concrete evidence to tell the police about.

As it was regarding last night, he'd had to lie to the women in his life about what he was doing. "Valeria, I need you to babysit tonight," he told her when she got back from work.

She was not happy: "Why? I was supposed to go to Ryan's house; he's having a 'Batman' marathon." she said. "You said it was OK; his mom's going to be there."

"I didn't know he was showing those movies," he said, looking for an excuse. "You know I don't like you seeing George Clooney in that huge codpiece. It's disgusting."

"Oh, Daddy, no one watches those anymore!" she said, hoping she could save her night. "It's the one with Christian Bale, you know the one where he drives through Chicago all the time."

"The answer is still, 'no;' I have to work on that lake house deck."

"Tonight?" she said, now clearly knowing something wasn't right. "You've been over there for days, and now you're going to work on the top of a house in the dark?"

"I think I know what work I have to do, and that's that," he said, with finality.

"Working on a roof in the dark," she said dismissively as she stormed off to her room. "I'm beginning to think you're Batman."

"And I'm beginning to think you're getting too much like your mother!" he yelled to a door now long closed.

Two hours later he hadn't felt any better about lying to Valeria or making her babysit. He liked that she was spending time with the Norloffs. Besides, anything was better than Paxton Dell.

But ever since the nail salon had bought out the day care center, finding child care in the city had been a nightmare. Both Soledad and Julio were now constantly scrambling to find a babysitter, and a decent pedicure.

But his desire to catch Paxton Dell in the act forced his

guilt aside, and after telling Valeria through her bedroom door he was leaving, he was gone. He was only at Paxton's house for 10 minutes when the boy came racing into his driveway, which seemed to be the only way he ever arrived or left.

Like yesterday, the scene was a weird one. Running into the house, he came back out with two rolls of duct tape and what looked like a pile of sheepskin. Within ten minutes he'd covered both the seats and dashboard. The completed effect looked like a sheep had exploded in his car.

Finished, he ran back inside for about ten minutes only to return wearing what looked like a tuxedo while carrying a backpack and a picnic basket. Climbing into the car, he once again peeled out in the driveway and made his second stop at the grocery store in two days, this time buying something he brought out in a thermal bag and a huge bouquet of flowers.

From there, he went to a house on the north edge of town, where he met a girl Julio recognized from the cheerleading squad. Portia McDonald, was it? Whoever she was, she didn't look the least bit interested in Paxton, the flowers, or at the chariot that awaited her. Indeed, she looked horrified as she sat down in the car, perhaps noticing that Paxton's clothes were covered in the same fuzzy substance as her seat.

Finally, they drove to the end of the dead end street near the jetty, where Paxton parked and began unloading the car. Fully encumbered with a picnic basket, cooler and giant framed backpack, he began making his way down the beach with Portia reluctantly following.

Waiting a couple of minutes, Julio got out of his car and

found a spot among the rocks on the jetty were he could keep watching the strange procession with his binoculars. He wasn't disappointed: Paxton managed to carry all of his goods while kicking crab shells and dead leaves out of Portia's path.

She still did not look impressed.

Her arms crossed, she said not a word as Paxton stopped and unpacked everything from the bag and started a fire. Clearly, he was going to grill whatever he'd bought at the store, although what he was now trying to inflate with his lungs and lips, Julio had no idea.

Noticing that Paxton had picked a spot just below the 45th Street bluff, Julio decided to leave his spot on the jetty and head up there instead. There, he could hide in the bushes where the road ended at the cliffs and watch with his own eyes, instead of having to stare through binoculars all night.

My God, maybe he was Batman, Julio thought, as he climbed back in his truck.

Parking about a block east on SW 45th Street, he arrived at his new spot just as the last peeks of sunlight disappeared, and Paxton finished blowing up what looked to be a six-foot-tall Empire State Building.

Once again, Julio decided Paxton Dell was the strangest person he had ever seen. But as Paxton unpacked a stereo and turned it on to some romantic pop music, Julio suddenly realized that he was feeling strange as well. It was something akin to anger for his daughter, instead of just at Paxton Dell.

Stunned, he found he was mad that Paxton Dell was cheating on his daughter, which of course made no sense because the last thing he wanted was that freaky kid anywhere near his daughter. But there it was: this kid was going to break his daughter's heart.

Now he was even madder at Paxton. Half tempted to go down and tear the kid a new one, he stopped only because he still wanted to send Paxton to jail, as well, for being a drug dealer.

Wondering again just when Paxton might make a move in that direction, he had already decided it wouldn't be tonight when Paxton began suddenly dancing around the fire. Thinking this might be another one of his bizarre signals, Julio looked around to see if a white van was anywhere nearby.

But after another 30 minutes or so the van never came, and Julio realized all Paxton had managed to do was both burn the end of his nose with one flaming marshmallow and burn a hole in his inflatable building with the other. Even as mad as he was at Paxton, it was extremely funny, and Julio had to keep himself from laughing — which is why he was surprised when he heard laughing anyway.

But then he saw the source: Several people gathered at end of the fence on the southern edge of the cliff. Squinting his eyes to help him see better, Julio saw what looked to be six or seven teenagers dressed all in black hiding in another set of bushes. Julio would have missed them entirely had they not been bathed in the glow of three different L.E.D.s on the video camera one was using.

Just how many people were watching Paxton Dell?

Chapter 55
Poe

Six miles north of the spot where Paxton Dell was being surreptitiously watched on and off by ten different people, Jackson Poe and Callista Walker realized they were being watched as well. And Poe was not happy that he'd put them in such a situation — though it was pretty much par for the course since he'd entered the house.

Climbing in the same unlocked door he had last time, he had been through every room, examined every piece of furniture and discovered that all of it was cheap replacement crap. Every board Walter Kauffman had nailed down, every piece of furniture he'd built, every fixture he'd installed was gone, replaced by faux knock offs and cheap look-a-likes, save for the still-inexplicable new stove.

That he had confirmed what Shabazz was up to still didn't tell him why; the economics of destroying what was almost literally a livable work of art just didn't compute. It was driving him crazy, and — he'd just now discovered — to distraction.

"Poe!" Callista said in a voice that was loud but still hushed at the same time. "There's someone out there!"

And there was; three someones in fact. He could hear each of their voices trying as well not to be heard, but failing miserably: "Joey! Get your ass around back and cover the backyard! We're goin' in the front! ... Goddamnit! I don't care if it didn't work in 'Star Wars'! Don't make me kick your ass!"

Less than 30 seconds later came the sound of a key in the door.

Poe used the time to process his options. They could try to go out the way they'd come, but with someone in back they'd have to fight their way out. Or they could stay where they were at the top of the stairs and wait for Shabazz and his boys to walk in the door.

He chose option two.

Poe really hated fighting people.

But a passive responsive didn't mean a defensive one. "Get behind me, out of sight," Poe whispered to Callista. She did, and when Shabazz and Bobby opened the door, all they saw was Poe leaning casually against the wall at the top of the stairs with his hands in his pockets and a giant smile on his face.

"Hello, Cornhuskers!" he said loudly.

In front, Bobby saw Poe first and spoke first, as well. "Cornhuskers are from Nebraska, you Oregon dip-shit."

"Oh, I know, but I figure one ignorant redneck from wheat country is pretty much like another," he said still smiling, but now beginning to look past Bobby at Shabazz, behind and to the left of him. "And you must be Shelton! You know, you really shouldn't leave that vinyl-covered piece-of-Detroit-crap car of yours out where people with taste can slice it up. Some people might start to think you actually know how ugly it is."

Poe knew he was playing a dangerous game, even before he saw Shabazz's face start to turn red. But he also hoped that by going on the offense he'd keep them off balance long enough to figure out just what the hell he was going to do. But even he was surprised by what he did next.

"Now, gentlemen, you see this bulge in my jacket pocket? It is not because I am happy to see you," he said now standing up straighter. "This is a gun, and I'm going to be leaving."

Again, Bobby spoke first. "How do we know that's a real goddamn gun? How stupid do you think we are?"

"There is no possible answer to that question, my wheat-shitting friend," Poe said, now starting to form a plan, hoping desperately that one of them would move to one side or another. "But as to whether or not this is a gun: are you willing to be wrong and get neutered by a .22-caliber bullet?"

By now, Poe could see that Shabazz was finally beginning to breathe again, although the vein on his head looked like it still might explode at any minute. The shock of discovering that all his problems had been caused by one man starting to wear off, Shabazz finally spoke.

"Listen, Union Jack-off, I don't care if you do have a gun, I'm gonna kill you for what you did to my car," he said, and Poe had to concede he sounded like he meant it. "But first I want to know what you did with my mail. Where is it?"

"Oh, that?" Poe said, realizing that his window of opportunity was getting smaller by the minute. "That's at my house," he said, now lying; it was still in his car.

"'Tiberian Shores'? Is that the latest piece of shit you plan to unleash on the planet? What, your car wasn't enough? You've got to spread your shit to other parts of the coast?" That's when Shabazz smiled — and Poe got worried.

Whatever Poe had said, he'd overplayed his hand, and Shabazz knew it. So much for offense.

" Sperm-shine, you don't know shit," Shabazz said, now smiling even bigger. "And now Bobby and I are going to beat you senseless. And when we're done with you, we're going to trash that piece of British shit out front you call a car." And with that, Shabazz fell in line behind Bobby and began walking up the stairs.

It was just the chance Poe had been waiting for.

Launching himself into the air from the top of the stairs, he yelled, "Run!" to Callista just before his body slammed into Bobby. As he'd hoped, his momentum knocked both Bobby and Shabazz to the bottom of the stairs in a jumbled clump of arms and torsos, with the legs still pointed up the stairs.

Pushing himself off them — he put his boots onto Bobby's face for traction and fun — he grabbed Callista's hand as she ran down the stairs and onto Bobby's chest. Not even stopping to look back, they bolted out the door — and ran right into Joey, knocking him to the ground.

Knowing he was about to be grabbed around the legs, Poe figured his plan had just been blown out of the water.

But instead of trying to stop either of them, Joey just stared at Callista.

Poe, taking just a split second to look back into the house, saw that Shabazz and Bobby were still cussing at each other as much as they were getting untangled. But Poe knew that wouldn't last much longer, and having no idea what Joey was doing, Poe jerked Callista's arm and began running for the car.

As they jumped over Joey still lying on the ground, Poe noticed Joey's now-huge eyes never left Callista. And talking clearly to himself, he'd been repeating the same thing ever since Poe knocked him to the ground: "She's alive … Just like Obi-Wan … She's alive … Just like Obi-Wan …"

Now fully sprinting down the street, Poe pulled his car keys from his pocket and remotely unlocked the Jag's doors. As they hopped in the car, Callista asked him if he had any idea what Joey was talking about.

"Unless you were in 'Star Wars' and didn't tell me," he said, clearly out of breath, "I have no idea." And he gunned the engine as they sped away from the curb.

"Speaking of which, you never told me you had a gun!"

"That's because I don't," he said, now pulling out the piece of redwood from Alice's shattered doorframe. "It was still in my pocket from the hospital."

"You bet our lives on a piece of wood?"

"I told you, I've gotten a mother of a splinter from these things …"

Poe let his voice trail off as the car raced past Shabazz's beach house. Bobby was well behind them by now, quickly running to his truck, while Joey remained down in the front yard, still clearly stunned by whatever he'd seen. Shabazz, meanwhile, was unleashing all his anger on his fallen nephew.

"So, what do we do now?" she said, remembering how they'd chased her. "I know they're not just going to give up."

"Yeah, I kind of have to figure that out, but I do know what to do first," and he started pushing the buttons on the steering wheel. In seconds, the CD changer in the trunk had brought up another one of Poe's mysterious musical choices.

This time, though, Poe knew Callista wouldn't bother to ask what it was: "Theme to James Bond, miss?" he asked in his best British accent.

And the car roared off towards Highway 101.

Chapter 56
Joey

Joey couldn't believe it: She wasn't dead.

The girl that he'd left for dead to die in the ocean wasn't dead. If he hadn't been so stunned he would have leaped for joy. Instead, he'd just stared at her, from the time he saw her flying down the stairs like an angel to the moment she looked at him as she sped by in the green car. "She's alive … Just like Obi-Wan …" he said to himself over and over again, becoming happier with every utterance.

It was a testament to his joy that his uncle had to scream at him for a full 30 seconds before he actually heard anything he said. But once Joey did, he recognized his normally disparaging comments were worse than ever.

"What the hell is wrong with you, cow-diarrhea?! They run right into you, and you do nothing?! I should slice off your balls and throw them in the goddamn ocean right now!"

Unlike a lot of his threats, Joey thought this one might be possible; he'd never seen his uncle this mad. So when his brother pulled up with his truck and honked the horn, Joey ran and jumped inside, although he had no idea if that's what his brother really wanted.

And he didn't care.

Barely able to breathe, Joey looked over at his brother who was also letting his breath come in rasps. But whereas Joey was just scared, Bobby was clearly furious.

"You asshole" he yelled at his uncle. "I knew he didn't have a damn gun, but you just had to keep yappin'! You didn't learn shit from James Bond: just kill the son-of-a-bitch!"

Too tired to argue himself, Shabazz shot back: "Just shut up and follow them, catch them, beat them, and bring them back to me so I can do it all again," he said to Bobby. Joey marveled that his uncle seemed to be too tired to even cuss.

Wrong. Again.

"Sheep-gleek! What are you doin' with that goddamn seatbelt?!" he yelled at Joey as he buckled up. "What did I tell you: Scientists say ..." But he never got to finish his sentence, because Bobby suddenly grabbed his seatbelt, buckled it, and sped out in the direction of Highway 101.

Looking in the rearview mirror, Joey could see Bobby's stunt with the seatbelt had it's intended effect: his uncle was still in the deserted street screaming at the top of his lungs as they went around the corner to the east. And he knew it was a stunt; Bobby never wore his seatbelt, either.

"Keep a look out for that green car, Joey," Bobby told him. "I think they're gonna try to make a run down the highway, thinkin' they'll find a cop or somethin'.

"And that's how we're gonna catch 'em, 'cause I don't care how many laws I gotta break to get that bitch. If she thinks she's gettin' between me and my $50,000, she's got another thing comin'."

It was then that Joey realized two things: One, his brother's rage wasn't directed at the man driving the car, it was focused on the woman riding in it. Her failure to die in the ocean had the potential to ruin everything for Bobby.

And two: Joey clearly had no idea what "everything" was. It was the second time today Joey had heard Bobby's $50,000 deal come up, and he had no idea what it meant. He sure wasn't getting any money; he'd just come along for the ride — an expression that was taking on an all-new meaning in the past two minutes.

"There! There's that bitch!" Bobby yelled, and he was right, at least about the location. Sitting at a stoplight just a little over halfway through town, the stair-diving driver and the ghost girl had gambled that they'd find help on Highway 101, and they'd lost. And now, gunning the engine and pressing down on his securely attached "horn cover," Bobby was going to make them pay.

"Be glad you buckled up, little brother, 'cause we're gonna take this Ram right up their ass."

Chapter 57
Poe

Poe had gambled, but he had not lost.

With only two cops on duty on a fall evening, he didn't think he'd find a cop on Highway 101. Chances are, they'd be off busting one of the high school parties somewhere in the woods. (The kids did that a lot when it wasn't raining.)

But he had hoped the public nature of America's most famous scenic highway would give him some protection. He just couldn't see anyone doing anything that stupid in the middle of a federal highway on a Saturday night, even if it was the slow season.

But as he heard the horn blaring and saw the headlights rapidly approaching in his rearview mirror, he realized he'd grossly underestimated Bobby's stupidity. He was going to get a beat-up redneck truck right up the tailpipe of his $100,000 car.

That, and they might get killed.

Gunning the engine, Poe checked both cross streets to make sure no one was coming and then blew through the red light. Bobby was about 100 yards behind him, going right through the same red light, although Poe doubted he'd been as careful.

"You know, it's beginning to piss me off that our friend isn't checking before crossing the street," Poe said, trying to pull Callista back from the edge of terror. "They must not have manners in Kansas."

"I'm beginning to think they don't have traffic laws here," Callista said, still holding onto the armrest with a death grip. "Are we just going to drive until they hire another cop?"

"Absolutely not; I plan to stop well before I turn 50," Poe said, still trying to keep the mood light. The truth was, Poe did have a plan, he just had to get through town to execute it, which was another three miles; unfortunately, that was plenty of time for Bobby to hit and kill any number of things.

The problem was, in a flat-out race, Poe could have left Bobby in the dust without ever getting out of fourth gear. But in the city he was limited by curves, other cars and a genuine desire not to kill anyone, and perversely, it was this last concern that kept him on Highway 101. Because only on Highway 101 did pedestrians on the sidewalks and drivers pulling out from the cross streets expect someone to be speeding by. (Even when there weren't seemingly homicidal maniacs on the loose, it was fairly common.)

But if Poe went onto the side streets, the people there would have no clue what was coming. Expecting nothing more than to be horrified by what phallic arrangements the high school kids could put plastic flamingos into, all it would take was one inattentive driver or pedestrian, and Bobby would kill someone.

So, Poe drove on, in a high-speed dance where he kept Bobby just far enough off his rear while periodically running stoplights and constantly blowing through the speed limit. But his plan was working: just another quarter mile and he'd be out of the city and onto the long stretch of Highway 101 where there was virtually no one. Bobby would be just a memory in less than a minute.

Or he would have been, had not a crowd of kids suddenly filled the crosswalk up ahead on SW 51st Street. "Goddamnit!" Poe yelled as he pounded on his steering wheel. "Why aren't these kids out drinking in the woods?!" Forced to come up with a plan B, Poe slammed on his brakes and quickly turned down SW 45th Street.

"What are we going to do now?" Callista asked, because while she didn't really know the plan, she knew something had gone wrong with it. "They're getting closer."

And they were; turning had slowed Poe down greatly, and now Bobby was just 150 feet from his bumper. Poe now had one more card he could try to play: his car cornered like it was on rails, and the truck did not.

So, speeding up as much as he dared while still scanning the sidewalks and side streets, Poe sped up, and eventually came to a spot where SW 45th Street began to climb the east side of the Harrison Bluffs. Accelerating where he should have been braking, he eventually came screaming to the top of the hill at close to 60 miles per hour. Now, slamming on his brakes again, he spun the wheel hard to the right — and immediately realized he'd made a mistake.

All the cosmic rationalizations he'd made about buying this car were about to bite him in the ass. "There's no karma like car karma," he thought to himself, and it would have been funny, if he hadn't been about to kill them both by rolling his car.

If it hadn't been raining that morning, he might have. But instead of the edge of the tires catching on the asphalt and flipping the car, the rubber just slid and skipped across the street as Poe turned onto SW Jetty Avenue, the automatic stability control and anti-lock brakes trying desperately to get Poe back on course.

For nearly 100 feet flying down the road, Poe knew what it felt like to completely lose control of his car. He'd done this more than once in his Toyota, but in his Jag it was terrifying, and gripping the steering wheel and slamming his foot onto the brakes harder than he could have ever thought possible, he desperately prayed they would survive Plan B.

Finally, they did, and the car rolled to a stop nearly a hundred yards up from the intersection.

"Tell me you planned that," Callista said, her face darkening from white as a sheet.

"Tell me you love sea lions," he replied, the blood finally returning to his face as well.

"That's what I thought," she said, and Poe rolled down the

windows to let some fresh air in.

Finally exhaling, Poe did something Callista had never seen him do: he turned off his CD player. Seeing her stare, Poe said simply, "The sounds of silence aren't just for Simon & Garfunkel."

Starting to move again, Poe looked back in the rearview mirror to see if they'd lost their pursuer. As he'd gone up the hill, Poe could see Bobby falling further and further back, but everything that had just happened would be for nothing if Poe didn't get off this street. And that's when Poe saw the profiled slice of headlight beams starting to crest the hill.

"Oh, shit," Poe said, as he hit the gas pedal, while still keeping an eye in the rearview mirror. But instead of Bobby's truck rounding the turn as it was supposed to, the truck instead kept going. Slowing to be sure, but it never did turn, never did stop.

Now just listening, Poe could hear the sounds of locked brakes and skidding tires, broken only by the sound of the truck sliding west through the same puddles that had just saved his life. Then, he saw people running, at least a half-dozen big guys, all headed east.

And then it was quiet.

"Uh-oh," he said, and he shifted the car into reverse.

Chapter 58
Paxton

Ever the optimist, even Paxton Dell knew he was in the middle of the worst date in history. Briefly fantasizing again about saving Portia aboard an out-of-control 747, he decided that would be easier than trying to make her happy here on the beach.

God knows he had tried.

Riding back on the bus he'd had plenty of time to think. Normally, a three-hour bus ride from the Portland airport, it had taken nearly twice that long when immigration officials pulled the bus over and searched the luggage compartment. As always they found nothing, except for a piece of luggage with 13 smuggled Chihuahuas, enough tranquilizers to kill a horse and 39 bootleg copies of "The Dog Whisperer" on DVD.

But that extra time had allowed him to create the ultimate date: A night on the beach in New York City. (True, he wasn't sure New York City actually had beaches, but he figured they had to be one close. It was on the Atlantic Ocean, wasn't it?) A little Sinatra on the CD player, some grilled seafood like in the nicest restaurants, heck, he even had an inflatable Empire State Building, left over from when King Kong played the Bijou downtown.

The car, however, was still a problem: he had an ugly, white 1992 Sentra, and while the license plate might say, "WYT NYT," he was still frustrated that he wasn't driving a Corvette to pick up his princess, his goddess, his everything. So he pondered: what made a car great, that he could possibly hope to replicate? And then he had it: leather seats. He'd seen Poe's car, it was the nicest in town, and it had beautiful leather seats.

The problem was, Paxton didn't have any leather, save for a funny pair of pants he'd found in his neighbors trash once. (No wonder they threw them out; they didn't have anything to cover the butt.) But he did have sheepskin, from a failed attempt to make his windbreaker into an insulated jacket (For the record, it did look cool when fighter pilots did it to their jackets.)

So he lined his seats and dashboard with sheepskin, using duct tape to hold it down. He figured one animal covering was the same as another.

He'd realized his huge mistake when he'd stopped at the grocery store. Running out with his scallops, jumbo shrimp and flowers, he'd noticed his suit covered with sheep fuzz. Not even the cummerbund he'd stolen from his dad's closet to make his suit look like a tux would make him look cool, now.

By the time he'd gotten to Portia's house, he looked like a horrifying hybrid of that Nuzzle Bear from the TV commercials and Dean Martin. And while at first he was disappointed that Portia had not worn a dress, he was at least relieved that her nice clothes wouldn't share his fate.

That, and she was wearing those tight jeans that still somehow always managed to pooch out in back. Consciously, he always made an effort not to look, but sometimes …

Upon parking at the beach, Paxton carried everything down to the site he'd chosen 20 feet below the fence at the end of SW 45th Street, despite its problems. (It was the clichéd spot everyone expected him to use, and it was a long walk, made harder by his attempts to sweep every errant leaf, crab shell and used condom — a lot of people came here — out of the way.) Portia followed like she'd been here a thousand times and helped him not a bit, and while he'd admit it would have been nice if she had, he was also happy to be a man doing everything for her.

Setting up, Portia just stared out at the ocean with her arms folded as he set out the chairs, the stereo and then got the fire started. Starting to inflate the Empire State Building, he stopped several times to try and engage her in conversation: "It's the biggest building in New York, 'cause, you know, it's a night in New York." Or: "It used to have a big King Kong on it, when I got it at the movie theatre, but I took it off so I could use it for show-and-tell in middle school science." And: "You know, they say Frank Sinatra is the most romantic singer in the world to, well, you know …"

But nothing he said resulted in more than a grunt, and soon Paxton moved on to getting the CD player working, which suddenly refused to operate, no matter how many times he pounded on it. Once again, he was frustrated — and once again, he refused to give up.

Turning his back to Portia, he pulled out his cell phone to make a call on speed dial. Upon finishing, he went back to the CD player, and instead engaged the radio function, which was set to maximum volume from its previous use. (He'd been practicing the Macarena and Electric Slide for tomorrow; he and Portia were going to dance on the dock!) Badly startled, he fell back on his behind before he could turn it down.

"Good evening, I'm Ron Blaine, and I'm happy to sponsor 'Love Lines,' Oregon's favorite song dedication show. And remember, when you're ready to buy a home, now you've got a friendship you can build on."

Turning down the volume, Paxton was happy to hear them play one of his favorite Celine Dion songs. Later on, they'd promised to play Sinatra for him. As one of the most frequent callers — they were number two on his speed dial, after Valeria — they said they'd try to get to it within a half-hour or so.

With the music and the atmosphere finally taken care of, Paxton was ready to get started on dinner. Portia was finally even speaking to him: "Is that a blanket? Give it to me, because I'm frickin' freezing. And when's dinner?" Not exactly the melody of the angels, he conceded, but it was a start — and the clock was ticking.

That Portia's presence here was only because of a bet

didn't bother Paxton at all. Given how horribly everything had gone, it was probably the only reason she'd stayed. But now he was making his amazing garlic shrimp and scallop kabobs. Even people who hated him would let him visit when he promised to make them, although in the future he'd vowed that he would ask not to be seated at the kids' table anymore.

As Paxton served up dinner, Portia finally exposed more than just her nose to the air. Indeed, as she ate, she actually let her whole face show. "This doesn't suck," she said.

She likes it! And entranced by the firelight, Paxton was once again reminded that while she could be a huge bitch, she was absolutely gorgeous.

Now pulling out some unwound coat hangers and marshmallows, Paxton prepared to make some s'mores. In his dreams this is where he'd imagined himself licking the melted treats from her fingers, so he was praying this part of the meal would go as wonderfully as the first.

It was not to be.

First, Love Lines played not Sinatra but the worst song in the history of the world.

"And this one goes out to Paxton and Portia, having a barbeque on the beach, and lifting themselves to all new heights of love. Portia, this one's for you: 'The Wind Beneath My Wings.'"

"Augh!" Paxton cried. "I hate this damn song!"

"Figures you'd hate the most wonderful song ever played," she said, her nose now fully in the air. "Every guy on the football team has sung me this song."

"Oh, sorry, I guess it is a great song …" Paxton said meekly, now returning to the only success he'd found all night: the food. But as the wind filled Bette Midler's wings, it also seemed to fill the fire, and soon his marshmallows had become tiny, sticky torches.

Trying to put out the flames, he waved them quickly through the air. But instead of going out, they simply came off. One flew through the air and landed on the Empire State Building, where it did more damage in two seconds than Kong had done in two different movies. The other landed on his nose.

Dancing about the fire, no matter how much flaming mallow he pulled off, the more the blazing treat seemed determined to hang on. Finally, he managed to get it all off, but not before making his hands and face a sticky mess covered with burned flecks of marshmallow. Coupled with the sheep fuzz still stuck to his clothes, he looked like one of the aliens on Star Trek — the first one, with no money for special effects.

Staring at him with her mouth open, she seemed stunned. Taking her shock for concern, Paxton asked her for help. "Could you get me some ice out of the cooler?"

"Could you get any weirder, boner boy? God, I am in HELL!"

At this point, any normal man would have given up and gone home, and indeed Paxton knew his night was a complete bust. But still, if he could just get that one kiss before the football players tackled him, it would be worth it. One kiss … and maybe it would be the kiss that would change everything. Just one kiss …

Beach Slapped

Paxton lost track of how long his mind held him in his reinforcing circle of hope. It might have been five minutes, or maybe ten, he wasn't sure. But he sure knew when it was over.

"Listen, freak, are you going to kiss me or what? You know you want to, and I figure there is no way in hell I'm getting out of here unless you do," she said, now looking at her watch. "So tell you what, I'm going to just sit here in the sand, back from the coals so you don't light your ass on fire or something, and you can kiss me. And then I can frickin' go home. Got it geek-shit?"

My God! She wanted him to kiss him! His dream was going to come true!

So, getting down on his knees about a foot in front of her, he pursed his lips and leaned forward, ready at last to be her prince.

Which was when a truck fell in her pants.

Chapter 59
Poe

Poe's car was only in reverse about two seconds when he heart the first screams coming from the beach on the other side of the houses. Gunning the engine once again and turning off the traction control, he spun the wheel and executed a perfect sliding turn.

Racing now back to the top of the hill where SW 45th Street and SW Jetty Avenue came together, he looked off to the right towards the top of the cliff but could see nothing. The boys he'd seen racing away from the intersection were now back, all staring over the edge. He was surprised, however, to see Julio Cruz running from the scene.

Weird.

But then, what wasn't? And indeed, it said something that as Poe parked his car just up from Fuzznut's house and ran onto the beach, he saw exactly what he expected: the White brothers' truck nose first in the sand at the bottom of the cliff, totally engulfed in flames. Rushing back to his car, he grabbed his cell phone and called 911, hoping that Pete Polanski would be the one handling the call.

This was going to be hard to explain no matter who arrived: the house, the chase, the wreck, although if it wasn't Pete who came he'd be a lot less forthcoming. It had been a long night, and he didn't need it to be any longer than necessary. Telling Callista to wait in the car — a directive she was happy to take — he ran back to the beach; he had to believe someone had been hurt.

He was not, however, expecting it to be his young mascot friend, Paxton Dell.

Paxton was lying in the sand about 20 feet from the burning truck. Poe had no idea if he'd been injured in the accident, but he figured he wasn't going to live that long anyway, the way the girl standing over him was beating him.

"You son-of-a-bitch! You worthless freak! You almost got me killed!" Portia screamed as she pounded on Paxton's chest. "Oh my God! You can't torture me enough with your 'New Jerk, New Jerk,' theme? Then you have to put me in the middle of a blazing car wreck?!"

Soon, the half-dozen large young men whom he'd seen at the top of the cliff were standing by her side.

Now sitting up on his elbows, Paxton began to speak. "I'm so sorry, I don't know what … I just wanted to –"

"Shut the hell up, boner boy! I hope you know this whole thing is on tape! See that camera right there," she said pointing to one of her football buddies still filming, "he got all of it, and by tomorrow it's going to be on YouTube, and everyone in town — in the world! — will know what a complete loser you are!

"God, I wish you would just die, Paxton!" Now breathing heavily, she finally had to stop and stepped away her victim to address her friends. "OK, guys, I'm done. Turn off the camera and paint him like a skunk. Not that he could look any worse."

As they advanced on him, the look on Paxton's face was one of sheer dread.

"Gentlemen, if I were you I'd get away from him," Poe said, finally having gotten to Paxton. "And before you even think about touching either one of us, just remember I know your principal, I know your parents, and I have a car that I'll make sure blows off your testicles one by one next time you make the walk to the football field."

Whether they believed him or not, Poe wasn't sure, which was fine with him. But it did achieve his goal: gathering up their things and Portia, they began walking back down the beach towards the jetty where they'd left their cars. Mumbling as they went, Poe had a feeling Paxton's problems were going to be waiting for him on Monday no matter what Poe did.

"Thanks, Mr. Poe," Paxton said as Poe gave him a hand up out of the sand. "I think you saved my life."

"Well, everyone needs a hand once in a while; I got saved once when a guy tried to stuff me in my locker in high school."

"Really?"

"Yeah, he was about to lock me in when another football player came by and threw him into the other wall."

"Wow, you must have been really popular."

"No, I was pretty much a geek, and the guy that saved me was just drunk and looking for a fight," Poe said, chuckling as he remembered one of the "highlights" of his freshman year. "My point is, everyone needs help once in a while, even if it is from weird places."

"Yeah, I guess so ..."

Listening to Paxton, he had a feeling the young man's problems went far beyond just tonight. Unfortunately, that was going to have to be a problem for another day.

"Paxton, did you see two guys get out of that truck after the wreck?"

"I think so, you know it all happened so fast ..."

"Just tell me what you saw."

"Well, when the truck came down, the truck's bumper went right into the back of Portia's pants. Not her underwear or anything like that," he said noticing Poe's raised eyebrows. "Just the back part, where her jeans kind of stick out, you know where ... Well, uh, anyway, the truck came down mainly in the fire and just sort of stood there upright, just like it is now."

Taking a moment to look back, the fire in the truck had almost burned itself out. What remained was a smoking chassis, body panels and four tires that the heat had oddly left intact. If anyone had stayed in there, they were certainly dead now.

"So, the truck crashed into the fire and you pushed Portia out of the way?"

"Ha! Don't I wish! That's why she was so mad! She fell back from the truck after the bumper snagged her pants. All

I did was roll out of the way and keep rolling. That's what everyone's going to see on YouTube tomorrow — Paxton Dell: coward."

"Well, maybe it won't be so bad …" Poe said, trying to make him feel better.

"Would you want to be me?" He asked, plaintively. "Have you ever seen that Star Trek episode where there's like a million different universes and in every one things are different?"

"Uh, yeah," Poe said, wondering where this was going.

"Would you want to be me in ANY of them?"

"Yeah, I see your point," Poe said, conceding that even if he put his mind to it, there was probably nothing he could do to help Paxton Dell. But still, he needed to know what happened, so he kept talking.

"After you rolled away, what happened?"

"That's when I saw the two guys in the truck, I think. They were both alive, but I think the guy in the driver's seat was unconscious. He had his head on the steering wheel, even though he was held in place by his seatbelt. They both were."

Looking up at the top of the bluff, Poe could see where the truck had crashed through the wooden fence at the end of SW 45th Street. As slow as he'd seen the truck sliding when it went through the intersection, it was entirely possible that it had basically slid off the cliff with little or no momentum whatsoever. And if they really had been wearing seatbelts, a fall of 20-or-so feet wouldn't necessarily kill them, " … but I wouldn't go buying any lottery tickets," he said to himself, quietly.

"Oh, hey, yeah! How did those lottery tickets I bought you ever turn out, you know for journalism class?"

Oh, great … Time to change the subject. "Hey, Paxton, you said one was unconscious. How did they get out of the truck?"

"Well, as the fire got bigger, the guy that was awake started slapping the guy in the driver's seat, telling him to wake up," Paxton said, his mind now back on his story. "Finally, he did, although the flames were really up against the windshield at that point. It must have been hotter than hell in that truck."

"But then they got out?"

"Yeah, they both got out, kind of staggered around a little bit, and then the guy that had been awake the whole time had the other guy put his arm around his neck and they walked off," he said, now distracted by the emergency personnel that had finally arrived. Thankfully, Pete was leading them.

"Well, Paxton, thanks, you've been a lot of help."

"Yeah, I hope so. I'm glad I could help someone tonight. I don't think Portia will see it that way, though," Paxton said with a sigh.

"Well, just between you and me, Paxton, I think Portia's a bitch," Poe said, and continued on: "Take it from me, you can do a lot better than the meanest person in the universe."

"Oh, I know she's a bitch," he said, now smiling at what he could finally admit to himself. "But definitely not the meanest person in the universe. I think that title goes to the guy that was unconscious in the truck."

"Why's that?"

"Because the whole time that other guy was helping him out of the truck and down the beach, he was cussing him out: 'My forehead's on fire, asshole, 'cause you didn't stop 'em! I can't wait to get home and shove a mini-barbell up your ass!'"

"Oh yeah, that guy was really mean," Paxton said, once again managing a small smile. "Maybe we could set him up with Portia."

Chapter 60
Callista

SUNDAY

People who live in places that are drier than Surfland, Oregon — which is to say most everyone, everywhere — are often incredulous that anyone can live in a place where it rains more than 100 inches a year.

In all fairness they are not without cause. Bushes grow sometimes as much as an inch a day, making yard work a neverending battle. If you don't power-wash your roof at least once a year, moss growth will destroy it, and that's assuming powder post beetles haven't eaten it already. Even age-old axioms like "put your things away," die in the humidity, since putting a pair of wet shoes in a closet usually means they'll mold before you wear them again.

There are plusses, however, and on the morning of November 5, Callista Walker was enjoying one of them. The torrential rains of the past two days had scrubbed the air as clean as any she had ever inhaled. There was not a cloud in the sky and she could see up and down the beach for miles.

To the south there was the jetty, Lenobar Bay and the aquarium on the other side, and to the north Ageya Head and the lighthouse perched on top of it. In between, she could see hundreds of out-of-season tourists already starting to flock to the sand, drawn by the unexpected sun.

The view closer up, however, wasn't quite so spectacular. Because in front of the normal rolling cliffs of the Harrison District and the cute little beach homes perched atop them was the charred remains of the truck that had now pursued her through the streets of Surfland — twice.

This was getting ridiculous.

When Poe had told her to stay in the car last night, she was more than happy to oblige; she was tired. When Poe returned to the car near midnight, she realized she had in fact dozed off in the seat and was more than happy to get back to The Seabiscuit and go to bed.

A night's sleep and a hot shower for both of them later, Poe was back. As always, he was wearing a brightly colored Aloha shirt, his rain jacket and a smile on his face: "How about some coffee before we return to the scene of the crime?" Within five minutes and what Callista recognized as the complete pre-Merle Haggard soundtrack from Monday Night Football, they were in the drive-through at Bendovren Coffee.

"Hey, Cheryl, my usual plus a shot — No, don't give me any crap — one cup of that crap Pete drinks, and a skinny 12-ounce latte, one Splenda. Anything exciting going on?" Poe asked, wondering just how much the town already knew about his night on the beach.

"Well, between the three-car wreck on 101 in the Duver District and the truck flying over the cliff in Harrison, I don't think any of the fire guys or cops have slept in a day," she said, while still managing to steam a quad-shot of espresso. "So, no, pretty much a normal night in Surfland."

"I didn't hear about the wreck," Poe said, glad to hear there wasn't more than the normal chatter about him this morning. "No one seriously hurt, I take it?"

"No, nothing that a little plastic surgery won't fix," she said, with a heavy, fake sigh. "When will these young brides learn to stop 'looking in his lap' while he's driving?"

"Thank you, Cheryl ..." Poe said, as she finished the story and his drinks. Handing her a $20 bill, he told her to keep the change.

Heading back through town to where Poe had parked last night, the daylight revealed to Callista what last night had not: this was the same road where she had ditched her van after the first chase. And when they got out of the car and went down to the beach, she noticed their path took them next to the house where she'd woken up.

Not for the first time, Callista tried to reassemble just how she had gotten out of the water and into someone's backyard. Recognizing the gate helped somewhat; at least now she had a sense of just how far down she'd floated from the jetty. But it still didn't answer just who had plucked her out of the water, let her sleep in their house, made her lunch or why she remembered them smelling like her old teddy bear.

"Hey, Poe!," she called after him, hoping to get some answers. "Whose house is ..." But before she could finish, Poe was out on the beach. With the mailing tube in one hand, and Pete's coffee in the other, he was making his way back to the wreck and Pete Polanski. Still fully outfitted in his turnouts, Pete was wrapping a cable around the frame of the truck so it could be pulled onto a flatbed tow truck.

Although Poe and Pete had spent hours together last night after the accident, neither had really had a chance to talk about the bigger picture. As Callista wrapped her hands around her coffee to keep them warm against the morning chill, Poe unrolled the drawings of Tiberian Shores. And while both men agreed it showed an unholy ugly box — "You know, if we were in Chicago, I could have the designer of that killed," Pete offered — neither of them had any idea just why Shabazz would want a picture of it so badly.

Then, Poe explained everything that had happened since they'd last crossed paths in front of Pete's house. It had been only yesterday, and yet it seemed like an eternity to both of them.

"Pete," Poe said, now remembering the coffee he'd brought for Pete was still in his hand, "have this. You look like crap."

"I've been on scenes for 15 hours," he said, sipping the coffee gingerly. "You're this ugly all the time. My God, does your mother know you wear those shirts everyday?"

"You make it sound like you work for a living," Poe said,

smiling. "Not everyone gets to go to work and see two people who've been living a porn movie in the front seat of their car."

"Don't even ... You know, after four or five of those a year, the thrill really is gone," he said, now taking a longer drink of his coffee. "Besides, I missed the best part. I guess right before I got there some guy screamed at everyone on scene before peeling out. Something about 'duck mucus' and a variety of obscenities I try not to use — much."

"Was this guy driving the world's ugliest Ford Mustang?" Poe asked, now worrying all three of them that Shabazz was very much loose on the streets of Surfland.

"Yeah, now that you mention it, they did say the guy was driving a green car with a cloth top," Pete said. "A giant asshole with a ton of horsepower: not exactly the most comforting thought, is it?"

Callista was the first to respond: "Only if you get used to it."

What alarmed Callista most about everything that was happening was that it had happened before.

Not on this beach, not with these people. But it was all too familiar, and it had been bothering her even as she ran out on the jetty fleeing her pursuers.

She was always running from bullies.

She remembered the first time she'd run from her father and sister. It was when she was 9 years old and they'd been skiing Heavenly at Lake Tahoe.

Well, she'd been skiing. Her father and sister were sitting

in front of a fireplace back at the lodge, he sipping his brandy and she a Perrier, or some over-priced water that came from a hole in the ground.

Skiing alone all day, Callista had met another family on the gondola and brought them back to meet her dad and sister.

They were surrounded by people enraptured by the latest words of the "Liberal Leopard," and couldn't wait for him to pounce on someone else. Having kept court all day in front of the fireplace, he was enjoying being the center of their universe.

"Daddy, this is my new friend, Jackie, and her mommy, Mrs. Jensen," she said, excited to have made new friends. "Can they come with us to dinner? They're alone, too, because her Daddy's in the Army in Korea."

"The Army?" her father asked, clearly winding up. "Is that the same Army that invaded Korea?"

"Excuse me?" Mrs. Jensen said, wondering what this hairy man with a ponytail halfway to his ass was talking about. "Do you mean the Korean War in 1950?"

"Well, that's when you started," he said. "Clearly if your husband's still there, we're not finished." Noticing that he now had everyone's undivided attention, he went on, no longer completely hinged by the facts or reality.

"Do you know how many men have died over there for your husband's sins?" he said, now taking a pronounced sip of his brandy. "Those men would still be alive if it wasn't for invaders like the Army!"

Jackie Jensen and her mom were gone before Callista's

father could continue. And as Callista ran back outside the only laughter that rang louder in her ears than her father's was her sister's.

More than a decade later Arianna was still hanging out in that lodge and still not skiing, preferring instead to spend her time and education humiliating people who had the audacity to not agree with her. Wielding her intelligence like a club, Arianna was as much a bully as her father and probably the reason Callista had kept her athletic interests well away from the mountains.

It also spurred her to do other things: Like have sex with Jerry Dixon.

She'd met Jerry her junior year at USC. He was a year younger than her, probably an inch shorter, and had the annoying habit of playing with his utensils during meals. Even eating pizza, he would use a fork, knife and spoon, usually to build some type of tripod for balancing the salt and pepper shakers.

To say he was not exactly Callista's type was an understatement. But he had two traits that she knew would make her father and sister nuts: He was in ROTC, and he was the youngest captain of the Trojan debate team ever. They had been lab partners in mammalian physiology, and despite his tendency to get bodily fluids on her — the mammals', not his — she was taken with him immediately.

"Jerry, what are you doing next weekend?"

"Well, I've got a test to study …" And he cut himself off as he realized he'd just sent the viscous fluid of a narwhal eye squirting right onto Callista's left breast. "Oh, God, let me clean that up ... or wait, maybe you should ... Oh, no, you look like you're lactating ..."

"Jerry, shut up," Callista said, laying a piece of paper down on her shirt. "I needed to burp a baby here next class, anyway. Come home with me next weekend."

Jerry had never had such an offer in his life and immediately said, "yes." On the seven-hour drive north, Callista told him everything about her father and sister, and just how she was hoping Jerry could take them both apart. "Just tell him you want to serve in Korea," she said.

And so Jerry did, and Callista's father and sister immediately began to pounce on their dinner guest even as the spaghetti and meatballs hit the table. "Those men would still be alive!" her father asserted.

"Actually, Mr. Walker," Jerry said, simultaneously trying to work his spoon and fork into some type of contraption, "that's not true. The rate of casualties in Korea is lower than the number of casualties suffered during normal training exercises."

Callista was thrilled. Too bad they couldn't have all met at Heavenly; Callista had gotten an e-mail once offering her free lodging for life if she could get her sister to stop coming up on weekends.

Not that the future FASCIST, Now! leaders were giving up.

"Well, that may be, but that doesn't excuse all the Koreans we've killed," Callista's father said.

"Oh, yes, Jerry, you can't possibly excuse the number of Korean lives lost working with our military over there," Arianna now chimed in. "Are you going to tell me they would have died in America, too?"

"No, I wouldn't, and those losses are tragic," he said, now attempting to balance a meatball on the back of his freestanding spoon. "But most experts agree that the security the U.S. military has given South Korea has enabled them to become the economic powerhouse they are today, one that has one of the longest average lifespans in the world. On the whole, there's been a lot more lives saved than lost."

For the first time in her life, Callista saw her father and sister speechless. It gave her goose bumps — and a tingling that she was surprised to find went a whole lot deeper than that.

For all she knew Jerry was making this stuff up — she'd have to ask him later — but what she was feeling now was almost orgasmic. No one had ever actually questioned them before, and like most bullies, they had no idea how to respond.

"You clearly have been brain-washed by the military-industrial complex conspiracy!" he cried, his mouth now wide open and his fist pounding on the table. "I am going to have to ask you to leave my hou…"

But that was as far as got, for all his pounding had finally succeeded in toppling Jerry's utensil creation. It wasn't a complicated design, but it was just good enough that the spoon acted like a catapult, one that plugged the mouth of Dr. Emerson Quincy Walker, Ph.D. with one mother of meatball.

Laughing hysterically, it was all Callista could do to grab

Jerry and go running out the door before her father or sister could react again. But when she got them to her van, she didn't head for the front seats, and Jerry Dixon got the best debating prize he would ever earn. For her part, Callista got a twofer: her family had been humiliated, and she learned a move that no one would come close to duplicating until her bizarre encounter with the world's horniest sea lion.

But thinking about the sea lion was rapidly bringing Callista back to the present, and her memories of Jerry humiliating her father and sister grew ever more distant. Recalling the sight of Anderson Cooper finishing what Jerry had started, she smiled a little as she noticed Poe and Pete walking back from where she and Poe had entered the beach, stopping once to pick up something near where the truck had been.

Their public humiliation on basic cable notwithstanding, it bothered her that even though her father and sister had finally gotten what was coming to them, she had never stopped running. The last time she'd left the house she'd been defiant and ultimately vindicated, but she'd still been running away from them.

And it pissed her off.

"Hey, Callista!" Poe called to her across the beach. "Here's your favorite license plate!"

Walking up to him, she could see his hands were full once again. In one was a charred license plate, all the paint gone. But the letters were clear enough: "HYSPLY."

In the other hand was a hair brush and a piece of paper,

folded into quarters.

"Let me guess," Callista said, "It's beach clean-up day."

"Only after criminals with perpetually bad taste in vehicles, let's hope," he said now unfolding the piece of paper. "I found this about 50 feet down the beach among the set of tracks the Whites made when they were limping out of here last night. I have no idea if it means anything; it's just a list of a bunch of numbers, but you never know."

Callista's train of thought was broken when Pete's fire department pager went off. "Oh great," he bemoaned after listening. "So much for getting home; somebody just jackknifed a truck across 101 just north of town."

"Injuries?" Poe asked, knowing that a 'yes' meant a much longer day for his friend.

"No, but it's full of raw sewage from a busted pipe near the bay," he said. "I swear, when are they going to stop feeding those fat German tourists all that rich food? Highway 101 could be closed for hours."

With that, he told Poe and Callista goodbye and headed for his Jeep. Even Pete's fake dog looked tired, although Poe was grateful to see that Pete hadn't gone so far as to put a dog bed in the Jeep.

Stuffing the list in his pocket, Poe and Callista headed back to the Jag. Noticing that he still hung onto the brush in his right hand, Callista decided to start haranguing Poe again; it seemed to make them both feel better.

"Going back to beauty school, Poe?" she asked. "Or is that for you?"

"I snagged this at a friend's house, he forgot it and asked me to bring it to him at work," Poe said, giving her a half-assed smile. "It seemed like a nice break. Running from the bad guys all the time is getting so five minutes ago."

"I know what you mean," she said.

I know exactly what you mean, she thought.

And with that, Callista Walker decided she had run from the bullies in her life for the last time.

Chapter 61
Poe

Leaving the beach, Poe was distracted again.

Thumbing through discs seven and eight, he finally settled on the battle theme from "Toys." It had been a terrible movie — never trust any film whose entire trailer consists of the star yammering in a field — but it was a combative, soaring piece, and it got his brain working quickly.

First of all, there was still something missing with the whole Shabazz deal, although he'd known that for at least the past day. The answer was there; he just couldn't quite get it. Knowing that Rip was still doing some digging into Shabazz's background, he hoped there might be some answers coming soon.

Next was the piece of paper he'd found on the beach. It was a handwritten series of four groups of numbers, three numbers apiece. Written too neatly in a row to not be a list, the only printing on the paper was black-and-gold writing in the lower right-hand corner: "Hays Printing and Office Supply."

One of the White brothers had obviously dropped it. But unless he could puzzle out just what those numbers meant, it was as nebulous as Shabazz's drawings of Tiberian Shores, and just as boring.

But as Poe drove himself and Callista back up SW Jetty and onto SW 45th Street (it was so much nicer turning at 20 miles per hour than three times that), he was mostly distracted by the lie of omission he'd dropped on Callista.

Had he technically lied to her? No. But he had heard her ask whose house they were passing. And he ignored her, because he didn't know what he'd tell her. His vow to maintain Fuzznut's secret would always be paramount, but at some point Callista was going to start figuring things out, and there was only so much his conscience could stand.

Unless it was lying about the car; that was different, he could rationalize that all he needed to. Because someday, he really did plan to tell someone, probably Aly …

"Damn! The plans!" he said to himself, another sign that his head wasn't really all there. He must have left them at Fuzznut's when he went in to get the brush. "I left them at my friend's house."

"Yeah, about that friend …" Callista said, only to get cut off again by one of Poe's exclamations.

"Damnit!" Poe said, grabbing his still-silent cell phone from where he kept it between his legs. "Who the hell sent me a text message?"

"Do you always get this upset at a text message?" Callista asked, trying to lighten Poe's mood while he drove. "Or are you just unfamiliar with the sensation of something vibrating in your crotch? They have toys for that, you know."

Laughing again, Poe was straightforward for once: "No, I just hate text messages. I've never really understood why you can't just call. Like now," he said, hitting one of the numbers on his speed dial. "Now I have to call Rip back ... and he's not answering," Poe said, as he pulled the car into a parking space outside Bo's Crab & Anvil.

After telling Rip to call him back, Poe finally checked the actual message. It said little, but it did portend more was coming: "Call me, got Morton's location — Rip." Checking the time stamp, he found it was more than two hours old.

This gave him a whole other reason to rant — and to hopefully keep from having to answer Callista's questions.

"I hate these things! I swear to God, a century ago, damn near everyone on the Titanic died because all they could do was type out funny little messages on funny little keys because they hadn't invented a way of just talking to people!"

Listening to this, Callista was smart enough to know that the SOS issued by the Titanic had saved hundreds of lives, and she suspected Poe did, too. But he was on a tear, and it seemed to make him feel better, so she let him go.

"So, what do we do now that we all have phones? We go back to typing out funny little messages on funny little keys! It makes no damn sense, especially when you don't even get the message for two hours? You can't even feel the thing vibrate half the time!

"My God, if Jack had texted Rose, neither of them would

have ever gotten off the damn ship!"

Having absolutely no idea now what the movie "Titanic" had to do with texting — Poe didn't really care — he listened as Callista tried to bring the conversation back to planet Earth.

"Couldn't you just set the phone to ring when you get a text?" she offered, searching the car to make sure all the coffee cups were out of reach of Poe's waving arms. "That way you'd know right when you got one."

"Yeah, I could do that," he said. "But then I'd have to admit I need to get them. Which I don't."

"You don't need to, or you don't need to admit it?" she asked.

"The second. I hate the damn things, and I hate to give in," he said, now starting to smile again. "Yes, I know, it's not real mature."

"Well, as long as you're happy," she said, pretending as if she was scolding a 5-year-old. "You don't have to live in the 21st century and text people while driving around in your spaceship car if you don't want to."

"Damn right, because I hate those people, too," he said, now clearly trying to egg her on. "People who text and drive should be shot. Hell, I think people who regularly drive and talk on cell phones should be castrated."

"Yes, I know, you never do anything with your phone and drive. Except for, like, just now, when you got the text," she said, playing along.

"That's true. But you'll notice I always pull over, and that I always keep the phone right here between my legs, so when I answer it I don't have to do all those crazy-assed gymnastics at 60 miles per hour trying to get my phone out of my pants."

"Actually, that makes a lot of sense," she conceded. "Have you always done that?"

"No, Aly made me do it, and it just sort of stuck, even after we broke up," he said, sounding a little more wistful than he intended.

"That, and when I stuck it in my cup holder I was always forgetting it in the car. That really made her crazy."

Quiet for a moment, Poe thumbed down through his call log and punched the redial button for Paxton Dell. He wanted to see how the kid was doing and also to remind him that his homework was still in Poe's car. Once again, Poe had to leave a message when no one answered. (Poe had thought about mentioning it last night, but Paxton seemed to be having a crappy enough night without talking about homework.)

Next, he tried Rip again, but still no one answered.

"Argh!" he yelled, this time letting his hands go so far as to send the hairbrush flying off the dashboard and out of the roofless car. "Well, that's just delightful," he said. "I guess I'll take that as a sign I should just deliver the brush."

"Here?" Callista asked. "What's so urgent that someone needs a hairbrush in a seafood restaurant?"

"Not what, who. Wait here," he said.

As he climbed out of the car, she saw him pick up the brush and then head out onto the pier next to Bo's. And there, as clear as day, was a giant teddy bear shooting T-shirts into the sky.

After waving with both hands at the giant cream-colored teddy bear to signal he'd arrived with the hairbrush, Poe found himself with one pissed off mascot as they both stood behind the dumpster outside Bo's.

"Damn kids," he said grabbing the brush. "They got water all over me, and it's water from the bay. You never know what's in that shit."

"Actually, I think that's exactly what's in it, if that wreck up on Highway 101 means anything," Poe said, once again amazed at his ability to have a normal (OK, semi-normal) conversation with what was to all appearances a giant plush toy. Not that he'd always been so sanguine.

When he'd first started running into Fuzznut's furry alter egos, their private conversations in places like dumpster shelters, bathrooms and dark corners of the mall had made him crazy. For one thing, Poe never knew where he should look to talk; half the time the eyes on Fuzznut's costumes were fake.

"Hey, Poe," Fuzznut told him once, when he was dressed as a neon-green-haired troll. "Stop looking at my chest; you're making me feel like a sorority girl. My eyes are up here, in the hair."

After a while, he'd learned to listen to Fuzznut first, and then look about three inches above where the sounds came from. That usually worked well, except when he wore the giant plastic heads. With the echo in those things, Poe could be speaking to Fuzznut's testicles and he'd never know it.

The Nuzzle Bear costume, however, was pretty

straightforward: Fuzznut saw through the eyes, shot the gun with his mitted fingers and one thumb, and walked on two legs. (The fish costume he'd worn at the Salmon Slapping Festival had been a real bitch in that respect.) It was basically a giant teddy bear that just happened to have a zipper in the back someone could crawl into.

And at the moment, it also had two very wet legs, which Fuzznut was trying hard to brush out. "Bo's just better hope that truck got all the shit first," he said. "This is the second time this week I've had to brush the water out of a furry suit, and I'm getting cramps in my hands."

Knowing it unlikely Fuzznut had jumped in the water to save another woman in distress, he waited to hear how it had happened this time.

"It was that damned T-shirt gun," he said, not forcing Poe to wait more than a few seconds for his answer. "That thing's got to be shooting 300 feet today; maybe it had a bad CO_2 cartridge in it when we tested it, I don't know."

"And this got you wet, how?" Poe asked. "Did you shoot yourself in the bladder and wet yourself?"

"Shut up, Poe, I'm getting to that," he said, now working out another furball, down on his inner right thigh. "My plan was to shoot the shirts from the dock to the back deck, and have the kids catch them. But they keep overshooting the deck and crashing into the water."

"And the kids go get them anyway..." Poe said, now seeing where this was leading.

"Damn right!" Fuzznut said, still keeping his volume

below wandering young ears. "And then they all have to come back and give me a hug, to thank me!"

"Well, you should be happy that so many kids think you're swell," he said. "Hell, you even make teenagers happy, from what I hear."

"Don't even get me started on the teenagers," he said, now almost growling. "I swear, if one more teen comes up and tries to whack me on the head with one of the wooden crab-cracking mallets from inside, I'm going to stuff them in the T-shirt gun. Besides, what the hell are you talking about?"

"Oh, I ran into Paxton Dell last night; he was out there when that truck came rolling off the cliff. Hell, it landed in his campfire," Poe said, laughing a little in spite of himself. "Afterward, despite having the worst date in the history of hormones, he was still thanking me for what you did when you gave that $700 to the boosters."

"That freaky kid with the inflatable building was the mascot?" Fuzznut said, shaking his furry head and glad he'd slept through all of it. "No wonder people think we're all nutballs."

Finally finished brushing out the wet spots in his costume, Fuzznut was ready to go back out. With an unlimited supply of T-shirts, he was ready to shoot again, although he'd decided now to shoot the shirts down the beach; the tide was going out, leaving him more room than he'd had earlier. "Well, thanks for the brush, I suppose now I owe you dinner," Fuzznut said.

"Oh! That reminds me; I finally placed that voice from the football game," he said, his Nuzzle muzzle moving all the while. "You'll never believe it."

"It was James Earl Jones; he does everything," Poe deadpanned.

"Smart-ass. It was Ron Blaine, the 'You've got a friendship you can build on' guy who's on the radio all the time, I'm sure of it," Fuzznut said.

"You're absolutely sure? Isn't he like a mutant, or something," Poe said. "I've always imagined him looking like Two-face in 'The Dark Knight,' only all over."

"It was him, I'm sure of it," I heard it last night when that kid-friend of yours was playing his radio on the beach," Fuzznut said, starting to head back to the dock. "He was listening to that song dedication show; I think he did 'Wind Beneath My Wings.' I almost threw up in my otter head."

Momentarily stunned that Paxton could like what was easily the worst song in the universe, he immediately moved on to more important matters: What was Shabazz T. Morton doing with Ron Blaine? It must have something to do Tiberian Shores, of course; both of them seemed the kind of people to be drawn to something so damned boring.

But before he could think about it any further, he heard Callista calling his name as she ran towards him: "Poe! It's Rip on the phone for you!"

Patting down his pants, he cursed himself: Yep, left the phone in the damn car again. Smiling a little, it still amazed him how well Aly had known him — and apparently still did.

At first, Poe was afraid that Callista would recognize Fuzznut, until he remembered that Fuzznut was in giant bear suit. He spent so much damn time talking to the guy in fuzzy suits he'd forgotten his friend was even in them. Of course, he'd also stopped noticing when Fuzznut was naked, and it occurred to him, again, that he needed to start finding other friends.

But even if Callista had been able to place Fuzznut, by the time she arrived at the dumpster, Fuzznut was already gone, well on his way back to the dock, the flying T-shirts, and too many teenagers let loose on the world with four-inch long mallets. When Callista thrust the phone at him, he was more than ready to take the call.

"Damnit! He's gone!" Poe yelled. "I swear to God!" he said, shaking the phone, "No, I cannot hear you now!"

Quickly pressing Rip's number on the speed dial, he was ready to explode again when Rip's phone sent him straight to voice mail.

"Maybe he'll call back," Callista said quietly, interrupting him. But it wasn't what she said that got his attention. It was what she was doing.

Because as Poe had been bemoaning the current — and literal — disconnect between the marketing world and real world of his cell phone company, Callista had been crouching down on the ground and picking up the wet fuzzballs that Fuzznut had brushed out of his costume. Whereupon she smelled them, and her eyes went wide — before they went back to squinting at Poe.

"OK, Poe," she said in voice he knew would have come sooner or later. "How did a teddy bear save my life?"

Chapter 62
Joey

Joey would never regret saving his brother's life. They were family, and that would always matter.

But when his brother brought his Hays Supply Athletic Club workout bag into the kitchen, he began to wonder if his brother hadn't been serious about shoving a barbell up his ass. Last night had changed Bobby, in more ways than one.

The destruction of his truck had seemed to uncork a reserve of rage that Joey wouldn't have thought existed. His brother had already seemed pissed off all the time; it was hard to believe human organs could stand more stress without rupturing something important.

Joey watched as Bobby walked around the house at a perpetual boil, now two beers in his hands whenever possible. So, as he went to the garage to check out his "new" set of wheels — the old flatbed they'd been driving to the house every night — Joey said absolutely nothing.

Just as he'd done last night, when Bobby's need to finish what he'd started with that woman had nearly gotten them killed. Even as they flew up the hill completely out of control, Joey said nothing and hoped his brother would come to his senses. To the credit of Joey's faith in his brother, Bobby did.

Unfortunately, that faith was more than outstripped by Bobby's misunderstanding of physics; when he finally hit the brakes, there was no chance they were going to stop before going off the cliff. And so they slid, first on asphalt, then on water, and then even on the tossed-aside sweatshirts of a group of young men who were suddenly running for their lives. As they approached the cliff, Joey was fully prepared to die, and he seriously doubted he'd get any second chance like Obi-Wan Kenobi, Captain Kirk, or any of those other people who seemed to die on a regular basis in the movies.

To his surprise, they did slow down enough that the truck's flight through the air wasn't so much a launch as it was a tip over the edge. (He finally understood how the cows felt.) And when they crashed into the fire below, their seatbelts kept them from being injured, although from all the screaming around him, he was pretty sure someone had been killed. (He hadn't heard lungs like that on a woman since his mother discovered their father with the farm's prize Hereford.)

His thrill at being alive quickly turned to horror, however; Bobby was unconscious, his head resting on the steering wheel just inches from rising flames on the other side of the windshield. Realizing now that the entire truck was starting to burn, Joey fought to unbuckle both him and Bobby and get them out of the cab, which seemed like the inside of a furnace.

Somehow, Joey did it, and throwing his brother's arm around his neck, he dragged them both off the beach to the north. Finally regaining coherence, his brother began cussing him out, making a variety of promises about sporting goods equipment, tongue depressors, condoms, and the carrying capacity of his rectum. None of them sounded appealing, yet he dragged his brother on.

Because Bobby had been right about one thing: his forehead really was on fire. Having rested his head on the metal horn cover while unconscious, the heat had left a large, nasty burn right above his eyebrows.

Knowing he had to get water on Bobby's burn while at the same time staying clear of the cops that would inevitably descend on the beach, Joey solved both problems at once. Following a trail of beer bottles and used condoms, he found a now-vacant Jacuzzi in the back of someone's unused beach house, and they both submerged themselves in the water. There, they both waited for an hour before they made the eight-mile walk back to the lake house.

Sodden and sullen, it was not a quick one. Within two miles, Joey's feet had started to blister. Even more painful, however, was his brother.

All the way home Bobby did nothing but talk about revenge and killing the woman that was ruining his life. Back in the kitchen, he continued his verbal assault on a woman Joey prayed he would never see again.

"I tell ya', after I carry out the plan and get my money,

I am gonna buy a new truck, run her over with it, and then drown her again," Bobby said, tossing an empty beer can over his shoulder. "That bitch has given me nothin' but headaches since we saw her."

Unfortunately for Bobby, that wasn't the only thing giving him headaches, a fact that once again stared Joey right in the face as his brother paced about the kitchen.

Bobby's time spent pressed up against the super-heated belt-buckle had left his skin charred all across his forehead. Even worse than where the burn was, however, was what it said — a fact that his uncle had spent all morning reveling in.

"Hey, pussy-face," his uncle said one more time as he returned to the kitchen, now carrying a small paper-wrapped package under his arm. "You know, if you'd just listened to me and not fastened your seatbelt, that burn would be on your stomach, your chest, hell it might even be on your balls. But it sure wouldn't be on your goddamn forehead." Now laughing even harder, his uncle went on as he grabbed his keys and left the house. "Hell, you look like a billboard for a porn shop."

And Joey had to admit his uncle was right. Because burned across Bobby's forehead were the letters, "PUS SY," and while they were all backwards, there was no mistaking the scars left by the middle five letters on Bobby's belt-buckle turned horn cover.

Yes, Joey thought, Bobby literally was a pussy face.

Thinking into the future, Joey realized Bobby's job at Hays Supply was likely over. After all, who would want to even deliver goods to a guy with "pussy" on his head? Tattoos were one thing, even when they were those bizarre Asian things he could never read, but that?

His brother was definitely scarred for life, and unless he could convince the porn shops along I-70 to hire him — always a possibility; he'd frequented all of them — his brother's life had suddenly taken a permanent turn for the worse. Which somehow made him all the scarier.

Oh yeah, Joey thought, I have got to get out of here.

Chapter 63
Poe

"Actually, it was Leon the Lion that saved your life," Poe said to Callista as he backed the car out of the parking space. "You know, the furry guy with the nice biceps on the cereal boxes."

"Poe, no more of your titanic diversions, and I mean that literally," she said.

"No, seriously, when that guy in the bear suit lifted you out of the ocean he was dressed in a furry lion suit," Poe said, now turning the car south on Highway 101. "It was the furballs, wasn't it? They say when it comes to recalling memories, the sense of smell is the most intense."

"Yeah, it was … Uh, where are we going?" she asked. "Town's the other way."

"I need to do some thinking on a nice road somewhere, and East Nelta Lake Road on the other side of the lake is still flooded," he said, as if that explained everything. "So we're going to my other favorite, it's south ..."

"No, no," she said. "You are not distracting me again. That's what you were doing on the beach, wasn't it? You know, when you didn't answer me this morning?"

"Guilty as charged, on both counts," he confessed. "So, you smelled the wet furballs..."

"Yeah, although those were really just the last straw," she said, now staring absently out the window as the car raced down the highway. "I've been getting bits and pieces for days, but when we went down to the beach today, that helped me start putting it all together ..."

"Poe, are you even listening to me?" she said, finally beginning to get fed up as she watched his fingers once again dancing through the CD changer controls on his steering wheel. "Or are you just rhapsodized by your music again?"

Truly apologetic, Poe stopped what he was doing with his fingers. "I'm sorry," he said, "but I just got a hunch; I get a little distracted by those."

"Yeah, I've noticed," she said. "I don't need to secure any valuables do I? If anything goes flying out of this car at this speed, we may not get it back."

Although even as she said it, Poe was pulling onto a side road and stopping.

"I swear, I'll explain everything in a minute," he said. "But first, I need to check something out," and pulling out his phone from between his legs, he hit the button that allowed him Internet access.

Calling up Google as he pulled the note he found on the

beach from his pocket, Poe had to be honest with himself that what he was thinking wasn't so much a hunch as it was an insane long shot. Typing "Hays Printing and Office Supply" into the search window, he confirmed what he had noticed before: the typeface on the paper was black and gold. Nothing inherently weird about that — unless you were in Kansas.

Because as anyone who lives even 20 minutes in Missouri or Kansas knows, black and gold are the colors of the University of Missouri, the century-long rival of the Kansas Jayhawks. And he was hoping that the choice of the much-hated colors would be distinct enough in Hays, Kansas, that the print shop might remember where they had come from.

"Find what you're looking for?" Callista asked him after a minute.

"Yep, that Hays Printing and Office Supply is closed on Sundays," he said, dejectedly, having actually convinced himself that his long shot would actually pay off.

But before he put the phone away, his eye caught the second listing Google had given him: "Hays Supply." And suddenly that charred license plate on the beach began to make a little more sense. Clicking on their number, he was thrilled to find they weren't closed on Sundays and that they did have stationery with black-and-gold lettering.

"Yeah, we got bunches of that from a misprint they did," the employee said. "We only use it in back and for toilet paper. Black and gold will get you killed around here."

Stabbing his Tiger soul in the heart, Poe confirmed that he understood perfectly: "Oh yeah, when we see tigers on Animal

Planet we like to flick pork rinds at the screen!" he said, before changing the subject: "Uh, listen, I was wondering if you could help me out …"

And having won the heart of the employee on the other end of the phone, Poe further explained how his idiot Missouri brother-in-law had written down some numbers on a shopping list, and now he had no idea what it meant. Quickly, the employee confirmed what Poe had hoped, that the numbers were a list, and from the sound of it, a list of locations in the store.

"Let me look in the book to be sure," he said, the sound of his fingers flicking through a heavy notebook easily audible over the phone. "Now, tell me those numbers again," he said, and Poe did.

They revealed a pay-as-you-go cell phone, (aisle 6, shelf 3, section 12) a cheap digital watch, (13•4•9) and some basic copper wiring (24•3•10). The fourth number was a little messier, however (11•5, 3) and it would keep its contents a secret: "He must have written something down wrong; we don't have an aisle 11," the employee said. "But what do you expect from a retard tiger? You know, no offense, but your sister really could have done better."

"Oh, don't I know it, but she's always been a little off," he said, his teeth now grinding together. But having figured out most of the list, Poe could at least get off the phone, and after saying his goodbyes and secretly wishing eternal damnation on the entire state of Kansas, he hung up.

"I am going to burn in Tiger Hell forever," Poe said to

Callista as he put his cell phone back between his legs. "But it will be worth it if I can get any idea what it means," he said, starting the car back up. "I just need to think."

"Not to be a self-centered bitch about this," Callista said, mostly kidding, "but what about me?"

"Oh, don't think I forgot," he said, with his fingers once again manipulating his CD player. "I never forget when it's time for a drive," he said with a smile, and just 10 seconds later they were flying down the road at more than 70 miles per hour.

Chapter 64
Poe

More than anything in the world, driving relaxed Jackson Poe.

More than watching football. More than drinking beer in his favorite chair on a rainy football Sunday or drinking multiple daiquiris on the beach on a sunny Saturday. More than sex, even, which was a good thing, since he hadn't been with anyone since Vivian left.

But that's what Vivian had never understood: more than anything in the world, Poe liked to drive. It relaxed him and enabled him to think clearly like nothing else.

He had always been this way. Even in high school when all he had to take out driving on the farm roads of eastern Boulder County was his beater '75 Celica, he could go out and drive for hours until everything made sense. Relationships, Euclidian geometry, plans for the weekend: there was very little that couldn't be solved by taking a broadly curving 90-degree turn at 50 miles per hour and a straightaway at double that.

There were side effects, of course. He'd been pulled over more times than he could count, and while he could usually talk his way out of them (there were some plusses to being a geek with glasses in a decade-old economy car), he had gotten enough tickets to make insurance fairly expensive in his youth. He also had nearly killed himself several times, which was definitely not a plus to owning a decade-old economy car, no matter how sporty they might look.

And that's why he bought the Jag and continued to rationalize it: without it, he'd probably be dead.

Because when Poe drove, it was like he detached himself into two parts: the thinking part and the responding part. The first enabled him to puzzle things out, and the second to drive the car exceedingly hard on just about any road, which was why a car like his Jag was necessary.

It was critical that the car respond to every move he made instantly and without compromise, and while someone like Vivian would never understand that, it was true.

Designed by people like him for people like him, when Poe got behind the wheel, he wasn't so much driving the car as he was a part of it. And in the entire time he'd driven the car, even on roads like this one that twisted and curved through some 25 miles of canyon out to the town of Ageya River, he'd never worried about taking the car beyond its limits.

Until last night anyway, when he'd nearly sent his car tumbling into a beach cottage and gotten himself and Callista killed. Which was why he owed her the truth, as least as far as he could tell it. "His name is Fuzznut," he said, hoping she'd be content with just that for a name. "He's a mascot, and he saved your life walking home from work."

From there he told her how Fuzznut had found her in the surf, brought her into his home, and then called him to pick her up off the porch. He told her about Fuzznut dressing as a skunk at the game. And he told her how Fuzznut asked about her frequently, although she was never to admit to Fuzznut she knew anything, should she see him again.

Because, he continued, Fuzznut was a hermit and he never went out in public without a costume. And here Poe freely admitted that even he didn't know why that was, and likely never would.

After several minutes of curves and silence, Callista spoke up: "Fuzznut: Is that your name for him, or his?"

"His actually: made sense to me: he's fuzzy much of the time, and he's clearly a nut," he said, laughing affectionately. "It's the only thing he's ever asked me to call him, from the first time we met, which is a story for another day."

But that was only half true.

Yes, the story would wait for another day, but in truth he did know Fuzznut's name: Lane Pruett. He'd read it on Fuzznut's hospital record that very first day they met, when Poe had taken him to the hospital in the Valley. Not that Fuzznut knew that, and Poe planned to keep it that way. Whatever secrets his strange friend wanted to keep, that was OK with him.

"So, let me get this straight," she said calmly, (while still holding onto the arm rest for dear life). "After being chased into the surf by two rednecks from Kansas, molested by a sea lion, and nearly drowned in the ocean, I was rescued from near death by a cereal mascot on his way home from work, only to have him dump me on his porch and call you, a lunatic with a fetish for weird music and driving insanely fast."

"You forgot that he made you some really nice crab cakes," Poe said. "He's never made those for anyone but me."

"And you think that's normal?" she asked him, incredulously.

"No, just Surfland."

Chapter 65
Poe

With the car now taking most every curve at more than 60 miles per hour, Callista was gradually getting used to the feeling of multiple G-forces pressing her body into the seat. It was like a roller coaster ride with more trees — and much stranger music.

"Poe," she said optimistically, hoping his newfound openness would keep going for a few more minutes, "just what is this stuff you keep playing on your CD player?"

"This is the City of Prague Philharmonic performing John Barry's theme from 'Raise the Titanic,'" he said.

"Oh God, 'Titanic' again? Are you serious? You know, I really never pegged you for the Celine Dion type."

"Not 'Titanic,' although I have the Celine Dion-free theme from that, too," he said, now drumming his fingers lightly on the wheel as the road began to finally straighten out. "'Raise the Titanic,' a wonderful book that was made into a terrible movie that just happened to have a killer soundtrack."

"How many soundtracks do you have," she asked, recalling all the many different songs she'd heard in the four days she'd been riding in Poe' car.

"I don't know, really," he said honestly. "I know I've got all 20 discs full in the CD changer in the trunk, and there's like 20, 25 songs on each one …"

"Four hundred soundtracks?" she asked incredulously. "No wonder all your friends think you're a freak."

"And don't forget the Aloha shirts," he said, as he started to slow the car with their approach to the speed zone outside of Ageya River. "I've got dozens of those, too."

"My God, you're as crazy as Fuzznut. Do you ever play anything like actual music?" she asked, recalling his rejection of her favorite CD. (And one which she reminded herself, again, to take out of her jacket when she got back to the B&B.)

"Oh yeah, I've got some of the more traditional music," he said, pulling a CD down from a holder attached to his visor. "As long as it's loud, bombastic and inspirational."

"I know I'm going to regret this," Callista said, "but I'll ask: Why?"

"As long as I could remember, I've thought life should have a soundtrack," he said. "When I was a kid, before there were Walkmans and all those things, I used to hum my own theme songs," he laughed. "When 'Superman' came out, I thought I'd died and gone to heaven; I sung that thing to myself as I mowed the yard for months," he said, as he put the CD in the stereo console.

"So now, I just like to have music playing all the time," he said. "Anytime I see a movie, I listen for the score to see if I'd like it. Not that I have to go to a movie to find songs I like," he finished, turning up the CD player again to a booming track that Callista instantly recognized.

"The '1812 Overture,'" she said. "I love hearing this on the Fourth of July!"

"Most Americans do, some even think it's from when the British burned the White House in the War of 1812," he said, knowingly. "But, really, Tchaikovsky wrote it as a piece to celebrate Russian victory in a completely different war."

"Are you this intelligent about all your music?" she asked, more than a little impressed.

"Nope; I was one of the people who used to think it was written by the British," he said. "I'd play it every time I got pissed off at our government. It made me happy to think of someone burning the White House."

"Why's it in you visor, then?" noticing that this was the first time Poe had played from a CD that wasn't in his changer.

"I don't need to play it near as much," he said, with a big smile on his face, "now that Bush is out of office. That, and I'm just not a huge classical music fan, I guess."

"Surely, you have Wagner's 'Flight of the Valkyries' on there," she said. "That's classical, but it was also in a movie, I think."

"Oh yeah, I got it; it was in 'Apocalypse Now.' It's probably the greatest song ever recorded," he said, but making no effort to shuffle through the songs to get to it. "It's at the end of the disc."

"So, how often do you play that? All the time, I'd guess," Callista said.

"Never, actually," he said. "I've got to be honest: that song always makes me think someone's going to die. Maybe it's a German thing; I've never seen people seem so damn angry when they talk."

Laughing again, Callista was happy to see they'd finally arrived in Ageya River. It wasn't a huge place, but it at least looked like civilization after the last 25 miles in the canyon.

But as Poe had said, the drive had left her feeling relaxed and refreshed — and desperately in need of a bathroom. Wondering how Poe managed to drink all the coffee he did and seemingly never go the bathroom — he was like a TV character that way — she was about to ask Poe to stop when his phone rang.

"Thank God," she said, out of the car before it even stopped moving near a gas station. "Saved by the bell."

Chapter 66
Poe

"Rip, it's about friggin' time," Poe said. "If you send me one more text message ..."

"Oh God," Rip replied, "you're not going off on that damn 'Titanic,' crusade again, are you?"

"Well, crap, Rip," he said somewhat frustrated that he was becoming far too predictable on this subject. "You know how I hate those things. Why can't you just call like a normal non-teenaged person?"

"I was trying to be nice," he said. "I heard you had a late night, and I didn't want to wake you up."

"Uh ... OK. So, now that I'm done being an asshole, tell me where our friend Shabazz has been spending his personal time," Poe said, knowing how lucky he was to have friends that put up with him.

Rip ran through it quickly: Searching all kinds of records, he'd found that one of Shabazz's distant Portland cousins owned the giant grey house with the six-car garage that sat on Nelta Lake, just across and north from Yacht Club park. Poe knew it well: he could see it every time he drove up West Nelta Lake Road. Owned by a noted science-fiction author and professor at Surfland's Anchor College, she'd been in Europe for several months on a book tour.

It was Rip's theory that she didn't even know he was there. "Although he's got to know that can't last forever," the private investigator said, sounding very proud of himself.

"Why's that?" Poe asked. "Let me guess: you hacked into the Lufthansa database and discovered she's coming home today."

"No jackass, that would be illegal, mostly …" he said cryptically. "I checked her website. She's got a speaking engagement tonight, November 5, at Powell's Bookstore" now fully giving Poe the crap that he deserved.

"If you ever decide to start texting and want to save money," Rip chided, "that's 'POWelllllllllls,' 'Eee'-'Leh'-'Vehn'-'Dash'-'Five.'"

"You're hilarious," he said, conceding that Rip had the comedic high ground. "Too bad you still have to steal my shirts to have any fashion sense," he continued, now trying to get back the upper hand in their war of words.

"Don't you wish; you copied me and Magnum, just remember that," he said. "Anyway, she's speaking in Portland tonight and tomorrow afternoon. So, if he really is there without her permission, he's got to be out of there by tomorrow night, at the latest."

That suited Poe just fine; the apparent deadline gave him

ample time to talk to Pete and then have both of them explain the whole mess to the police.

"Well, it looks like I may have to send the local law enforcement authorities to pay Mr. Morton a house call," Poe said, as Callista returned from the bathroom.

God, Poe thought, it felt good to finally be able to put this mess in the past, even if he still didn't quite understand everything. Whatever; better the police get chased through the streets than him and Callista.

"Anything else I should know?" Poe asked to wrap things up. "Any more websites I should be checking?"

"Well, no," Rip said, "But I did find out some more background on Morton's childhood. I got someone to crack open his juvie file."

"I thought those were legally sealed," Poe said.

"They are, but when I promised someone a personal escort around Colter County in a professionally driven Jaguar XKR Convertible, they decided a little peek couldn't hurt," he said, with a smile Poe could virtually hear. "Kansas must really suck."

"You have no idea," Poe said. "Now tell me what you learned after prostituting me out."

"I don't know if it means anything," Rip said, "but it is kind of interesting …"

Ten minutes later, Poe was in shock, stunned by his own stupidity. "Holy shit," he said. "I am the biggest idiot in the world.

"It's all about the stoves," he said. "He's going to take out the whole block."

"What?" Callista said, more alarmed by Poe's suddenly changed demeanor than anything she'd been able to make sense of. "What do you mean, 'he's going to take out the whole block'?"

"Tiberian Shores: It's not an ugly box he plans to build somewhere else!" Poe exclaimed. "He plans to build it in Surfland, right there where the houses are!"

"What do the stoves have to do with it?"

"They're defective; all he's got to do is make one of them blow, and the rest of the block will go with them as the gas pressure surges," he said. "That's why he took everything out of them: he gets to sell all the stuff made of redwood, and then make the insurance claim like it's all still in there."

"Are you sure? That guy doesn't seem bright enough to pull off all of this," she asked, hopefully.

"He doesn't have to be. All he has to know is how to blow things up, and Ron Blaine will do the rest."

"Who the hell is Ron Blaine?" Callista asked, now thoroughly confused.

"Buy satellite radio and pray you never find out," he said, knowing that didn't really help. But it was all coming together now, and even the supplies from Hays Supply made sense. But trying not to be a complete ass, he rewound his train of thought and explained everything to Callista.

"You really think he can make a trigger out of just those three things?" Callista asked.

"You heard Rip: he would have gotten away with it in Kansas if he could have kept his mouth shut, and you've heard Shabazz's mouth."

From his initial shock, Poe was finally starting to calm down. The circumstances had certainly changed, but one thing had not: he still had time to get back to Pete and get the police involved, which was all the more critical now. Hoping to give Pete a heads-up, however, he tried calling his friend, only to get sent direct to voice mail. Figuring Pete must still be on the accident scene, Poe resolved to try him again just as soon as they got to the other end of the canyon road.

Glad that Poe seemed himself again — he drove wildly enough even when he wasn't crazed — Callista commented on what looked like the end of their adventure.

"Well, I will surely mark November 5, 2010, as a day to remember. I solved a mystery: What the hell Jackson Poe listens to. Oh, and that whole homicidal-arsonist thing, too," she said, glad she and Poe could finally get back to the banter that had made the last three days so much fun, in spite of it all.

"And how about you? Do you want me to put this in your phone?" she said, to Poe's now smiling face. "Or, wait! I could text it to you: 'Eee'-'Leh'-'Vehn'-'Dash'-'Five.'"

But just as soon as she said it, she knew something was wrong. Poe's face fell, and almost instantly he slammed on the brakes and began talking to himself as much as Callista.

"No, no, no, no …" he said worriedly, as he pulled the Hays Supply list from his pocket and unfolded it. "Oh, God, it's not bad handwriting, at all! It's a date: '11•5, 3.'

"Today, 3 p.m."

Tossing Callista his cell phone, he told her to keep trying Pete until they got out of cell phone range. She managed to connect with his voice mail one more time before they were back in the canyon, but that was all. Placing the phone back into Poe's lap, she then held on for dear life. Because if the trip out had been hair-raising, it was nothing compared to the speeds they were doing now.

Maybe it was the music.

Poe had cranked the 1812 Overture on the stereo, now an anthem for his efforts to keep the car on the road. What he was racing to save was far more important to him than the White House.

Chapter 67
Shabazz

The first time Shabazz T. Morton met with his parole officer after he was released from prison, the officer commented on how well Morton had adapted to life behind bars. After Shabazz's previous history of outbursts with African-Americans, figures of authority and, indeed, just about any living thing above a banana slug, the officer was stunned that Morton hadn't been violated by more than a parking meter in downtown Portland.

Hearing this observation, Shabazz did what came naturally lately for the last 10 years when surrounded by authority figures: he smiled, shut up, and bided his time until he could leave and go unleash his rage on someone else.

The truth was, however, that everything Shabazz needed to know about keeping his secrets around people who could screw up his life, he'd learned long ago after blowing up that Toyota in downtown Topeka. The lesson was simple: shut up.

Because if he'd done that after his "legendary crime," he'd

never have been caught, been thousands of dollars richer, and would never have been deported to the world of perpetual mold and mildew.

When he'd bought the used car in Topeka, it was loaded. But by the time he parked it just a few blocks from the dealership a few days later, it was pretty much a gutted shell, Shabazz having sold off everything inside of any possible value. The stereo, the seats, the mirrors: they all brought him money, with even the gear-shift knob putting $25 in his pocket when he convinced one of the blind kids in his class that it was actually burled walnut.

So, when he'd set the car ablaze with a self-designed combination of wires, his cell phone and his dad's Casio watch, there really wasn't much left to destroy. But the insurance company didn't know that, and when it was revealed that a nearby fire hydrant had been turned off to keep homeless people from using it as a long-distance shower, the perfect crime was complete.

Young Shelton was so proud of himself. Having made the trigger out of common household items, there was absolutely nothing to indicate foul play. He'd even selected the site on purpose. Having heard on the news that the city had turned off one of the fire hydrants when a derelict accidentally blew out both his eyeballs standing too close to the makeshift shower, he knew by the time any water actually hit his burning wreck, there'd be nothing left but a shell.

He was so proud, in fact, he had to tell everybody in his remedial math class — and one of them ratted him out. (It had never occurred to him that blind kids might actually use their ears more than most people.) Within days, he was busted, sent to juvenile detention and sentenced to multiple visits with a psychologist. They were convinced that Shelton was well on the way to becoming a sociopathic firebug, never a good idea in a state with millions of acres of dried wheat.

But instead, Shabazz came clean to his psychologist, who instead recommended that Shelton be sent far away. Clearly, he needed a change of environment, and his parents were more than happy to provide him one. His entire juvenile file legally sealed, he walked onto the plane, the "legend" of his crime already starting to grow.

In truth, he was glad to be away from boring-ass Kansas, his horny brother, and dozens of terrified cows. Getting away gave him a chance to make a clean start — one that started with vowing to never again tell anyone what the hell he was really up to.

That's why as he drove through the streets of Surfland on a sunny Sunday morning, he wasn't terribly concerned about what had happened the previous night. Certainly, he'd taken precautions; the fact that he'd put the gun from his brother in the car was proof of that. He couldn't say he was happy it was there — not after the exploding raccoon incident — but should he run into any more problems, he wouldn't hesitate to use it.

But neither the girl nor the man who was with her knew anything, really. Sure, they had Shabazz's drawings, and if he could, he still planned to get those back. But right after everyone had gone racing away last night, he'd checked one more time to make sure his timing contraption was still in place behind the stove. It was, and even if someone could identify the pieces after the blaze, they'd never be able to track the immolated parts all the way back to Kansas and then back to him.

Further, no one but Bobby and Ron Blaine knew his entire plan, and they had as much to lose as he did. Knowing neither one of them would talk, he was actually fairly relaxed as he drove to the high school to meet Ron and pick up his last payment of $20,000. He'd been getting payments for months, in various amounts, but this one was special: it brought him right up to a cool million.

Soon it would be over, and when the houses went up, Shabazz would be sitting nearly 100 miles away in a coffee shop talking quietly with his parole officer as he did every Sunday afternoon. It was a meeting time he'd kept for months, and while his parole officer didn't usually meet with his charges on weekends, he was just glad Shabazz had chosen a county with fewer than one percent African-Americans. It was a nice calm arrangement for the officer — and the perfect alibi for Shabazz.

Shabazz hadn't been this pleased with himself since Topeka; he had to say something, to someone.

He decided to cuss out an old woman in a wheelchair on the way home. "Hey! Wrinkle-wheels! You're in the way of a millionaire!" he screamed out the window as she crossed Highway 101 at West Lake Nelta Road. "How can anyone so close to dying go so damn slow?!"

Indeed, he was actually glad the direct road to the house down East Nelta Lake Road was still flooded. He even chose the most congested route home; it gave him even more chances to scream at people. Taking care there were no cops around, he yelled obscenities to at least five different people before he hit the northern edge of the city.

He'd never felt so good.

Chapter 68
Bobby

Bobby had never felt so terrible.

Looking in the mirror at his PUSSY scar for what seemed like the hundredth time, Bobby wasn't sure it was worth $50,000. Hell, he wasn't sure it was worth a million dollars, but he had to admit getting paid $50,000 just to sit on a street and make a phone call so his uncle could blow up a whole block of houses was a pretty sweet deal.

Truth was, he'd have probably done it for free, especially after his uncle told him it would happen fast enough for him to watch all 18 go up before the fire department got there. After a lifetime spent blowing up spiders and toilets with M-80s in his backyard, watching 18 houses go up would probably give him a hard-on.

Hell, as many problems as that old bitch in the middle house had caused him, he'd have paid to blow that one up. And what if that chick that wouldn't die could be in there as well?

Hell, he'd give up all $50,000 for that.

Thanks to her, he'd lost his truck, his horn cover, and most of the epidermis on his forehead. He'd pay real money to meet her again, and he started to fantasize about just how he could make that happen. Maybe if he waited at the beach: he could attack her while she was surfing. Of course, having no idea how to swim, that could be a problem ...

Still thinking, such as it were, he walked back into the kitchen and began digging through the refrigerator for a couple more beers; he'd found if he doubled his intake it dulled the pain in his head. He briefly noted he was down to his last two Milwaukee's Best. But at that point he was so thoroughly buzzed he immediately got distracted and went mindlessly back to his earlier task of finally packing up all his stuff, and more. (He'd decided the microwave would fit quite nicely into his athletic bag.) But before he could even begin, Joey walked in and began to open his mouth.

"Before you start, asshole: Is this about space men, dark forces, dead people who aren't dead or any of that other shit?" he asked. "Because it's your fault that bitch got me this burn on my head, and nothing you say or do is going to keep me from someday killing you in your sleep."

Turning back to the problem of how to actually get the microwave in the bag, he was moving the four mini-barbells into the outer zip-up pockets when he noticed Joey was still standing there. "You know, ass-wipe," he said dismissively, "I meant it. You may be my brother, but I hate your guts."

"I know," Joey said. "That's why I think I'm going to just

leave. I think it would be …"

But Joey never got a chance to finish. His brother had knocked him to the ground with a flying barbell.

Chapter 69
Paxton

Sitting at the edge of Yacht Club Park high over Nelta Lake, Paxton lamented the date that could have been as he stared at the water 150 yards below. And while he had finally admitted to himself that Portia McDonald was indeed a raging bitch, he knew after word about last night got out, no girl in school would be doing the "Macarena," the "Electric Slide," or anything else dockside with him for a very long time.

Slumping down against his car, he began to cheer up, somewhat, when he saw Valeria. He had called her, hoping she could do something — anything — to keep him from trying to crawl into the bowels of a crab boat and shipping off to Alaska. (He'd always thought the story an urban myth, but lately he was really hoping it wasn't.)

"Hey there, Valeria. So, how bad is it?" he asked, knowing she'd been in church this morning with a lot of people from school.

"Well, let's just say I wouldn't Google 'Beach Slapped in

Oregon' and 'YouTube' anytime soon," she said, as nicely as she could.

"Oh, God, the whole accident is really on there?"

"The whole date, actually," she said, dreading that she couldn't spare him the truth. "It's about 45 minutes long, from what I've heard."

"Please, kill me now," he cried, as he slumped his head up against Valeria's shoulder, and lying there, he actually sobbed.

Finally, he stopped, and when he looked up he saw that she had been crying, too. And for the first time, he noticed how beautiful she really was, as she brushed the hair out of his face and used the tip of her fingers to dry both of their tears.

Smiling a little now, he began to blush. "You don't think anyone's filming this," he said quietly, trying to make a joke because he had no idea what to do next, "do you?"

"Nope," she said, now seeing the same things he was. "Not a lens in sight," and both of them rested their foreheads against the other.

Naturally, she was wrong.

Chapter 70
Julio

Julio Cruz had a perfect view of his daughter and Paxton Dell through his binoculars. Watching them from the lakeside roof-top deck he'd been working on all week, the binoculars got him close enough to actually read lips.

Once again, he had not been planning to spy on his daughter.

Although the whole family had gone to church together, within five minutes of Reverend Shields last words, they had all split up. Julio was off to work on the deck, Soledad and the two youngest girls were off to Bo's to try and catch free flying T-shirts from Nuzzle Bear — just who the hell that was he had no idea — and Valeria was off to work, he presumed. She always worked the busiest days at Bo's.

But now he could see that wasn't true at all. She was with Paxton Dell. How she had found him here, he had no idea; maybe she had spotted his car alongside West Nelta Lake Road.

That was what had first captured Julio's attention.

Taking advantage of the clearest day he'd seen in weeks, he'd brought his new binoculars up with his work tools so he could take in a view he'd never find anywhere else. And as he swept from north to south, east to west, he could see half the city.

There was the giant house along the lake, (their dock looked pretty worn, maybe he'd make an offer). The still-flooded East Nelta Lake Road, although the water over the road finally seemed to be getting shallower. And a very familiar-looking white 1992 Nissan Sentra, parked right next to West Nelta Lake Road at the top of the park.

And with it his daughter, who was now actually touching heads with Paxton Dell.

Having seen what had happened to Paxton last night, he actually felt sorry for him — though not because he still had some sheep fuzz on his shoes. But because after all the kid had gone thought last night, it was a shame the police hadn't just arrested him then, because Julio was calling them now.

Chapter 71
Callista

As Poe roared back onto Highway 101, Callista looked at her watch: they'd covered the 25 miles in 24 minutes, and it would have been faster had they not been caught behind a manure truck. Between the delay and the smell, Callista thought Poe might just explode in the car.

Now headed north towards Surfland, she tried with her phone what hadn't worked on Poe's: contacting Pete Polanski. But it still went straight to voice mail, and both she and Poe began to wonder just how bad the sewage truck accident had been.

"Maybe he's got his phone off," she suggested.

"Do you know any volunteer firemen who leave their phones off?"

"I don't know any volunteer firemen," she said, meekly.

"Unexpected phone calls are the same thing to Pete Polanski as they are to high-priced Thai prostitutes: pure gold," he said. "Believe me, that man doesn't know how to turn his phone off."

"I don't know any Thai prostitutes, high-priced or otherwise," she said, now looking at him strangely.

"Oh, neither do I," he said, the grin never leaving his face. "Screw it, I know where the accident is, let's just go find him."

As they approached the outskirts of Surfland, they were easily doing 100 miles per hour, still led by Tchaikovsky's cannons.

Chapter 72
Shabazz

Shabazz's good mood had disappeared along with his luxury of time.

Still a mile short of the north end of East Nelta Lake Road, he ran into the traffic backup left by the jackknifed sewage truck. Then, behind him, the driver of a 36-foot Winnesaurus Lux Macrocruiser tried to do a three-point turn in the middle of the road, stopping completely when someone yelled, "God damnit, you land-yacht-driving prick!"

It was not Shabazz, however, which was a testament to just how bad things were getting.

Getting more irate by the minute, Shabazz looked at his watch again and realized he'd lost nearly 45 minutes time. Much later, and he'd never make it to his appointment with his parole officer on time.

So, sparing the RV driver his thoughts — they started with "Winne-bung-hole" — Shabazz pulled over onto the right-hand shoulder and drove the nearly quarter mile up to the northern end of West Nelta Lake Road at close to 45 miles per hour. He cursed everyone he passed, with exception of the cop on the corner, who he immediately slowed down to pass.

Not daring to cuss out anyone that had any kind of flashing lights on top of their vehicle, Shabazz instead flipped him the bird below the dashboard (it just made him feel better). And once he was out of the cop's sight, he started speeding south on West Nelta Lake Road.

His only choice now was to go the south end of the lake and try and take the Mustang through still flooded East Nelta Lake Road. But with the car's ground clearance only a few inches, he knew he ran the very real chance of drowning the engine. "God!" he screamed, as he began to pass Yacht Club Park. "How I hate this flooded shit-hole of a tow…" But he never finished because he suddenly found himself lined up to plow into a little white car parked on the side of the road.

Slamming on the brakes and slowing down, he was about to unleash another filth-laced tirade when he realized he could see his house across the lake from the park. And as he slowed and looked further, he decided to drive down to the dock at the park.

His salvation was at hand.

Tied to a private dock next to the park was a small skiff. To a man used to stealing speedboats from crowded yacht clubs, hot-wiring an outboard motor next to an empty vacation home was a piece of cake.

Taking care that no one was looking — he saw only two kids sitting at the top of the park, and they looked far more interested in each other — he put the $20,000 in the trunk and walked down to the boat. One minute later he'd sliced the rope holding the boat to the dock, and two minutes later the wind and water were racing over the bow.

Three minutes after that, he was pulling up to his own dock.

Chapter 73
Poe

By the time Poe had turned right onto West Nelta Lake Road to avoid the city traffic, he'd been doing a rough approximation of the speed limit for more than three miles. As much as he was in a hurry, the only person he planed to maim today was Shabazz T. Morton.

Once again passing the mayor's house, he saw she was raking more leaves, but this time Poe did not bother to say hello. Hoping to find Pete home, he did slow as he passed his house, but not seeing the red Jeep out front, Poe gunned the engine again. As he passed beneath the parabolic mirror at the top of hill, Poe sped up as the road curved north, convinced Pete was still at the accident scene.

Mindful of cross traffic, he slowed again as he passed Yacht Club Park, and was happily surprised to see Paxton Dell sitting near his car with a girl. They appeared very serious. "Dude, good for you!" he said, mainly to himself. "Get past ol' what's-her-name."

Callista, of course, gave him another one of her looks. But before he could explain himself, he suddenly discovered Shabazz's green Mustang parked near the lake.

"I'll be damned," he said. But this time Callista needed no deciphering; she'd seen it, too. They immediately drove down to the Mustang and exited the Jag. They were wary that Shabazz might still be around, but quickly realized he was nowhere to be found. A brief look around the area, however, revealed the cut rope and gave Poe a pretty good idea of just where Shabazz had gone.

"Callista," he said tossing her the keys to the Jag. "I'm going to wait here."

"I must have missed something," she said. "How did I miss the part where you went insane?"

"See that big gray house across the lake over there?" he asked, now pointing northeast. "That's where Shabazz is. For some reason he stole a boat, but if his car's still here I've got to believe he's coming back."

"And you're going to just take him out when he gets here?" she asked incredulously. "Have you lost your mind?"

"A long time ago, actually, but as related to this? No," he said, still looking at the lake house. "I'm going to wait here in the bushes while you go up the road and get Pete, since he apparently has no interest in high-end Thai prostitutes."

Rolling her eyes, Callista still wasn't convinced. "What if he comes back before I get back?"

"I'll just wait, and if he goes anywhere, I can follow him in

Paxton's car," he said, genuinely having no desire to deal with Shabazz again. "In any case, he won't be able to burn down all those houses."

"Now, go," he told her, pointing at the Jag.

Sliding behind the wheel, she looked at Poe like he'd just given her the controls to a spaceship. He appreciated the look; he'd had it the day he picked it up at the dealer.

"It's just a normal car," he said. "Accelerate, brake, clutch, shift: you know, all the stuff you ignored in driver's ed."

Starting the car, she let the engine purr for a moment, before she finally began to smile. "Well, then," she said, "let's actually do something normal for once." And before he could do anything she'd ejected the classical music CD and slipped in one she'd apparently had in her pocket. After handing him his own CD, she cranked up the stereo and hit the gas. Poe could barely hear her yell as she drove out of the park: "I'll be right back!"

Smiling as he watched her turn north onto West Nelta Lake Road, he found he was talking to himself again: "Oh well, at least it's the Beatles."

Chapter 74
Shabazz

Although running the shallow-drafted skiff across the lake had been a bit of a balancing act, Shabazz managed to do it without capsizing. Yes, he had thoroughly soaked feet from all the water that had settled in the bottom of the boat. But at least he was here, and once he got the $980,000 still up at the house packed up, he knew he could get back to his car and out of this watery hell of a town.

The plan was simple: Bobby would blow up the houses with a phone call while Shabazz was having coffee with his parole officer. Then, Bobby and Joey would spent the next 48 hours moving the redwood out of the garage to a storage area while Shabazz "grieved" in Portland over the loss of his property. By the time his distant cousin the science-fiction writer got home from Paris, or some damn place in Texas, his and his nephew's presence in Surfland would be just a memory.

And it couldn't happen a moment too soon. Because as Shabazz walked into the kitchen carrying his stacks of bills from his bedroom, he found his now perpetually drunk nephew standing over Joey. Bobby was waving a barbell with one hand, holding a beer with another, and screaming with what seemed like at least three lungs.

"You want to leave? You ungrateful shit!" he yelled. "I bring you all the way out here, you scar me for life, and now you want to just walk away?

"Screw you, you ain't done yet. Or did you forget that?"

Secretly, Shabazz was impressed; that kind of volume usually made him go blind in his left eye. But there was still work to be done, and his trip across the lake had made him realize his plan needed a couple of changes.

"Pussy-face!" he screamed, now knowing that was his favorite insult ever. "You and your brother get over here! We got work to do!"

As they both walked over to the table, it was clear to Shabazz that neither of his cousins had ever seen so much cash in one place. There were nearly 100 stacks of $100 bills in $10,000 increments. Joey looked fascinated, while Bobby seemed nearly on the point of drooling.

"Which $50,000 is mine?" he asked, already spending the money in his head.

"None of it. Not one damn dime until you make that call and get all that shit moved out of the garage," he said. "And then we'll meet, just like we planned, at the Popeye's at exit 278 on I-5."

"I told you, I ain't gonna eat any of that mutant KFC bird-shit!" Bobby yelled.

"Cock-grease! It's Popeye's! There are no goddamn mutant birds!"

"Well, good! I guess I can meet you inside there," he said. "You know how I like fried chicken when they use real birds. The grease keeps my hands from gettin' all scaly."

"Not inside," Shabazz reminded him. "They still keep my picture behind the counter in that place. I'll just give you the money in the parking lot and you can do whatever the hell you want with it on your way back to Dundernuts, Kansas, or wherever the hell it is you're going."

Placated for the moment by the thought of fried chicken (Surfland's choices sucked), Shabazz saw Bobby go right back to being furious with what Shabazz did next. Just as he knew he would, when he started tearing open Bobby's condoms.

"What the hell are you doing?" Bobby screamed. "Those are limited editions! You can't open the damn package!"

"We're going to finally put this Hays Supply shit to use," Shabazz said, now tearing open even more packages.

"Those are mine, damnit!"

"Listen, rooster-spew, I paid for this shit. And now I'm going to use it," he said, virtually daring Bobby to question him again. "Now, start putting those stacks of dollar bills into the condoms, and then stack them in that athletic bag."

The wind and the water of the boat ride had reminded Shabazz of a basic tenet of boating: even stuff inside the boat could get really wet. One minute on the lake had reminded of that, and he realized he'd better do something to keep his bills from getting soaked and flying across the lake.

"I can't believe yer tearin' up my genuine Hays Supply condoms for this!" Bobby complained. "They ain't even going to fit around those stacks!"

"Listen, clit-lips," Shabazz said, liking that name almost as much as Pussy-face. "First of all, these are just normal condoms, or didn't you notice there was nothing written on the packages you just opened?"

Taking special joy at Bobby's realization that he'd been ripped off, he went on. "And second, even though your dick has probably never given you reason to stretch one of these out, the bills will fit just fine." At which point, to demonstrate, he put his hands inside the rim of one of the condoms, stretched it out, and pulled in down over Joey's head, all the way to his lips.

"So just shut the hell up and get to work, and be sure to use three layers. I don't want any of my money molding in this God-forsaken swamp. And you," he said, now pointing to Joey, "Get that condom off your head. You look like a sperm."

Chapter 75
Joey

Joey didn't know what was worse: the disrespect, his brother throwing a barbell at him, or having a condom stretched over his head. Dispatched to the garage to fetch his uncle a dry pair of boots, he pondered all of this. Honestly, if his feet hadn't been such bloody messes after his walk from the night before, he'd have just walked out.

At least that what he told himself.

"Sperm-cap!" His uncle bellowed from the house. "Where are my damn boots? Don't make me come out there!"

Yep, the condom was the worst. Darth Vader had done a lot of shitty things, but he'd never tried to put a condom over Luke's head. That's probably where even Luke would have said the hell with it...

But his thoughts never got beyond that. Because there she was: the not-dead girl from the ocean. She was standing there at the edge of the garage in the open door. Why she was here, having escaped from them twice, he had no idea. But he couldn't let her get caught now, or any chance he had to walk away from all of this would be gone forever.

"Miss!" he called to her in as loud a voice as he dared. "You have to get out of here!"

"What?!" She said, clearly caught by surprise. "You!"

"You have to get out of here! My uncle could come out any ..." but it wasn't Shabazz who came looking in the garage.

"Hey, shit-bro! What lawnmower did I stuff my beer into?" he said, as he walked into the garage. "I think it was the riding one, for drivin' down to the ..."

"Well," Bobby said, so pleased he even forgot about his Milwaukee's Best. "Hello, bitch."

Watching in horror, he saw the woman try to run, but she tripped over a redwood windowpane, and by the time she got untangled, Bobby was on top of her. "Let go of me, you goddamn bully!" she yelled.

But Bobby's prayers had been answered, and he had no intention of letting go. As he dragged her into the house, all Joey did was watch. "Hey, Shaaaaabaaaaazzzzzz!" he heard Bobby yell as he took her into the kitchen. "Guess what I caught me in the garaaaaaage?"

Following Bobby and his prisoner into the kitchen, Joey could see that the process of rubberizing and stowing the money in the athletic bag was largely finished. The arrival of the girl, whom Bobby had now forced into a chair, could only bring a bigger smile to his uncle's face. "Where are my drawings, bitch?" he asked, coldly.

"Why? If you want to stare at an abomination of God,"

she said, clearly not cowered, "just look at Pussy-face here, he's bad enough." With that, Bobby grabbed her hair again and began to pull. But surprisingly, to Joey, Shabazz called him off.

"Bobby, if you want to see a dime, let her go," Shabazz said, before turning back to the woman. "That's my favorite name for him, too, actually. But I still want my plans back. If I have to, I'll drive all over this town until I find your friend's pretty green Jaguar. Then I'll take my plans back, and burn him and his car to ashes."

"They're not even in his car, you asshole!" she said, more defiantly that ever. "He took them out to keep them away from you!"

And that was the mistake Shabazz had been hoping for.

Smiling as he left the room, he returned less than a minute later with a package that looked very much like the one he'd taken out to his car earlier. Almost eerily calm, he began talking to the woman again.

"Well then, you can take us to get them," he said, now turning to Bobby. "I'm sure she's got a car out there. Get it, have her drive, and go get those plans."

And that's where Joey decided he had finally had enough. He was sick of being bullied. He was sick of being told he was retarded. He was sick of trying to save his brother and being treated like crap for the effort.

"No!" he cried, and swinging his arm like he never had in his life, he smashed his brother across the face and knocked him stunned to the ground. It was the best Joey had ever felt in his life, and it was just the chance the woman would need to get out of here. "Run!" he screamed, as he grabbed her arm to hustle her out of the door.

"One more step and I'll put so many holes in your heads," Shabazz said menacingly behind him, "not even a space doctor will be able to figure out what species you are."

And that's when Joey noticed the package in Shabazz's hand had become a gun.

Chapter 76
Shabazz

In truth, Shabazz hated guns.

When he was just 6 years old, his father had made him come into the barn while he "took care" of a raccoon. Why that required young Shelton carry a shotgun while his dad carried a .22 pistol, his tiny brain couldn't figure out. But his dad had said Shelton was about to learn something about "learnin' varmints," so he eagerly went along.

Seeing the raccoon running under the pig fence, his father fired the pistol several times, missing every time. Even with six shots, all he managed to do was chase the raccoon up the corner post into the corner by the ceiling. Cornered, the raccoon was now just hanging on for dear life. That's when his father gave Shelton the pistol, took the shotgun, and fired it.

It was the loudest sound Shelton had ever heard in his life. And as his sense of hearing recoiled from the sound, his eyes did the same as the raccoon was virtually vaporized in the corner of the barn. (As did the barn wall and part of the roof, to the surprise of no one but Shelton. His dad had been kicked out of the Hays chapter of the NRA for trying to get baby robins out of a tree with a pistol.)

Horrified, Shelton ran screaming from the barn, only to trip and send himself flying head-first into a giant trough of pig sludge. Submerged head-first up to his hips in liquefied pig fecal matter, it took two days and 23 showers to finally get him clean enough for church. The taste in his mouth seemed to stay much longer — like a lifetime.

This had its effects on the man that was now Shabazz T. Morton. For one thing, he refused to eat anything with pig meat, and in fact, gradually stopped going to places that served it all together. When he was banned from Popeye's and KFC, his dining options whittled quickly.

The other thing was, he hated guns. Even touching one brought back memories of that horrible day, and its violation of every one of his senses. On the one day a year it got really hot and humid in Surfland, he twitched incessantly because it felt like he was surrounded by pig poo again, giving him another reason to hate the town.

But the last time he'd talked to his brother and told him that he had huge plans afoot that would make him a millionaire, Denny insisted he should have a gun handy for insurance. Reluctantly, Shabazz agreed, and had Denny sent him two in a lockbox.

Standing in the kitchen, Shabazz was glad he'd listened to his brother. While they'd sat unused in the box Bobby brought out from Hays until this morning, with everything that had happened in the last day, he'd decided to put one in his car — and the second one in his hand.

"Bobby, get up and go get that damn rope I bought," he said, never taking his eyes off Callista and Joey. "It seems your brother has decided he's not going to return to Kansas. You can throw him in the trunk once you go get her car."

Within five minutes, Bobby had completed the first part of his task. Using his no-longer "Official Hays Supply Super Rope," he'd bound up his brother and headed out to find the car the woman came in. Not once did Shabazz ever take his eyes off either of them, even when Bobby came running back into the house.

"I got me a god-damn 'Jag-Oo-AR!'" he screamed. "She brought that guy's goddamn car!"

Looking at the woman with a bit more appreciation, he said, "I can't imagine you stole it. Where's your London-broil friend?"

"He's with the police, telling them all about you, you shit."

"Fine by me," Shabazz said, unperturbed. "By the time they get done with that wreck out there, I'll be long gone. And so will you.

"Bobby, after you get the plans back from her, go ditch this car at that deserted boat dock a couple of miles up the river — with them still in it," he sneered. "You can walk back to town and catch the casino bus back to the north end; that thing runs all the time."

As always, Bobby had to complain: "How the hell am I supposed to get back here to the flatbed truck?" he asked.

"That's a long goddamn walk. And who's gonna help me get all of that shit out of the garage?"

"You can hire those Mexicans again, I don't care!" he said. "But let's just take one thing at a time. Because you're right, it is a long walk, Pussy-face," he said, fully enjoying the moment. "So, here's a new toy to make you shut the hell up," and he gave Bobby the gun.

Bobby looked like he'd been promoted to upper management.

Chapter 77
Callista

For Callista, watching Shabazz hand Bobby the gun was like watching one psycho pass the key to the asylum to another, and she was once again reminded she'd been really stupid.

Again, and again, and again.

The first time was when she'd gotten to where Poe said the wreck would be and she didn't see Pete. She should have tried calling him again or even told a cop her story. But she didn't, deciding instead to go find the lake house instead.

At the time, it seemed like a good idea; she would stake out the house just as Poe was staking out the boat dock. She could call Polanski or Poe from there and tell them what was up. Besides, she was enjoying listening to the Beatles — the early years, not that later drug-fueled hippie stuff her father liked — and with the top down and the sun out she was enjoying the drive.

Once she was there, however, she made stupid decision number two. Parking the car just out of sight of the house, she decided to get out and poke around a bit. If she could get some good, hard evidence, she'd have that much more to tell Pete and the police.

But then she'd gotten caught, witnessed a momentarily promising brother-on-brother civil war, stared down the barrel of a gun, and realized she could very well get killed in the near future. She also realized mistake number three.

"What kind of dumb bitch leaves her keys in a car like that?" the man she'd come to realize was named Bobby sneered at her. Not answering, she realized she'd never seen such crazed hate and decided from this point on to say as little as possible.

The next few minutes were relatively quiet. As Bobby went into the back of the house again with the gun, Shabazz held the back of her hair, quietly promising to snap her neck if she moved. Returning to the kitchen, Bobby picked up his trussed-up and now-gagged brother and slung him over his shoulder to take him out to the trunk of the car.

"He won't fit in that goddamn tiny trunk," Bobby said, returning now to the kitchen, happily brandishing his gun. "So I threw him in the backseat. Don't make no damn difference, still can't see him."

"Let's go, bitch," he said, leading her out to the car as Shabazz followed. "You're driving."

Walking to the car, Callista still hadn't given up, but she had to admit she was running out of options. Wondering if her sudden refusal to give in to being bullied and pushed around hadn't come a bit too early, she scrambled to do something —

Beach Slapped

anything — that might stall things. Hoping for Poe or Polanski to suddenly have the cavalry screaming over the hill was a stretch, but it was really all she had.

"Why should I drive you anywhere?" she asked, sounding more frightened than she'd intended. "You're just going to kill me after I do."

"If you don't, I'll simply kill him now," Bobby said, and without even thinking about it shot his brother right through the top of his shoulder. "See how easy that was?"

Listening to Joey's gagged screams in the back seat, Callista realized she was prepared to do a lot of things, but watching Bobby torture his brother wasn't one of them. "All right! All right! I'll drive you," she pleaded. "But do not hurt him again."

"Bitch, I'd worry a lot more about your own skin than that piece of shit," he said. "My kid brother's never been nothin' but a geek loser, and now he's going to die that way, too.

"Hey, since you're goin' to die together, why don't you introduce yourselves," he said, now laughing even more.

"'Course, my brother's a little busy, so I'll do it for him: That piece of shit bleeding in the backseat is Joey White. And you are ..." he asked, now tickling her chin with the gun.

"Callista ... Callista Walker," she said, now sounding even more frightened.

But this time at least some of it was an act, because she'd realized she did have one final chance to at least slow this disaster down. "Can we please just go..."

Finding his captives seemingly terrorized, Bobby smiled

as Callista drove the car from the driveway. In her rearview mirror, she could see Shabazz smiling ever bigger as she pulled away from him, his visage only disappearing as she turned south onto East Lake Nelta Road — and towards her last hope.

Poe had told her earlier the road was still flooded. She figured, whether Bobby made her try to cross it and she killed the engine, or he made her turn around, either one gave her more time. As they approached the still-watery road, she could see the 100-foot-wide flooded portion was down to maybe nine inches deep. She hoped it would be enough.

"Gun it, bitch," he said. "And don't bother puttin' the top up. Let's make some waves."

Speeding up, Callista hoped she was keeping her speed still low enough that the water would rise through the low-slung car's engine and flood it. Indeed, as she hit the water there was a flood: two giant waves curled off both sides of the car and soaked Joey in the backseat. The car, however, continued like nothing had happened.

"Yee-hah!" Bobby screamed. "That was more fun that sneakin' in to see Lee Greenwood with a 12-pack of Milwaukee's Best and a half-naked drunken rodeo queen!

"Damn! I almost forgot," he said, as he pulled a CD from out of his jacket. "I brought this just for us, honey! I don't know what shit it was you were listenin' too — sounded like a bunch of girls singing — but this here is real music. Figure you oughtta die right," he said, pulling Callista's disc out of the CD player. "Who the hell are The Beatles?"

Chucking it over his shoulder as they cruised into the city, he put his own CD in the player, and within seconds everyone within a city block knew that Lee Greenwood had once again God-blessed the U.S.A.

Shit, Callista thought, even if I survive this, Poe's going to kill me.

Chapter 78
Shabazz

Shabazz's second trip across the lake would prove to be every bit the disaster his first trip had not.

After seeing Bobby off, he still felt relatively content that everything would work out fine. Yes, getting rid of the car, Joey and whoever this Callista Walker was was a complication he hadn't foreseen or needed. But he'd dumped enough cars into Pacific Northwest rivers to know that once it hit the current, it would be underwater and soon buried with silt, never to be seen again.

Besides, he thought, once again staring at his near-million-dollar bag, I've come this far: I can't possibly fail now. Hefting the bag into the boat, he was once again surprised by how much the money actually weighed as he carefully placed it on the front seat to keep it out of the water.

Restarting the engine, he took the boat back out onto the lake, when the boat began to rock harder than it ever had before. Immediately slowing off the engine, however, only made it worse, and before Shabazz could even react, the unthinkable happened.

"Noooooooooo!!!!!" he screamed, as he lunged for the bag, which was now sliding off the side of the boat. For the briefest of moments, he thought he had caught his money as it slid down the port side and around the back of the boat, the air in the bag managing to keep it a float.

But as he thrust his hand into the water, it began to sink quickly. Still screaming, his hands still in the water, he watched as the bag sank out of sight through the murky water — the nine pounds of barbells Bobby had zipped up in the pockets speeding it's trip.

"Shiiiiiiiiiiiit!!!!" he yelled, even though there was no one to hear him on the lake. Horrified, he simply laid there, his hands hanging in the water — which was when his left hand drifted into the still-spinning propeller.

"Auuuuuuuuugh!!!!" he screamed, as he pulled his sliced-up hand from the water. Miraculously, he wouldn't lose any fingers; he probably wouldn't even need stitches. But as his hand bled from a hundred small cuts, which were seemingly everywhere, he took off his boots and used his socks to wrap up what had been his dominant hand.

Just then his phone rang.

"Goddamn it, Bobby, if that's you, you goddamn goat-scrotum," he said to himself, awkwardly fishing his phone out of his pocket, "I'm going to ..." But it was a sentence he never finished, because he suddenly realized only Bobby could help him get his money out of the lake.

Not today or tomorrow, but maybe Tuesday. The entire lake was usually less than ten feet deep, and sitting in the bag, it wasn't going anywhere. Wet money was better than no money, and as he answered his phone he prepared to tell Bobby his $50,000 was going to require a bit more work after their meeting at Popeye's.

"Listen, Bobby," Shabazz said, deciding for once that 'Pussy-face' and all the things he usually would call him might not be the best idea. "We got a problem."

"Bobby? Can't you read your goddamn caller I.D.? This is your brother, Denny."

"What?!" Shabazz couldn't believe he was calling now; it was Sunday! Oh, wait, he always called on Sunday, Shabazz suddenly realized. That's when they let you do that in jail. Still, he had bigger things to think about.

"I can't talk right now, damnit. I just dropped a million bucks in the goddamn lake," and he hung up. He had to get back to his car.

First confirming his location on the lake, Shabazz re-engaged the motor. He found it hard at first to steer the boat with his right hand. He definitely was not ambidextrous, and he went slow as he headed back to the dock.

Finally looking around the lakeshore, he was glad to see there didn't appear to be anyone who had actually seen what happened. No one on the docks, no one standing on their decks, no one: except for one man standing on the very dock he was headed for — and Shabazz caught his breath.

For even though Shabazz was still some distance off from

the shore, and the figure really only a small silhouette against the reflected sunlight off the water, Shabazz still had no doubt who it was.

He never forgot a man who called him Shelton.

Chapter 79
Poe

Nearly half-an-hour after sending Callista off with his car to get Pete, Poe was getting really bored sitting in the bushes by the lake. Trying Pete's cell phone one more time, it took him again straight to voice mail. Beginning to think Pete might never answer, he was all the more perplexed when he saw Pete's red Jeep heading south along the road right past the park without even slowing.

Why the hell didn't he stop? Where in the world was Callista?

But before he could think any further on the subject, he heard a faint scream come from the direction of the lake — and then another, and then another. Someone clearly was in trouble, but from his obscured vantage point in the bushes, it was impossible to know who or where.

Walking down to the dock, he squinted against the sun, only to see the figure of a man drop into a boat halfway out into the lake. Suddenly, the boat lunged forward, and piloted as if by a drunk, came flying across the lake. As Poe ran down to the water's edge, the boat continued without slowing, eventually surging out of the water and sliding nearly all the way up the concrete ramp.

As it came to a rest mere feet from Poe, he ran down to the boat, where he could see a man on his knees in the bottom. He was slumped over a seat covered with blood, not moving. Hesitant to touch him, not knowing his possible injuries, Poe stood just next to the man and spoke loudly: "Are you OK? Do you need help?"

Which is why he was totally unprepared when the still-slumping figure punched him in the jaw and sent him sprawling back into the lake. Lying in the water, Poe then watched as the figure quickly leapt from the boat and ran up to the hill towards the Mustang. Struggling to rise from his own personal fog, Poe was almost out of the water when the now all-too-familiar man came walking back down the hill with a slightly waving gun pointed right at Poe.

"Well, hello, Shelton," Poe said, now rubbing his jaw. "I see you drive a boat about as well as you decorate your car."

"Kiss my ass, Jag-whore," Shabazz said, very pleased with himself. "I'm the one with the gun and a million bucks."

"And all you had to do was beat up a little old lady, terrorize a young girl, burn down a whole block and build the ugliest, most boring piece of shit building ever," Poe said, wondering how much longer Shabazz would let him go on. "You must be the pride of Kansas; although I suppose that's a beautiful building where you come from."

"Screw you, shit & chips," Shabazz said, still moving the gun in front of Poe. "That building doesn't look any different from any other building up and down the coast."

"Well, at least we agree on something," Poe said under his breath.

"All right, enough talking about this mold-zoo of a town," Shabazz said. "I got better things to do, and you're my ticket out of here."

"How's that? I wouldn't drive that piece of shit anywhere," he said, sorely hoping Shabazz wouldn't actually shoot him in broad daylight. "I'd rather you shoot me."

"Yeah, that's what your friend said, too, before my nephew shot her would-be savior," Shabazz said with a little too much certainty for Poe's tastes. "Joey should have never tried to save her, 'cause now they both get to die."

"You're bluffing," Poe said, more a wish than a statement.

"'Callista Walker,' name sound familiar?" Shabazz said, now gesturing Poe to walk in front of him back up the hill to the car. "I expect any time now Bobby will be calling to let me know he's on his way to drown both of them in that piece of British shit you call a car.

For Poe, there was nothing to say. Shabazz had been happy to prattle on because he knew he had the hand, if not always a steady one.

"Say, you know what, Winston Church-whore? Let's just call Bobby and see how that's going," Shabazz said, now clumsily fishing the phone out of his pocket with his bad hand. "I expect he should be picking up those plans of mine you stole

477

right about now."

As Shabazz slowly worked his phone with his mangled hand trying to call Bobby, Poe realized this had gone far worse than he ever could have imagined. Bobby had Callista, and if he'd been willing to shoot his own brother to get the plans back, he had no doubt Callista would take him right to them. Depending on the timing, Fuzznut might even be in danger, although Poe had no idea when he was getting back from his job at Bo's.

As long as Shabazz needed Poe alive, he might be able to get out of this mess. But that wasn't going to help Callista, Fuzznut or Joey, although how the hell he had come to be Callista's ally, Poe couldn't even begin to guess. Apparently, however, he was bleeding all over Poe's upholstery, and that was never a good thing.

He had to get help to Fuzznut's house. But how?

"Goddamn, Pussy-face," Shabazz said into his cell phone, having finally managed to dial Bobby's number. "Answer your goddamn phone. Pick up!"

Poe thought Shabazz was going to explode, until his phone rang back at him, at which point he calmed down. Until Shabazz read the caller I.D., and then he went nuts again.

"Goddamn it, cow-semen!" Shabazz yelled. "I don't care if it's Sunday, I told you I'm busy!"

Poe had never seen anyone get so angry, all the time. As someone who had screwed up large portions of his life saying the wrong thing at the wrong time, he recognized a part of himself he was glad he'd — largely — put behind him. And he also saw his chance.

"Oh, Shellllllton!" he said loudly, "Do say hello to your brother for me! Is he a complete scumbag, too?"

"You better shut the hell up, cock-knees, or I will shoot your ass right here."

"Now Shelton, you can't shoot me," Poe said, hoping to hell he was right. "I'm your ticket out of here, remember. Shit, I'll bet after punching me in the boat, you can't even do that again. I'll bet your hands are too tired from masturbating and embroidering those ugly ass initials on your car.

"You know, I took the time to cut each one with …"

But Shabazz had had enough, and punching Poe as hard as he could across the jaw, Poe's head snapped back and he collapsed. His body rolled all the way to the base of the hill, eventually coming to rest in a crumpled heap facing the lake.

Poe was exactly where he wanted to be.

He'd taken more of a hit than he'd planned, yes, but most of his head snapping had been an act, as had his tumble to the bottom of the hill. And now, hoping that his hands were still out of sight under him, he pulled his phone from his pocket.

Briefly, he considered trying Pete one more time. But figuring he might only have seconds until Shabazz started threatening him again, Poe decided he couldn't waste what might be his one chance, and thumbed down to the next number on his call log.

Chapter 80
Paxton

How long had passed as he and Valeria Cruz gazed into one another's eyes, Paxton would never know. It could have been thirty seconds, thirty minutes or thirty years: it was timeless, and it was wonderful.

But now it was getting weird.

Because what had gone from quiet giggling, and then moved into thoughtful silence, was now becoming just a little awkward. Certainly, he was still lost in her eyes. Even when he'd heard a boat come racing into the dock and then two fishermen arguing about it, he'd pushed it to the back of his mind. Everyone knew he could live in his own little world. But for the first time ever he wasn't there alone, and he had no desire to screw that up.

OK, what was he supposed to do now?

Should he try and say something romantic? Damn! If only he'd memorized that Emily Dickinson like he was supposed to in English class, instead of thinking about how he could save

Portia from Rodents Of Unusual Size!

Should he wipe more tears from her face? No, she didn't have any more. That would be stupid.

Should he kiss her? Oh dear God, should he actually kiss her? He'd never actually thought about how that worked. Yes, he was supposed to kiss Portia last night, but he supposed he'd always really known that was never going to happen.

And this was Valeria! She was his best friend, not some ethereal and completely non-existent woman in the cockpit of a 747. Should I use my top lip first? Or the bottom? Yeah, maybe the bottom …

Mercifully, his phone rang. Checking the caller ID first, he opened it up.

"Oh, thank God! Mr. Poe! I m so glad you called! Look, I swear I'll get that paper back …"

"Paxton! Just shut up! OK?"

"Uh, OK. But Mr. Poe, you should know I can barely hear you."

"I know. Just listen."

"OK."

"You see that body lying at the base of the hill by the lake about 150 feet down from you?"

"Uh-huh …"

"Well, that's me."

"Oh my God! Are you dead?!"

"Paxton: breathe," said the voice on the other end, with what Paxton began to recognize as frustration. It was a tone he heard a lot with his parents, teachers, friends — well everyone

— and he resolved to say nothing else unless he had to.

"Paxton, no I am not dead, but believe it or not, some people will be unless you can help me. Now listen…"

Quickly, Poe told him which house was Pete's and to drive there immediately. He was to tell Pete to send police cars right away to 4649 SW Jetty Avenue for a possible hostage situation. Then, Pete was to keep West Nelta Lake Road clear, from the top of the hill to the beach, and then follow the green Mustang discreetly once it passed.

"You got that?"

"Yeah, but what if he asks me why?" Paxton asked, trying to be quick. "I mean can he just clear a whole road like that?"

"Yes he can, especially when you tell him the guy who tried to kill me last night is trying to do it again. I want the residential streets cleared."

"Listen, you could even help," Poe told him. "Go down to the beach and keep people from driving up onto the access ramp at the end of West Nelta Lake Road."

"Are you sure about this? I mean, what if he's not home? What if I screw this up like everything else? What if …"

"Paxton! Breathe!" Poe said, immediately bringing Paxton back to his previous vow of silence.

"Paxton, listen to me: you will not screw this up! And if Pete's not home, simply call 911 and go to the police station, they'll know what to do," Poe told him. "I know you can do this. It's your chance to be a real hero."

"Oh, great," Paxton said. "Now we're all dead."

Chapter 81
Julio

Only in a town of less than 10,000 people could you call the police and get put on hold, Julio Cruz thought.

His first mistake had been telling them it wasn't an emergency. With everyone still cleaning up — he hoped that was only an expression — the sewage truck accident scene, there was no officer available to listen to his complaint.

So, he waited.

And waited, never for one second taking his eyes away from the binoculars: he saw everything Paxton Dell did, which he had to admit, seemed to be not much of anything. Even as he heard voices coming nearby from the lake, he remained completely focused on his daughter, even though she was more than a quarter mile away.

Finally, after what he figured to be a half-hour, he hung up. The hell with it, he'd go down there and get his daughter away from that drug-dealing Paxton Dell himself.

He had no desire to admit to his daughter he'd been spying

on her and Paxton for days, but enough was enough. It wasn't his job to be his daughter's friend; it was to be her father.

But just then, he saw Paxton move from his daughter and open his phone. Talking quickly, he hung up after less than a minute and grabbed Valeria by the arm, forcing her into the car. Again, he was forced to read lips through his binoculars. (These things really need to come with microphones, he thought.) Most of it was a jumble, but one word right before he got in the car and drove away was nearly unmistakable: "Beach."

Either that, or "Bitch." But for now he'd go with the former. And then, once he found Paxton Dell on the beach, he'd presume the latter and beat him senseless for grabbing his daughter, dragging her into a life of crime, and all sorts of things.

Running down the stairs, he tried calling 911; if his daughter possibly being kidnapped wasn't an emergency, what was? But just as they answered, he dropped the phone, sending it tumbling off the stairs and into the lake.

"The hell with it," he said, not even breaking stride, as he finished running to his truck. He'd steer his four-wheel-drive truck right down on the beach if he had to. Now, if he could just remember how to get down there on these damn winding streets from this part of the lake. Who the hell designed this idiot city anyhow, he thought as he spun the gravel from underneath his tires.

Chapter 82
Poe

Poe had just finished his desperate phone call to Paxton when Shabazz started screaming at him to get back up the hill. Walking slowly, Poe tried to look like a man who'd been thoroughly beaten. He didn't want Shabazz to have any idea that Poe still had hope.

"Get behind the wheel, blood-nuts," Shabazz told him. "Since I can't get ahold of my sheep-skid mark nephew, we're going to go get the map."

Walking in front of the car, Poe watched as Shabazz never once took his eyes off his intended target now buckling up behind the wheel. Taking advantage of Shabazz's distance, he tucked his cell phone into his lap, while never taking his eyes off his target, as well.

Poe noticed something else, as well: Shabazz's hand was shaking — again. Not the coffee shakes, like when Poe had ordered that six-shot latte after chaperoning the all-night graduation party. But rather, the kind of shaking and slight waving that happens when something doesn't feel quite right in your hand. Maybe he wasn't used to holding a gun, he thought, or maybe it was something else.

"Thank God, I'm right-handed," Poe said in as subservient a tone as he could manage. "Or I don't think I could shift the stick on an engine this powerful."

"Damn right, you cockney-cock! You think I'd even need you if my hand wasn't so messed up? Goddamn boats. Only good use for them is crashing them into a bridge abutment and sinking them in the Willamette," he said, his mind — and, Poe noticed, his gun — starting to wander.

"But I dealt with being left-handed in prison, and I'll deal with it now," he said, unknowingly giving Poe the information he wanted. "So just drive and shut the hell up.

Trying to follow Shabazz's directions, but still give Paxton and Pete time, Poe drove slowly up the hill out of the park. His only prayer was that Pete was actually home. If Paxton had to go the police, he'd never be able to buy himself enough time.

"Why are you driving so goddamn slow, pussy-foot?"

"I'm just not used to driving a car this powerful," he said, knowing full well his car could leave this one in the dust. And not for the first time he silently prayed he would see it again.

"You sissy-lick, you better speed the hell up," he said, starting to slowly open and close the fingers on his hand inside the bloody sock. "Any more shit from you, and I'll drive this thing myself. Even with a mangled left hand, I got more balls than you.

"Damn, your car must get bored with a shit-cream like you behind the wheel!"

Right then, Shabazz's phone rung again — and this time it was the call he'd been waiting for. Putting it on speakerphone, he wanted Poe to hear what he was sure was bad news for his captive.

"Where you been, flax-phlegm? I've been calling."

"Hey! Don't give me no shit," Bobby's unmistakable drawl barked back through the phone. "This town's got the most ass-backward streets on Earth, you know that! It takes forever to get goddamn anywhere!"

"Just shut up. Is it done? You got the plans?" Shabazz asked. "Because I got Callista's friend right here, and I want him to know his friend and his car are just about to take a swim."

" I got it all covered, you just make sure you got my money."

"Uh, yeah, I got it," Shabazz said, sounding to Poe like he wasn't all together sure. "You just meet me where I said. Now get to the damn river."

Hanging up the phone, Shabazz smiled, and spoke as slowly as Poe had ever heard him: "Well, I guess I don't need you anymore, do I?" And once again curled his fingers underneath the sock, this time a little faster.

Chapter 83
Callista

Callista's last two hopes after the Jag had gone through the water were failing, as well. One was literally walking off waving, while the other was proving to be made up of people so clueless she couldn't believe she'd ever actually dared to hope.

Rolling through town with Lee Greenwood's "God Bless the U.S.A." playing over and over again — Bobby kept skipping the CD back — she'd decided to go out of her way and drive in front of Bo's. Her main hope was that she would attract Fuzznut's attention, and when he saw her making panicked faces at him in the car, he would call the police, pounce on the car, something. If he and Poe were as close as Poe had told her, he would have to know Callista driving his car with a strange man was a bad thing.

That hope disappeared as soon as she arrived, however, when she saw a giant fuzzy bear walking west. A good 200 feet away from Bo's, he was well onto the beach with no chance of seeing that anything was amiss with Poe's car, even if he saw it.

Her second hope was that the throngs of tourists walking around Bo's would notice someone lying bleeding in the back of the Jag. True, Joey was largely out of sight, but with the end of Bo's event, there were dozens of people walking mere inches from the car.

And they did absolutely nothing. Maybe they didn't feel right looking into the car, or maybe they were just too busy mindlessly singing along with Lee Greenwood to notice anything was wrong. Indeed, she noticed most were doing just that.

This song should be banned outside of the first four days of July and ballparks, she thought.

But whatever they did, they didn't help. And with a gun still pointed at her side — another thing no one noticed — she was grateful the heavy traffic she normally despised was giving her at least a few more minutes to think.

"You drove down here on purpose," Bobby said accusingly, jabbing her in the side with the gun. "You were thinkin' one of these people might rescue you, weren't ya'?"

"No, I swear, I just got lost," she said pleadingly. "You know how these streets are."

Mumbling something, he acted like he might be agreeing. "Whatever, but if you don't have us next to those plans within five minutes of us gettin' out of traffic, I'm gonna plug Joey again.

Beach Slapped

"Cause I'm getting' real tired of sittin' in this damn slick leather seat," he said, shifting around. "It's makin' the staples in my underwear go up my butt-crack."

Ten minutes later, they were finally out of traffic and on their way to Fuzznut's house. Any thoughts she'd had about delaying again were batted away when she'd seen Bobby hit his brother with his gun and smile, just for the hell of it. Worse was the realization that not only had she gotten Joey hurt again, but by the time she got to Fuzznut's house, he'd actually be home. The realization sickened her.

She had just killed Fuzznut, too.

As they went up SW 45th Street and turned towards Fuzznut's house, she was worried that Bobby might recognize this intersection as the one that almost killed him, and shoot her right there. But having turned up the stereo even louder, he was oblivious, singing loudly about how if all the things he'd worked for all his life … blah, blah, blah.

Forget July and baseball: God, she hated this song.

Pulling up in front of the house, she noticed the curtains were open. With her skewed view upward through the window, she couldn't see anyone. But the sight of a giant bag of Bo's T-shirts hanging high on a post let her know Fuzznut had made it home, much to her regret.

"Hey! Don't give me no shit!" Bobby barked into his cell phone after calling his uncle. "This town's got the most ass-backward streets on Earth, you know that! It takes forever to get goddamn anywhere!"

Listening to just one end of the phone call, it was clear

Shabazz had been calling. Bobby had obviously never heard it ringing over the rhapsody that was his nonstop blessing of the U.S.A.

But what she heard next chilled her: Shabazz had Poe. My God! Who wasn't going to die because she had decided to go surfing?

Now fully involved in self-pity, she barely heard the end of the phone call: "I got it all covered, you just make sure you got my money," Bobby said, and Shabazz answered back: "… Now get to the damn river."

Hanging up the phone, Bobby got out of the car and closed the door, but turning back to Callista before he went into the house, he threatened her one more time. "Don't even think about going anywhere, honey," he said. "Because if you do, I'll pop Joey right here in the head and then call my uncle and make sure he does the same to your friend."

And with that, he walked to the door. Discovering it was locked, he wasted no time kicking it in and going into the house. Morbidly, Callista stood up in the driver's seat to get a full view through the window.

Sweeping the room with his gun, Bobby walked inside. Seeing nothing more than a giant teddy bear sitting on the couch, he lowered his gun, and began to scream at Callista outside: "Hey, bitch! Get in here and show…"

Which was when the bear shot him right between the eyes.

Chapter 84
Fuzznut

Rising up from the couch, Nuzzle Bear walked over to the unconscious form lying on his floor. Looking from the T-shirt gun and back at Bobby, surprised less that it had knocked him out and more that it not taken off his head entirely. The gun could launch a T-shirt 300 feet. God only knows how fast it was still going after hitting a forehead 10 feet away.

Or a "PUS SY" after 10 feet. Who the hell would tattoo that word on their forehead? Damn, Poe was right, Fuzznut thought, this guy was a whack-job.

Suddenly, he realized he wasn't alone. Standing in the door was the woman he'd rescued from the surf, and she was crying. "Oh! Thank God you're all right! I thought I had killed you," and she ran forward and crashed into him, giving the bear a bear hug. "How did you know what to do?" she asked.

More worried about Callista than his continued need to be a hermit, Fuzznut explained: He'd just walked in the door and hung up his bag of shirts, when he heard "God Bless the

U.S.A." screaming down the street. Opening the curtains to see who it was, he was stunned when Poe's green Jag starting rolling into the driveway.

"I knew anyone that would play that song in Poe's car had to be a terrorist," Fuzznut said, still a bear head-to-toe. "So, I just figured I'd shoot them and figure it all out later.

"Poe's going to love the part about the gun," Fuzznut laughed. "After all the shit he gave..."

"Oh my God!" Callista cut him off. "Shabazz has him. We have to let Poe know everything's OK!"

"Can't you just call him?" Fuzznut asked as he walked away into the room where he kept all his costumes.

"No," she said. "Shabazz might know what we're up to."

"What about the cops?" he yelled, still from the back room. "Although from the sounds of all those sirens getting closer, they're all in this end of town."

"Wait! We can text him, Fuzznut! His phone never rings when he's texted!" she said, thrilled — and now starting to laugh a little at a thought. Just how pissed would Poe be that a text had saved his life?"

"But what do we tell him?" Callista asked. "He might think it's just Bobby on our phones. Shit!"

"Get me my phone," Fuzznut replied. "It's in that bag on the floor. I know what to put."

Now back in the room, he moved to grab the bag from Callista. Looking up to pass it to him, she suddenly dropped it again when she saw him standing in his birthday suit costume.

"Well," she said, regaining her composure at the sight of

Fuzznut standing buck naked in the living room. "I can see being an eccentric mascot isn't the only reason they call you Fuzznut."

Chapter 85
Poe

"Well, I guess I don't need you anymore, do I?"

Shabazz's words hit Poe like a sledgehammer. Not because he was dead, but because his friends probably already were. As Shabazz continued to test the worthiness of his hand to drive the car, Poe realized that even if he could get away from Shabazz, nothing was going to bring them back.

Dropping his hands to his lap, Poe noticed for the first time that the CD Callista had pulled out of his car was still very much intact in his pocket. Pulling it out slowly out, he looked at it with a grim smile: it was the soul survivor of the audio collection in his Jag.

But as he looked down, he felt something vibrate under the CD in his lap. Goddamnit, he thought, one of my last moments on Earth is going to spent getting a text. But as he moved the disc aside to look at the message, a giant smile spread across his face. The words were the most beautiful he'd ever read:

"All 3 OK. Cops here. Kick some ass. Lane Pruett."

That son-of-a-bitch, thought Poe as a smile spread across his face, he knew that I knew...

Looking at Shabazz again now with a new thought, Poe nevertheless continued his scared-stupid routine. "I don't want any more surprises. I just want to take you where you want to go," he said, as he pushed Pete's number on the speed dial, praying that he'd finally turned it on. Holding his finger over the speaker, he was thrilled to see Pete finally pick up — and that this time it wasn't Vivian on the end of his phone's freakishly good microphone.

"Why don't I just drive you right up *West Nelta Lake Road* here? It will be *all clear all the way through to the beach*, and then we can go wherever you want," Poe said, hoping that Pete was listening and getting the message, and knowing Pete either got the message or he didn't, Poe hit the disconnect key.

"Forget it, Brit-snot," Shabazz sneered. "You're going to drive me to the ramp on the river to make sure my nephew does his job right. Then, we'll see if I let you live."

From his tone, Poe knew that would never happen. But that didn't matter, because Shabazz's plan — and this car — were about to be done far sooner than the arsonist could have ever imagined.

Timidly, Poe asked one more favor: "Would you mind if I put my CD in? It helps keep me calm in traffic."

"Sure, fairy-puke, whatever," Shabazz said, still dangling the gun in his right hand. "What is it, 'Taps'?"

"Nope," Poe said, now smiling ear to ear. "Just some Wagner."

Chapter 86
Pete Polanski

Pete had gotten Poe's message loud and clear, just like he had from Paxton. Thank God he'd decided to plug his phone into his car charger on the way home. The nearly 24 straight hours he'd been on duty had drained it long ago, and apparently nearly gotten Poe and his friends killed.

First thing tomorrow he was getting two extra batteries.

But now, he had to keep the street cleared. Because if Poe's two oddly emphasized phrases meant what he thought they did, this street was about to become truly dangerous.

Looking through his binoculars, he could see Paxton Dell right where he told him to be less than two minutes ago: parked in the middle of Highway 101, his car and cones blocking all the traffic coming from the north.

He'd also placed cones all the way across the south side of the intersection. Normally, that wouldn't be enough to stop traffic, but coupled with the bullhorn Pete had given him, Paxton and his friend Valeria had brought both sides of the busiest highway on the coast to a dead halt. "By order of Surfland Fire & Rescue, you are ordered to stop," Paxton was yelling at the cars.

After a rough start, the kid had really come through. "Paxton Dell," Pete said the name aloud, and he vowed to ask his high school-aged son about his fellow Harrison skunk.

Now putting down his binoculars, Pete smiled again as he saw Paxton had also managed to block off the few side streets between the top of the hill and the beach. He'd done that after delivering Poe's first message.

Whatever Poe was going to do, Pete was ready. Still feeling guilty as hell for not having answered his phone for the last few hours, but ready. "Mayor!" he cried down the street. "Do not get near the street! Training exercise!"

"Whatever you say, Pete," she called back. "Just raking leaves."

Turning again to look at where West Nelta Lake Road curved off to the north, Pete raised his binoculars again. In the distance he could hear a car, and it was coming quickly, if the sound of peeling rubber was any indication.

Chapter 87
Poe

Just before the first notes of "Flight of the Valkyries," Poe gave one last suggestion to Shabazz T. Morton: "Fasten your seatbelt."

"Seatbelt? Listen you coastal-strap-nugget, seatbelts are for…" Shabazz snapped back. And kept going on a tirade that to Poe was becoming very familiar — and, this time, genuinely welcomed.

Poe had assumed his mere attempt to tell Shabazz what to do would ensure Shabazz would scream and not do it, even if Shabazz was inclined to do so in the first place. That his suggestion would set off another self-induced shit-storm of this magnitude, well, that was just a bonus. The more Shabazz lost control at this point, the better. And as Shabazz began to scream and flail more, Poe was satisfied he'd covered all his bases this time.

As a writer, Poe relied on no skill more than his ability to observe and successfully analyze people. It had made him a better writer than most other reporters his entire life — and now it was going to save that life. Because if there was one thing Poe was sure of, it was that Shabazz was not comfortable with the gun in his right hand.

Hell, the guy was so uncomfortable with the gun, he might not be capable of wielding it in either hand. And with satisfaction, he saw that Shabazz dropped the gun as Poe took the special-edition Mustang from zero to 60 in five seconds flat.

It might be ugly as hell, Poe thought, but it still hauled ass.

Fumbling around for his gun, Shabazz was now screaming at Poe: "Crack-moist! You stop this goddamn car! Now!"

But Poe was beyond listening to anything but the rising swell of Wagner. Taking the broad sweeping curve of West Nelta Lake Road to the south and west at more than 70 miles per hour, his fingers tapped the volume controls to make his Flight even louder.

By now, Shabazz had the gun back, and had returned to his threats. "I will shoot you in the head! Right now!"

"What, Shabazz? No more insulting names?" Poe shouted at his shotgun passenger, now knowing he had the upper hand. "Besides, don't you think shooting me at near 100 miles per hour, right here, might cause you some problems, too?"

And suddenly Shabazz saw what Poe had been seeing all along: the top of the hill racing towards them at an unholy speed. Dropping the gun again, he began grabbing desperately for the seatbelt.

But between his mangled left hand and his right hand being too close to the door, Shabazz could not find the belt.

It also didn't help that not having used a seatbelt in his entire life, he looked for it in the wrong place. Watching out of the corner of his eye with grim amusement, Poe smiled as Shabazz searched the base of the seatback to find nothing but change and one empty box of Banquet Fried Chicken.

Now screaming nothing but noises and guttural sounds, Shabazz was still digging like a dog on the trail of the world's last bone when Poe took one last look at the parabolic mirror at the top of the hill. Seeing the road on the other side was clear, he hit the gas one more time and let the final crescendo of Wagner's Valkyries fill every eardrum for 100 yards.

When the car went airborne, Poe judged himself to be doing about 130 miles per hour; he wasn't sure as the speedometer topped out well below that. How far he flew off the top of the hill he didn't know; indeed, later on when they measured the skid marks, he asked not to be told.

Because unlike the Duke boys flying around Hazzard County, Poe did not want to be here in this car flying through the air, grimly pondering all the dead people in "Apocolypse Now." He knew he could very well join them soon.

But Poe was counting on something the much-lamented General Lee never could: the road he was landing on was as steep as the one that launched him. If he'd done it right, the Mustang would crash down hard, but flat and somewhat in control. And hopefully, if he could bring the car to a stop jarringly enough, Shabazz T. Morton would slam into the dashboard so hard it would knock him senseless for a week.

Anything to keep that damn gun out of his hand.

Despite it all, however, Poe took in the view as he sailed through the peaceful air, thrilled all the more as he regaled in Wagner's building waves of accompaniment. Even Shabazz's noises had retreated to a feral sort of whining, and as his ass stuck straight up in the air, Poe found the canine reference delightfully more appropriate.

No one had ever been this high above the highest hill in Surfland without a helicopter. Not for the first time, he marveled just how beautiful the beach and the ocean were on a sunny day like this.

Even the ugliest places in Surfland looked good from up here: the gravel pit, the crappy motel on 101 with no vowels in its sign, the RV dealer who insisted on only installing tires as an option. And the beautiful parts looked even better: just as he began his descent, he could make out the rooftops of Alice's neighborhood. At least he'd saved that.

Even in the moments before impact, he still took the time to appreciate the little things.

"Hello, mayor!" he screamed out the window. "I'll see you on Monday!" To her credit, she never actually dropped the rake as Poe flew by her house. Or registered surprise when the wheels of Poe's car suddenly stopped turning in mid-air.

Chapter 88
Poe

When the Mustang hit the pavement again, it was still moving at more than 100 miles per hour. Slamming on the brakes in mid-air, Poe hoped that when he hit the ground, the car would be jarred so hard that Shabazz's braining would be inevitable.

Unfortunately, it also served to tear the car apart. Although the flat landing had spared the frame being bent to hell, it wreaked havoc on nearly everything else. The tires blew out as the wheels crashed up into the wheel wells. The shock absorbers punched straight up through the fenders. Even the axles broke as they bent and contorted around everything above them. Apparently, it had even destroyed the airbags, something Poe didn't think was possible.

Poe was stunned.

And not just a bit horrified. If someone had told him that he would finish the foul process of destroying Steve McQueen's "Bullitt" progeny that Shabazz had started, he never would have believed it. Sicker still: the only part of this car he hadn't destroyed was the roof; the vinyl was right where Shabazz had left it.

Asking for God and Steve to forgive him, Poe turned to Shabazz, the hope that seeing his insensate body crumpled in the seat would be worth it.

What he saw, however, was another surprise: Shabazz was flying through the windshield, ass first. He tried to hold on, of course, but even if he'd had the hands of The Hulk, nothing could have stopped him as his flailing arms slid over the dashboard and out the window after his oddly silent mouth.

His mouth was, in fact, the last thing Poe ever saw of Shabazz T. Morton's face. Because before he had barely realized Shabazz was gone, he saw the arsonist's bent form suddenly spring straight across the depth of the hood. Within moments, he slid off the front and under the car.

"Well, that's certainly not what I had in mind," Poe said to himself in the oddly quiet car. (The CD player had also been destroyed in the impact.) He'd much rather have seen Shabazz in prison than dead. Morbidly, however, the only thing he could think as the car continued to slide down the road, was that he hoped Shabazz's body wedged under the car wouldn't prevent the Mustang from continuing to slide straight.

Because the car was slowing quickly now, the friction of steel on asphalt stopping it faster than the brakes ever could. (Not that the car actually had those anymore; they'd been sheared off on impact, as well.)

By the time he started to slide across Highway 101 on his

way to the beach, he was only moving what he guessed to be about 30 miles per hour. (The speedometer was busted, too.) Thrilled that he had survived without killing anyone, he began to relax and close his eyes as the car hit the sand.

He never saw his friend Julio on the beach run right in front of the car.

Chapter 89
Paxton

Picking up where he'd left off when the phone rang at the park, Paxton once again wrapped his arms around Valeria. He knew now how to kiss her: Just do it.

At least that's what he figured, and after what he'd accomplished in the past ten minutes, why the hell not? He hadn't been a hero, but he'd definitely helped Mr. Poe and Mr. Polanksi.

He'd started at the top of the hill, he and Valeria doing everything they'd been asked. Armed with nothing but a bullhorn and several dozen highway cones that Mr. Polanski kept in his garage for some strange reason, they drove down the hill and blocked off every side street that they'd been asked to. Valeria even ran on ahead to clear the beach.

Not that there weren't some moments of panic. When Mr. Polanski had called him just a few minutes later, telling him to bring Highway 101 to a halt in both directions, Paxton told

Mr. Polanski he couldn't do it. But Mr. Polanski told him that wasn't an option. People could die if he didn't — so Paxton came up with a plan.

He started with parking his car across Highway 101. The magnetic flashing red light Mr. Polanski had given him — another item he seemed to have plenty of — helped a lot. Then, with the careful placement of cones once the stoplight had stopped traffic anyway, Paxton managed to create a traffic jam that now basically maintained itself.

In his fantasies, he'd always been the man in charge, and as he yelled, "By order of Surfland Fire & Rescue, you are ordered to stop," though his megaphone, he was once again finding the world he usually lived in delightfully intersecting with the real one.

He didn't even hate his car anymore. With that red light on top, it actually looked kind of cool. Well, no, it actually still looked like a piece of shit. But the light was nice. Maybe he could keep it.

That was when he finally let himself walk down to the beach to Valeria. He was more sure himself after the last 10 minutes than at any moment in his life. Walking to her side as she yelled at people to get off the beach near the ramp, he felt a surge of pride as he once again directed people through the bullhorn, "By order of Surfland Fire & Rescue."

Within minutes, whatever stragglers had been left cleared the area.

Their mission was complete.

And now, here he was, standing on the beach at the end

of the ramp, both he and Valeria smiling at one another. Their foreheads once again touching, they both turned to look east as the sounds of screeching metal echoed off the houses on the side of the hill.

It was spectacular to be sure; Paxton hadn't seen that many sparks since the Fourth of July. But as the car slowed, he realized it was going to slide to a stop on the sand well behind them, just as Mr. Polanski had planned.

To anyone else watching, it would have seemed crazy.

But after all his wishing and trying, screw-ups and embarrassment, this was as good as his life had ever been. Taking one last look around to make sure the beach was still clear, Paxton turned back to Valeria.

Just do it, he thought, and stepped back to gaze in her eyes one more time before he kissed her.

Which is when he screamed and threw her to the ground.

Chapter 90
Julio

When Julio Cruz finally found his way back to Highway 101 via NE 20th Street, he found it completely backed up. Taking a quick glance south before he crossed the highway towards the beach, all he could see was some idiot waving a megaphone and yelling next to a flashing red light.

This town has more crazy damned accidents, he thought.

Reaching the beach, Julio turned left onto the sand without even stopping. He had no idea if Paxton Dell had brought his daughter to the beach here, but this was as good a place to start as any. Driving slowly, he looked for both Paxton Dell and wandering tourists. They weren't the most observant people, he'd discovered, and running them over would be bad for business. Especially since driving on the beach was illegal as hell.

Approaching the West Nelta Lake Road beach access ramp, Julio curved toward the ocean, as all of a sudden every tourist in the world seemed to be heading away from the ramp. Stopping entirely now, Julio looked to see what was going on.

Dios! It was Paxton Dell! Waving a megaphone like a crazy person, he was yelling at people to get off the beach!

Gunning his engine, Julio turned towards his nemesis — only to find he'd buried his truck up to its axles with his sudden acceleration on the soft sand. Cursing again, he jumped from his truck to see that Paxton now had his hands around Valeria!

Julio charged, and putting his head down, he began a dead sprint towards Paxton.

He had never run so fast in his life. The need to get there quickly, combined with the desire to slam into Paxton like a bull, gave him seemingly inhuman speed. He stopped only when he suddenly heard a scream. Dear God, what …

But before he could even complete the thought, he was stunned to see a wrecked green car sliding inexorably toward him. Looking for the driver to take control, his disbelief continued: behind the wheel was the screaming face of Jackson Poe. His friend's hand was furiously slamming a horn that had long-stopped working — and Julio could do nothing, the car now just mere feet from crushing him.

Frozen in fear and shock, Julio knew just one thing: He was going to die.

But just a split second before the front of the car broke every bone in his body, another force slammed into him from the side. Not even registering what it was, he was thanking God even as the wind was knocked out of him.

Rolling through the sand, he came to rest staring straight

up into the face of his deliverance.

"Hello, Mr. Cruz," it said, extending its hand. "It's nice to meet you. I'm Paxton Dell."

Chapter 91
Pete

Just as soon as Poe's car had flown past him, Pete had called Colton County Dispatch and had all available units respond to the beach at U.S. Highway 101 and West Lake Nelta Road. Seconds after that, after seeing Paxton's flying leap save some clueless fool, he was racing down the road in his Jeep, sirens screaming and lights flashing.

The first thing he saw was Poe standing next to the wrecked Mustang, talking to both Paxton Dell and the bruised and battered clueless fool, who turned out to be his friend Julio Cruz. (Oops.) Next to Julio was his daughter, or at least that's what Pete assumed from the way Julio held her protectively. Everyone seemed to be laughing, although maybe Julio a little less so.

"Julio, you thought Paxton was a drug dealer because of the white van?" Poe was in hysterics now. "No! No, my friend, not even close, although I can see why you'd think that. Let me explain ..."

Five minutes later, Pete could see that Julio seemed to have relaxed somewhat. He still hadn't let his daughter go entirely, but it was down to a left hand on her shoulder. Poe's explanation, as convoluted as it was, seemed to explain everything to his satisfaction — and then some.

Julio's right hand now finally free, he extended it to Paxton Dell, who gladly shook it in return. Using the lull, Pete walked closer and spoke: "Hate to interrupt, but Julio, do you mind if I check you out a bit? I think Paxton may have broken one of your ribs as he kept the car from breaking all of them."

Smiling, Paxton gave a little wave to Valeria. Staying with her father, she returned his gesture. Smiling as he tried to leave the moment to them, Pete recognized the sign of a blush beginning to bloom, as Paxton walked off with Poe.

Chapter 92
Poe

"Well, you're certainly a hero, now," Poe told Paxton as they walked back to the wreckage of the Mustang. "I'll bet the cheerleaders are all over you now, although you seem to have already taken care of that."

"Uh, yeah," he said, blushing slightly himself, while looking back at Valeria. "I kind of have to figure all that out."

"You at least not dreading going to school tomorrow?" he asked, clearly concerned about Paxton. "Word about this will be all over town in about 20 minutes."

"Dreading? No. Looking forward to it? No," he said, now staring back down the highway toward the school. "This story will last about one day on the grapevine. That video will last forever on YouTube."

"Well, that's true, but there are other things that are just as permanent in high school," Poe said. " Like the thrill of having the nicest car in the parking lot."

"I don't think a flashing light's going to do it," Paxton

said. "I tried really hard, and my car still looks like shit — oh, sorry — crap."

"I wasn't thinking your Nissan," he said, putting his hand on the sprung trunk of the Mustang. "I was thinking you could drive this."

"Um, thanks, but even if I could get the title to this car, I'm not sure I'd want it," he said, looking over the still-smoking wreck. "I don't just have $20,000 lying around to put this thing back together."

"Funny, I do," Poe said, and as he lifted the trunk lid, Paxton saw two bundles of money, still very much intact despite all the beating they'd taken. Poe went on: "Now, before you do anything stupid: slip that money into your shirt, get it into your trunk, and deposit it first thing tomorrow.

"And don't worry about the paperwork, I've got a friend who can take care of all that."

Stunned beyond words, Paxton did just what Poe had told him. Returning to Poe, he was almost in tears.

"What can I possibly do to say thank you, Mr. Poe?" he asked genuinely.

"Promise me three things," Poe said.

"One: you will never play 'The Wind Beneath My Wings' on that stereo.

"Two: You will return that God-awful top to its original green.

"And three: You will get your stuff in to your editor on time from now on," he said with a smile.

"In fact, I think your homework is here now."

Chapter 93
Poe

Led by a police car, Callista driving his Jag down the street was one of the most beautiful things Poe had ever seen. Finally stopping in the intersection, she jumped out of the car and gave Poe the biggest hug he'd had since he and Aly split up.

Selfishly, he first checked the back seat, happy to find most of the blood had dripped on the floor mats. Then, fishing Paxton's homework out of the glove box, he shook the young man's hand and told him he'd see him class on Tuesday. As Paxton skipped off, Poe was surprised to hear him singing.

And they say my music's weird, he thought.

Sitting down on the hood as she waited for Poe to finish with Paxton, Callista seemed virtually bursting to tell him what had transpired. So she did, everything from what had happened after she left him in the park until Fuzznut had sent his text message. Even here, however, she had to admit she didn't know the whole story.

"What message did Fuzznut send you?" she asked. "He never told me."

"You know, in the heat of everything, I really don't remember," he said, hoping to protect at least a few of Fuzznut's secrets still. And whether she believed him or not, she seemed content to let his answer be. Which was good, because now Poe was itching to ask some questions of his own.

"Where's our disgusting friend and the brother he tried to kill?" he asked, hoping they'd both survived, although for very different reasons.

"The police showed up about three minutes after we texted you," she said. "It was just enough time to get Bobby tied up and out onto the corner, and Joey untied and sitting next to him. Fuzznut hoped they'd keep out of his house that way.

"It seemed to work, because they got both brothers off to the hospital right away and just asked me a few questions before escorting me over here.

"They're both supposed to be OK after a day or so. I think Bobby's stay is going to be shorter than Joey's, but I'll bet Bobby's headed for a much shittier spot," she said, her tone turning nastier than Poe had ever heard it. "I hope he makes a lot of special friends there."

Talking about the other brother, however, Poe noticed Callista's tone was completely different, even affable: "Joey tried to save my life," she said. "More than once, I think, and I'm going to tell the police, the judge, everyone.

"I think he's been bullied his entire life, and I know what that's like."

Beach Slapped

Confused by her last comment but content to let her mystery rest, as well, Poe walked Callista down to the Mustang and a remarkably empty beach. Surprised that the wreckage of the car hadn't become a nut-site crawling with tourists, he had just one question left.

"Where's Fuzznut? Did he just stay in the house when the cops showed up?"

"Oh no, with all that excitement, he said he had to get out and do something," she said. Turning her head, she led Poe to look down the beach, which also solved the mystery of the missing tourists.

Standing in a crab costume, Fuzznut was making animal balloons, stopping occasionally to look up and wave at Poe and Callista. Laughing at his old friend, Poe said: "I think you've got a new friend. He never waves at me."

"You think he'll even do that when he's naked?" she asked, jokingly.

"That's what friends are for."

Turning back towards Poe now, Callista did have one final question. "Speaking of 'friends,' where is Mr. Shabazz T. Morton, anyway? Off to jail, I hope?"

"Nothing quite so glamorous," and kicking away the sand he'd put in place to keep the car from becoming a spectacle, he revealed Shabazz T. Morton. The lower half of him anyway.

"Oh my God! What did you do?" she said, though not truly displeased at all.

"Don't look at me," Poe said, turning his smiling face back to the ocean. "I told him to fasten his seatbelt."

Barton Grover Howe

Epilogue

Alice Kauffman: Released from the hospital the same day that her assailant was arrested and brought to St. Gangulphus, she took great pride in flipping him the bird as he was wheeled into the emergency room. She enjoyed even more suing the estate of the late Shabazz T. Morton, and was awarded nearly 100 percent of its assets when the only non-incarcerated heir that would admit to knowing him — a nephew — refused to contest the suit. With her award, she put all of her husband's houses back together and sold them back to 12 original neighbors who wanted to return.

Rip Rockford: While still wearing Aloha shirts and trying unsuccessfully to get his 1976 Ford Torino to work, Rip ensured that the title to a 2008 Limited Edition Bullitt Ford Mustang was transferred to one Paxton Dell. Discovering that serial-text-message-bitcher Jackson Poe had been saved by one, he began sending Poe 20 a day until Poe told him it was costing him 50 cents a text. Rip them doubled his messages to 40 a day.

Pete Polanski: After spending another 12 hours on his feet trying to clean up the mess Poe's flying Mustang left behind, Pete went home planning to sleep for nearly a day-and-a-half. He left strict instructions not to be disturbed — unless something unusual happened. He was in bed approximately two hours before a boat flew off of a trailer and imbedded itself in a very awkward position between two football players sleeping on the beach, who explained with great animation that they were not gay. He also, over his wife's objections, finally bought his fake dog a bed.

Fuzznut Pruett: Having discovered the illicit joy of a T-shirt gun, Fuzznut still fights the urge to shoot it at teenagers holding crab mallets, 3-year-olds that hit him in the crotch, and other annoyances. Still experimenting with crab dishes — he sees real possibilities in white pizza — he now cooks far more often for three than he used to. He still spends all of his time in his house naked, although Callista does ask that he wear the longer aprons when she eats over.

Portia McDonald: Having returned to school fully prepared to make Paxton Dell's life a living hell, she enjoyed approximately 30 minutes of joy before she discovered the 45-minute version of she and Paxton's date had gone viral — on BiggestBitchEver.com. By Christmas, she had been voted the sixth biggest bitch in America — and number one among non-drunken celebrities. Transferring to another school at semester's end, she discovered everyone there knew she was a bitch, too.

Paxton Dell: After working with Ryan Norcross and spending $19,820 putting his new Mustang back together — including the original roof — he gave the first ride to Valeria Cruz. They remain best friends, deciding mutually that romance just screws everything up. Together, they spent the last $180 buying every last copy of "Wind Beneath My Wings" they could find and burning them on the beach on New Year's Eve. Also: having discovered that all the people who used to hate him now want to be his buddy because of his car, Paxton refuses to give any of them rides unless they agree to be the mascot with him. As of this writing he has had no takers.

Julio Cruz: Relieved beyond words that his daughter does not want to date anyone, he did concede that when she does get married someday — he hopes sometime after he is dead — she will marry someone as kind and brave as Paxton Dell. He is currently babysitting every night, whether his wife works or not, as his punishment for stalking his own daughter. He still has not told his middle daughter what a penis does.

Ron Blaine: Absorbing the loss of a million dollars as just the price of doing business, he thanked God every night for a month Shabazz's disaster could never be traced back to him. To help him recoup his losses, he built two more hideous condo developments in the Portland area that sold out in weeks, and began advertising twice as much to make himself feel better. He now has all six top spots on the list of Portland's worst commercials, the saleswoman's creepy dog having died.

Arianna Walker and Emerson Quincy Walker, Ph.D.: Following her complete meltdown on Anderson Cooper 360, which included her trying to steal Anderson's leather shoes as "the spoils of cow murder," Arianna now works behind the scenes writing press releases for fringe animal-rights groups so crazed even PETA wants nothing to do with them. The only time she appears in public is dressed as the grim reaper, where she is only given a plastic scythe for fear she may stab herself.

Professor Walker resigned from Berkeley when, after his and his daughter's episode on CNN, he was fired, lunging at talk show hosts not being an act protected by tenure. He currently works as a late-night talk show host in San Francisco, where according to Arbitron Ratings, some 18 percent of his listeners find him too conservative.

Bobby White: Convicted of kidnapping and armed robbery, Bobby White was sentenced to life in prison without the possibility of parole as part of the three-strikes-and-you're-out law. A favorite target for all-male parties in the shower, the burns on his forehead have made him particularly popular with dyslexic inmates. Every holiday season, he still receives an anonymous Christmas card from Surfland, Oregon, with a picture of a sunset and the words "You suck" on the back.

Joey White: Begging leniency from the court, and supported by the testimony of Callista Walker, he was sentenced to 100 hours of community service, which he served by starting a science-fiction reading group at the Surfland library. Special dispensation was also granted as a result of him granting Alice Kauffman all of his uncle's assets, save for the one beach house his family had always owned. He lives there now and works as the assistant manager at the sci-fi bookshop his distant cousin owns in Surfland. Asking that people call him "Joseph," he no longer thinks "Tiberius" is a cool name for anything.

Jackson Poe: After having arguably the most desperately-needed massage of his life on Monday, he returned quickly to his normal job routine: writing decent-paying stories for people he can't stand and poorly paying ones for people he actually gives a damn about. His life, as well, went on pretty much as it had before the incident that has come to be known around Surfland as "Flight of the Bullitt," save for two things. One: He painted his house yellow with blue trim, after discovering no one else in town had ever done it. Two: He vowed to never listen to any Wagner again — ever.

Callista Walker: Hoping to stay in Surfland, Callista moved into one of Alice's beach houses once it had been put back together. As a thank you for being instrumental in saving her neighborhood, Alice gave Callista the house just down from Joseph's and next to the beach access ramp. She still surfs everyday, sends the occasional postcard to a prison, volunteers at Harrison High School when she can, and works with the otters at the Surfland Aquarium of the Pacific.

She still prefers not to work with the sea lions.

Barton Grover Howe

Beach Slapped

Author's Notes

Although it is hard to believe, one ancient old-growth redwood can be used to build multiple buildings, or one very large one. For an example, check out the Curly Redwood Lodge in Crescent City, California, at www.curlyredwoodlodge.com.

"Tell to Sell" is a fictional show. However, the duplicity involved by the producers of the program in getting home owners to lie about their homes did in fact happen on the coast of Oregon in the summer of 2008 with another nationally known home-improvement show.

The behavior of sea lions and their anti-social — and at times very social — behavior has been documented, and is largely accurate as described.

The town of Surfland is entirely fictional, as are the bad and evil people described in this novel. All of the good people are based upon decent people that no doubt live somewhere, and if they are lucky, on the Oregon coast.

Barton Grover Howe is a high school teacher and humor columnist who has spent most of the last 10 years teaching, being a mascot and generally not being near as funny as he thinks he is. He currently resides in a small town on the Oregon coast within shouting distance of Surfland.

If you liked "Beach Slapped" go to www.BartonGroverHowe.com for more of Barton Grover Howe's writing.

Made in the USA
Charleston, SC
28 September 2011